The Astonishing Color of After

The Astonishing Color of After

Emily X.R. Pan

LITTLE, BROWN AND COMPANY
New York Boston

Copyright © 2018 by Emily X.R. Pan

Ornament copyright © iktash/Shutterstock.com; feather and art palette copyright © Mary Volvach/Shutterstock.com; smoke copyright © Weerachai Khamfu/Shutterstock.com; hourglass copyright © Frolova Polina/Shutterstock.com

Cover art copyright © 2018 by Gray318. Cover design by Gray318 and Sasha Illingworth. Cover copyright © 2018 by Hachette Book Group, Inc.

Little, Brown and Company

Hachette Book Group

1290 Avenue of the Americas, New York, NY 10104

Visit us at LBYR.com

First Edition: March 2018

Little, Brown and Company is a division of Hachette Book Group, Inc. The Little, Brown name and logo are trademarks of Hachette Book Group, Inc.

The publisher is not responsible for websites (or their content) that are not owned by the publisher.

Library of Congress Cataloging-in-Publication Data
Names: Pan, Emily X. R., author.
Title: The astonishing color of after / by Emily X.R. Pan.
Description: First edition. | New York : Little, Brown and Company, 2018. |
Summary: After her mother's suicide, grief-stricken Leigh Sanders travels to Taiwan to stay with grandparents she never met, determined to find her mother who she believes turned into a bird.
Identifiers: LCCN 2017022920 | ISBN 9780316463997 (hardcover) |
ISBN 9780316464000 (ebook) | ISBN 9780316464925 (library edition ebook)
Subjects: | CYAC: Suicide—Fiction. | Grief—Fiction. | Artists—Fiction. | Racially mixed people—Fiction. | Grandparents—Fiction. | Secrets—Fiction. | Supernatural—Fiction. | Americans—Taiwan—Fiction. | Taiwan—Fiction.
Classification: LCC PZ7.1.P3573 Ast 2018 | DDC [Fic]—dc23
LC record available at https://lccn.loc.gov/2017022920

ISBNs: 978-0-316-46399-7 (hardcover), 978-0-316-46400-0 (ebook)

Printed in the United States of America

LSC-C

10 9 8 7 6 5 4 3 2 1

For 媽媽 *and* 爸爸 *and Loren,*

who always believed I could do this

If I should see a single bird
　　　　　　　　—Emily Dickinson

1

My mother is a bird. This isn't like some William Faulkner stream-of-consciousness metaphorical crap. My mother. Is literally. A bird.

I know it's true the way I know the stain on the bedroom floor is as permanent as the sky, the way I know my father will never forgive himself. Nobody believes me, but it is a fact. I am absolutely certain.

In the beginning, that mother-shaped hole was made of blood. Dark and sticky, soaked to the roots of the carpet.

Over and over again, I rewind back to that June afternoon. I walked home from Axel's just in time to see my father stumble out onto the porch, clearly looking for me. I'll never be able to erase that image: his hands slick and shaking, maroon smeared across his temple, chest heaving like it was iron filings getting sucked into his lungs and not air. At first I thought he was injured.

"Leigh—your mother—"

He choked on the sentence, face puckering into something

awful. When he finally got the words out, his voice crawled through an ocean to get to me. It was a cold cerulean sound, far away and garbled. I couldn't process what he said. Not for a long time. Not when the police arrived. Not even when the people came to carry my mother's body out the front door.

It happened on Two Point Fives Day. *Our* day—what had become an annual tradition for me and Axel. It was supposed to be celebratory. The school year was almost over and things were finally going back to normal, even with Leanne in the picture. We were already making plans for the summer ahead. But I guess the universe has a way of knocking *supposed-tos* right on their asses.

Where I was that day: on the old tweed couch in Axel's basement, brushing against his shoulder, trying to ignore the orange wall of electricity between us.

If I pressed my mouth to his, what would happen? Would it shock me like a dog collar? Would the wall crumble? Would we fuse together?

And Leanne—would she disappear? Could one kiss erase her?

The better question was: How much could it ruin?

My mother knew where I was. That's one of the facts that I still can't get over.

If I could have climbed out of my goddamn hormones for just one minute, maybe my neurotransmitters would've signaled for me to go home. Maybe I would've shaken off my blinders and forced myself to take count of all the things that had been off-kilter, or at least noticed that the colors around me were all wrong.

Instead, I withdrew into my shell, let myself be one of those self-absorbed, distracted teenagers. During sex ed, our teachers always made it sound like the guys were the horny ones. But right there on that couch I was certain that some crucial detail about the female body, or at least *my* body, had been left out. I was an already-lit firework, and if Axel came any closer, I was going to barrel into the sky and rain back down in a million pieces.

He was wearing the brown plaid that day. It was my favorite of his shirts—the oldest and softest against my cheek when I hugged him. His boy smells wafted over: the sweetness of his deodorant, the smoky floral of some other product, and, beneath all that, a scent like the quiet grass at night.

In the end, he was the one to take off his glasses and kiss me. But instead of bursting into sparks, my body froze. If I shifted a millimeter, everything would break. Even thinking that word—*kiss*—was like touching an ice wand to my chest. My ribs seized, freezing solid and spiderwebbing with cracks. I was no longer a firework. I was a thing frozen deep in the Arctic.

Axel's hands stretched around my back and unlocked me. I was melting, he had released my windup key, and I was kissing back hard, and our lips were everywhere and my body was fluorescent orange—no, royal purple—no. My body was every color in the world, alight.

We'd been eating chocolate-covered popcorn just minutes ago, and that was exactly how he tasted. Sweet and salty.

An explosion of thoughts made me pull away. The cloud of debris consisted of remembering: that he was my best friend, that he was the only person I trusted a hundred percent besides Mom, that I shouldn't be kissing him, *couldn't* be kissing him—

"What color?" Axel said quietly.

This is the question we always ask to figure out what the other person's feeling. We've been best friends since Mrs. Donovan's art class—long enough that that's all we need. One color to describe a mood, a success, a failure, a wish.

I couldn't answer him. Couldn't tell him I was flashing through the whole goddamn spectrum, including a new dimension of hues I'd never before experienced. Instead, I stood up.

"Shit," I breathed.

"What?" he said. Even in the dim light of the lone basement bulb I could see how his face was flushed.

My hands—I didn't know where to put my hands. "Sorry, I gotta. I have to go."

We had a no-bullshit rule with each other. I kept breaking it.

"Seriously, Leigh?" he said, but I was already running up the stairs, grabbing at the railing to pull myself up faster. I burst into the hallway outside the living room and gulped down breaths like I'd just broken the surface after the deepest dive.

He didn't follow. The front door slammed as I left; even his house was pissed at me. The sound rang out puke green. I thought of the hard cover of a book smacking shut on a story that wasn't finished.

2

I never saw the body up close. The police arrived and I raced ahead of them. Up the stairs two at a time. Burst into the master bedroom with a force that nearly cracked the door. All I could see were my mother's legs on the floor, horizontal and sticking out from the other side of the bed.

And then Dad was behind me, pulling me out of the way while my ears rang with the shrieking. It was so loud I was certain it was a noise brought by the police. Only when I stopped to catch my breath did I realize the shrieking was coming from me. My own mouth. My own lungs.

I saw the stain after they removed my mother, after someone had made a first attempt at cleaning it out of the carpet. Even then it was still dark and wide, oblong and hideous. Barely the shape of a mother.

It's easier to pretend the stain is acrylic paint. Pigment, emulsion. Water soluble until it dries.

The one part that's hard to pretend about: Spilled paint is only ever an accident.

Spilled paint doesn't involve a knife and a bottle of sleeping pills.

The day after *it happened*, we spent hours searching for a note. That was the surreal part. Dad and I floated around the house, moving sloth-like as we pulled at drawers, flipped open cabinets, traced our fingers along shelves.

It's not real unless we find a note. That was the thought that kept running through my brain. *Of course she would leave a note.*

I refused to go into the master bedroom. It was impossible to forget. Mom's feet sticking out from behind the bed. My blood pounding, *she's dead she's dead she's dead.*

I leaned against the wall out in the hallway and listened to Dad riffling through papers, searching, moving from one side of the room to the other, sounding as desperate as I felt. I heard him open her jewelry box and shut it again. Heard him shifting things around on the bed—he must've been looking under the pillows, under the mattress.

Where the hell did people usually leave their notes?

If Axel were there with me, he probably would've squeezed my shoulder and asked, *What color?*

And I would've had to explain that I was colorless, translucent. I was a jellyfish caught up in a tide, forced to go wherever the ocean willed. I was as unreal as my mother's nonexistent note.

If there was no note, what did that mean?

My father must've found something because everything on the other side of the door had gone intensely quiet.

"Dad?" I called out.

There was no response. But I knew he was there. I knew he was conscious, standing on the other side, hearing me.

"Dad," I said again.

I heard a long, thick intake of breath. My father shuffled to the door and opened it.

"You found it?" I said.

He paused, not meeting my eyes, hesitating. Finally his hand swept out a crumpled piece of paper.

"It was in the garbage," he said, his voice tight. "Along with these." His other fingers uncurled to show a pile of capsules that I recognized immediately. Mom's antidepressants. He crunched them up in his fist and went back downstairs.

A cyan chill seeped into my body. When had she stopped taking her medicine?

I smoothed the paper out and stared at its whiteness. Not a speck of blood to be found on that surface. My hands brought it to my nose and I inhaled, trying to get at the last of my mother's scent.

And finally, I made myself look at it.

~~To Leigh and Brian,~~
~~I love you so much~~
~~I'm so sorry~~
~~The medicine didn't~~

Below all that, there was something scribbled over with so many pen strokes it was entirely unreadable. And then one final line at the very bottom:

~~I want you to remember~~

What had my mother been trying to say to us?

What did she want us to remember?

3

I started spending the nights downstairs on the sofa, the farthest I could get from the master bedroom. I was having a
lot of trouble sleeping, but the old leather sofa swallowed me
and I imagined myself cradled in the thick arms of a giantess.
She had my mother's face, my mother's voice. Sometimes if I
managed to drift into an uneasy slumber, the determined tick
of the clock above the television became the beat of the giant's
heart.

In between the heartbeats, my dreams pulled up slivers of
old recollections. My parents laughing. A birthday celebration,
chocolate cake smeared over all of our faces. Mom trying to
play the piano with her toes, at my request. Dad with the sing-
song rhymes he liked to make up: "Little Leigh, full of glee!"
"Oh my, what a sigh!"

It was the night before the funeral: I woke around three in
the morning to a sharp rap on the front door. It wasn't a dream;
I knew because I'd just been dreaming that the giantess was

humming over a piano. Nobody else stirred. Not my father, not my mother's cat. The wooden floor stung with cold and I stepped into the foyer shivering, baffled by the drop in temperature. I dragged the heavy door open and the porch light came on.

The suburban street was purple and dark, silent but for the lone cricket keeping time in the grass. A noise in the distance made me look up, and against the murky predawn sky, I could make out a streak of crimson. It flapped once, twice. A tail followed the body, sailing like a flag. The creature swept over the half-moon, past the shadow of a cloud.

I wasn't frightened, even when the bird glided straight across the lawn to land on the porch, those claws tapping short trills into the wood. Standing at full height, the creature was nearly as tall as me.

"*Leigh,*" said the bird.

I would have known that voice anywhere. That was the voice that used to ask if I wanted a glass of water after a good cry, or suggest a break from homework with freshly baked cookies, or volunteer to drive to the art store. It was a yellow voice, knit from bright and melodic syllables, and it was coming from the beak of this red creature.

My eyes took in her size: nothing like the petite frame my mother had while human. She reminded me of a red-crowned crane, but with a long, feathery tail. Up close I could see that every feather was a different shade of red, sharp and gleaming.

When I stretched out a hand, the air changed as though I'd disturbed the surface of a still pool. The bird launched into the sky, flapping until she disappeared. A single scarlet feather stayed behind on the porch, curving like a scythe and stretching to nearly the length of my forearm. I rushed at it, accidentally kicking up a tiny gust. The feather took to the air lazily, scooping a little, bumping to a stop. I crouched low to catch it under my palm and angled my head to search the sky. She was gone.

Would she come back? Just in case, I set out a bucket of water and left the front door wedged open. I brought the feather inside, and back on the sofa, I fell immediately into true sleep for the first time since the day of the stain. I dreamed of the bird and woke up certain that she wasn't real. But then I found the feather in my fist, gripped so hard my nails had bitten marks into my palm. Even in sleep I had been afraid to let go.

4

The funeral was open casket, and when I walked up to that wooden box, I almost expected to see a mound of ash. But no, there was a head. There was a face. I spotted the familiar brown birthmark in the hollow above her collarbone. That was my mother's blouse, the one she'd bought for a recital and then decided she hated.

Before me lay a body grayer than a sketch. Someone had applied makeup and colors to try to make it look alive.

I didn't cry. That was not my mother.

My mother is free in the sky. She doesn't have the burden of a human body, is not made up of a single dot of gray. My mother is a bird.

The body in the casket didn't even have the jade cicada pendant I'd seen my mother wear every single day of my life. That neck was bare—further proof.

"What color?" Axel whispered as he came up next to me.

It was our first time speaking since the day Mom died,

since a week ago. He must've found out from his aunt Tina, after Dad called her. I know I shouldn't have shut him out, but I couldn't bear the thought of us having a conversation. What would I say? Every time I tried to imagine the words, everything in my head went cold and blank.

Standing there at the funeral, he looked terribly out of place. His usual clothes—plaid over a screen-printed shirt, worn pair of jeans—had been replaced by an overlarge button-down, cinched with a shiny tie and worn above a pair of dark slacks. I saw how he glanced nervously at the casket, how his attention carefully shifted back to my face.

If he looked in my eyes straight on, he would know how he'd pierced me with an arrow, how its shaft was still sticking out of my chest, twitching each time my heart contracted.

And maybe he'd see how my mother had sliced up everything else. How even if he could wrench that arrow free, the rest of me was so punctured and torn that nothing would ever be able to suture me back together.

"Leigh?"

"White," I whispered back, and I could feel his surprise. He'd probably been expecting a glacial blue, or maybe the dying vermilion of dusk.

I saw him reach for my elbow and then hesitate. He dropped his hand.

"Will you come over later?" he asked. "Or—I could go to your house?"

"I'm not sure that's a good idea." I could sense the pink rising up through him.

"I didn't mean—"

"I know," I said, not because it was true but because I

couldn't bear for him to finish that sentence. What didn't he mean? For us to break through that sizzling wall and connect one mouth to another in the same moment that my mother was dying?

"I just want to talk to you, Leigh."

That was almost worse.

"We're talking right now," I said, my insides curling even as the words came out.

Bullshit bullshit bullshit. It echoed in my mind, and I tried to shove the word somewhere I couldn't hear it.

It was only as Axel turned away that I noticed how his shoulders shook. He reached a hand up to yank his tie loose and walked toward the other end of the room. In a flash like a vision of the future, I saw the distance stretching between us, unfurling like a measuring tape, until we were separated by miles and miles. Until we were standing as far apart as two people can get without leaving the surface of the earth.

What did Axel think talking could accomplish, after all that had happened to my mother?

What could we fix?

5

I hadn't yet decided if or how I was going to tell Dad about the bird, but as we were walking back to the car after the funeral, I stumbled over a crack that had made the sidewalk hideously uneven.

That silly childhood rhyme sang its way into my head:

Don't step on the crack or you'll break your mother's back.

My brain snagged on the words. I blinked and fell half on the grass and half on the edge of the sidewalk. Dad helped me back up. There was a greenish spot on my knee, and it brought on a longing for the past, for a simpler time, when grass stains were among my biggest worries.

"What's that?" said Dad, and at first I thought he was asking about the stain. But no, he was pointing at a long, slender spot of red a few feet away from me.

In my fall, the feather had made its way out of my dress pocket. It uncurled on the sidewalk like some kind of challenge.

I swiped it off the ground and shoved it back in my pocket.

Dad asked about it, of course. And I couldn't lie. Not when it had to do with my mother.

"It's from Mom," I tried to explain as we got in the car. "She came to see me."

Dad was silent for a few beats, his hands white-knuckling the steering wheel. I saw the millisecond in which his face twisted with grief. His expression was loud as a roar, though outside of us there was only the sound of the car rolling over pavement. The muted noise of the pedals shifting beneath his feet as he braked.

"She came to see you," he echoed. The concern was obvious in his voice.

"She came as—she turned into—" I swallowed. Now that they were on the tip of my tongue, the words had the taste of something ridiculous. "She's a bird now. Huge and red. And beautiful. She landed on the porch the other night."

At Mill Road, he turned left, and I understood that he was taking us home the long way, dragging out this conversation. I was trapped.

"What's the significance of her being a bird?" he said after a long stretch of nothing, and I knew in that moment that he didn't believe me, and there was nothing I could do or say that would change his mind.

I didn't answer, and he sighed through his nose very quietly. I heard it clear as anything. I turned my face out the window, my thumb stroking the vane of the feather.

He drummed the steering wheel a few times with the pads of his fingers, as he often did when he was thinking. "What does red mean to you?" he tried again, and it sounded almost textbook, like some technique he'd learned from Dr. O'Brien.

"I didn't make the bird up, Dad. It's real. I saw her. That was Mom."

The rain came then; we had turned directly into the path of the storm. The water drummed loudly, slanting into us and cutting straight down the image of my face mirrored in the window, slicing me apart again and again.

"I'm trying to understand, Leigh," said Dad as he pulled the car into our driveway. He didn't push the button to open the garage door. He didn't shift the car into park. We sat there, idling, and the little tremors from the engine were starting to make me feel sick.

"Okay," I said. I thought I would give him a shot. If he was making a real effort, so would I. If he wanted to talk this out, fine. I just needed him to *try*, for one second, to believe me.

I watched his fingers tap-tap-tapping against the steering wheel as he searched for the right words. He closed his eyes for a beat.

"I also wish . . . I could see your mother again. More than anything."

"Right," I said, and my mind went blank, like a computer screen shutting down. I clicked my seat belt loose, threw open the door, made my way out of the car.

The rain clung to me as I dug through my bag for my key to the house. It was a warm rain, and it looked gray as it came down from the sky. I imagined it to be liquid armor, shaping itself to my body where it made contact. Shielding me from everything.

Caro didn't believe me, either. I tried to tell her after we'd both changed out of our funeral clothes and made our way to Fudge Shack. We sat on the high stools, a slice of Rocky Road untouched on my square of wax paper. She sucked up mouthfuls of her chocolate milk shake and swallowed slowly, letting me finish. She was being all quiet in that way she has of disagreeing. There in the patient nod of her chin and the glassiness of her eyes I could see I was losing her with each new word that came out of my mouth.

I reached the point where I couldn't stand to look at her face any longer. Instead, my eyes drifted up to the bit of blue dye in her super short hair. It had faded to a color like broken sea glass. She'd had strands of blue since we met freshman year, and this was the greenest she'd ever let them get.

When I was done, she said, "I'm worried about you."

I dug a finger into my fudge, then pulled away again, staring hard at the indent.

"I know you're not clicking with Dr. O'Brien," she said. "But maybe it would be worth . . . trying someone else?"

I shrugged. "I'll think about it."

But I could tell she knew I was just saying that to get her to stop talking that way.

I made a show of checking the time on my phone and offered my hollow apology as I gathered up my fudge and slid off the stool, headed toward whatever imaginary thing it was that I was late for.

Later, I felt guilty. Wasn't Caro only trying to help?

But how could anyone really help me if they didn't *believe* me?

What I wanted was to talk to Axel about my mother, to skip a hundred days ahead of that kiss, try to wipe it from his memory and mine. I wanted to tell him about the bird. I sat on the sofa with my wanting, turning a charcoal stick between my hands—around and around and around—until my fingers were soot black and everything I touched ended up smeared and burnt.

Would Axel believe me? I wanted to think yes. But honestly, I had no idea.

After I didn't answer my cell, he called the house phone, just once. Nobody answered. He didn't leave a message.

We'd rarely ever gone so long without seeing each other. Not when I had the stomach bug, immediately followed by the regular flu, immediately followed by an upper respiratory infection—he came over anyway, braving the toxic air from my lungs to sit on the sofa beside me and paint. Not even when Dad made me go to Mardenn, that god-awful hellhole of a summer camp. I was so miserable that Axel rode the bus all the way up to help me sneak out and get back home.

He would never cut me off. This I knew. This was all on me.

To think about it was to twist the arrow between my ribs. So I let myself be swallowed by thoughts of the bird, my questions spiraling, like where is the bird now? What does she want?

I tried to draw her in my sketchbook, but I couldn't get the wings right.

6

The mother-shaped hole became a cutout of the blackest black. Something I could only see around. If I tried to look directly at it, I saw emptiness.

I had to fight that emptiness, that absence of color. I looked in the other direction, toward white, which is made up of all the other colors of the visible spectrum. White was a solution, or at least the smallest of Band-Aids. In the empty hours the morning after the funeral, I drove to the hardware store, winging through an obscure route to avoid being seen by anyone in the neighborhood who would recognize first the car and then my face. The need for white paint burned so hard I didn't think twice about driving unlicensed.

I did one coat on the walls of my bedroom—the paint was thin; the bright tangerine my mother and I rolled on years ago turned a sickly shade of Creamsicle—and was making my way toward the bathroom when Dad came out of his office.

He looked at the paint bucket by my legs, smears of white already staining my jeans, and said, "Leigh, come on."

He didn't understand about fighting the gaping black hole, the emptiness. Not that this surprised me. There was so much he didn't understand, would never understand.

"You're not bringing that in there," he said, pointing his thumb toward the master bedroom. Fine with me. No way was I going in there anyhow. He took the paint bucket, and I escaped downstairs and into a sketch pad and let my knuckles work against the paper.

I made dark, pooling shapes. I pressed my stick of charcoal down as hard as I could until my knuckles were stained and aching and a waxy puddle of black shined up at me. Maybe if I could draw the emptiness, I could control it.

But it was never dark enough. It was never the blackest black.

It'd been a long time since I colored anything in. Charcoal and pencil were all I was using, and I mostly stuck to outlines. I was saving the colors for later.

7

I knew what I'd seen. It was real. Wasn't it?

Each of those nights after that first appearance of the bird, when all noise upstairs had subsided, I went to stand on the porch and squint into the sky. The clouds blew in front of the stars. The moon shrank, giving up a sliver of itself with every passing day. I emptied and refilled the bucket so there was always fresh water, just in case. And when I went back inside, I left the door propped open by a worn sneaker. A breeze crept in through that gap to take its turn through the living room, and I fell asleep dreaming of the giant's breath on my face.

A week after the funeral, moonbeams reached through the living room window and the temperature suddenly plummeted. It was the type of summer night that should've been unbearably hot, but my every exhale sent a cloud of white billowing out in front of my face. I didn't hear a sound or anything, but I decided to check the front yard anyway.

As soon as I stepped outside, I saw a package slightly smaller than a shoe box waiting on the doormat. Dirty twine wrapped around the sides, crisscrossing in the middle, knotted to secure the lid. The corners were a little smashed, and the only thing on the box was my name in the bold black marker of an unfamiliar hand. There was nothing else. No stamps, no labels, not even an address.

I raised my head and the bird was standing in the yard with one leg tucked up just like the cranes I'd seen in paintings. The moonlight made her wing tips silvery and sharp, made the shadows in her body almost indigo.

"The box is from your grandparents," said my mother, the bird.

My first thought was *My grandparents are dead*. Dad's parents had been on the older side when they had him; both of them had been gone for a few years.

Unless...the bird meant my mother's parents? The ones I'd never met?

"Bring it with you," she said as I bent to pick up the box.

"Bring it with me where?" I said.

"When you come," she replied.

When I straightened again, the bird was already leaping up and away, this time leaving no feather.

There was nothing left to do but go back to the living room. For a moment, everything around me seemed to be melting, the colors darkening like something cooking over high heat. The windows and curtains losing their shape, furniture sagging and shrinking into the floor, even the light fixture up above turning to a murky liquid.

A couple blinks and it all looked normal again.

I sat down on the sofa, suddenly so exhausted I fell asleep halfway through trying to get the twine off the box. When I woke again, this time with a full sun buttering the windows, the box was still there.

It was real. It existed in the light of the morning. I took a deep breath and let my fingers curl around the lid.

8

I'm still trying to figure out what to do about the box. It's been nearly a week since my mother came as the bird and delivered it. It's agonizing to feel like I can't talk to Axel about this.

Will Dad believe me now?

I think of the way his brows furrowed, like there was something wrong with me.

I'm sitting on the sofa, cross-legged and directly above the spot where I've hidden the package. The stuff inside that box—it's different from the feather. It's so much more. Maybe this time I can get him to listen.

I stare straight ahead into the glossy finish of the upright piano like it's a crystal ball that will explain why my mother is a bird, or show me what I'm supposed to do next. I've been going through the house and drawing the things that feel important, but I haven't made a picture of the piano yet. It has so much history, and history means colors.

Once upon a time that instrument poured sound through

our home. When did I last hear my mother play? I'm not sure; I guess that should've been a red flag.

In hindsight everything seems obvious.

Year after year I promised that the next summer I would finally let her teach me so that a second set of hands might grace those keys. It was something she wanted. More specifically, it was something she wanted us to do together. I always imagined us learning some charming duet, my hands pounding chords in the bass, her delicate fingers tinkling in the higher octaves.

Mom used to leave the piano keys out in the open, gleaming like teeth. She said they needed to breathe. But my father put away the sheet music and pulled the cover down. The piano before me is bare, unsmiling, funeral black.

In the space where the music books used to sit, open to whatever sonata or nocturne she was working through, I find the ebony reflection of myself. Growing up, I always wished I could look more like my mother. More Taiwanese.

My mother had shoulder-length hair that she kept permed in loose curls, and big glasses that she peeled off when her headaches took over. I remember trying to see her through the eyes of strangers: the willowy, dark-haired woman with the disjointed grammar and mixed-up idioms. I only ever remember hearing her speak English. She even picked an English name for herself: Dorothy, which she ended up shortening to Dory.

I have some of the same shapes in my mother's face, but otherwise most of my features come from my father, the Irish American guy born and raised in Pennsylvania. I have a smudgier version of his hazel eyes, a replica of his sharp nose. I look a lot like his younger self—especially in certain pictures from back before I existed, when he was a bass player in a band called Coffee Grind. It's hard to imagine him as a musician—I've only ever known him as a sinologist, a scholar on all things related to China: the culture, economics, history, etc. He's totally fluent in Mandarin and makes regular trips to places like Shanghai and Hong Kong to give talks and meet other sinologists and economists.

I tug fingers through my shoulder-length hair—the one attribute that seems to be all my own. The stripe on the side is currently dyed mermaid green, but the rest of it is my natural color, a deep brown, exactly halfway between my mother's thick black strands and my father's mousy waves. It's a little thin, but it looked decent when Mom used to weave a French braid down my back; I wish I had bothered to learn how that worked.

There are a lot of things I wish I'd learned from her, while I still had the chance.

My reflection makes me sigh.

The piano tells me nothing about my mother, the bird. Nothing about the box. It only mirrors back the story of a desperate girl who's been getting up in the deadest hours to unlock the front door.

The sound of coffee spitting and bubbling breaks apart my thoughts. It means Dad is in the kitchen. I don't really want to face him. I'm tired of his doubting me, and I'm sick of the way he walks around emanating a murky Payne's gray. The colors of this kind of grief should be stark and piercing, with the alarmed brightness of something toxic. Not the quiet hue of shadows.

But my stomach is gnawingly empty, and once the coffee is made he'll sit there for ages. It's either face him or go hungry.

I shove my sketchbook under the sofa and pad into the kitchen to dig a piece of string cheese out from the drawer in the fridge. My mother's cat winds back and forth between my legs, mewing.

The newspaper crinkles between Dad's hands. "Ignore Meimei, I just fed her."

I lean down to graze her soft back with my fingers. She mews some more. Maybe what she's hungry for isn't food. Maybe what she wants is my mother.

If Axel were here, he'd say, *Hey there, Miss Cat.* He'd lean down and have her purring in a matter of seconds.

Axel. The thought of him sends a shard of phthalo blue into my center.

"What about you?" Dad is saying. "Would you like a real breakfast?" He sips his coffee. "I'll make oatmeal?"

I scrunch up my face, but my back is to him so he can't see. Doesn't he know I eat oatmeal only when I'm sick?

No. Of course he doesn't. He doesn't know shit.

Mom would have offered to make waffles with berries and cream. And if we were really going to keep up our Sunday morning tradition, Axel would be letting himself in through the back door any minute now. But he isn't going to come. He knows me better than anyone, knows when I'm trying to serve him counterfeit cheer, knows when I'm on the verge of shattering. Even if he can't see the self-hate chewing through my insides, he has to know that it's irreversible, this thing that's happened between us.

"No thanks." I busy myself with pouring orange juice into

Mom's favorite mug—the black-and-white one covered in music notes—to avoid looking at him. "So when are you going back to work?"

"Well, given what happened..."

My brain immediately begins to tune him out. *Given what happened.* I want to burn those words out of existence.

"...so, I'll be here."

"Wait. What do you mean?" I turn around. One of my charcoal sticks is dangerously close to his mug, and I make myself resist the urge to walk over and rescue it. Dad is known for being a klutz; plus he doesn't particularly care for my "habit" of drawing. (Like it's something detrimental to my health that I need to quit. Like it's crack cocaine.) "Don't you have another conference or workshop coming up?"

"I'm not going."

"But you have to. Don't you?"

He shook his head. "I'll be working from home for a while."

"You *what?*"

"Leigh," Dad says. He swallows audibly. "You sound like you *want* me to go."

Well, I'd assumed he would throw himself back into work. I've been waiting for him to call a car to take him to the airport. Waiting to have space to breathe again, put things in my sketchbook without being policed, figure out what exactly it means to grieve for a mother.

"*Do* you want me to go?" he says, and the fissure in his voice threatens to put a matching crack in my chest.

I steel myself, feeling ruthless. "It's just that...you used to leave for work things all the time. We got used to it. Why aren't you traveling anymore?"

"You had your mom to take care of you," he says, trying to mask the hurt in his voice.

"I'm about to turn *sixteen*. I've been staying home by myself for *years*."

"It's not about how mature or independent you are, Leigh. It's about . . . us needing some quality time together. Especially given what's happened. I want us to . . . talk more." His eyes take on the shine of guilt.

I gulp down a deep breath. "Okay. Then I have something I want to talk about."

Dad's eyebrows rise a couple millimeters, but he also looks relieved. "All right," he says warily. "Shoot."

9

It takes me just a second to retrieve the package from its hiding place under the sofa. "I know you don't believe what I said about Mom," I begin, setting the box on the kitchen counter and dragging a stool over to sit.

Dad closes his eyes and pinches the bridge of his nose between his thumb and index finger. "Dreams sometimes just feel incredibly real. No matter how badly you want them to be true, they aren't—"

"But can you just look?" I tell him. "The bird came again, and she brought this box."

He looks at me with a pained expression. "Leigh."

"I'm being serious!"

"There's no postage on the package," he says slowly.

"Just listen for a sec." I try to pull back the anger. "I get that this sounds ridiculous."

Dad shakes his head.

The cat meows by the sliding door in the back, and Dad

steps over to the glass to let her out. Meimei slinks through the gap in perfect silence, as if she can't bear to witness any more of this conversation.

The door slides shut hard. "How about we schedule another appointment with Dr. O'Brien—"

I clench and unclench my jaw. "Just *look in the box*, Dad. Please."

He makes a noise of frustration and tears off the cardboard lid. His hands slow as he sees the contents. Yellowed letters, neat in a bundle. A stack of worn photographs, most of them black-and-white. He loosens the drawstrings of a velvet pouch; a silver chain pours out, followed by a shiny piece of jade. It's a solid and weighty thing, only a bit smaller than Dad's thumb. An intricately carved cicada at rest.

My father draws a sharp gasp. He recognizes it, as I did.

That is the necklace my mother wore every single day of her life.

"How is this here?" he murmurs, tracing a wing. "I mailed this off."

"She said the box is from my grandparents."

Dad furrows his brow and blinks at me. He looks old and tired. Not just in his body, but in his face. In his eyes.

I hold up one of the black-and-white photos. There are two little girls perched on ornate wooden chairs with tall backs that stick up beyond their heads. I'd seen these two before, in a different photograph, one that Axel had helped me unearth in my basement. In this picture they're a little older. One of the girls has grown taller than the other.

"Who are they?" I ask, pointing at the girls.

He looks at it for a long time. "I'm not sure."

"Okay. Then what does the note say?" I prod.

"What note—?" he begins, but then it's in his hands and he's reading it and his eye is twitching.

I stared at the page for so long I can remember the inky look of the contents, characters with strokes that swooped down and hooked upward. I know the look of Chinese writing when I see it. It's all over my father's study.

When I was little, I would crawl around on the shaggy rug of his office while he drew on giant pieces of paper torn off an easel pad and taped to the wall. My fingers would trace the air as he taught me the order of the strokes. He'd break down the components of the characters, teach me to identify the radicals—*This one looks like an ear, right?* and *See how this is just like the character for* person, *but like if you were seeing the person from a different angle?*

Mandarin was like a secret language between us—the best was in grocery stores, or in restaurants, how we could talk about people around us and they wouldn't understand. *That boy has a funny hat*, I would tell Dad with a giggle.

It was something that Mom never wanted a part of, even though I couldn't help thinking of it as her secret language to begin with. It belonged to her in a way that it would never belong to me and Dad.

And like so many other things, our secret language faded away. I haven't spoken a word of Mandarin in years.

I still have a bit of it, of course. Like I remember *ni hao*, which means *hello*, and *xiexie*, which is *thanks*. There were times when I asked Mom whether she thought I should go to Chinese school on the weekends, like a couple kids I knew. She always stepped around the question.

Maybe next year, she'd tell me. Or, *You can take the class you want in university.*

I still remember the way she wouldn't meet my eyes when she answered.

If only I could read the language. Like, *really* read it. I still know some of the basic characters, like the ones for *wo* and *ni*—*me* and *you*.

And *mama*. *Mother*.

But I can't read who the letter's addressed to. I can't even figure out who wrote it—though I have a few guesses.

"Is it from my...*waipo*?" The syllables for *maternal grandmother* get stuck in my throat. *Why pwuh* is kind of what they sound like. I remember Dad teaching the words to me a long time ago, but I never imagined that I might someday use them in a context relevant to myself.

It's frustratingly ironic that I'm the one with Chinese and Taiwanese blood running through my veins, and yet my Irish American father is the one who can read, write, and speak the language.

Why was Mom so stubborn? Why did she reject Mandarin and talk to us only in English? The question has bothered me a hundred times, but never as intensely as now, looking at these strange letters. I always thought that one day she would give me an answer.

Dad clears his throat. "Your *waigong* wrote it, actually. But it's from the both of them."

I nod him on. "And?"

"It's addressed to you," he says with disbelief.

Excitement and fear and hope and dread churn together in my stomach. I've spent years waiting for the chance to know them. Is this finally it?

A photograph falls out of the stack. It's stiff, the edges crisp, like it's been carefully kept.

In the picture, my mother is wearing big thick-rimmed glasses, a pale dress, half a smile. She looks young enough to still be a teenager. It must have been taken before she left Taiwan to study in the US.

Was she happy back then? The question wraps around me, carrying with it a bluish slip of sadness.

There's the sound of air being sucked in quickly. When I look up, Dad's lips are pressed into a line. He seems to be holding his breath.

"Dad?"

"Hmm?" His eyes reluctantly break away from the picture.

"Will you read the letter to me?"

He blinks several times, clears his throat. He begins to read. Slowly at first and then settling into a pace, his professor's voice loud and clear.

Mandarin sounds so musical, the way the tones step up and down, each word rolling to the next in little waves. I catch phrases here and there that I recognize—but strung together, I can't quite decipher what the whole of the letter means.

Dad finishes, and seeing the expression on my face, he explains: "In a nutshell—your grandparents want you to visit. As in, go to Taipei to meet them."

Is that what the bird wants? My mother's voice echoes back to me: *Bring it with you. When you come.*

I turn toward him. "What about you?"

My father gives me a confused look. "What?"

"Don't they want to meet you, too?"

"We've met."

The words hit me in the chest. "*What?* You told me you'd never met them."

"No," he replies very quietly. "It was your mother who said that." The look on his face is unreadable.

How is there so much that I still don't know about my own family?

"They know about Mom?" I ask.

Dad nods.

I listen to the clock striking out each determined tick. If only I could rewind, go back in time and ask my mother every question about every tiny thing. How crucial those little fragments are now; how great their absence. I should have saved them up, gathered them like drops of water in a desert. I'd always counted on having an oasis.

But maybe that's why the bird came. Maybe she understands that there are too many things unanswered. A shiver ripples through my body. It occurs to me that Caro, who believes in ghosts, would probably call this a haunting.

Bring it with you. When you come. The bird meant for me to go somewhere. I'm almost certain that it could only be where my grandparents are.

Maybe that's where I'll find my answers.

~~I want you to remember~~

"So can I go? To Taipei?"

Dad shakes his head. "Things are more complicated than you realize."

"Then *explain* it to me."

"It's not the right time for any of this," he says. He tilts his head down in a way that says, *This conversation is over.*

The bird doesn't come back after that.

10

When I close my eyes to try to sleep, everything tilts and spins. Behind my eyelids, I see the bird landing again and again. I hear my mother's warm voice.

I crack my eyes open, gazing at nothing in particular, letting my vision adjust to the darkness. But the longer I look, the more things seem to change. The edges of the end table going soft, rounding. The other side of the sofa deflating, though I don't feel my body moving with it. The carpet below turning into a dark and wavering sea, reflecting back the lines of moonlight that trace the window edges. The entrance to the living room melts away, walls dripping down like a surrealist painting.

"Dad?" I call out softly.

The room resets. I wait to see whether he heard me, but there's no sound of him moving around.

Trying to sleep is pointless. It's not even what I need right now.

I sit up and pull my computer into my lap, let the harsh light of the screen wash the living room in a cold glow. It calms me to see everything more clearly, to note the sharp corners of the piano bench, the straightness of the curtains draping down against the window.

When I type the word *suicide*, my hands are slick with sweat and I am almost certain my father, upstairs in the makeshift bed in his office, can hear me tapping out each individual letter. The last thing I want is to go back to Dr. O'Brien's office, to endure his nasally voice and answer questions about how I'm "coping"—which is exactly what will happen if my father realizes what I'm searching for on the internet.

I sink back into the old sofa and tuck my bare feet under a pile of cushions before scrolling through the search results.

Link after link, page after page. The words crowd the screen, crawling everywhere, blurring like dots of rain gathering on glass, sharpening again to prick at my eyes.

My gut makes the sickening lurch like I'm at the top of a roller coaster, just starting to drop. Only there's no release. There is just that tension, coiling tighter and tighter, constricting my organs and seizing my breath and threatening to bring up my last meal.

What I learn is that all the odds were stacked against my mother actually dying. Someone should have caught her before she lost enough blood. Her stomach should have ejected everything she swallowed.

I can't stop myself from wondering about the physical pain of the experience. I try to imagine suffering so hard that death would be preferable. That's how Dr. O'Brien explained it. That Mom was suffering.

Suffering suffering suffering suffering suffering.

The word circles around in my head until the syllables lose their edges and the meaning warps. The word begins to sound like an herb, or a name, or maybe a semiprecious stone. I try to think of a color to match it, but all that comes to mind is the blackness of dried blood.

I can only hope that in becoming a bird my mother has shed her suffering.

Dad still doesn't believe me.

Would it make a difference if he did?

Isn't part of being a parent that you're supposed to believe your daughter when no one else does? When she needs your belief more than she's ever needed anything from you?

The more I think about it, the more that *believing* seems like the ultimate definition of *family*. I guess my family is kind of broken. Always has been.

Once, in the first grade, our teacher had us make family trees. I remember trimming out the shapes for Mom and Dad and Grammy and Grandpa. I remember making a trunk from an inside-out cereal box and cutting multicolored construction paper clouds to use as leaves.

I hated how it came out. My tree was imbalanced. Mom wasn't an orphan, but that was how it looked when the teacher stapled mine up on the bulletin board. Most of the other kids had made trees that were perfectly symmetrical.

After school that day I went home and asked, "How come we never see my grandparents?"

"What do you mean?" Mom said. "Every week we see your grammy."

"But *your* mom and dad," I clarified. "How come we never spend Thanksgiving with them?"

"They live too far away," she replied curtly.

I didn't understand what I could possibly have done wrong,

but I knew then that I wasn't supposed to ask about Grandma and Grandpa on Mom's side.

I tried again in middle school, when my social studies teacher did a unit on East Asian cultures.

"Mr. Steinberg asked me if anyone in our family has ever experienced foot binding."

"Why does he ask you that?" my mother said almost defensively, and I remembered her looking up from the knife and cutting board with a strange blue expression.

"I told him you grew up in Taiwan," I explained.

She paused and looked up into the corners of her eyes. "I think my grandmother in China—your great-grandmother— she did do foot binding."

"But not your mom?"

"No."

I waited a beat. "Why don't you ever call your parents on the phone? Or write letters?"

Mom gave me a look. "We do not have good terms. There was an argument."

"But can't you just make up?"

She looked so conflicted when she tried to answer. "It's difficult. Sometimes things not so simple. You understand when you are old enough."

I hated that answer.

11

Aweek after I show Dad the box, it happens close to midnight: Every window in our house unlatches and slides
open.

I'm on the sofa when I hear the scrape and slam of the window frames, and a second later, the noise of things softly *shush-
ing* against the screens. Things that sound like they're angry
and trying to get in.

People? Robbers?

The curtains in the living room curl toward me in fat bil-
lows. A whisper of wind sneaks in around the edges.

My mother?

Fear seeps through me, crawling toward my center like
cold water through fabric. I'm glued down, fixed in place.
One tiny nugget of logic in my brain fights against the freeze,
reminds me that sitting here with my back stiff against
the couch is not helpful.

"Mom?" My voice is all scratched and shaky.

It's like that one word halts everything. The *shush*ing is gone. The wind dies. The only answer is silence.

I do a circuit and check the kitchen. Nothing.

Then I hear the distant crash, and more *shush*ing far away. Whatever it is has moved to the second floor, where it sounds much worse. Up there the wind is whistling, high-pitched and sharp.

My father curses loudly from his office. I hear his heavy footfalls, listen to him creaking from one side of the house to the other and back again. More cursing.

"What's going on?" I call up the stairs.

He shouts back, "I'm handling it!" Which doesn't sound entirely true.

I don't want to go up there. But it sounds like he might need help.

With each step I take, the fear tightens around my legs, trying to anchor me in place, making my feet heavy and slow.

Aside from the white paint incident, I've tried my hardest to avoid going upstairs. Every time I climb these steps, I can't help thinking that I'm making my way toward where the body was.

The body.

The stain.

I'm halfway up when a second crash comes, this time loud enough that I cringe and slap my hands over my ears.

My eyes squeeze shut and I sit down hard.

The body the body the body. The stain the stain the stain.

"Leigh?" It's Dad, standing at the top of the steps, leaning on the banister like he's been defeated.

"What is it?" I ask.

He shakes his head.

That's when one last gust of wind comes funneling through the house, through every open window, crashing together above the stairs, creating a miniature tornado. Bits of red appear, sweeping into the current of twisting air. Dad tries to fight it, wheeling his arms into the tornado again and again.

The wind abruptly dies; everything settles. A torn window screen cartwheels along the hallway and down a few of the steps before coming to a halt. Pieces of red cling to my father; the look on his face stony and furious as he tries to brush them off.

"What are they?" I ask, squinting to see, but as soon as the words are out I know the answer. I don't even need him to say it.

"Feathers," he says. "They're goddamn feathers."

Days pass and we don't talk about it. No mention of the feathers or the bird. He pretends the strange wind never came. But he's quieter than usual—the event spooked him more than me. It's a long week full of cold silence, uncertain and carbazole violet.

After that, he books us two plane tickets.

12

Taipei is fifteen and a half hours away. It's a direct flight. I can't remember ever sitting still for so long in my life. Part of me wonders if it makes any sense, scraping across the sky toward these people I've never met. But the thought isn't worth it. This trip is almost too good to be true; I have the fear that at any moment Dad is going to stand up and somehow force the pilot to turn around.

It took over a week for him to get all his work things settled, then just one afternoon for us to pack. I was prepared to fly out by myself, but he didn't want to let me do that. It doesn't even matter. All I care is that we're doing what Mom wants. Or at least, what I *think* she wants.

On the car ride to the airport, Dad tried to give me all these "fun facts" about Taiwan. Suddenly he was invested in this trip. Like it was his idea or something.

"You're going to love it, Leigh. Taipei is such a neat city. There's a Seven-Eleven on every corner—people just call them

Seven. And like, their garbage trucks play music; it's so random. We'll definitely go to Taipei 101—it's one of the tallest skyscrapers in the world. Oh, and we're there in time for the Ghost Festival, if we want to make a day trip to Jilong—which is actually spelled K-E-E-L-U-N-G—"

"Neat," I said, using his word. My voice came out flatter than I'd meant it to. He stopped talking after that.

Right before we took off, I checked my in-box. Sitting at the top above all the unread messages of condolences, there was a new email:

FROM: axeldereckmoreno@gmail.com
TO: leighinsandalwoodred@gmail.com
SUBJECT: (no subject)

I didn't open it, didn't even look at the preview. There's a part of me that desperately hopes it's just one of his usual notes. I'll click it open to find a silly joke, a sketch he made with some new app, a goofy photo of him and his sister.

If I don't open it, I can pretend our friendship is the way it used to be.

If I don't open it, things will not have changed.

Next to me, Dad's asleep, with the latest superhero movie playing on the tiny screen in front of him. His eyes are shut, his face tipping down, the cheap airline headphones sliding off his head. In his unconscious state, his elbow scoots past the armrest and over into my side. He hasn't hugged me since before my mother turned into a bird. As though offering a hug would be giving into the grief. As though I'm a fragile shell and he's afraid of crushing me.

And I thought I had stopped wanting hugs. But that accidental elbow—I welcome its warmth, its company.

My fingers are ice. I curl them into the softness of my neck, seeking heat. Everything is cold. I imagine a diagram pinned up in a doctor's office, illustrating an electric-blue chill that starts at the outermost tips of the limbs and seeps in toward the center of the body.

Maybe that's what dying is like. Did my mother feel this coldness at the end? Maybe every time my fingers start to go numb, it's the shy beginning of death. Maybe my body just happens to be strong enough, alive enough, to ward it off.

Or maybe that coldness is the beginning of how someone turns into a bird.

13

The sky in Taipei is the kind of purple that makes it hard to tell whether the sun just came or went. Dad says it's evening.

My face is melting; sweat trickles down every inch of me. In a quiet alley between residential buildings, Dad scrolls through his phone trying to find the exact apartment number. The streetlamp stretches its long neck high above, casting down a harsh fluorescent light. The building doors are sheets of scratched-up metal. The windows, to their sides, are caged in by bars. It's so very different from our neighborhood back home. There are no brightly painted doors and windows with decorative shutters here. No yards or driveways or front porches.

Long red banners are glued above some of the doors, bearing Chinese characters in shiny gold foil, each word the size of my hand. And outside, sitting in the alley itself: a cluster of mopeds and bicycles, clothes clinging to drying racks made of bamboo poles, a dusty sedan. Smells drift around the corner to meet us—a combination of incense smoke and garlicky oil.

The few people who walk past turn their heads to stare. Now Dad's fumbling through his pockets, his hands noisy with his frustration.

"They know we're here, right?" Suddenly I'm questioning the decision to fly to Taiwan. I think of the way my mother's face darkened every time I mentioned my grandparents—is there a reason it was a bad idea to come?

The air is so thick I'm convinced a giant tarp covers the city, trapping the wet heat of our collective breaths. A breeze swims past, but it brings no relief, only brushes the hairs on my arms in the wrong direction. I rub my elbows nervously. Beneath the lamplight, I see my father's hands shaking. "Dad? Are you okay?"

"Just hang on a sec," he says tensely. He swings his backpack around to the front and paws through it.

I look out into the empty road and listen to the sound of his riffling. Papers fall to the concrete with a smack and a gasp, fanning out in a mess. Just as I stoop to help gather them, the next door over creaks open, pouring gauzy light everywhere.

A hunched little woman stands on the threshold, squinting out at us.

"*Baineng*," she says.

It takes me a minute to realize the woman is trying to say Dad's name. I stand up fast, but Dad rises out of his crouch more slowly.

The woman hesitates, then says, "Leigh."

I swallow a gulp of air, letting that one syllable tie a knot in my throat. The voice is both my mother's and not.

"*Name wan cai dao. Chiguole mei?*"

This woman clearly does not speak English.

"Leigh!" she says again, stepping forward.

Well, and what was I expecting? That after all these years, my grandparents had bought a copy of *Rosetta Stone*? Weren't all those letters from my grandparents written in *Chinese*? In some corner of my mind, I had imagined my mother's language skills passing up to them in a sort of backward inheritance.

Dad turns to me expectantly as if to say, *Don't you remember the manners I taught you?*

"*Ni hao.*" I can tell my tones are off as I slide up and down the words. It's been too long since I last uttered those syllables out loud.

"*Waipo hao,*" Dad corrects.

Waipo. Right. *Grandmother.* I figured out that much, but I'm still not quite ready for it. Too many extra beats are spent searching for Mom's features in that wrinkled face. "*Waipo hao,*" I finally say. My voice has never sounded so pink.

She says my name again, and a string of words I can't process. And then, miraculously, something I understand: *Very pretty.* She smiles at me. Her fingers gently follow a strand of my hair down my shoulder.

Pretty. *Piaoliang.* With my wide hips and tree-trunk thighs? My face, so much rounder than my mother's? The shape of my body not at all delicate the way I'd always wished it to be, and my hair brown instead of black?

Waipo ushers us in and the door squeals shut. Dad and I drag our suitcases into the small elevator. On the second floor, my grandmother stops and gestures for us to remove our shoes. She offers us foam sandals to wear inside.

We round the bend into a small living room. The man who must be my grandfather is perched on the couch with a wooden cane next to him. He shuffles across the room in a pair of faded blue slippers.

"*Waigong hao.*" My voice cracks.

He nods for a beat too long, then twists his head down to cough into his arm. When he straightens, he's smiling.

If only I could remember how to say, *It's nice to meet you.*

I try really hard to dig the knowledge out from my memory, but suddenly all I can think of is Axel at the funeral asking me, *What color?* and me answering, *White.*

White, like a blank page. White, like my teeth. I try to smile back.

14

I sip from my tiny cup of tea, grateful I have something to busy my hands and mouth with. The taste of the oolong is colored by the smell of smoke—salty wisps bending toward me from the altar.

Not an hour ago, we stood there before the bodhisattva statues, touching flame to incense and pricking the bottoms of the spaghetti-thin sticks into a bowl of rice and ash. Dad closed his eyes, and I tried to follow his lead, but I wasn't sure if I was supposed to be praying, or taking a moment of silence, or maybe listening for some distant sound.

In my head the words that circled were the ones crossed out at the bottom of that note.

~~I want you to remember~~

The bird wanted me to come, and here I am. I inhaled the salty smoke and tried to make up a prayer. *Please tell me what it is I need to do here. Please tell me what I need to remember.*

No answer arrived. Well, and what was I expecting?

Now we're all sitting in the living room. Dad and me in brocade armchairs, Waipo and Waigong on a couch made of wood and cushions. Beneath bright halogen lights I study their faces. My grandmother's thin lips are stretched in a perpetual smile, her cheeks lightly mottled, nose small and flat. She wears simple gold hoops in the lobes of her ears, her white hair pulled back in a loose bun. My grandfather nods as we speak, his gray hair military-short, teeth slightly crooked, skin freckled with little brown constellations.

I try to find my mother's face in each of theirs. How different did they look the last time she saw them? What caused there to be such a chasm between them?

Dad and Waipo carry most of the conversation. I catch a few words I understand. *Airplane. America. Eat. Weather.*

How strange this is. To sit here and talk like this, hold polite conversation over tea, when it's a tragedy that has brought us together.

Dad passes things back to me in English like a game of telephone: This is a new home; they moved here two years ago. Waigong hasn't spoken a word since he had a stroke. They've had decent weather the last few weeks, not as hot as usual, thanks to a typhoon out in the ocean that's carried in some rain. The sugar-apples and dragon fruits have been particularly good this season. The guavas, too, which Waipo makes into smoothies.

Who the hell cares about guavas when my mother is a bird? My knee jiggles fast and hard.

Dad tips his suitcase on its side and unzips it, the contents gleaming like the innards of a treasure chest. He pulls out packages of candy: Hershey's Kisses. Godiva chocolates. Tootsie Rolls.

Waipo's eyes light up, but then she shakes her head.

"What's wrong?" I ask.

"She's saying it's too much," Dad explains. "But I wanted to bring all her favorites."

The words sting oxide brown, the unfairness slicing at something deep inside me. Why is it that he knows what my grandmother loves, and I don't?

Now, at last, we've run out of things to say, and a paralyzing silence fills the air. No one speaks. No one moves, except Waigong, who sucks on a Tootsie Roll and nods vaguely to himself.

My body tautens with every passing second. I'm wound up, ready to burst.

Waipo reaches for the television remote, and in a panic I spit out a word in English: "Wait!" The words spiral up out of my memory: *"Deng yixia."*

Because how can the four of us sit here and watch TV together? Pretend like we're just having a normal night as a family? This is not how this is supposed to go.

Everyone watches me expectantly. I hold up a finger, uncertain whether that's even a universal sign, and run for the guest room. The box is in my duffel bag, carefully wrapped in a pair of jeans. I peel off the lid.

I hesitate for just a second—because is this what my mother wants me to do? But how would I know? I can't afford to waste time. If she's here, I have to find her.

"Leigh," my father says in a warning tone when I return to the living room holding the box.

I ignore him and kneel on the floor between the couch and the armchairs, carefully extracting the contents. Waipo says something; the lilt of her words form a question mark in the air. Dad doesn't answer. When my eyes meet his, I note his furrowed brows, the unhappy tug in the corner of his mouth. He doesn't want me to do this.

Well, I don't care. I didn't come all this way to keep secrets.

I turn to my grandparents and point down at my array. The letters, in a carefully balanced pile. The photographs, fanned out. The cicada necklace, which I pour out from the pouch.

Waigong has stopped nodding.

My grandmother kneels down beside me and fingers the silver chain, traces the edges of the cicada. *"Baineng,"* she says, and a fast string of words rolls from her mouth, the syllables coming out all silk and knots, peaks and valleys.

Dad replies slowly, keeping his gaze pointed at his feet. Whatever it is he's saying sets my grandmother shaking her head, her body trembling like a string yanked taut.

"What is it?" I cross my arms. "Tell me."

My father finally looks up. "Where did you say you got this box again?"

The anger lights inside me like a match. Fire burns fast along my ribs. "I told you. Mom came as a bird—"

"Stop. This is going too far, Leigh." His voice like a coil of something hot.

I stand up. "I'm not lying about this. I wouldn't lie about Mom."

My grandmother starts rocking back and forth.

"Tell me what she said," I demand.

Dad sucks in a deep breath and squeezes his eyes shut. "You should never have gotten this box."

I roll my eyes. "What the hell is that supposed to mean?"

The language slips out by accident. His face tightens, but clearly other things are more important because he lets it go. "They never sent this. There's no postage on it."

"I told you," I say, trying to curb my tone, "it didn't go through a mail service—"

"*No,*" he says. "Listen. Your grandparents put this package together, planning to send it. But they changed their minds. Instead, they burned it. The photos and the letters. The necklace, which I mailed to them. They burned all of it."

Waipo murmurs something, shaking her head.

"They burned it so that your mother could have these with her on her next journey," Dad translates, his voice dropping low.

"But Mom—the bird." I feel everything tilt and bump. I'm a top teetering at the end of its spin, a squeeze of asphaltum paint sullying zinc white. "You have to tell them about the bird."

Dad pushes himself out of the armchair. "We're done with this conversation."

I listen with disbelief to the sound of his feet creaking their way down the hall, the guest room door shutting behind him with a click.

Waigong closes his eyes, gripping his cane and letting out a long, lasting pitch that's halfway between a hum and a wheeze, almost too quiet to be audible.

I turn to my grandmother. "*Mama shi,*" I begin—but then it takes me a long moment to remember how to say *bird*: "*Niao.*" Did I get the tone right?

My grandmother blinks at me.

I grab a pen and pad of paper from the table next to the couch, wondering how on earth to communicate this.

The silence is back louder than ever. This time nobody tries to end it.

I start with a quick sketch of my mother's face. It's my first time drawing her since she turned into a bird, and it comes slowly at first. But my fingers remember—my muscles know how to draw the dark eyes, the freckle on her right cheekbone, the tilt of her eyebrows. Her face materializes out of the ink.

Waipo bends forward to see and I turn the pad around. My grandmother studies the drawing. She squints and blinks, and recognition blooms in her eyes. I point to a photograph from the box and then back at the face, just for confirmation. "*Mama,*" I say again. My grandmother nods, and then I draw an arrow. Where its tip ends I begin to make the bird.

Waipo stares for a long time, watching my pen work. The ink doesn't flow smoothly through the ballpoint, and I still can't get the wings right, but it doesn't matter. It's the bird. I look up, triumphant.

My grandmother's expression is apologetic. She shakes her head and murmurs something in Mandarin.

A different approach, then. On a new page, my pen works out the fat, fuzzy body of a caterpillar. A new arrow points from that to the other side, where I make a butterfly. Before I even finish, Waipo's already nodding. She understands. Her finger traces the arrow from one to the other.

I tear out the page with my mother and the bird, and place it beside the caterpillar and butterfly.

For a moment there is only the tick of the tiny alarm clock on the shelf. And then Waipo gasps with understanding. She pats Waigong's arm, and he opens his eyes, gazes down at the pages.

"My mother has turned into a bird," I say in English.

Waipo nods.

15

Raised voices startle me awake. I sit up slowly, feeling disoriented. Eyes achingly dry, muscles sore and prickly. It's my first time getting sleep again since the bird brought the box to our house. Trying to swim my way up out of the exhaustion feels awful.

My hand is in a fist, and when I unclench it, there's the cicada necklace warm in my palm. Dents are left in my skin from where the edges dug in. I don't remember picking it up when I went to sleep. The chain sticks to me; I shake it off on my pillow.

A tug of the curtain reveals the world outside to be still and dark. Not yet dawn.

Decibel by decibel the voices climb. Waipo, sounding rough and defensive. Dad, weirdly nasal, pitched higher than usual. Her voice burnt sienna, his kings blue. Their words crashing into each other so fast and hard I can't pick out a single recognizable phrase.

There's only one guest room, and when I turned in last

night, my father had already taken the floor—likely feigning sleep on top of those blankets—and left me the bed. I didn't expect to actually fall asleep, not after the shock over the box that should have been destroyed.

How long has Dad been up? What time is it? Purple confusion clouds my mind.

When I get to the end of the hall, Dad's back is to me, but I can tell from the way his shoulders hunch and how he has one fist pressed to his head: He's crying. It's the first time I've seen him cry since the funeral.

My grandfather, Waigong, is standing on the other side of the room—which might as well be across the Pacific Ocean—one hand gripping the back of the couch. There's a terrible look on his face. Waipo's in the doorway separating the kitchen from the living room, shaking her head at the floor.

Nobody sees me for a long, quiet moment. Then they all notice at the same time, my presence announced via some frequency I can't detect. Waipo's eyes snap up. Dad pivots around.

"I'm sorry, Leigh," he blurts at the same time Waipo utters a string of syllables. My father heads back toward the guest room, sweeping past me so quickly the air churns into wind.

Waipo ducks into the kitchen and reappears half a second later with plastic containers stacked between her hands. She calls out words that sound like music and like nothing.

"Sorry for what?" I turn to send my voice down the hallway after my father.

"She's asking what you want to eat," Dad translates over his shoulder.

I take a step toward him. "Dad, what are you doing? What's going on?"

Waipo gently takes my elbow, guides me back to the kitchen. She pulls bag after bag out of the fridge, stacks box upon box, showing me endless food options. Vegetables and uncooked dumplings and porridges and tofu and pickled things—

"Yao buyao?"

"Yao," I tell her. *Yes. Want.* It's a relief that I understand this at least.

My grandmother's eyes light up at my effort to speak the language. She grabs a pan, and I turn back into the hallway in time to see my father rolling his backpack and suitcase out of the room.

"Dad!"

He looks up at me guiltily. "I'm sorry, Leigh. I just can't do this."

"*What?*" I glance at Waigong, who's now sitting on the couch. His eyes are closed, his shoulders rigid.

"Your mother—" Dad's voice breaks. "She wouldn't want us arguing."

I jut out my chin. "*I'm* not arguing with anyone."

"She wouldn't want there to be this…anger. And resentment. Over her. Over the past. This is what she tried to avoid. And here I am, breaking the promises I made when we got married."

"You got married almost twenty years ago. Things change."

He gives me a tired look. "I thought so, too. But some things don't."

I cross my arms. "We *just* got here. You can't make me leave."

"I'm not," Dad hurries to say. "I'm not making you leave. Okay? You can stay. I'll head to Hong Kong for a little while—"

The disbelief shakes me like an earthquake. "Are you *kidding* me? You're just going to…*leave* me? Here?"

"You're in safe hands," he says, rubbing his temples. There are dark pouches beneath his eyes, flecks of gray in his hair. "You're with family. I'll be back to pick you up when you're ready to go home. In the meantime, I'll get a phone card. And I saw an internet café around the corner, so you can—"

"They don't even speak English! How am I supposed to talk to them?"

"Practice your Chinese," he says quietly. "Isn't that what you've always wanted?"

It sounds like a joke. Like he's mocking me. How much Chinese do I really have? Almost nothing.

Someone needs to make it illegal for parents to throw things you once said back in your face.

I watch him push his suitcase out the front entrance, kick off his slippers, and slide into his shoes without untying them. Before he shuts the door, he says in a voice so apologetically fuchsia, "I love you, Leigh."

I'm too pissed to say anything back.

Nobody even says goodbye.

16

More pieces of Chinese that I learned years ago are trick-ling back:

Shengqi = to be angry

Weisheme? = Why?

Hao buhao? = Is it okay?

Buhao. It's not okay. In fact, it's very bad.

I can't believe that not an hour ago I watched my father walk out of here. Part of me is relieved he's left; part of me is disgusted. How am I supposed to get my answers without him? How will I find the bird? Rage flares through me alizarin crimson, and a scream holds itself ready in my throat.

In the guest room, I sit on the bed, cupping the necklace in my lap. That cold silver chain. The stone pendant as real as anything can be. How is it here in my palms? How did this—and all those letters, those photographs—survive?

The act of burning destroys something. But these are not destroyed.

My anger hisses and sputters like a lit match hitting water, and suddenly all I am is exhausted.

Morning light peels in around the dusty edges of the curtain. I drag the fabric aside for a look at the city.

My gaze locks on two eyes, shiny and round, the color of flames, but inky in the centers. They're just beyond the bars outside my window, intensely focused on me. There's a beak, long and charcoal black and pointed. Bold red feathers curl up and back into a crest atop its head.

The air sticks in my throat; my stomach clenches. Panic and relief swirl in my head, a mess of oranges and yellows.

"Mom?" I reach for her and my fingertips land too hard against the glass. The bird snaps her head aside, startled. She angles her beak toward the clouds and opens it wide. Her scream rips across the sky, vibrates against the window.

She launches up and away, one claw slipping off the metal, tearing into the screen behind the glass.

My bedroom door bursts open, and Waipo stumbles in, looking about wildly.

"*Mama*" is all I say before I rush around her and into the hallway, my feet scrambling to find their place in a pair of shoes—any pair. I throw the front door open and skip the elevator, racing down the stairs, the sandals on my feet slightly too big and *slap-slap-slapping.*

"Leigh!" Waipo calls from above, but I'm already at the bottom, shoving my way out into the morning light.

Where is she?

I try to slow my breath, get enough air into my lungs so I can think. At the end of the alley, I swing right to get behind the building my grandparents call home.

Why is it so dark now?

My eyes search for the window with the slash in its screen.

The sky opens up and warm rain dumps down hard. Within seconds, the water has claimed every inch of me.

There's no sign of the bird anywhere. I look up and all I see is the wide, flat gray.

"Leigh!" Waipo's panting hard as she pulls a plastic poncho over me one-handed. She stretches out her umbrella, a pastel-pink thing with a broken spoke, and mutters something about rain. I can barely hear the words over the noise of the storm.

Back at the apartment, she finds me some fresh clothes. She towels off my hair, blows it dry, the air pouring hot and fast. How strange it is to have her fingers against my scalp, so gentle and certain. With my eyes closed, they feel just like my mother's hands.

The first thing I notice when I blink my eyes open is the fan on the chair buzzing as the blades spin. The sound makes me think of summer bugs skimming over grass, of sitting in a field and sketching trees with a charcoal nub, Axel making a face as he checked whether a spot on his leg was a tick, a blue sky smoothed out flat like a sheet.

Some strange, unexplainable compulsion makes me roll out of bed and walk over to the dresser. I pull open the top left drawer and find the inside empty except for two things:

A curved Winsor red feather. And a slim, rectangular box I've never seen.

The feather is what I pick up first. It's slightly oily between my fingers, smelling strongly of a wild musk. It looks so much like the other feather I have from the bird. Was this left as a message? How is it that I didn't know what I would find, but somehow I knew exactly where to look?

The box is approximately the right size and shape for holding a letter opener—or maybe a feather—and made of a stiff cardboard material that's so old and worn it's gone soft. My fingertips come away gray; it's coated in a layer of silty dust. The whole thing is a faded marigold orange with Chinese characters printed on it vertically in red:

最
難
風
雨
故
人
來

The only character I recognize is the one with just two strokes. *Ren*. It means *people*.

The lid comes away easily enough, just like the top of a shoe box, scraping away with a light *shush*ing sound as if to warn of its contents: long sticks smelling of smoke and wreckage and used-up matches. A scent like a mess of colors swirling into darkness.

Incense. Roughly the same size and shape as the sticks burning atop my grandparents' altar, except these are solid black. I lift one out carefully, overcome with the strong urge to light it. Between my thumb and finger, it's strangely hot, like it's been warming in the sun.

And then: the whispering. The tiniest, most hushed of voices. It's coming from the incense.

I bring it close to my ear—

A knock at the door makes me jump.

"Hold on—*deng yixia!*" I call, scrambling to shove the box and the feather back in the drawer, and dropping onto the bed just as the door squeaks open.

Waipo looks at me through the crack, her face hesitant.

"Hi," I say, my heart slamming in my ears. I don't know why I felt like I had to hide anything. Why I'm weirdly nervous now.

My grandmother beckons me out. *"Lai chi zaocan,"* she says.

Zaocan. Breakfast. Right. A stab of guilt—have they been waiting for me all this time?

Her gaze drops to something next to the bed. She makes a beeline toward the nightstand and picks up my mother's necklace, holding the cicada pendant up to a sliver of sun peeking out from behind the curtain. The light catches on the jade. She points at me and smiles as she says the next thing.

All I understand is *ni. You.* Before I can try to guess, she's leaning over me, sweeping my hair to one side, clasping the chain around my neck.

The weight of the cicada settles against my sternum. Waipo takes my hand, pulling me to my feet.

There's so much food on the dining table. I recognize the fried cruller sticks glistening with oil; *youtiao*—my mother's favorite, I remember with a pang. And the rectangular *shaobing* flatbread. Then there are all the things I've never seen before. Steamed rectangular cakes drizzled with a dark sauce. A bowl of some kind of vegetable, pale and spongy. Sliced pieces of a rolled crepe with a glistening white skin. A strange brownish soup.

My throat tightens up. It wasn't often that we would have a Taiwanese-style breakfast—only a couple times a year, when Mom felt like making the drive out to one of the Asian grocery stores—but that rarity made it such a treat. Axel and I, and Dad, if he was around, would stuff ourselves to the point of having to skip lunch.

I wonder about the days when she'd come home with all the ingredients for a meal like this. Were those the times when she missed Taiwan? When she missed her family? She'd had me almost convinced that she'd stopped caring about them.

Waigong is already seated, his wooden cane leaning against the table by his elbow. He picks up one of the sesame-dotted flatbreads, digs his finger into the side, and opens the two layers like butterfly wings. He stuffs it with a section of cruller, and dunks the whole thing in his soy milk—just the way Mom would have eaten it.

The pendant feels heavy, and my fingers trace the shape of the cicada. I try to imagine my grandparents thirty years younger, sitting at a round table just like this one, smiling at my mother instead of me.

17

In the heavy quiet of the night, I'm finally alone in my room again.

I spent the day melting under the sun, trailing behind Waipo through the open-air market where whole fish were laid out on piles of ice in bright plastic buckets, and pineapples were stacked high on metal carts, and one woman pushed her dog around in a stroller to go buy a whole black-skinned chicken. Afterward, Waipo bought us bubble tea, and we sat on a park bench people-watching as we sucked the tapioca up through fat straws.

It felt so different from the parks back home, full of thick trees draped with scraggly brown beards. Star-shaped flowers smelling like kumquats. Long leaves waving like flags, flapping their rusty undersides.

We watched children racing down a path toward a small playground. Kites sprinkled the sky like confetti—a butterfly, a phoenix, a winged monkey.

It was an Axel type of scene. He would've pulled out his

portable watercolors and made us stay until he'd gotten at least two good pages. And once he went home, his quick strokes of color would bake from raw visual into warm, delicious audio. The kites would be rendered in arpeggios. The children would become little timpani gods roaming the earth in seven-eight time. For Axel, watercolors are just his way of taking notes—his own form of shorthand. He uses the colors to guide his compositions, to produce pieces of what he calls opera electronica.

Even as Waipo and I walked home, even as we ate dinner with Waigong, I couldn't stop thinking about what Axel would do and say if he were here with us.

I didn't tell him we were going to Taiwan. In my head I see him standing on our porch, ringing the doorbell, knocking hard. I see him stepping back, counting the passing beats like a piano accompanist waiting to jump in again.

I blink and it all vanishes: the memory of the park, those imagined spreads of watercolor, Axel's unhappy face.

It's growing late, but something keeps me awake. My grandparents have gone to bed, the last of their sounds shuffling and clicking away into silence.

I wonder where Dad is now. Is he checked into some fancy hotel, paid for with all his travel points? Does he regret leaving us? My fury is still simmering, tinting everything a dark burnt umber.

The smart thing would be to try to sleep, get my body on schedule. I need to be operating at max levels of energy if I'm going to find the bird. I'm exhausted, and the heat makes it so much worse—every one of my limbs feeling thick and weighed down.

And yet. When I close my eyes, willing my body to relax...
I can't shut off my mind. Images rewind, replay, again and
again. I think of that red and feathered creature sailing across
the sky. The box of things that my grandparents said they'd
burned. That gray body, arranged in the casket like a doll.

And what about the box of incense? I'd never seen incense
sticks so black.

I hear them again: the whispery voices, words I can't decipher. The *shush*ing of syllables that slide up against each other.

Cold light puddles in the wide crack between the bottom of
my door and the linoleum. It seeps in from the window behind
the thin curtain, washing the walls in spectral beams. At first I
think it's the moon snaking down the alley, and then I realize
it's the streetlamps. My eyes settle; the darkness lifts. There's
just enough glow to see by.

My bare feet slide out of the low bed to find the floor, carrying me to the dresser. I guess I was expecting the whispers
to grow louder, but they abruptly halt the moment I touch
the handle. I pull at the drawer slowly, quietly. This is a small
apartment with thin walls; sound travels.

There's the feather. There's the incense. And this time,
there's also an old-looking book of matches. Where did these
come from? A shiver traces the curve of my spine. I can't help
checking over my shoulder. The light outside the window
flickers and dims, as if answering a question I didn't know I
was asking.

I'm convinced they're from the bird—the feather is like a
signature, telling me she sent these here for me to use.

Yank out a match, scrape the flame to life, touch it to the
tip of a stick dark as tar.

The end catches, lights up like a firefly. The smoke that rises is inky black, drawing lines through the air.

No voices. Nothing. I don't know what I expected.

But then the dark lines billow out fast, drawing ribbons that wrap around and around in the shape of a storm. I gasp, and smoke shoots into the back of my throat and down into my lungs. I'm coughing and spitting and trying to rub the sting from my eyes.

The smoke fills the room, until there's only black.

18

—SMOKE & MEMORIES—

The smoke clears, darkness melting away, and I find myself standing in a completely different room. A room I know all too well, in the house where I've lived my whole life.

Pear-green walls. An arched entryway.

My living room.

Mom's at the piano; a Beethoven sonata flies from her fingers, the notes turning and falling impossibly fast.

I'm looking at my mother. *My mother my mother my mother.* My ribs are on the verge of fracturing.

"Mom." The piano drowns me out.

Her hands roll over the keys, shaping wide arpeggios, her torso rocking to match the dark waves of the music. I remember this piece: "The Tempest."

There's a vaguely sweet scent hanging in the air—my mother's coconut shampoo, the only shampoo I've ever known her to use, the closest to a perfume that I'd ever smelled on her.

The colors in the room are muted, and there's a meditative

quality to the music, to its spinning rhythm. I'm nowhere near the piano but I can practically feel the smooth keys under my fingers.

"*Stop*," someone whispers behind me, giggling. I whirl around, and there on our sofa sits a dark-haired girl that is unmistakably me—but younger—grinning widely and elbowing a shorter, gangly version of Axel. The faces are a bit blurry, but it's definitely us. I'm standing directly in front of them, but they don't see me. This is so weird.

"What?" he says, his face a canvas of blank innocence.

My younger self rolls her eyes dramatically, shining all the while. Had I realized how I felt about him yet?

This is a section of the past, somehow preserved. I don't remember it at all; and then I realize by some instinct that this memory belongs to my mother. That's why it smells like her.

The stripe in my hair is purple, so this memory-Leigh is probably about twelve years old, still carefree. She and Axel hug sketch pads over their knees, kick at each other's ankles.

There's a thunderous noise above—footsteps coming fast down the stairs, and then my father appears, his face lit up. I'd forgotten that sound—the joyous stomping of feet. When did we become quietly padding people?

"What smells *amazing*?" says the memory version of my father.

A timer in the kitchen goes off and the colors shift as if awakening. My mother whirls halfway around the bench and leaps to her feet. She plants a kiss on Dad's nose and waltzes right past him into the kitchen. He turns to watch her, enchanted.

Once upon a time we'd been an almost perfect family. I wish we could rewind, go back to live in those years forever.

Everything turns even blurrier, and the smell of the

coconut shampoo fades slightly now that my mother isn't here. I walk into the kitchen and the edges sharpen, the colors brightening once more. Her face is glowing, and there's the hint of a smile as she slides the pan out of the oven.

"Enough with the suspense!" Axel calls from the other room. "Tell us what they are, already!"

"*Danhuang su*," says my father.

I follow Mom back into the living room, her arm stretched out ahead of her so that the plate leads the way. She's stacked it high with a dozen perfectly round pastries, gold and laminated, ornamented with sesame seeds.

This is the mother I want to remember. This joy. The way her glow filled a room. Her playfulness, her love of good food, her bright and bouncing laughter.

I step forward, desperate to touch her, but my hand disappears against her shoulder like I'm the one who's the ghost.

My parents share a pastry between the two of them, pulling the flaky layers apart with their fingers, catching the bean paste on their tongues. Mom lets Dad have all of the salted egg yolk at the center—his favorite part.

I stand there with my feet rooted into the carpet of that memory, watching until my ribs crunch together and pulverize my heart and send the heat of my missing everywhere. The grief spills out of me sepia dark.

All the colors invert. The light sucks away.

Flicker. Flash.

There's Leigh from the past, even younger this time, no color in her hair yet, crouched at the edge of a dark lake. My father comes up beside her, pinching a bouquet of green grass blades. The colors have changed their tint, like someone turned a dial to make them warmer. The scent completely different, like dryer sheets—the way my father always smells.

It's Dad's memory.

"So here's the trick. Take one of these—" He lays the blades out on a flat spot and selects a prime piece for my memory-self. "Now sandwich it flat between your thumbs. Press them together."

Little Leigh holds her hands out to show him. I don't remember any of this, either.

"Yeah, like that. Press harder. Then you go like this—"

Dad brings his thumbs up to his face. He puffs up his cheeks and puckers his lips, blowing hard just under the knuckles to produce a reedy squeal that sings out across the water.

I watch as the memory version of me imitates him, blowing into her thumbs. Her blade of grass flaps and squeaks.

"I cannot do it also," says my mother, who stands a few paces away, balancing on top of a rock, watching, holding her own blade of grass.

"Leigh's almost got it. Keep trying, kiddo." My father steps his way back from the edge of the lake to help my mother.

Memory-me blows and blows. She straightens the piece of grass. She tries a new blade, pressing her thumbs together even harder. At last, that thin pitch squeezes out loud and true, halfway between a kazoo and a duck.

She glances over her shoulder.

There's my mother, a silhouette against the fading sky. Her arms circling my father's waist, cheek against his shoulder. The two of them sway together in time to music only they can hear.

There's the flash. The colors invert.

When the room returns, I'm sitting on my bed in my grandparents' apartment in Taiwan. The memories are over.

My thumb and index finger are pinching together so hard it hurts. I look down: The stick of incense is gone. I click on the lamp to make sure: No trace of it anywhere. No ashes. It simply vanished.

Open my palms wide, look at my trembling hands.

I sit there like that, shaking, until dawn.

19

Whose fault was it? That's the question on everyone's mind, isn't it? Nobody will ever say it out loud. It's a question people would call *inappropriate*. The kind of thing where everyone tells you, "It's nobody's fault." But is that even true? It's only human nature to look for a place to lay the blame. Our fingers are more than ready to do the pointing, but it's like we're all blindfolded and spinning.

What makes a person want to die?

She had me. She had Dad. She had her best friend, Tina. She taught piano lessons to a third of the kids in our neighborhood.

Anyone who knew her would have said she seemed like the happiest. The most alive. When she laughed, her face bloomed and you felt warm at the center.

Those last few months her laughs came rare. I noticed it, I really did. But I chalked it up to moodiness; she'd always been in the habit of swinging from one extreme to the other. I excused it too quickly, too easily.

Was it my fault? If I had only—

Or if Dad had only—

If Mom had only—

What?

20

Even in the bright morning the air is heavy and presses too close, sticking to our skin, drawing out the sweat.

I turn to my grandmother. *"Niao."* Bird. I'm not sure what else to say. How do I tell her we have to find my mother?

Waipo nods, but I'm not sure she actually understands.

We walk out of the maze of alleys to a breakfast shop, where there's a woman making something I've never seen before. It's called *dan bing*. Her deft hand spreads a batter into a perfect flat circle, mashing an egg over the top, sprinkling it with scallions. I'm not particularly hungry, probably in part because I didn't sleep and my body feels sluggish—but even so, my mouth waters at the smell.

The shop sells *fantuan*, too, and those I do recognize: rice patties wrapped around sweet dried pork *song*, reddish brown, fluffed like cotton. There was one day, in elementary school, when I brought a *fantuan* for lunch. When the kids saw the *rou-song* center, they made fun of me for eating yarn, and asked if I was going to cough up hair balls like a cat.

The woman wipes her fingers on her apron, wraps up our breakfast order. Her eyes flicker over me, linger for a moment on my face, as purposeful as a touch.

"*Hunxie*," she says to my grandmother, who is pushing coins around on her softly wrinkled palm, counting out payment. Waipo launches into a chain of words so quick I can't catch any of them. The woman smiles at me, says something about being an American, something about being pretty. The few people eating at the nearby tables turn to point their stares at me. My skin prickles beneath the gazes.

Waipo and I eat as we walk. To-go cups of chilled soy milk are sweating in our hands, condensation gathering into drops, drops gathering into rivulets, the water rolling down my fingers from knuckle to knuckle.

"*Shenme shi...hunxie?*" I ask. Her eyes gleam. She likes when I try with my Mandarin.

"*Hunxie*," she repeats, and proceeds to explain the term.

Eventually, I gather that it means *biracial*. And then I recognize the parts, like finally seeing shapes in the clouds: *Hun. Mixed. Xie. Blood.*

Back at home, sometimes people say I look exotic or foreign. Sometimes they even mean it as a compliment. I guess they don't hear how that makes it sound like I'm some animal on display at the zoo.

One time these two guys at school asked, "What are you?"

When I only blinked, one of them said, "Like are you part Hispanic or something?"

I told them my mother was Taiwanese, and the other guy pounded his friend's shoulder. "That's a kind of Asian. You totally owe me five."

They didn't say anything else to me before they turned away, laughing to themselves.

It's not like it happens every day, but it happens enough to be a regular reminder: People see me as different.

And now finding myself so directly named—*hunxie, mixed blood*—like a label printed out and affixed to my forehead...it makes something twist in my guts in a dark and blue-violet way.

Back at the apartment, Waigong's lounging on the couch, hogging all the cushions under his back and his elbows. He stares into the television, watching a music video with the volume all the way down. A dozen Asian men are dancing in a hexagonal tunnel filled with flashing lights. The screen bursts into a drizzle of feathers.

Waipo hands him a *dan bing* and soy milk and steps over to the altar. Her shaky fingers are surprisingly firm with a match. The flame follows her hand like a comet tail, settling into a dot of light as she touches it to incense. The woody smell drifts across the room. I watch the lazy curl of the smoke and think of the black sticks sitting in that box in my room. There are no whispers out here. Had I only imagined those?

Next to the incense bowl, there's a wide ceramic vase painted with blue dragons, its glossy finish catching both light and shadow. Gray smoke pirouettes in front of the dragons. For a brief moment, one of them seems to swing its head around to peer at me through the haze, teeth bared, claws splayed. A blink, and the smoke shifts. The dragon is once more two-dimensional and unmoving, glaring off to the side in the direction of an unframed photograph that sits propped up against the edge of a fruit bowl.

I didn't notice the picture before. It's barely the size of my palm, black-and-white, worn and coated in fingerprints: two little girls sitting stiffly in high-backed chairs. A faded copy of the photograph I found in the box, the one I asked Dad about.

"Waipo," I begin to say. But before I can figure out the words to ask about the girls, a loud *chirp-chirp-chirp-chirp-chirp-chirp-chirp* fills the apartment. At first I think it's an actual bird, but there it goes again: *chirp-chirp-chirp-chirp-chirp-chirp-chirp*, too rhythmic, too exact. I've learned the precise and flattened quality of audio samples from watching Axel work on his compositions, and this is sort of the same—just a recorded bird vocalization on repeat.

Waipo swallows the last bite of her *fantuan* and rushes to throw open the front door.

It's a deliveryman, holding a brown parcel in his arms.

My grandmother immediately launches into a fast and animated conversation. Her words sound completely different— the vowels wider, the consonants coming faster, stronger, syllables clicking and turning. She's switched from Mandarin to Taiwanese. The phrases completely unrecognizable to me.

The deliveryman leaves, but as Waipo steps aside, a pale young woman comes into the apartment, her blouse printed with giant roses in shades of pink and green. She's older than me, maybe college-age. Maybe older than that. I shift in my chair, shrinking into my loose tee and jeans. I didn't pack much more beyond the things I usually wear at home, which all take into account the possibility that I might get charcoal or paint everywhere.

Waipo is still cheerfully rattling off words, now gesturing in my direction, saying my name. She tears into the box with a knife from the kitchen and begins to pull out packages of snacks, dried fruits, a tin of tea. For just a moment, she switches to Mandarin, throwing a sentence in my direction.

Your father is the only thing I catch. When I shake my head, she shrugs and turns back to the package.

The woman gives me an uncertain smile. "It's very nice to meet you, Leigh."

Her English hits me like a splash of cold water. She has no accent at all.

"My name is Feng, but I also have an English name, if that's easier—"

"Hi, Feng," I rush to say, prickled by the idea that her one-syllable name would be too difficult for me. "Nice to meet you."

"Popo says you speak a bit of Mandarin—would you prefer that?" Her hands flutter like moths, pale and nervous.

"English is fine." Even as I say the words I feel my shoulders tightening with a sense of inadequacy.

"Sounds good!" Feng smiles. "English is great for me, too. A new skill, you could say. Ah, there's green in your hair! Is that an American thing?"

"Um, I think it's an anyone thing."

"Oh. How unusual. People will probably think you're some pop star."

I'm dying to change the subject. "So how do you know my grandparents?"

"Well." She looks embarrassed, uncertain. "I've known them a long time. I'm an old family friend."

Waipo hands me a scrap of paper that was in the box—a pink piece of Hello Kitty stationery. There are two lines of Chinese words, but they're scrawled out in Pinyin, the romanization system that Dad taught me when I was little. Since the letters are all from the English alphabet, I can sort of guess at how to pronounce the words, even if I have no idea what they actually say.

"What is this?" I ask.

"My address—just in case. But I doubt you'll need it."

I nod. "You live around here?"

"Temporarily. I've been away from home for a long time."

And then she points my attention toward a stiff white gift bag that Waipo has just pulled out of the box. The front of the tote has Chinese characters printed across it in red calligraphic strokes. "I brought some fresh pastries, with different fillings—red bean, lotus seed paste, sesame. I made sure to get all my favorites for you to try. They're *delicious.*"

Waigong's already investigating the contents. He dips his head to smell one of the buns wrapped in waxy parchment.

My grandmother's speaking in Taiwanese again. She comes to stand beside Feng; it's clear the two of them are very close.

In the shiny glass of a picture frame, I can see the three of us reflected. Feng looks like *she* should be the granddaughter, with her sleek black ponytail, her dark eyes, her delicate features. I'm the one who doesn't match. Thin hair, brown plus the stripe of color, nowhere near as shiny and thick. My eyes too pale.

Feng nods at my grandmother and turns back to me with a smile. "There's a SIM card in that box, too. Do you have a smartphone? The card I brought gives you internet access. I thought that might be helpful."

She shows me how to use a bent paper clip to pull out my American SIM card and pop the new one in.

"All set," she says.

"Thanks." I think of that email from Axel that I still haven't read.

She beams. "If there's anything in particular you'd like to

see, just tell me. I know you'll need lots of help, and I want to do as much as I can for you."

I try to smile, but my face feels awkward and stiff.

"It's so rare to get the chance to see family, to reunite like this." She interlaces her fingers and pulls them apart again. "I want to make sure you have the best time."

"Thanks," I say again.

Feng grins brightly at Waipo and Waigong. They exchange more words, syllables that flit past too quickly for me to even guess whether they're Mandarin or Taiwanese. My grandmother makes some sort of joke—or at least, seeing the way Waigong and Feng laugh, I'm guessing it's a joke. Cold pewter envy curls around my stomach. Waipo doesn't know me well enough to joke with me. She can't even expect me to *understand* a joke.

Feng slips her shoes on and turns to wave at me, thin fingers fluttering back and forth, and as she leaves, my shoulders sink away from my ears, tension rolling off them, a weight disappearing.

Waipo heads to the kitchen and Waigong is back on the couch watching his music videos.

I sink into a chair at the dining table, where it smells overwhelmingly of oil and sugar. There's the paper tote full of pastries, with brushstroke words printed on its front. Tracing the bold characters with my fingers doesn't help me recognize any of them. I turn it around on the off chance that there might be English on the back of it.

But there isn't. Instead, there's a logo: a red circle drawn around a red bird.

21

I can't sleep, so I pull up my email on my phone. There's a message from Dad, which makes me roll my eyes. I'll read it later.

Below that: the thing Axel sent. No hesitation allowed. My index finger jabs at it hard.

> FROM: axeldereckmoreno@gmail.com
> TO: leighinsandalwoodred@gmail.com
> SUBJECT: (no subject)
>
> 4 minutes 47 seconds
> You breathe out all those lines of art like your
> life depends on it. Well my life doesn't depend
> on this but I guess it's how I process things…
> my sketchbook is like a journal. Converting it to
> music…that's me analyzing and processing it.
> This is the final piece in the Lockhart Orchard set.
> Titled "Goodbye"

Goodbye.

I read the message again, and that last word kicks my heart out of place.

What the hell kind of email is that? What's it supposed to mean?

Goodbye. The confirmation of all that I've ruined slams into me in waves of fluorescent hues. I was ridiculous to hope that one kiss would turn everything he had with Leanne to ash.

I think of how mad he got at the funeral. I know he didn't mean to, that it was the last thing he would've wanted on a day like that.

But it was my fault. I broke the no-bullshit rule.

I imagine Axel sitting on his tweed couch where we kissed, holding a thick pad and some watercolor pens. I imagine myself transported there by a magic carpet, swooping into the basement and crashing into the floor, my mouth already shaping an apology.

At the bottom of the email: a link.

It takes me to a private page where Axel's uploaded the track as an MP3: GOODBYE: ADAGIO IN ORCHARD GREEN. The final piece in the set. I know exactly what he's referring to.

The image he's used as the "album cover" on this page is a photograph of Lockhart Orchard that twists my stomach, sends a nostalgic red ochre rippling through me. It's a picture I watched him take with his phone, on a day I remember all too well.

I can't help wondering: Has Leanne listened to this? Has she asked him about the significance of Lockhart Orchard?

Does she know what's happened between him and me?

My thumb hits play. The piece begins with the bass section humming low and deep, legato lines that crescendo ominously. A piano comes in with soft chords, the cello arching after them.

Pieces of the past rise to the surface of my mind like little bubbles.

22

SUMMER BEFORE FRESHMAN YEAR

I would always remember my fourteenth birthday with perfect clarity, because it was one of the first times I realized that there might be something truly wrong with my mother. She cared that it was my birthday, but it wasn't enough to blow aside the storm. In the shadowy master bedroom, with lights off and curtains drawn, she spiraled all the way down. Her body was silent, but her darkness was louder than anything. Our home shrank to the size of a dollhouse, and the walls pressed up against me so that I couldn't breathe or speak or hear anything but her despair.

Axel and I went out riding bikes. We tried to get lost so that I could remember a different set of fears. At every junction where we would've normally turned down a familiar road, we went the opposite direction.

We wheeled through woods and past farmhouses, across fields and around parking lots. We raced toward the edge of the sky—we could see the crease where it touched our part of the earth—but we never made it. The horizon always ran ahead of us. We scraped to a stop when we found a line of trees we'd never seen. They seemed to stretch on endlessly.

"Are we lost?" I said.

Axel didn't answer. He hopped off his bike and threw himself flat on the grass. A fat bumblebee zigzagged over him.

"Everything looks different from this angle," he said.

I lay down next to him. The white streaks in the sky were like lines of foam across a restless sea. Birds crawled past. Something small buzzed in my ear, then took off again.

"We're not lost," Axel said finally. "We're just headed somewhere different."

We ended up in an apple orchard, and by then my mood had improved. The air was thick and sticky, faintly sweet. The trees rippled against the touch of a high breeze. I didn't yet know how much I needed to worry about my mother, and so I let myself be distracted enough to celebrate a birthday.

"This is a good one," I said through a full mouth, gripping a half-eaten apple, sitting in the wedge between two thick branches. Wind tugged at the bit of color in my hair—back then it was a streak of electric blue. "What's it called again?" I asked.

"Honeycrisp, I think?" Axel called from across the orchard. I ducked to look at him between branches. He was in another tree, his violet plaid peeking through the twists of leaves and fruit.

"Sounds like a breakfast cereal," I said.

"If you keep eating, you're gonna make yourself sick," he told me.

"Nope. I could eat a hundred more of these."

He wriggled out from between two tricky branches and settled into a new spot against the trunk, sighing contentedly. His already tan skin was extra dark from the summer sun.

"Why do people never climb trees anymore? This is glorious. I feel so alive up here."

"I love this," I told him, dangling my leg experimentally. "It *is* glorious. That's the perfect word for it. Glorious in a golden-rod sort of way."

"We should bring some back for your mom," said Axel.

Mom. That one syllable triggered a wave of sadness and worry. All I could think of was how my mother looked that morning, slumped over the kitchen table, her frame small and compressed, as though her darkness took up so much space in the house there was barely any room left for her body.

I couldn't help but feel a little angry that he had brought her up. Without her strange bleakness, it would've been an almost perfect day.

"What?" he said. "Don't you think she'd love these?"

I rolled my eyes. "Why do you have to be such a suck-up? She's not *your* mother."

He looked taken aback. The harshness of the words surprised even myself, but already it was too late for me to pivot, to try for a joke that might save the conversation.

Axel was just considerate like that. And so what if he was sucking up? His own mother had walked out on his family when he was seven. In the course of our friendship, my mom had become something of a surrogate parent to him.

My feelings peaked and then deflated just as quickly, and then I felt ashamed. Here he was, wanting to do something nice for my mother. And here I was, moping about the fact that she was in a bad mood on my birthday.

I took my half-eaten apple and lobbed it into the sky. The

Honeycrisp arched high and fell noisily into the branches of another tree.

We paid for the apples, minus the ones in our stomachs, and tucked them into our backpacks before unlocking our bikes, which we'd left side by side against the fence separating the orchard from the road. My bike leaned into his, both of them held in the embrace of heavy-duty locks that we'd threaded through the wheels and frames.

It occurred to me—sadly, pathetically—that those bikes looked romantic. They touched and bumped without hesitation, without thought. They'd shared in so many adventures; they had history. They belonged together.

I had to be losing my mind. I was personifying *bikes*, for crying out loud. Things of metal and rubber, without hearts or brains.

The road ahead was smooth and empty. The sun was fading; its glow cut across the horizon at a flat angle, springing loose these long, fuzzy shadows that followed us wherever we went. My bike was on too high a gear for going up the hill, but I gritted my teeth and didn't change it. My legs worked, pumping hard, calves burning. I kept my eyes fixed on the back of Axel's helmet.

"What color?" I shouted to him.

He didn't respond, but his bike gained speed. I pedaled harder to keep up.

"*Axel*," I tried again. "What color?"

The hill flattened out and he must have cranked up to a higher gear. I saw his legs working, saw the way his bike lurched forward and rolled like it'd gotten picked up by a wave. He sped to the end of the road and turned right. I followed, winding down a path into a park. Axel braked hard and jumped off, throwing his bike to the ground, not bothering with the kickstand.

"What are you doing?" I stopped beside him, straddling my bike and panting.

"Burnt orange," he said. "The color of being mad at you."

Sometimes Axel completely defeated the purpose of our color system by stating the obvious.

"I'm sorry," I said immediately. I hated that I'd been an ass-hole, that he was right to be upset. "I'm really, really sorry."

He threw off one strap of his backpack and swung it around. I watched him pull out a blanket and a Tupperware container.

"Well, it's still your birthday," he said grudgingly, and I knew I was mostly forgiven. "This is the second part."

"What . . . is it?"

"Sandwiches," he said, tossing the container over to me. "Sliced pear and Brie. Your favorite."

"What?"

"We're having a picnic," he said matter-of-factly. "You were complaining that we're too old for picnics. Well, we're not."

And that was why I was so grateful for Axel: because what other fifteen-year-old boy would ever plan a surprise picnic for his best friend? My throat was tight. After I'd been such a brat, how was he still so good to me?

"Pear and Brie is *your* favorite. My favorite is pear, Brie, and peanut butter."

"Oh, make no mistake," he said, "yours definitely has pea-nut butter on it. You big weirdo. I had to quarantine it from mine with aluminum foil."

I helped him spread the blanket out before kicking off my shoes and investigating the sandwiches. He'd used the smooth peanut butter. Perfect. I stretched out on my back with my knees bent and bit into my sandwich.

Axel reached into his backpack for his art things. A water-color pad, black pouch filled with brushes, small square of terry cloth. His Winsor & Newton paint set was a thing of plastic origami, unfolding out into a palette with mixing trays for wings. I watched him unscrew one of his portable watercolor brushes—they looked like futuristic pens. He carefully angled the lip of a water bottle, filling the pen barrel so that with the gentlest bit of pressure it would release fluid and gather up pigment.

He flipped open to an empty page in his pad and pressed the brush into a square of paint.

I had disappeared. When Axel reached this point, there was nothing left in the world except for him and the colors. Every time I watched it happen I couldn't help but feel left out. When he went to that place in his head, I couldn't follow.

My fingers were also itching to make art. But I held myself still. I wanted to take in this quiet. The sky had turned electric and the sun was cutting stripes across Axel's face, giving him a mask made of light. I sketched him in my head first—a meditative exercise I often did before I started on a realistic portrait.

Bold brows, defined cheekbones—then, as always, my gaze lingered on the eyes. They were so dark—almost darker than mine. I wondered if he'd gotten them from his mother. Axel had so much of his father that I'd always been curious what his mom looked like. There were no photographs of her on display in their house. At least not any that I'd ever seen. I suspected that his dad had hidden them all away.

Axel and I seemed to be the only two mixed kids in the

Fairbridge school district. When people saw us together, they sometimes called us the halfies, which only made me roll my eyes, but it bothered Axel way more.

There was almost nothing left of the Filipino side of his family in his life. Some days he got defensive about it. Some days he talked about his mother like she hadn't left.

Other days he seemed to wish people would just treat him as if he were a hundred percent Puerto Rican. Or he tried even to shed those pieces of his heritage, to blend in and look and act like everyone else in our school. I totally understood; I went through a period of striving for that, too.

Those were the things swirling around in my head as I fell asleep on the picnic blanket. When I woke up, it was with Axel's hand on my shoulder, saying it was time to go home.

Mom was already in bed, but there was a miniature Bundt cake waiting for me on the kitchen counter, with a note on a napkin that said only *Happy Birthday* in her slanted scrawl. She'd mustered enough energy to bake for me; the thought made me feel a little bit better. I set the apples Axel had picked out on the kitchen counter for her.

That night I went to bed thinking of how school was about to start. The previous year—eighth grade—had been a hard one. I thought—or maybe more like hoped—that it had been just as hard for Axel. Since he was a year older, he'd gone across the street without me to begin high school. We still rode the same bus, and we still spent time together outside school. But both of us felt that we'd lost an ally in the halls.

I was about to be a freshman, and Axel a sophomore, and everything would go back to normal. I'd have my best friend at school again. We would at least have art together, because

Axel had skipped it his freshman year, for reasons I still didn't understand. A small part of me wanted it to be because he knew that if we started in Art I at the same time we could guarantee that we'd have at least one class together for three years.

The next day he came over for dinner. Dad was back, and Mom made chive dumplings for a belated birthday celebration— a sign that she had climbed out of the darkness. Afterward, Axel and I sat on the couch drawing each other's feet. When it was time to leave, he handed me a thick, folded square.

"Your birthday present," he said.

"It's late," I teased, to hide my pleasure.

"I needed the extra day," he said. "You'll see."

I watched him shuffle down the steps of our porch, tucking his hands into the pockets of his hoodie. The trapezoidal light poured out our open door and spilled onto the road so he had to have known I was still standing there, still watching him. He didn't look back.

The thick square unfolded into several pieces of watercolor paper. At the center of them all was a thumb drive and a note:

MADE THESE YESTERDAY WHILE YOU
SPENT YOUR PICNIC NAPPING. THINK
OF THEM AS THE SHEET MUSIC.

It was one of Axel's first experiments with translating his art into music, and it blew me away. There were four MP3 tracks on the drive; I couldn't believe he had done all of these in just a day. The paintings were numbered to match the tracks, and I stared at them until my eyes hurt. He had captured more than the colors. Each piece was a snow globe of emotion and instinct.

And the music—that was another language entirely.

He'd done the park in heavy splotches of ink. Yellow dashes of merry-go-round turned to the jagged runs of an electric guitar. The imperial-blue playground was sketched out by the spiccato of a double bass. An arpeggiated synthesizer rose out from under the heavy notes, buoyant and energetic like the rouge strokes used for highlights. Thin swirls of aubergine matched the high vibrato, which he later explained was meant to be a solo operatic voice—he'd maybe one day source a real singer because it was the weakest line sampled digitally.

He'd painted me as well: oranges and reds and yellows layered over lines sketched in India ink. And one other color: a Pacific-blue stripe running through my hair. All these were described through the legato of a cello, a solo clarinet wending its way in and out of a swell of strings, a low timpani, and an ethereal bending pitch later pointed out to me as a theremin.

While I had been napping out in that park, while I'd been playing back my memories of him in the low-lit corners of my mind, he had been excavating me, digging to the center of my soul.

I listened to the four tracks on repeat the entire night, certain that it was a confession of love, convinced that the next time I saw Axel everything would be different. I don't know when I fell asleep, but I woke up wrapped in chrome yellow and Spanish red, feeling like that streak of blue was the core of myself worn as a token of love.

High school started, and I was right. Everything *was* different. But not in the way I'd expected.

The second day, I found out through the grapevine of gossiping freshmen waiting to pay for their cafeteria lunches: Axel had asked this girl named Leanne Ryan out on a date.

23

We try so hard to make these little time capsules. Memories strung up just so, like holiday lights, casting the perfect glow in the perfect tones. But that picking and choosing what to look at, what to put on display—that's not the true nature of remembering.

Memory is a mean thing, slicing at you from the harshest angles, dipping your consciousness into the wrong colors again and again. A moment of humiliation, or devastation, or absolute rage, to be rewound and replayed, spinning a thread that wraps around the brain, knotting itself into something of a noose. It won't exactly kill you, but it makes you feel the squeeze of every horrible moment. How do you stop it? How do you work the mind free?

I wish I could command my brain, say to it: *Here. Go ahead. Unspool, and let the memories go. Let them be gone.*

24

FALL, FRESHMAN YEAR

As I was trying to navigate the strangeness of freshman year, my mother's moods kept nose-diving again and again, twisting and turning as she crashed to the bottom.

It happened so frequently that it started to feel almost normal. Or maybe that was just a mind trick, a way to convince ourselves everything was okay. But I grasped that normality tightly in my fists and I ran with it. I tried to be a normal teenager. I let myself fixate on the embarrassingly trivial things.

Like the question of: When was Axel going to dump Leanne Ryan? Weeks passed. Suddenly they'd been together a whole marking period.

There was one day when Axel and I were standing in the kitchen while his aunt Tina was showing Mom how to clean off the algae growing on the side of our house.

He hadn't been over in a while, and watching him drum his fingers in that familiar way against the countertop felt weird. He was telling me how Leanne thought the lemonade he made from powder was disgusting, how she demanded he make "real" lemonade. How she refused to drink from a jar, the way we always did at the Morenos' house. He told it all like a joke, but there was nothing funny to me about any of it.

"What is it about her?" I blurted.

He held his face very still and turned his gaze toward me slowly. "What do you mean?" he said, which was kind of the exact bullshit he was allergic to, because he knew just what I meant.

"What's so great about Leanne Ryan?" The real question was, *Why the hell are you dating her?* She seemed like everything that he should hate.

He waited a long time before he answered shortly, "I like her."

It turned our conversation chilly. Mom suggested Tina and Axel stay for dinner, but Axel made an excuse about too much homework. I went back upstairs thinking, *Whatever whatever whatever,* the syllables bouncing in my head like staccato triplets my mother would pluck from the piano keys.

And suddenly, I didn't see very much of Axel at all. We still had art class, but every time I opened my mouth I was at risk of saying something horrible about Leanne. It was safer to stay quiet. If Axel noticed my silence, he said nothing.

I carried the silence home with me.

One afternoon Dad's return flight was delayed, and after he called to tell us, Mom slunk upstairs and stayed there. Dinnertime came and went—I inhaled a stick of string cheese and then wandered up to see if she was in the mood to order pizza. She was in bed, cocooned in an oversized quilt. I stood there watching for a long time until she shifted and muttered words that were indecipherable. There was something disturbing about seeing her in that loneliness-induced sleep.

This was early on in the time when Dad had started traveling for work. I guessed—*hoped*—that things would get better as we got used to his being gone. But it stuck in my head, that memory of her sleeping sadly, pining after my father.

Everything in my life seemed to be changing. It felt like things in my house were falling apart in direct proportion to the rate at which Axel and I were crumbling.

My father flew home just in time for Thanksgiving, so Mom went overboard with the cooking. When I showed him the things I'd made for art class, he nodded without smiling. "Is this your last year taking art?"

"No?" I said, thrown off by the question.

"Oh. I just thought maybe you would grow out of it when you got to high school."

Grow out of it? The words shocked me so much I didn't know what to say. It was the first time I realized that maybe it was what Dad actually wanted. For me to grow out of art, get over it. Move on to something different. How could I?

The next week, Axel was out sick. Leanne Ryan sauntered into our art class asking for his folder. She saw me but didn't smile, just let her eyes slide right off my face. No pretense necessary; no Axel around to witness anything.

"He has mono," she told Dr. Nagori. "So it's hard to say how long he'll be out."

Hearing that made me want to puke. How much more clichéd was he planning to get?

Since Axel was absent, Carolina Renard moved into his

chair. I liked her immediately—maybe because we both had a bit of blue in our hair, or maybe because I could tell right away that she was my kind of person. We were partnering for an assignment: an acrylic painting on a piece of shared canvas. The point, Nagori said, was to try to learn from your partner and see through their eyes. Consistency was key. He didn't want to be able to tell which sections were painted by which artist.

Ours was already getting really intense. Caro—*Please don't call me Carolina; that name was a terrible mistake*—was into this jagged pattern like lightning; it split our picture in half. On the left we'd painted a long-necked blue figure on bent knee, offering an anatomical heart. The lover was on the right, holding out hands to receive, except the lightning divided it so that you could see with X-ray vision. Inside the lover floated all manner of orange evil. False promises swirled and toxic thoughts twisted. We made both figures androgynous.

Friday afternoon rolled around and our painting still wasn't finished.

"You going to turn this in on time, girls?" said Nagori as he watched us pack up.

"No sweat. We're working on it over the weekend," said Caro. "I've got everything we need at my house. Right, Leigh?"

"Yup," I said without missing a beat, though this was the first I'd heard about going over. I watched as Caro carefully slid our painting off the table and held it by the wooden frame underneath.

"Can you help me get this into my mom's car?" she said. "We'll give you a ride so you don't have to suffer the late bus. If you could just grab my backpack for me—"

I followed her out to the main parking lot, where she marched straight up to a boxy white sedan.

"Hey, Mom," she said, sliding into the shotgun seat. "This is Leigh. She needs a ride. Her house is over on Larchmont, right when you make the turn."

I threw our bags into the back of the car. "How'd you know that?"

Her mom snorted. "Caro makes it her job to know where all the ladies live. Nice to meet you, Leigh. I'm Mel."

Caro craned her head around to roll her eyes and say, "My mother is convinced I flirt with anything that's got boobs. Which is not true." She turned back, checking that she hadn't smeared the painting. "Anyway, we're actually in the same neighborhood. And you're just a few houses down from Cheslin."

I racked my brain. "Who?"

"You don't know Morgan Cheslin? She moved onto your street a couple years ago."

"Cheslin goes to Stewart," Mel added.

"That explains it." I was bad enough at keeping track of the people in my high school class, let alone any other schools.

"Cool if Leigh's over this weekend to finish our painting?" said Caro.

"Of course," said Mel. She winked at me in the mirror.

Caro saw the wink and made a noise of irritation. "It's not like we're going to be making out, Mom."

Mel shrugged dramatically. "I didn't say anything!"

They dropped me off and were already pulling out of my driveway—Caro giving me one last eye roll through the window—when I discovered the front door was dead-bolted.

As far as I knew, we never touched the dead bolt, and I

didn't have the right key. Some instinct made me feel the need to do a performative search through my pockets and backpack. Mel had paused the sedan in the middle of the street, and they were watching me. I turned around and waved, shrugging, hoping that that would urge them onward, that as they pulled away, my mother would hear me ringing the bell and open the door in time for Mel and Caro to glimpse me entering my house like a normal human being.

But nobody opened the door. There were no sounds from the inside. I banged louder, and when that seemed useless, I gave the door a few hard kicks.

My embarrassment swelled as Mel rolled back up the driveway and put her window down.

"Nobody home?" she said. "You can always come with us if you can't get in."

"I mean my mom definitely *should* be home." I huffed a nervous laugh.

"Is there another door?" said Mel.

"Um, a sliding door," I said, "but it's usually locked...."

I wanted them to go, but Mel insisted on waiting while I went around to the back of the house to check.

The door wasn't locked, in fact. I had just yanked it wide open when I saw her: my mother down on the floor of the kitchen tiles. Curled into a ball, small and helpless.

"Mom!" I ran to her, feeling like I was about to vomit, imagining the worst.

I was able to shake her awake, but she seemed terribly groggy and confused. Everything in my chest pounded as I tried to run through the possibilities. A heart attack? She fainted?

"What happened?" I said. "Are you okay?"

She didn't answer me. "Who are they?" She was squinting up at Mel and Caro, who had gotten out of the car and run over to find us when they heard me scream.

"They gave me a ride," I replied.

"Should we call someone?" said Mel. It took me an extra beat to realize that by *someone* she probably meant 911.

"No," said my mother. "I am fine. Everything okay."

It took a thousand years for Mel and Caro to leave. I couldn't even look at them—the embarrassment was spiraling inside me, firing up crimson, turning hot like a kind of anger.

After they were gone, I watched my mother like a hawk. The way her hands shook as she reached for a pan. The slowness of her footsteps as she moved.

There was a new weight pressing down upon me. What had she been doing passed out on the floor?

"Dad's flight get in soon," Mom said later, when she seemed to have recovered from whatever it was. She gave me a small smile. "Don't need to worry him."

I thought for a long time about those words. She meant that I didn't need to tell my father about being locked out, about finding my mother on that cold tile floor. The way she said it left me unsettled. *Don't need to worry him.* But what about me? What about my worry?

My worry expanded like a coral balloon, its color growing paler with every breath that filled its belly, until the worry was almost see-through, little more than the hint of a shadow, but nevertheless still constant, still there.

25

Here it is," says Feng. "This is the store where I got the pastries."

Waipo taps my elbow and points at a shelf. *"Ni mama zui xihuan,"* she tells me. *Your mother's favorite.*

My eyes find the row she's pointing to, and I recognize the *danhuang su.*

"Yiqian…" Waipo begins to say—*in the past*—and I don't catch anything else. Her eyes are sharp and intense. She's saying something significant, but I can't understand.

Feng jumps to translate before I even ask. "Popo says years and years ago this was a pastry shop owned by a different family. It was your mother's favorite because of their *danhuang su,* which are these round—"

"I know what they are," I tell her, my voice coming out slightly sharp.

"Oh. Right." Feng fidgets with her hands, curling and uncurling her fingers. "Did your mother make them for you?"

"Yeah. I used to watch her when she baked," I reply quietly, and suddenly I'm lost in an indanthrene blue, heavy with remembering.

My mother shaping the patties of dough, pale and flour-dusted. Scooping dollops of maroon bean paste. Setting the salted yolks, little drops of sunlight, into the middle of the red.

She'd brush a lock of hair from her forehead and leave a streak of flour running across her temple like a shooting star. She'd paint the pastries with a thin layer of egg and sprinkle a few dark seeds over the top, little sesame winks.

All around us are shelves bearing trays of baked goods. Which of these would my mother have picked out for herself? The cheery yellow tarts? The fat buns? Or the strangely shaped rolls, embedded with corn and scallions?

Feng inhales noisily, and the sound grates on my nerves. "Doesn't it just smell so *wonderful*? I could stand here smelling all this forever." She points to a tray full of buns shaped like panda heads. "Look how cute these are! The ears must be chocolate. What I love is how pastries like these aren't too sweet. The flavors are more subtle...."

She's been talking incessantly since breakfast this morning, smothering me under her commentary, the cadence of her voice making my temples throb.

I try to block her out and just *think*.

It can't be a coincidence that this was once my mother's favorite shop. But why is their logo a red bird?

"The bird is a new logo," says Feng, making me jump. "They started using it a couple weeks ago. It used to just be a crescent—now the circle is meant to be a full moon."

The hairs on the back of my neck stand up. "Why did they change it?"

"I asked the owner the other day. Apparently she's always loved birds, and in the last few weeks she's seen this red bird high up over the city. She thinks it's good luck."

The bird. My mother. So other people have seen her, too.

My heart swells with raw-sienna hope. I knew I needed to come. I knew that I would find her.

If the woman saw the bird in the sky above the city, then maybe what we need is to go somewhere with a good vantage point. I have to see her for myself.

Dad's words echo back to me. *One of the tallest skyscrapers in the world.*

"Feng, you know the really big skyscraper?"

She blinks for a moment. "You mean Taipei 101?"

"Yeah, that. Are tourists allowed up at the top?"

"Oh, definitely!" She looks cheered by my sudden interest. "You can see the whole city from every direction—"

"Great," I tell her. "Can we go there? Like right now?"

We've barely stepped back out onto the street when an apple rolls right to my ankles. There's no one in the direction from which it came.

Waipo stops me from bending to retrieve the fruit, muttering something in an urgent tone.

"She says not to touch it," Feng translates. "It might bring a ghost after you."

"A ghost?" I repeat.

"They like to latch on to people."

I look back at the apple as we walk away. It catches the light of the sun, that waxy skin shining like a smile. I can't shake the thought that it looks just like a Honeycrisp.

Waipo calls my name, and for a second her voice sounds like my mother's.

She doesn't realize that the ghost is already with us.

The eighty-ninth floor of the Taipei 101 tower is the observatory deck, where you can look out at the entire city through walls of glass. Buildings in miniature. Mountains layered in the distance like gentle strokes of watercolor, the farthest ones fogged and fading into the clouds. It's a strange juxtaposition: the city so tightly packed, everything built so closely together—and beyond that, the sprawling greens and blues of lush forests.

Feng won't shut up. She's going on and on with all sorts of tourist facts. "So it's the only wind damper in the entire world that's on exhibit for people to see. The steel basically balances out any movements in the building caused by wind. ..."

We've circled the floor four times, and there's been nothing. No sign of the bird.

Feng says brightly, "Hey, how about we take a picture together? Want to use your phone, Leigh?"

Reluctantly, I pull out my cell. I lean in toward my grandmother and force my mouth into a smile. Feng squeezes close on Waipo's other side, and I can't strike the thought that they look like a proper grandmother and granddaughter.

I just look like the tourist.

On the little screen I can see my hair sticking out in annoying directions. I comb a few fingers through, try to reshape it. Behind our heads is Taipei and its wide sky, pale and overexposed.

"Smile!" Feng says.

Something red soars past our heads, and Waipo and I both gasp.

"That was her!" I squeeze my grandmother's arm. She's shivering a little.

"Wait," Feng is saying. "You didn't get the photo. . . ."

I whirl around and press close to the glass. "That was the bird!"

Beside me, Waipo is silent, her hands knotting together, eyebrows tight and drawn. She looks out over the city. She saw it, too. For the sliver of a second, those red wings beating past us—she saw it just as clearly as I did.

We wait and watch for a long time, but the bird is gone.

Did she see us? Does she know that I'm here?

My heart is still slamming into my chest, shaking my veins with a heavy violet rhythm. An idea makes me turn to Feng. "I need to go to all of my mother's favorite places in Taipei. The places she went when she was younger. Can we do that?"

Feng begins to translate. Waipo's face is hard as a rock, but she drinks in the words, her expression softening. Her features sink into her wrinkles, crumpling like tissue paper, turning fragile.

"*Hao*," my grandmother says. She nods.

We have to find the bird. And then my mother can tell me herself.

I want you to remember

26

My mother's hands have turned to wings. Her hair, to feathers. Her pale complexion now red as blood, red as wine, every shade of every red in the universe.

The bird. The bird. The bird.

That's all I can think about.

Crawling into bed is like swimming through something thick and murky. My every limb weighed down. Brain hazy with sleep deprivation. Eyes aching, the periphery of my vision dull and watery.

I should be able to sleep. I'm exhausted.

But the moment I close my eyes, they flutter. I have to strain to keep them shut.

The bird the bird the bird.

My mother the bird.

I catch myself rubbing my thumb in circles around the edges of the jade cicada.

Funny how when you can't sleep the brain turns itself

inside out, becomes a desperate and hungering thing. All I want right now is to fall headfirst into the blackest black. All I want is for everything to shut off so I can finally rest. Make the colors stop. Send the thoughts away.

Let everything go still.

Is this what it feels like to want to reach the end? Is this the kind of existence that led my mother to become a bird?

There's a rhythmic sound outside—growing louder and louder. The flapping of wings. I bolt upright, yank the curtain open.

Nothing. Only the bright coin of a moon, and the hint of coffee-dark clouds beside it, unmoored.

Maybe if I step outside, she'll come to me like she did back home.

Without turning on any lights, I make my way through the apartment, my bare feet lending me an extra bit of quiet. I only pause to hook my fingers into the straps of a pair of sandals, waiting until I'm out the door before I slide them on.

The outside air is still thick and muggy, the fluorescent streetlights casting their ghostly beams down into the alley. I stand at the nearest crossroads and wait to see if I hear the wings again. Wait for some sort of sign. A sound, or a smell. A vision. Anything.

Even when I squint my eyes, I can't see anything moving across the sky. Everything is dark and murky and still. The nearby alleys are all quiet, but I can still hear distant sounds of traffic, of cars wheeling past.

I'm so settled into the emptiness that when I turn and see a man standing across the street under a tree, I nearly jump with surprise. He stares at me long and hard, barely moving, his hands at his sides. I keep waiting for him to walk away, but he doesn't, and so at last I'm the one to break eye contact and turn back toward the apartment. I hate the idea of him seeing where I live, but when I glance over my shoulder again, he's gone.

There's no breeze, but the tree where he stood rustles slightly, and for a second I think I see something like a mist shifting across the branches. And then it's gone. The tree is still, and it's just me alone in the alley.

Upstairs in my dark room I sit down on the bed. It happens in a flash, in a blink: My eyes close, and when they open again, the room is bright as day, the ceiling so white it's glowing—except for the inky cracks branching off in all different directions above me. They're as jagged as lightning, like something heavy has struck down from the other side and begun to break into my room. The in-between lines so thin, so black—like there's nothing beyond that layer of ceiling but a gravity-defying abyss. Wind loud in my ears, goose-bumping my skin.

It makes no sense.

I blink again, and the room is dark once more. My fingers fumble to click on the lamp: The ceiling is perfectly fine. Not a crack to be seen. No wind, no sound. Just my heart drumming, drumming.

27

The hands of the clock glow alien green: It's 4:12 in the morning. Is there any point in trying to sleep? The seconds tick past, louder and louder, echoing in my ears.

Then, over the sound of the clock, I hear it again. The flapping of wings, faint in the distance. Click the lamp on. Swing my legs out of bed.

The noise is gone.

My feet carry me across the moon-cold floor to tug open that same drawer as before. I reach past the flattened pastry bag for the box of incense. The feather is still there, slightly curled, like something asleep. I take that out, too, pinching the shaft between thumb and finger.

I'm still trying to figure out why the bird brought me the incense—if it'll lead me to her. Or if it's to help me understand.

I want you to remember

Light the match. Touch the stick of incense—its tip alight and calm as an ember—to the vane of the feather.

What follows is a sizzling. It starts between my hands and rises up like a cloud, the noise surrounding me and filling the room. The feather suddenly oven-hot, but I can't let go; my fingers are stuck.

Black smoke ribbons out, pulling like taffy, riding some wave of air that I can't feel—

Here are the swirls. Here are the turns. Here is the changing of the light and colors.

The room goes dark.

28

—SMOKE & MEMORIES—

All I see is black. Black, and the feather. My finger and thumb closed over a red stem.

A jolt of pain hits me: It's all light and noise and emotion flooding my head, throbbing in my temples.

A burst of cold light. The colors invert.

There's my mother alone at the kitchen counter, and at her elbow is an empty orange bottle next to a rectangular array of capsules. It's dark outside and around the edges of the memory; the only light that's on washes her in a stale yellow glow. Her index finger slides each pill one at a time into the perfectly dotted rows, her lips moving silently, counting.

When was this? Not from this year. She looks too young. Her face pale, but her forehead smooth and relaxed, eyes reserved. Had she already made up her mind?

The colors spark and flicker. The smell changes.

There's my father on the phone, calling everyone he can think of, his voice shaking as he asks, *Have you seen Dory?*

There's me on the couch, knees tucked into my chest, eyes unfocused, listening to his strained words.

All the curtains thrown wide, windows dark, clock ticking past dinner, ticking away the time that Mom had been gone.

Dad saying, *No, we haven't seen her in fourteen hours.*

Saying, *I don't think we can call the police yet.*

I remember this, I do. But here it's the chemical smell of dryer sheets, and my face is a blur. This is a memory from my father, and everything is so dim and muted, the hues of his worry, the umbra of his fear.

Finally, white beams cut through the heaviness. Headlights roll into our driveway, a car with a dent in the side.

Mom headed out that morning to get a gallon of milk. That was what she said. *Be right back.*

Dad, hanging up the phone.

Me, pushing up off the couch.

The two of us in stunned silence as we watch through the window. My mother walks up to the front door, her hands empty but for her car keys, no milk or anything, feet dragging heavily along the concrete.

There's the flicker. There's the flash.

Coconut shampoo in the air again. The colors muting themselves.

There's our kitchen lit by the gray predawn light, the sound of water running in the sink. There's my mother, sliding against the cabinets to the cold floor.

She curls up on the tiles, tugging her bathrobe around herself. The sun has started climbing its way in through the edges of the window, warming everything except the shad-owy figure that is my mother. The sky outside painting itself a brilliant and mocking blue.

Footsteps creaking on the stairs, and then Dad shuffles into the kitchen, finding her on the floor.

"Dory," he says. His voice so quiet.

He asks what's wrong, how he can help, what she needs. Her words come out in shattered pieces, unintelligible, thick with hopelessness, heavy under the weight of something that's taken me years to even begin to understand.

Nothing is right, she says. The only three words I catch.

If someone had asked me, I would've said that every-thing seemed right except for my mother, who seemed totally wrong, and that in turn made everything else feel dark and stained. I would've carved out my heart and brain and given them to her just so she could feel right again.

A flash of light, a flash of dark, and then a burst of better times, shuttering past:

My mother, smiling a real smile at my father for the first time in years.

Quiet and calm and playing Debussy, fingers roving over the keys, making the piano tinkle and shine.

Waking up early again instead of sleeping through the days.

Sliding on a satiny dress and doing her makeup and hair, looking rejuvenated, looking alive.

Reviving the tradition of Sunday waffles with me and Axel.

We thought she was better. We were convinced.

And then, unfairly, a memory of that body in the coffin. Me, standing there at that funeral. Axel at my elbow. *It's not her,* a voice screams from the corner of my mind. *My mother is a bird.*

Bird bird bird bird bird. That one word echoes on and on.

The colors invert and go dark. I blink myself back into the room. The incense is gone. The feather has crumbled to silty ash in my palm. My hand turns, the dust falls, and before it can touch the floor, it vanishes.

29

We thought she was better.

What can you do when all you see behind closed eyes are the flashes of your mother, your mother, your mother, miserable, alive, beautiful, sick, warm, smiling, dead?

But not dead.

Not exactly.

My mother is a bird.

30

What makes a person—one who is so deeply loved—decide to do such a thing?

A sudden recollection: my mother and father standing on opposite sides of the kitchen, talking to each other with their mouths but pointing their focus elsewhere with their eyes. They were out of sync. Mom with her arms crossed. Dad nodding vaguely in the direction of the floor, slumped with his back against the fridge.

I can't even recall what they were talking about—something logistical, probably, to do with groceries or whatever—but I remember trying to *see* the love between them, waiting for a spark, or even a faint glow that might be hovering in the air, however dim. I remember squinting to see *something*.

It had to be there. Some slight color, no matter how bleached the hue—or even just a pale wash wrapping around them.

Did we love her wrong?

How did we fail?

Sleep is what I need. Sleep will end all these thoughts, this viridian spiraling. But with my eyes squeezed shut, lashes twitching against my cheeks, all I can do is think about the past.

31

FALL, FRESHMAN YEAR

I'd never felt so intensely jealous of another family until I met the Renards. Later the guilt for having the thought would come in heavy fluorescent-green waves, as if I'd committed the worst kind of betrayal.

First I fell in love with Caro's house. Their garage was amazing, crammed with easels, paints, jars of brushes, tarps and fabrics stained with colors, a hamper full of smocks. All Mel's. I couldn't help the thought: *What would my house be like if Mom were constantly cheerful, and if Dad also made art?*

Down in the walk-out basement Caro had her own workspace. Wooden bookcases lined the walls, but instead of books the shelves were packed with cameras and lenses and other gear.

"This is incredible," I said. "You're a photographer?"

"Oh," she said bashfully. "Most of this was originally my grandfather's. He got me into it." I followed her into another room. It was much darker there—no sun, just two bulbs fixed directly into the ceiling.

The walls were covered in black-and-white photographs, portraits of girls doing various things. One knitting. One crouched down to tie her shoelaces. Another in the middle of shaving off her hair. A few arcing their bodies, mid-dance.

"Wow," I said. "You did these? They're amazing."

"Thanks," said Caro, sounding embarrassed.

One girl appeared over and over again, and she looked familiar. Something about her was different from the rest—something more sensual in the way she was positioned, torso twisting, hands curling gracefully. The pucker of her lips, the lowered gaze of the eyes. She was photographed the way da Vinci might have painted a lover.

Caro saw me looking. "That's Cheslin."

I thought I detected a bit of color in her cheeks. "Are you guys...?" I trailed off because maybe it was rude to ask.

"What?" she said with a certain sharpness.

"Dating?" I said hesitantly.

"Oh." Her shoulders sloped down. "Yeah. Isn't it obvious? I mean, my mom thinks I'm dating nine girls at the same time, but Cheslin and I have been together since the beginning of the summer."

"Whoa," I said. "That's...a while." I thought about Axel and Leanne, and tried to imagine them together that long. My stomach churned.

"I meant to say sorry about my mom," Caro said. "I hope she didn't make you feel uncomfortable. I came out to her pretty recently, and I think it was such a surprise that she's been overcompensating."

It took me a moment to realize she was talking about Mel's jokes when they gave me a ride home. I wondered if it was my turn to apologize for *my* mother. For her being passed out on the floor. For causing Caro and Mel to wade knee-deep into a swamp of awkwardness. Was I supposed to try to explain what had happened, when I didn't have a clue myself?

I took a breath and made myself smile. "No worries. Your mom seems really cool."

Caro rolled her eyes. "Everyone says that. She's the biggest weirdo nerd."

"And what are we?" I gestured at the art and equipment all around us.

"Touché," said Caro.

Relief settled around my shoulders. It didn't seem like the subject of my mother was going to come up, thank god.

In the other room, we set everything up where the light was best. We spent the day painting the details swirling in the body of "Evil Lover," as we had taken to calling him. Her. Them. Caro told me how she first found her papi's original SLR camera. How she figured out she liked girls when she watched *Titanic* and couldn't stop staring at Kate Winslet's breasts. Then there were the moments of silence, when we mixed colors and focused on our brushstrokes.

We painted until the sun tucked itself away. I was mixing to get the perfect teal and caught myself squinting.

"Is there a lamp or something?" I asked.

Caro looked up. "We should probably stop, really. I have a light, but it makes all the colors look off. We can finish tomorrow."

"Yeah," I agreed, though part of me was reluctant to leave. Painting had been meditative.

"You should totally stay for dinner, though," she said. "My grandparents are over. They love meeting my friends."

Friends. The word echoed in my skull and sent a ray of warmth into my chest. I hadn't made a new friend in years.

"I'd love to," I said.

"I'm warning you, though, they're kind of gross."

Gaelle and Charles Renard made me feel like I'd been a part of the family forever. They told me the story of how Mel kicked her boyfriend out two days before Caro was born.

"And we haven't seen the bastard since," said Gaelle with a wink, walking in from the kitchen bearing a casserole. "Good riddance."

Mel shrugged and topped off her wine. "At least I didn't marry the guy."

While Grandma Renard sounded entirely American, Charles had a touch of a French accent. "And at least all your rolling around in the hay gave us the gift of Carolina." The way he said her name, the R turned in the back of his throat, making the syllables sound special, like they belonged to a Hollywood actress in a black-and-white film.

Caro made a loud, drawn-out noise of pain.

Mel wrinkled her nose. "We never *did it* on the *farm.*"

"You sure smelled like it, though," said Gaelle. She reached for Charles's hand across the table, and the two of them chortled.

"Never *do it* on a farm," said Charles in a mock low voice, leaning toward Caro like he was saying this in confidence. "No matter how beautiful and sexy your girl is." There was extra emphasis on the word *sexy.*

"*Papi,*" Caro pleaded. She looked mortified.

"What are you so embarrassed about?" said Gaelle. "I loved a few women back in my day."

"More than a few," said Mel, "the way I heard it."

Caro's grandmother ignored this. "You love who you love. There's no changing that. You do your loving whenever, wherever you wish—"

"Except on a farm," Charles interjected.

"If you *do* do it on a farm," said Gaelle, "just don't tell your papi."

"*Chérie*, you are the most terrible of them all," said Charles to his wife.

Gaelle giggled and leaned in to rub her nose against his.

"*Ugh*," said Caro.

"Seconded," said Mel.

I ducked my head down for a bite of green beans to hide my smile.

"Leigh, what about your parents?" said Gaelle. "I'm always keen on a good love story."

I chewed fast and swallowed, suddenly hyperaware of my grip on my fork. "I'm not even sure I've heard the whole story. When I was little, I used to ask how they met, and they would just say they'd known each other since the beginning of time, for hundreds of lives."

"Life after life," said Charles. "Very romantic."

I smiled, but inside I was wondering if *romantic* was the right way to describe it. Once upon a time, maybe. I thought of how Dad used to sit on the couch while Mom puzzled out new pieces on the piano. There'd be something work-related in his lap—papers he was pretending to grade—but I knew he was really listening to the music, watching my mother move like a wave. His eyes stayed glued to her, and a soft smile tugged up the edges of his mouth.

That had been romantic. But something had changed in the last several months, the most obvious of which being that Dad started flying off to conferences and things. He was too busy now.

He'd shifted his work toward economic sociology, whatever that meant. He was gaining recognition and being invited to speak, join research projects, be a visiting professor. He was coauthoring a book with a fellow sinologist—it sounded like a big deal.

My mother was so loudly supportive and enthusiastic of everything. It was obvious: She was overcompensating for the guilt she felt whenever he suggested we move to Asia. He'd asked about China and Taiwan and Hong Kong and Singapore, and every time her answer was *Maybe in a few years*, or *What about Leigh's schooling, we cannot afford international private school*, or *I moved here for a reason*.

"Leigh?"

Caro kicked me under the table. I'd missed something Gaelle said. "Sorry, what?"

Everyone smiled politely like I hadn't just zoned out.

"Did you ever find out how they actually met?" said Charles.

"Right," I said. "Yeah. My mom was still a college student in Taiwan, but she came over for a summer music program in Illinois. My dad had just started his PhD there, and both of them got dragged to a mix-and-mingle event. They dated for almost the entire summer . . . and then kept it up long-distance after that."

"Wow," said Mel. "Long distance is tough."

"Yeah." I imagined my mother waiting for his call, snatching up the receiver on the first ring.

"And then?" said Charles.

"He proposed over the phone, and she flew to Chicago, and they eloped."

Gaelle was beaming. "I love it."

"You would love it if they'd met falling into a septic tank," said Mel. "As long as they ended up together."

"Yup, she's a hopeless romantic," Caro told me with an eye roll.

"There's got to be at least one of us in this family," said Gaelle.

"Lucky for you, there are two." Charles reached out to pinch his wife's chin and then her nose. Gaelle dissolved into musical giggles.

I tried to remember the last time I'd seen my mother laugh like that. The last time she'd looked so happy. I focused on Gaelle's wide smile, the crow's-feet wedging cheerfully into the corners of her eyes, and tried to mentally transplant my mother's features onto that carefree face.

As we painted the next day, my brain replayed the conversations from that dinner. I couldn't stop thinking about my mother. My father. About Axel and Leanne.

Caro was lucky to have these amazing grandparents in her life, to be so close they could joke about things like sex. The construction-paper family tree I'd made all those years ago stretched across the surface of my mind. That project was long gone, probably recycled as soon as it had come off the bulletin board, but it lived on in my brain. I pictured it going through a shredder, the kind that spat out squares so tiny they were impossible to reassemble.

"What's on your mind?" Caro asked.

"Hmm?"

"You've been weirdly quiet. What are you thinking about?"

"Nothing." I was so caught off guard by the question I couldn't even think of a good lie.

"Doesn't seem like nothing." She set her brush down and wiped her hands on her smock. "Come on. Spill."

"I was just...thinking about your grandparents."

She didn't say anything. She just sat there, waiting for me to continue.

"I've never met my grandparents on my mom's side. I don't even know what they look like."

"Why's that?" said Caro.

"That's the frustrating part," I said. "I have no clue. My parents won't offer any explanation for it. It's just like...a given. That I'll never get to know them. I don't have a choice in the matter. I'll never know if they're super in love, if they hate each other, if they're weird, if they pick their noses over breakfast—nothing."

"No offense," said Caro, "but that sounds pretty messed up."

"You're telling me." I ran a hand through my hair and realized I was probably streaking paint everywhere. "Even if they're terrible human beings—if they're sociopaths or something—I still want to meet them and judge for myself. At the very least I should know *why* I'm cut off from them."

"So what are you going to do about it?"

"My parents aren't going to tell me anything," I said.

"Then there has to be something you can dig up yourself."

My instinct was to shrug it off, but then I thought about it. *Was* there something to dig up?

I nodded slowly. "Maybe."

"You at least have to try," she said, picking up a tube of paint and squeezing out a liberal amount of orange. "And keep me posted."

"Can I ask you something else?"

"You just did," she said.

I rolled my eyes. "You and Cheslin were friends before you ended up together, right?"

Caro eyed me as if she knew what was coming. "For a while. Why?"

"Was it ever . . . weird?"

"This is about Axel Moreno," she said.

It wasn't exactly a question, and I did not confirm or deny.

"Listen, Leigh. If you've got shit to work out with him, you work it out with him. You can't work it out with me. I'm not Axel."

I took in a slow breath. "You're right." *Work it out with him.* It sounded easy, but I wasn't sure how. I couldn't even be sure what *it* was, what exactly I was feeling. I sighed and cleaned off my brush.

I'd never snooped on my parents. Even the thought of it sat in my stomach like something I shouldn't have eaten. I thought it was worth at least one more conversation before I really began the *investigation,* as Caro called it.

It was an evening that Dad was home for dinner. He'd be flying out again the next morning, but for the night he was ours. He was a husband and a father. Mom cooked his favorite things. I put on his favorite Nachito Herrera tracks and cranked up the volume. We sat down to eat and it actually felt normal. It was the kind of dinner we hadn't had in a long time.

I wanted to catch them in a good mood, so I waited until we were halfway through, laughing at a story about one of

Dad's students. My mother had a smile on her face and my father was spooning more fried rice onto his plate.

"When will I get to meet Mom's parents?" I said, trying to sound nonchalant.

Dad put down the rice. "Leigh," he said in a warning tone.

My mother stopped chewing; her smile melted off. "Why ask this now?"

I shrugged. "It's not like it's the first time I've asked. Why haven't we ever gone to visit? I don't know anything about them. That's pretty damn weird."

"You have bad tone, Leigh," said my mother. "You do not speak like this to your parents."

Guilt curled its fingers around my gut, but I refused to cower. "It's just not fair."

"Many things not fair. Many things hard to fix." She pushed her chair back and left the room, the food on her plate unfinished.

"*Dad—*" I started to say.

"Leave it, Leigh. It's complicated. Stop asking. You'll stir up things that aren't any good for anyone."

I slumped back in my seat.

Dad took a few lackluster bites. "I, uh, have some emails I need to take care of." He picked up the plate and headed to his office.

"Right," I said. I stayed at the table, listening to the sounds upstairs: Mom turning on the shower, Dad settling into his creaky office chair. It was hard to believe that only moments ago this room had held a family full of laughter.

Overhead, one of the yellow lights buzzed and flickered.

"Hang in there," I said to the bulb. It went out anyway.

32

My mother is a bird.

And I am only a girl.

A girl, human and wingless—but what I have is the beginning of a plan.

Because why was the incense given to me, if not to guide me? There must be hints in those memories. There must be answers to my questions.

Waipo promised we'll go everywhere that's important. The places my mother loved. The places that were her habits, where she walked, where she found inspiration, where she dwelled on things that made her sad, where she might have left traces of herself.

We'll visit all those places. I'll burn those inky black sticks. Search out every last clue, gather all of them up like the torn pieces of a map.

The bird wants to be found. She has something to tell me. And this is the way I'll get to her. I'm absolutely certain.

33

We're on our way to a temple, and the dust-colored brick road is thronged with people. Every so often a slow moped noses its way through, and for the briefest moment there's a gap and I can glimpse what's up ahead. Milliseconds later the space disappears. People pour back together like granules of sand sliding into a crack. I can't imagine anywhere back in the States looking like this, with mopeds and motorcycles sharing the pedestrian walkway.

I follow closely behind Waipo, with Feng tailing me, as we squeeze our way through tight clusters. Heads turn; gazes track over me.

"*Hunxie,*" I hear someone say, not bothering to lower their voice. *Mixed blood.*

"*Shi ma?*" someone else asks, not quite believing.

I suck in a deep breath and quicken my steps to press closer to my grandmother. Her proximity feels like a shield. If only I didn't stand out so obviously with my lighter eyes, with my lighter hair and its streak of green. If only I had been raised more Taiwanese, and could somehow prove to these people that I belong here. This was my mother's home for the first half of her life—can't it feel a little bit like home to me, too?

I imagine a carbon-black veil dropping down around me and curtaining me off from the rest of these people. Blocking me from view and giving me a few moments of cool and quiet aloneness.

The crowd seems to grow denser with each step we take. I wonder if this is why Waigong shook his head when we asked if he wanted to come—because he knew that it would be crowded to a hellish degree.

Red bricks on either side of us shape archway after archway, gaping mouths that lead to the shadowed fronts of little shops and stands selling all sorts of things. I crane my head to see better: calligraphy brushes, scrolls of paper, carved blocks of dry ink. Vintage trinkets and retro postcards. Snacks like steamed buns and pastries and what looks like tofu floating in white soup. We get stuck against a wall of people, and the nearest archway begins to warp and twist. Its shadows darken, going black and pitchy. They shift into the silhouette of a bird with outstretched wings—

"Leigh?"

My grandmother is tugging at my elbow. The crowd ahead of us has thinned a bit.

I blink and glance back—the archway looks normal. My head's all heavy and fogged up. It must be the lack of sleep.

"Are you okay?" says Feng.

I nod. "Fine. Tired."

"Jet-lagged?" she asks.

"I guess so." *Or maybe just losing my mind.*

We cut down an alley that's cool and gray, untouched by the harsh sun, and emerge once more onto the open road.

Waipo points to the magnificent temple. Sweeping red roofs curve up at their square corners. Stone dragons guard the highest points with open mouths and hooked claws. Fire-bright lanterns hang down from the eaves, strung together like lines of planets, their tassels angling in the wind.

We weave our way past the smoke and crowd to get onto the steps. The thick columns holding up the temple are intricately carved, capturing the vivid details of humans and creatures.

"They all show different events," says Feng, pointing at the closest one. "Every panel tells its own tale. When I was a kid, I used to make up my own stories about them. Usually there were two people falling in love and making their way through a world of monsters in order to find each other and be together."

Waipo gestures around, her fingers grasping at invisible things in the air as she tries to tell me something. I don't under-stand a word of it.

Feng jumps to translate, and I have to stop myself from sighing. I know I need the help, but I wish it were coming from someone else.

"This was your mother's favorite Taoist temple. She would come here when she needed guidance, when she was looking for an answer."

My grandmother points up at the ceiling. The undersides of the roofs are domed, made from carved pieces of wood that are stacked together in complex systems of interlocking circles and octagons. It's beautiful, and even a bit dizzying.

In the heart of the temple, people bow before a crowned statue with a face of black stone, and dressed in imperial reds and golds.

Toward the far side, a young man is tossing things into the air, letting them arc up in flashes of red and fall back to the ground. For a second I think they're feathers, just like the ones from the bird—but they're dropping too quickly. The wrong shape, the wrong weight, clattering against the floor. No, they're pieces of wood shaped like crescent moons, painted cherry red. The percussion of their falling makes them seem almost like toys.

Part of me wants to ask what those are and what he's doing, except I'm reluctant to encourage Feng. The way she talks to me makes me feel like a tourist, like someone who doesn't belong. And, well, maybe I don't belong. Still, I don't need the constant reminder.

But it's like my thoughts are painted on my forehead, because she says, "In Taiwanese they're called *bwabwei*. He's asking his god a question. If one lands faceup, and the other lands facedown, the answer is yes. If both land facedown, it means the god doesn't like what he's asking. If both land faceup, it means the god is laughing at him."

"What kind of question?"

"He might be trying to make a decision. It has to be a yes-or-no-type thing."

The man steps over to a bucket of red sticks, raising the whole thing up like a drum and shaking them loudly.

Feng leans close. "So first he was asking whether his answer can be found here in these sticks. The god must have told him yes."

Having selected one of the sticks, he reaches for the *bwabwei* again.

"Now he's confirming whether that stick is the correct answer."

The red moons fly up, turning in the air, clacking and skipping when they hit the floor. He throws them again. He throws them a third time.

"The answer is yes," Feng explains. "So now he can use the number on the stick to find its corresponding poem. The poem will explain what the god is trying to tell him."

I've never seen anything like this temple back home, never seen Mom do anything religious. Is this what my mother needed? Would having a place to go to ask questions have saved her?

I make my way over to where he was throwing the *bwabwei*, right in front of the crowned statue.

A teal curiosity settles in my stomach and my fingers itch to give a toss of my own. What answers could I get here? What questions would I ask?

Am I going to find the bird?

Is my mother happy, finally?

Was it my fault?

Waipo wanders over to the other side of the temple, and Feng follows her.

The relief of being alone comes like the cold side of my pillow on a restless night. When their backs are turned, I reach for the *bwabwei*. The moment my fingers touch the two moons, a shiver blooms against my neck.

Fear makes me hesitate. I throw the blocks anyway. As they turn in the air above me, I ask:

Is the bird here?

One lands faceup. One lands facedown.

The answer is yes.

34

The moon blocks said the bird was there. But I walked every inch of that temple, even the little offices where it didn't look like I should be allowed in, and still I found nothing. Not one sign of my mother.

After lunch and back at the apartment, Waipo stands over a bamboo tray, cutting into a vacuum-sealed package of tea. It's the tea from Feng's box. She's saying something, but I don't understand.

"Popo says every set of leaves has their own story," Feng translates.

My grandmother holds the package to her nose and inhales deeply, sighing the air back out. Her face full of cobalt contentment.

"You never drink this in America, right?" says Feng.

"I do, actually. You can get Asian teas in the States. And, like, Chinese restaurants always serve tea." I try to swallow the instinct to be defensive.

"Well, you probably haven't had this. This is Dong Ding oolong tea," Feng explains eagerly, her eyes gleaming. "I got it because it's Popo's *favorite*."

The way she grins at me as she says that last word makes my jaw clench. Is she trying to prove a point? Show that she knows my family better than me? It's hard not to look at her since she's sitting directly across from me, but I drop my gaze, try to ignore the sap-green irritation dripping through my insides.

Waipo arranges the cups in a line, handling them like fragile pieces of art. There are only three cups out; Feng made a big stink about how tea has been disagreeing with her stomach. I guess she brought the tea just to suck up.

My grandmother distributes the brew by pouring a continuous stream from left to right, excess water trickling down the sides of the cups, through the slats of the bamboo tray.

I reach for a cup, but my grandmother shakes her head.

"*Hai mei*," she says. *Not yet*. With wooden tongs, she tips each cup by its edge, empties it over the tray.

"That was just a wash," Feng explains, setting a hand on my arm, her long floral sleeve tickling me. "These are the steps in the *laoren cha* tradition."

I shift out from under her touch. "Right."

Waigong traces figure eights against the surface of the table, his finger tracking through a spot of water, dragging it left, dragging it right. He catches my eye and winks, and a bit of my tension ebbs.

Another round of water from the kettle. This time my grandmother lets the leaves sit. The usual tremor in her hands gone—in making tea they're deft and stilled by certainty. She stands over us with a confidence in her shoulders I've never seen. Her fingers are older and softer versions of the hands I knew so well, hands that shaped the dough for *danhuang su* and mixed batter to pour into the waffle iron.

My grandmother. My mother. Both of them so careful, so full of love. How did they end up so cut off from each other?

When Waipo pours the tea again, the stream that flows forth is reddish brown.

Feng takes in a deep breath. "Mmm. It smells divine. Did your mother brew tea for you a lot?"

Mom was never this particular about the tea she made, but once I caught her standing at the kitchen counter for a long and quiet moment, sifting through the wet leaves with her fingers. She dug them from the belly of the pot, rubbed at the pieces in her palms. It seemed that she was deep in thought, trying to remember something.

The idea hits me then—the tea. The leaves my grandmother carefully spooned out of the foil. The leaves she so lovingly handled, whose smell she inhaled through her knuckles, pressing her fingers to her nose and closing her eyes. Nobody will notice if I take them.

Waipo brings out trays of passion fruit with the tops sawed off. The pulp inside is sunny and glistening, tart like citrus but also refreshingly sweet, and we scoop it out with tiny silver spoons.

"I think this should be a new family tradition," says Feng, watching me crunch on the dark seeds. "Afternoon tea and passion fruit."

The green feeling goes hot, and closes around me like a shell, like armor, and I swallow and set my spoon down. "Why?"

"Why not?" she says, her voice a tad too cheerful. "I think family traditions are important."

"We've got plenty of traditions," I reply.

"But you don't have any with Popo," she says.

I don't know what to say to that. Waipo and Waigong look at me almost expectantly, even though I know they haven't been following the conversation. They can't understand what Feng and I have been talking about.

"It can be a tradition for all of us," Feng tries again.

The thought of her inserting herself into this family that I already barely feel a part of turns me coppery and mean. I pick up my tea and exhale into the cup, letting the steam press against my face.

When the husks of fruit are empty and we've all had about eight servings of tea, I follow Waipo back into the kitchen. Together, we wash the cups and the spoons, return things to their cabinets. As she reaches for the teapot, I wave her off, and she smiles, understanding that I'll take care of it.

When she isn't looking, I gather the used leaves in my fist and wrap them in a rag for later.

35

We head out again in time for the evening service at a Buddhist temple, one that Feng says is very important. Walking behind my grandmother, I can see the tension in the set of her shoulders. Her hand slides along the top of the balcony, dropping away only when she nearly runs into the glittering silk of a spider's web.

This temple is built of clean white stone and muted green roofs. Dragons and other mythical creatures crown the top edges of the eaves, gazing down like guards. One dragon narrows its eyes.

I blink hard, try to send the image away. I can't shake the feeling that it's watching me. Warning me.

A nun in brown robes bows to all of us, presents us with sticks of incense. *"Amituofo,"* she says, pressing her palms together and dropping her chin to her chest. *"Amituofo,"* her voice so calming, as if those four syllables smooth out the wrinkles of the world, set everything right again.

"Popo says they used to always come here together," Feng tells me. "This is the temple where your mother spent the most time. This is where her spirit is."

That last part snaps my attention back into sharp focus. "What does that mean?"

Waipo points into a small room where a golden bodhisattva sits in a glass case, stretching from floor to ceiling, glowing like a piece of treasure. On either side of it: hundreds of wooden plaques, painted the color of marigolds.

"Those yellow tablets bear the names of the dead," says Feng. "Including your mother's. She knows her name is written here. This is where her spirit lingers."

Where her spirit lingers.

My eyes sweep the room, looking for the slightest bit of red, hunting for a feather, a shadow, anything.

My mother my mother my mother.

There's the sudden thunder of a low drum rumbling across the floor. The round tone of percussive bells arching in the air, rainbows of sound. And then a monk's amplified voice rises up like a wave. A hundred voices follow in a chorus, tracing the ups and downs of a song without a real melody.

"They're chanting sutras for the ones who have passed. Especially those still within the forty-nine days," Feng says.

I shake my head, not understanding. "Forty-nine days?"

"After a person's death, they have forty-nine days to process their karma and let go of the things that make them feel tied to this life—things like people and promises and memories. Then they make their transition. So the temple will keep each yellow tablet for forty-nine days. After that, they're burned."

The thudding in my head matches the thudding against my ribs. "What transition?"

"Rebirth, of course," says Feng.

Forty-nine days. Is that how long she'll be a bird? How many days has it been? There can't be much time left. I can't believe nobody told me about this sooner.

Let go of the things that make them feel tied to this life. But I don't want her to let go. I don't want her to forget about us. Forget me.

Waipo gathers all our incense in a bouquet, dipping their tips into a well of flames. The wispy smoke hangs in the air like cobwebs. They look nothing like the black incense hidden in my drawer, the black smoke of the memories unfurling.

Feng and Waipo kneel upon the low, cushioned bench, like they've practiced this. Like they come here together, and often. Their eyelashes meeting their cheeks, chins bowing in sync.

I wish Feng weren't here. The thought has been burning quietly in a far corner of my mind all day, but now that it's risen to the surface, I can't tuck it away again. Doesn't she have better things to do? Why is she always tagging along? Does Waipo invite her because it's weird to be around me by myself?

The two of them kneeling together there . . . it's perfect and picturesque, like something Axel would paint. If I joined them, I would only make it look odd. This strange American girl, who doesn't really speak the language of her ancestors. Her hair not dark enough, and hands gripping the incense uncomfortably. Her faith uncertain.

I wish I felt more Taiwanese. I wish I knew these traditions, knew what to do.

I don't belong here. I should just walk away.

Waipo turns her face toward me. *"Lai,"* she says, beckoning earnestly.

And so I kneel on her other side, coming down hard and clumsy, my shins aching from dropping too heavily onto the bench.

It doesn't matter, I tell myself. It doesn't matter if I don't belong, if I'm a fish out of water here. I just need to find the bird. I need to get to her before the forty-nine days are up.

We wind our way back out into the boiling air. I'm still trying to mentally count out the passage of time when I hear the screech, shrill and high-pitched overhead. People around us are shading their eyes, tipping their heads back. Waipo and I turn our faces toward the low sun, and I think I see the last of a red tail disappearing around the edge of a building.

The bird.

My heart's slamming and fingers are trembling and there's smoke stinging my eyes, but I can't close them, can't miss her if she circles back around.

I need to get to her, talk to her. Why is she flying away? Why won't she come down and speak to me, like when I was back at home? The urgency and longing wrap around me in swirls of aureolin and splotches of violet.

We stand there long enough for people to begin flowing past us like a river around boulders.

How many days left? I go back to counting.

36

The night stretches on, quiet and endless. I have a theory, and it's spurred me into action. The theory is that the longer my mother has been a bird, the more she has begun to forget her human wants and needs—the more she's forgotten *me*. Why else would she fly past without stopping?

We're forty-one days in.

That's what I've counted, and count again to check, trying to sharpen my memory of all that's passed since the stain.

What would I give for a remote control with a button to slow down time, or even rewind a little bit? Forty-one days since my mother became a bird, which means when the sun rises, it'll be the forty-second morning. Including tomorrow, that's eight days before my mother makes her transition.

Eight days.

I have to work even faster. Burn the incense, see the memories. Find the clues. Find my mother.

I've pulled out all the T-shirts and sweatpants I can spare, and found myself a pair of scissors. There's something very meditative about opening the steel wide and slicing into the fabric, *snip snip snip*. When I was a kid I learned to weave these baskets out of shirts by first cutting the material up into long strands. It's pretty easy—the way you cut just spirals up the shirt starting from the bottom, so that one shirt becomes one long piece of string. I need all the pieces I can get.

I'm weaving a net—as big a net as I can make, so I have to cut the clothes as thinly as possible. I don't think it'll hurt the bird, since the material is soft, and I'm hoping she'll recognize the scent of me, or the particular brand of laundry detergent she always bought. If all goes according to plan, then once the net is over her, she'll notice those familiar smells and see me, her daughter, her own flesh and blood from before she was a bird. She'll settle down and tell me what it is she wants me to remember.

Snip snip snip.

My brain won't stop tracing shapes and rewinding through memories. Sometimes, when it gets all cyclical like this, I try to calm myself down by inventing new colors in my head.

I found this video online once about these scientists who unintentionally invented a new shade of blue. They called it YInMn blue.

I thought it was cool but at the same time hard to believe, because how is it possible that YInMn didn't exist before?

YInMn, they said, was supposedly fade resistant. I scoffed a little when I saw that part. Everything fades.

Everything in the physical world, like paper and furniture, but also things in the mind. Memories, emotions. Life.

Friendships. Those fade, too. It's just a matter of time.

The creepy thing is, right as I'm thinking that, my phone lights up on its own and starts playing that track Axel sent before. "Goodbye."

37

WINTER, FRESHMAN YEAR

When the house was empty, I searched for clues, starting with my parents' bedroom. My hands were careful. The drawers made a loud *shush* as they slid open. The closet door creaked in warning.

What was I expecting—

A letter? A diary? Anything in Chinese would be useless. But Caro was right. I had to try.

Nothing looked unfamiliar or mysterious until I hit the storage section of the basement, where a shed's worth of cardboard boxes were stacked in the corner, lined with dust, untouched for who knew how long. I'd never given them much thought before.

I asked my mother what was in the boxes.

"Not sure. Some is mine, other might be yours. Maybe your old homework. I don't remember. Probably none your father's—he always throwing away stuff he don't use. Why you ask this?"

The lie came easily. "I need to find some projects from, like, elementary school. It's for an assignment. Can I go through them?"

"Okay. It's very dusty. Maybe when you're there you also do some vacuum and clean."

"Sure." I tried to look reluctant, though I was glad for the excuse to spend more time with the boxes. "I can do that."

There were so many, their insides completely disorganized. I slowly pawed my way through the mess of each one, paranoid that if I sped up I'd miss something. There were random bank and insurance statements, grade-school spelling quizzes and essays and social studies tests, old postcards from Dad's parents, ancient pieces of computer software. Just in case my mother actually asked, I pulled out some of the old school projects I came across.

If I was lucky, a weekday afternoon—while Mom was busy teaching piano—could get me through half a box. Weekends were utterly unproductive. If I stayed in, she'd try to chat for endless stretches. Or, if her dark mood took over, the house shrank down so that I felt like I was being choked.

I started going to the Renards' on Saturdays and Sundays, helping Caro set up her photo stuff so she could get macro shots of water drops and the faces of dead bugs. When we got tired of that, we played cribbage with her grandparents.

I hadn't had a real conversation with Axel in ages. Even Mom asked why he hadn't come over when she made chive dumplings or waffles.

"He has a girlfriend, Mom," I snapped. "He has better things to do."

Her face flashed a maroon shade of hurt before smoothing again. "I see."

The first morning of winter break brought a familiar rap on our door, the rhythm drifting upstairs like a dream. I was lying on my stomach, sketching an antique camera borrowed from Caro.

The knock was something I'd imagined—I was certain of it. All the wishful thinking was manifesting in some form of psychosis. My knuckles dug the charcoal harder into the page.

Then came the same knock on my bedroom door. It was so jarring I nearly tore a page out of my sketchbook.

"Come in?" I hated how the words leaped out as a question.

The door opened and there was Axel in his forest-green plaid. His hair was dark and wavy, longer than I'd ever seen it. It draped nicely, framing his face. A few strands fell against his forehead like arrows trying to direct my gaze to his eyes.

"Hey, Leigh," he said, as though nothing had happened in the last few months.

I stared at him.

"Oh, I like the pink." He gestured toward the streak of color in my hair. "Did you just do that?"

I meant to respond in the most detached voice I could summon. What came out was "Why are you here?"

His mouth twisted. He tried for a tight smile. "I'm not allowed over anymore?"

"No, I mean, you're allowed." I sat up and wondered if my hair was a mess. Had I brushed it today? I decided I didn't give a crap. "Looks like your mono's gone. Did you give it back to Leanne or something?"

He looked pained. "That's not how mono works."

"Right," I said. "I wouldn't know. So how is she? Leanne? Or do you call her *Lee* for short?"

He opened his mouth and closed it. When he finally spoke again, his voice was very quiet. "I would never call her that."

"Is she the reason you're growing your hair out?"

Axel barked out a mirthless laugh. "Are you kidding? She hated it. She was into the military look. *I'm* the reason I'm growing my hair out."

"*Hated? Past tense?*"

"I broke up with her," he said with a shrug. "Last week, actually."

Half of me was relieved and the other half was pissed as hell. I slid off my bed and drew myself up to my tallest height. "I'm supposed to be your best friend, you know."

Axel's face went gray. "Leigh—"

"I'm not a replacement, I'm not someone *to be replaced*."

"You're right," he said.

"It's ridiculous that just because you went and got yourself a girlfriend you stopped being my friend."

"You're right."

I actually heard it this time. "What?"

"You're absolutely right," he said. "I was an ass. I pushed you away. I guess I didn't want you to see the way I was when I was with Leanne."

I didn't really understand what he meant, but I also wasn't sure I wanted to hear more. "So why'd you dump her?" I asked instead.

"I couldn't figure out who she was."

"What's that supposed to mean?"

"I used to think she was interesting. But when we started dating...she just became this weird mirror image of me. Everything I liked, she liked. Everything I wanted to do, she automatically wanted to do. It started driving me up the wall. I wasn't dating her so I could be in a relationship with myself, you know? And half the time, those weren't even the real things that I liked and wanted. Hell, I just wanted to sit in my room and work on music. But that wasn't a *couple activity*." He put air quotes around those last two words, rolling his eyes hard. "Plus, and this will sound terrible—"

"What?" I said. Terrible was exactly what I wanted to hear.

"Well, she was kind of obnoxious about…money. Not like her family's rich or anything. But the way she spent it. Like one day she bought a soda at lunch. And then she left it in the science hall—and when she went back, someone had already taken it. So she bought another one…and didn't even finish it. Just threw it out half full. Around her I just constantly felt…poor, I guess."

"Ah." I didn't know what else to say.

"Okay," he said, "can we change subjects now? I'm overdue for a dose of normal."

I gave him a weird smile.

"What?"

"Nothing," I said. "It's just that…it hasn't exactly been normal over here, either."

"What's going on?"

He'd known about the weirdness with my grandparents for forever, so I jumped right into how Caro got me thinking I should do something about it.

"How far are you into the boxes?" he asked.

"Not even halfway. But I'm hoping I'll find something when I get to the older ones buried in the back."

Axel nodded. "Can I help?"

The question surprised me. Even Caro hadn't offered, but

then that was probably out of respect for my privacy. That was the kind of person she was—careful and considerate, especially when it came to personal stuff.

But this was different. Axel was practically family.

"Of course," I said.

He let out a breath that sounded like relief. "So, I'm forgiven? We're okay?"

I picked up my charcoal. "I'll let you know the color when I figure it out."

Half of winter break was gone in a blink, swallowed by the basement. With Axel's help, we were cutting through the boxes way faster.

Caro and her family were snowboarding in Colorado for the week, and I'd promised to text her if I found anything interesting. Every once in a while she'd send a random photo. I smiled at the shot of her high in the air midjump, and one of Gaelle and Charles fallen in the snow but still holding hands, and later rushed to hide my phone when she sent her snow sculpture of a giant vulva.

"Your cell is awfully busy these days," said Axel.

"Jealous?"

I was only teasing, but the uncertain look on his face made me wonder if my words hit the mark. He straightened out his expression with a roll of his eyes.

"You'll like Caro," I told him. "When she gets back, you'll see."

Bad weather messed up Dad's flight. It was our first Christmas without him. His absence was like a crack we stepped over so often we usually forgot it was there—but not on Christmas. On Christmas it was an empty black pit gaping up at us. We weren't religious or anything, but this was Mom's favorite time of year.

All morning she wore around this false holiday cheer like a garish sweater. Dad called from his hotel—I talked to him for about twenty seconds before my mother took the phone and carried it upstairs. I stood in the hall with my ear turned up, waiting to hear the crest of an argument. But she was back in the kitchen after just a few minutes, frying up a batch of pot stickers.

Axel came over after dinner so we could do presents. We turned off all the lights except for my winking icicle strands, and settled onto my bed cross-legged and facing each other. It had been an unspoken rule since seventh grade: Our gifts had to be homemade.

He unzipped his backpack, and what he dumped out was the last thing I would have expected: a projector from school. I recognized the last name of a history teacher scrawled on its side in Sharpie.

"You stole a projector?" I said.

"Borrowed indefinitely. For presentation's sake." He'd opened up his laptop and clicked through folders. "Close your eyes."

I snorted.

"I'm serious!" He folded the laptop halfway shut. "Close your eyes, or you don't get your present."

I threw myself back so I was horizontal and held a pillow over my face. I could hear him typing away.

"It's hard to breathe like this, you know."

"You're bad at following directions. I didn't say to smother yourself." More typing sounds. Some clicking. "Okay. You remember that thumb drive I gave you? With the Lockhart Orchard tracks?"

"Of course." I immediately wished I'd said something more casual.

"This goes with those. You can come back."

I sat up. It took my eyes a minute to adjust: He'd turned the light of the projector up toward the ceiling and placed the mouth of a glass fishbowl upside down over the lens to distort the projection. Bold watercolor strokes domed against my ceiling and walls.

"Ready? Set. Listen." Axel's finger came down on his space bar. The music started up, and I immediately recognized it. The swell of strings, the cutting edges of electric guitar. The watercolors shifted. Royal-blue sketches of playground spun around us. The music darkened and the playground crumbled. Black streaks of lightning stabbed down from the ceiling in time to the jumping notes of the low bass.

The world was made of jagged pieces that spun and twisted. He'd somehow taken his watercolors and spliced them into elements that tiled and tessellated and fit themselves back together again.

"I made a video to go with every track," he said, sounding almost shy.

"It's incredible," I told him. "Seriously. I don't even know how you came up with this."

"I designed them to work best like this, projected in a bubble," he said with a grin. He pushed a button, and the next piece began to play.

I fell onto my back and lay there hugging my pillow as the

images bent and shifted. After a few seconds, Axel let himself go horizontal, too, tucking his sweatshirt under his head. I could smell his shampoo. It was a comforting scent and made me want to touch his hair. I snuck a glance at him.

But he wasn't watching the projection. He was watching me. Our eyes locked and heat surged up into my face. I didn't look away.

38

Every time I rise up out of those memories it's like coming up for air. I try to shake the feeling of reliving my life. Try to think about something else, something that doesn't have to do with Axel. Because to think about Axel is to think of that day on the couch in his basement, the same day my mother became a bird. The day that everything changed irreversibly.

What I need is a different kind of remembering. My hands are aching from all the cutting now, so I set down the shirts and the scissors and yank open the drawer with the incense and matches.

Since the feather burned up and showed me the past, I've been trying to puzzle out how it worked. The first stick brought me things I'd nearly forgotten. But when I lit the incense with the feather—it triggered something in the smoke. Something different. It mixed in memories that weren't mine, moments I didn't know had happened.

Alone in my room, wrapped in the quiet of insomnia, I light a new stick of incense. Unfold the damp rag, take up my handful of tea leaves—

39

—SMOKE & MEMORIES—

There's the spark, the colors of time changing.

There's a burst of light and a smell like woodsmoke.

Slowly, my eyes settle into the dimness. I'm in a small cottage where a low fire burns in a pit carved out of the wall. As I turn and look, some pieces are blurrier than others, their colors faded like in old photographs.

There's a woman shifting under a ragged blanket on a thick bed of dry grass, her face red with effort and shining with sweat.

"It's a girl," the midwife announces from the foot of the bed. She's definitely not speaking English, but I understand her as if she were.

She holds up a gleaming pair of steel scissors, opens them wide like teeth, severs the umbilical cord with a resounding slice.

The mother reaches for the kicking mess of little limbs.

"A daughter," her husband says. "Do we keep this one?"

The woman brushes away a bit of gunk sticking to the baby's nose. "No. This one we sell."

The colors change, go dark. A glimmer and burst bring new light.

The same woman in the doorway of her hut, rocking the baby, who is small and unknowing and swathed in rags. The woman's face smudged and empty, her husband beside her looking broken. He takes a filthy wad of money from a balding man in the grass just outside their home. The man takes the child. An easy transaction, hearts aside.

The balding man carries the baby across the field and into the trees. Out of the trees and up a mountain. And inside his own run-down mud cottage, he shows the baby girl to his wife. She rocks another tiny body in her arms, helping the mouth find her nipple and feed.

"What should we call our new daughter?" says the man.

"Yuanyang," she says, rocking.

"Like the birds?" says the man, sounding not at all surprised.

"Just like the birds," she says.

"Yuanyang," the man repeats to himself.

Something about the smoke, the careful way he says the name—I suddenly understand. This is my grandmother. Yuanyang is Waipo.

"Yuanyang," the man says again, carrying her across the room to see the other child. "See who Mama's holding. Meet our son, Ping."

Flicker, darkness, flash. New colors come; the smell of this memory is earthy and green.

Yuanyang, seven years old, watching everyone greet the

uncle who has come to celebrate the Lunar New Year. I can see into her mind, can hear her thoughts, feel what she feels.

"Ping! You are getting so tall! Soon you will be taller than your mother." The uncle laughs deep in his belly as he steps through the doorway. "Eight years old. That's a lucky number. This will be a good year for you."

Ping smirks. "Thank you for coming, Uncle. Happy New Year."

"Thank you for coming," Mama echoes. "You must be tired after your trip. Yuanyang, bring the tea out for your uncle!"

Every corner of the tiny kitchen is crowded with the aftermath of Mama's preparations. Dried spices dusting the splintery slab of wood used for a table. Bowls ringed with sauces and oil. There are roasted yams, stir-fried yam leaves, rice porridge. Noodle soup—no meat in it but made with pork bones, so close enough, a rare treat. A handful of water spinach, thanks to a neighbor who made a trip down the mountain. There are even a few tea eggs; if Yuanyang is lucky, she'll get a bite of one.

She wonders how they are able to afford all this food. Lucky for Ping that his birthday coincides with the biggest holiday. Only once a year do they eat like people who deserve to survive.

Her eyes hunt for the clay teapot she heated only moments ago. There it is, on a tree stump beside the large pail in the back of the kitchen, the house's only source of water. She wraps her hand in rags so the pot won't burn her.

Yuanyang sets a cup before the uncle and pours the red tea slowly, careful that her elbow angles away from him so as not to be rude. He taps two fingers on his knee in thanks, and she shrinks away. Her job is done best when she turns invisible, blending into the wall, becoming one with the sparse furniture.

She heads for the kitchen knowing Mama will want her to clear away the mess. But as she leaves, she hears the uncle chuckle and say, "When the time comes, Yuanyang will make the perfect wife for Ping."

Little Yuanyang stiffens, nearly trips on her way out. She hears Mama say faintly, "I just hope that her hips get wider, or she won't be fit to bear a healthy child."

The darkness drops like a veil, followed by a sweeping beam of light, opening up into new colors.

On the sloping side of a hill, nine-year-old Yuanyang stands among bushes reaching as high as her shoulder. She wears a ragged scarf tied around her head, and a leather strap presses over the fabric around her forehead to dangle a straw basket against her back. Sweat beads at her temples, trickles down the sides of her face. Her quick hands pluck at leaves and buds from the tops of the bushes.

As Yuanyang moves across the mountain, she wonders who her birth family is, what life with them might have been. She imagines a mother sewing her beautiful dresses, weaving elegant braids. A father teaching her songs, accompanying her voice with a bamboo *dizi*, his fingers running adeptly over the holes, lips stemming the air. Yuanyang wonders: Would she have any siblings? Perhaps a sister to share a bed with, and whisper secrets to?

With a hand, she swipes the perspiration from her brow. This work is exhausting but easier than school. Easier than studying characters by scratching them into the mud, worrying that a mistake might bring the teacher's biting stick down upon her hand. Here among the leaves the only punishment to be had is the burn of the sun, the occasional itch or sting of a bug. But it's quiet. Nobody telling her how to think. Her hands are busy, but her mind is free to roam.

She clutches a handful of tea leaves to her nose and inhales deeply, letting the green smells tell her the secrets of the land.

40

Was it real? It had to be.

My brain turns these new pieces around and around.

Yuanyang.

I think of the careful way my grandmother brewed the pot of tea. The way she gazed intensely into that foil bag brimming with stiffly curled leaves.

I say her name out loud to feel the shape of it on my tongue. "Yuanyang."

Yuanyang, who is my waipo.

Does that make Ping...my waigong?

Everything in my brain is glimmering with wonder, with iridescent hues, like the colors pinned by the sun against an oil-slicked surface. Wonder, and sadness. Because I'd always imagined that one day it would be my mother telling me the stories of her family. Not memories materializing from wisps of incense smoke, memories that feel stolen.

And somehow—I'm absolutely certain of it—these glimpses of the past will lead me to my mother, the bird. These pieces will help me find her, will bring her to me.

And when the time comes, I'll be ready for it.

I pick the scissors back up, thread my fingers and thumb through the plastic loops to find a good grip.

41

I've cut up all the shirts, and my hand is sore, so I decide to try to get some rest.

My body is heavy with exhaustion, but my brain won't stop. It flutters like a restless animal. When I close my eyes, the past dances across the darkness in spurts and swirls of light.

Sleep is a thing I can't remember. The face and smell and texture of it all forgotten, as if it's been wiped from my mind.

I think of the temple, the people chanting, the melody of their words dark and lilting.

I think of that tail sweeping past us. What I need is for her to come down out of the sky and stay awhile.

I want you to remember

I'll throw that net—gently, lovingly, so that she senses that I don't mean to hurt her. I'll catch her in it, and then she'll talk to me. She'll tell me what I need to know.

I blink, and the ceiling turns shadowy. The cracks are there again, widening, spreading farther. They've stretched across the entire surface and begun fissuring down the walls. An entire corner's missing, like someone just took out a chunk of it. There's nothing to be seen there, only oblivion made of the blackest black.

Blink again, and it's gone.

42

In the early morning darkness, the display of my phone glows like lightning, white-hot as the latest email loads.

Axel.

FROM: axeldereckmoreno@gmail.com
TO: leighinsandalwoodred@gmail.com
SUBJECT: (no subject)

Sometimes I got to your house for Sunday
waffles before you woke up. Those mornings
your mom and I would sit and have coffee before
she started the waffle batter. There was this one
Sunday when she said out of the blue, "Do you
like Emily Dickens?"

I asked her if she meant the poet Emily
Dickinson, because this was right after we had
gone through those boxes. She said yes, and then

she started to recite poems in this calm and
steady voice.

I think about that morning a lot. There was
one poem that I'll always remember:

> *I lost a world the other day.*
> *Has anybody found?*
> *You'll know it by the row of stars*
> *Around its forehead bound.*

I'm not even sure if that's the whole poem.
But I think about it a lot. I wonder what she lost.

43

WINTER, FRESHMAN YEAR

By the end of winter break, Axel and I were down to the last couple boxes.

"Ack! Oh my god!" he shouted, leaping to his feet and shaking his arms.

"What?" I stood up, alarmed. "What is it?"

"*That* was a spider. Definitely a spider. It went under there." He pointed at the box he'd been halfway through opening.

I rolled my eyes so hard. "Seriously? Unless it's poisonous—"

"No—*ugh*, I think it was a daddy longlegs."

"Oh my god, Axel. A *daddy longlegs*. Those are, like, the tea-cup wiener dogs of the arachnid family. I thought you'd gotten over this by now."

"It—is—not—funny," he said, gritting his teeth. "Will you just kill it already?"

"Sure, if you'll help me pick up the box so we can find it?"

"Ugh. *Fine.*"

He took two edges of the box and I grabbed it from the opposite side. We moved three paces to the right and craned our necks to peer down at the square indentation in the beige carpet. It was flat and empty.

"I don't see it."

He squeezed his eyes shut. "Oh my god. If it's *on this box*—"

Right at that moment I saw the legs peeking out from the bottom edge, not far from my left hand.

"Don't look—" I began to say, but I was too late.

Axel yelped and dropped his side, leaping away. I let go, too, the weight shifting too fast for me to hold it up all on my own.

And then I couldn't help it: I doubled over, cackling mono-azo yellow, laughing so hard spit flew from my mouth. I laughed until my stomach hurt and my throat was dry and my eyes were leaking. I laughed because of the spider, but also because I hadn't felt so at ease and normal in months.

He cracked a sheepish grin. "It looks dead."

"Happy now?" I was still trying to gulp down the last heaves of laughter.

"I will be once you dispose of the body."

"Christ on a bike." I hunted around for a tissue.

"You don't believe in Christ."

"I don't believe in killing things, either, and look what I just did for you."

We tore into the box together. It was immediately obvious: This one was different from the others. Instead of folders and paperwork, this box mostly contained envelopes.

Axel grabbed a stack and spread them out in a fan. "They're all unopened."

I picked one up. It was addressed to Dorothy Chen, but there were three Chinese characters next to that. The return address was written all in Chinese, except at the bottom, where it said: *Taiwan (Republic of China)*.

We sorted the envelopes by the dates stamped on them. The latest ones were from almost a decade ago.

"Holy crap," I said. "I can't believe she never read these."

"Who do you think they're from?" said Axel.

I shook my head. I wished I could ask Dad . . . but there was no way he would tell me anything.

"You think it's them?" said Axel. "Your grandparents?"

I grabbed a stack of letters and examined their corners. The return address said *Taiwan* again and again. And the name—or what I guessed to be the name, made up of those swooping strokes of pen—was the same on every single one.

I nodded slowly.

Axel reached into the box to pull out more, and something heavy fell from his handful. He fished it out: a bracelet. Little rounds of cloudy green jade set in yellow gold, the pieces linked together. I clasped it around my wrist; the stones were heavy and cold against my skin. Who had this belonged to?

"*This* is random," said Axel. He held up a worn leatherbound book. On the front it said THE POEMS OF EMILY DICKINSON.

It had the sour and musty smell of something old. Something once loved but then forgotten. I hoped for notes in the margins; there weren't any. But things were underlined, boxes had been drawn around certain words, entire stanzas circled. Some of the pages were missing, others stained. The corners

floppy and weak from being dog-eared. I opened to somewhere in the middle:

> *You left me boundaries of pain*
> *Capacious as the sea,*
> *Between eternity and time,*
> *Your consciousness and me.*

"That's the only English thing in here," said Axel, peering into the box. "Assuming all the letters are in Chinese, of
course."

And were they? It was an important question. But if I tore
open an envelope, it would be crossing a line. What I was
doing right now, looking through boxes—this was simply
explorative. But the moment I opened someone else's mail,
it was snooping. It was trespassing. My body felt orange with
preemptive guilt.

The thought hit me: What if my grandparents didn't even
know I existed? What if they had no idea there was a half-
Asian, half-white descendant of theirs out here in the town of
Fairbridge, dying to meet them?

That would be messed up. I could hear Caro's anger churning away in my rib cage, and Axel's curiosity spreading down
my spine.

What did *I* feel, independent of everyone else?

Only the stiff mint-green cold of being unable to process
what was in front of me.

I tore open one of the letters from Taiwan before I could
change my mind.

Lines of pen flowed across the paper in thin and wispy strokes. It *was* all in Chinese. I couldn't read a word. I thought I would at least recognize something—a *you* or an *I* or an *of*—but nothing looked right. This writing was not like what I'd been used to seeing, back when Dad taught me some of the basics. It seemed to be the Chinese equivalent of cursive. Elegant. Moving like water. Hard to read.

As I riffled through the last stack, a stiff little rectangle slipped out from between the envelopes. It landed facedown by my knee.

A photograph. Black-and-white—or more like brown and yellow, for all that time had faded it—and it showed two little girls side by side, peering straight into the camera, unsmiling. Both of them in pale frocks and dark Mary Janes. One girl's hair was in a long fishtail pulled in front of a shoulder. The other had high braids that hung in loops on either side of her head. They looked like sisters.

Axel leaned over to see. "Who do you think they are?"

"I have no idea."

"Maybe one of them is your grandmother?" he said.

I squinted like when I was trying to identify the lightest and darkest points for a sketch. My eyes searched for something in one of the faces to call familiar, but what was there to see? It was just two little girls, probably both under the age of eight. I tucked the photo into the poetry book.

That night I saw the little girls from the photograph. In my dream they had the same faces, the same frocks and shoes, but they'd grown taller. The rest of their bodies were old and wrinkled from the neck down. They hunched as they walked.

Who are you? they demanded without moving their mouths. *Who are you?*

I'm Dory's daughter, I answered.

Dory doesn't have a daughter, they said.

They reached out hands that gripped blackboard erasers, the kind with felt on the bottom, and began erasing me, starting with my feet and working their way up. Once my knees were gone, I was stuck in place, forced to watch as my body disappeared.

I jerked awake right as they were about to erase my head.

44

At last the air is not so sticky and a chilled velvet black arrives.

It drapes over me, settles like a blanket. It darkens everything in the room so that I can no longer see the ceiling or the walls. There's just me and the rhythm of my breath. My chest rising and falling. My fingers uncurling.

"Leigh."

I'm not in my room. I'm drifting in an empty sky, cool and cloudless, free of gravity. I'm floating through the blackest black.

When the noise of gentle flapping reaches my ears, I know exactly what I'm about to see.

"Mom?"

The bird glides toward me out of the dark, majestic and graceful, her red wings gleaming.

I stretch my arms out to hug her.

She flaps once, twice.

She falters. Her feet scratching wildly, trying to find purchase. As one set of sharp claws closes over the air, it crumbles to ash. It disintegrates, burning away into dust, just like a stick of incense.

The bird gasps. "Leigh!"

My heart lurches into my throat. I blink and sit up, and she's gone.

A dream. Just a dream. But the sound of her voice echoes in my ear until morning.

45

My heart is still pounding when the pale dawn light washes into the apartment.

The night passed both too quickly and too slowly, an agonizing turn through all the dark and muted colors.

Forty-two days now. I know exactly what the dream meant: With every day that passes, my mother diminishes. I *have* to find her.

Forty-two days.

Out in the living room I find Waigong by the door, kicking off slippers, pulling on outdoor shoes. He leans with one hand against the wall, the other hand tugging on his sneakers and Velcroing them tight.

My grandfather smiles at me when our eyes meet. He reaches out a hand with the palm facing down and waves it toward the floor. It takes me a moment to process the gesture: He's inviting me to join.

Forty-two days.

Maybe we'll see something. A hint of the bird. A clue.

Waigong is slower than Waipo, with his long cane, his off-kilter hobble. The sky is still grayish when we leave, but it opens up to the watery colors of morning as we walk. We end up in the park, winding our way through greenery, pausing to watch bugs crawling into the hollow bells of flowers.

At first the silence is strange. But once I get used to him being quiet, I start talking to him in English. It's kind of nice, pretending he understands me.

"I had a dream," I tell him. "An awful one."

My grandfather gives me a long and steady look. He leads us to a bench, where we sit for a spell, watching two little kids chase each other around the small playground. On the other side, there's a gazebo over a table. Two old men sit opposite each other, gazing down at something between them. Some sort of game. They take turns moving around flat pieces.

"What are they playing?" I ask.

Waigong says nothing, but I imagine it to be something like backgammon, or maybe checkers.

While he watches them, I study him for a little bit, search for Ping's features in his face. Was that him? I try to imagine Waigong growing up alongside Waipo, as a brother.

The wrongness of the idea makes me squirm a little. Even if she *was* adopted. Still. Brother and sister, engaged, and then married. Didn't *they* think it was weird?

A flat buzzing fills the air. It takes up a percussive rattle, quickening its beat, finding a steady pace. The noise halfway between a scrape and an electrical hum.

My eyes do a quick scan but find nothing to land on. "What is that?"

Waigong points with a trembling finger.

There it is, on the thin branch of the nearest tree, almost the size of my thumb, brown and unmoving.

A cicada.

I watch it for a long moment before I realize it's far too still. This is only the shell, a husk left behind like an empty house.

We can't see the one that's singing, but it buzzes louder and louder. The tempo changes, quickening, slowing. It gathers up like a wave, retreats like a falling tide. We listen until the song dies.

Before we head home, my grandfather stops us near a patch of purple flowers. He touches them, tracing their silky edges, nudging each one aside until he finds the perfect blossom. His knuckles travel down the stem to the base near the grass, where he pinches tight and breaks the green.

When he holds it up to me, I tell him, "That's lovely."

The most perfect flower. We bring it home to Waipo.

46

The first thing I see when Waigong and I step back into the apartment is Feng, wearing another one of her floral shirts with colors so sharp they hurt my eyes—sunflowers painted in neon hues. She's sitting at the dining table, where there are bowls of snowy rice porridge, and chatting gaily with my grandmother in quick Taiwanese. The television is blasting loudly, but she talks over it. The noise scrapes into my ears. Without breaking her sentence, Feng turns to wave to us, her grin a sharp and blinding crescent.

I swallow a sigh. Don't Waipo and Waigong get sick of her?

Feng describes something with her hands, drawing wide circles, looking almost like a caricature.

And across from her, just outside the kitchen, Waipo is clutching her stomach, eyes squeezed shut, leaning heavily against the doorway to the kitchen, laughing like it's all she knows how to do.

On the TV an audience is also laughing. It's like the

universe has perfectly timed some ridiculous joke to sync up everywhere, and I'm the only one not in on it.

I kick my shoes off loudly.

"Leigh," says Feng, "*lai chi.*"

Come eat. Like she's the host. Like she belongs here more than I do.

I yank my chair out from under the table as loudly as possible.

"Maybe we should put on some *yinyue*?" Feng says, looking pleased with herself for mixing English and Mandarin. "*Yinyue* means—"

"Music," I say before she can finish. "I know." My good mood from the walk with Waigong is completely ruined.

"Oh." She studies my face for a moment, and I try to make my features hard as stone. "Is everything okay?"

"Sure," I say. "Yeah."

Feng turns back, saying something in Taiwanese. At first I wonder if she's calling Waipo's attention to me being horrible. But my grandmother responds by gesturing excitedly with a hand in the air. She makes her way slowly across the living room to click off the TV and turn on an ancient CD player.

Strings croon like a wave. A glockenspiel joins in above, the spare notes delicate, like bells hung from stars. A woman begins to sing, her voice buttery and warm with slow vibrato. The words are in Mandarin.

Feng sings along—she has a surprisingly good voice, and she smiles through the lyrics, her face taking on more color and radiance.

"This song was very popular back in the day," she says during a part that's just instrumental.

And then I realize the melody is familiar to me—somehow I recognize it. But at the same time I'm certain I've never heard it before, because never in my life have I listened to lyrics that weren't in English. Could it have been something I heard as a baby? Does memory even work that way?

And then it strikes me. I haven't heard this song *sung*, but I've heard it played on the piano. This very melody turning in the upper octaves, an accompaniment rolling beneath the left hand. When I close my eyes, I can see my mother leaning over the piano, eyes squeezing shut, hands feeling out the song. All I knew was it was improvised—it was one of the pieces she would play that never came out the same way twice.

In the chair beside me, Waigong draws little smiles back and forth in the air with a finger, moving in time to the music, like he's the one conducting the orchestra.

"The name of the singer is Teresa Teng," says Feng. "Deng Lijun. Have you heard of her?"

"*Ni mama zui xihuan,*" Waipo says. *Your mother's favorite.* She brings over the CD case. The album cover shows a rosy-cheeked woman, her black hair curled and fluffed, the expression on her face soft and demure.

How many other songs would I recognize if we listened to this whole CD?

Waipo fills the table with dishes full of toppings for the congee. There are the sugary black pickles and silky slivers of bamboo shoots dripping with oil—I used to love those. I can't remember the last time I had them. There are also sautéed greens I don't recognize, red sausage slices, and ruddy blocks of either a paste or tofu. In the last bowl, there are little knots of something brown and squishy soaking in a syrup, with cooked peanuts crowding the edges.

I follow Waigong's example, reaching with chopsticks to help myself to a little bit of everything.

"Waipo, *ni zai nali*—" I start out with my voice strong and firm. *Where were you . . .* I struggle to find the words in Mandarin. I want to ask her myself, to see her face as the question registers.

"Just say it in English," says Feng, watching us eat. "I'll translate for you."

I'm barely able to bite back the harsh response boiling up into my throat. I want to snap at her that I don't need a translator—but that's a lie. I do. I need her if I'm going to get the answers to my questions.

"I want to know where she was born, and where she grew up," I say reluctantly, dragging the words out of my mouth, hating the sound of them in English. "What it was like, with her—with her family."

Feng spins it into Taiwanese. I wish she would stick to Mandarin so I can hear how things are said.

Waipo looks directly at me as she answers. I'm grateful for her gaze.

"She says she was born just outside the Alibung Mountain district. Her parents had no money, and they already had a son. She was just a girl. So they sold her to another family."

I shake my head. "But you"—I turn toward Feng—"she was their daughter."

"Once she came of age and married into another family, she'd be *that* family's daughter. So it wasn't economical for her parents to keep her, to have to feed and raise someone who would leave. It made sense to sell her off."

My grandmother nods matter-of-factly.

I think of the woman in the memory. The balding man carrying the baby. "Was this a . . . commonplace thing?"

"It was," says Feng. "In fact, Popo's adoptive parents sold their own daughter to have the money to purchase your grandmother. It was a good deal for them—Popo would grow up to be the wife of their son."

"Even though she was growing up *with* him? Even though that made him her brother?"

"Living with them, Popo would learn all the habits and preferences of their family," Feng explains. "They could raise her to be the perfect daughter-in-law. And then when she married their son, there would be no need for a dowry."

"So Waigong—" I begin to ask.

Waipo smiles and jumps to say more, the words tumbling from her mouth fast.

"The betrothal didn't exactly go as planned. Her adoptive father died, and Popo was just a child then, but she quit school and started working, picking tea leaves so they would have the money to survive. She became their main source of income."

"What about her brother?" I ask.

Waipo shrugs.

"He didn't know how to shoulder any kind of responsibility. He wasn't bad at heart . . . just a wild boy who lost his father too young. When Popo came of age . . . her mother pulled her aside and said, 'Yuanyang, you don't have to marry him. You've been such a good daughter. You have such a good heart. Do what you want. Live your life and be happy.' So their betrothal was broken."

I try to imagine a provincial life spent on the mountains,

picking tea, not going to school. If I were my grandmother, I think I would have run away. "Did she leave?"

Waipo shakes her head.

Feng translates, "She stayed. Popo's mother taught her to cook and sew. She taught her how to coax the chickens back after they'd had a scare, how to bind up strands of firecrackers to sell for Lunar New Year. They understood each other. They were each other's true family. So your grandmother stayed with her, in the same house where they'd always lived... until the day a young man came and knocked on their door. A man who Popo had never seen before."

"Waigong," I say, glancing to my left. He smiles at me and shakes his head slightly.

"No," Feng continues. "Not your grandfather—this was before he moved from China to Taiwan. When your mother opened the door, the man said, 'Eighteen years ago I lost my sister. She was only a baby when my parents sold her to a family on the mountain. I'm trying to find her.'"

I blink in disbelief. "Was it really her brother?"

Waipo's face pulls into a faraway smile.

"It was. After years of struggling, her biological family had claimed a plot of land and built their own hotel. They were thriving."

"So then what?"

Waipo's expression changes. Her voice grows quiet.

Feng explains, "Her mother told her to go with her brother, back to the family who birthed her. And your grandmother listened. She did exactly as she was told. So Popo went down the mountain with her brother. She started working in her family's hotel. At first she went to visit her mother every week, but then she was too busy. A month passed, and then two. Your waigong came to stay at the hotel, and they met and fell in love, and time disappeared. And when Popo went back to visit again, her mother had grown terribly ill."

My lungs tighten; I don't move. If I hold myself still, I won't feel the pain in my grandmother's expression.

"It was clear that life wasn't the same in that cottage on the mountain. Popo thinks that when she left, she took something away with her, something invisible but necessary. Her adoptive mother fell into rapid decline. Popo brought her medicines and herbs. She offered to move back in, but her mother didn't want that. She said, 'Your new life is down in the city. Go live it, and be happy. I'll be fine.' And in that moment her mother looked almost normal, healthy again. Popo visited her just one more time after that."

I let the air back in. My eyes are aching.

Waipo's voice drops low.

Feng hesitates. She sucks in a breath between her teeth. "Your grandmother knew she'd died when her son—as in Popo's adoptive brother—came to the hotel searching for her. She knew it the moment she saw him. She opened her arms and he fell into them and cried. It's the only time she can remember ever touching him. She tried to get him a job at the hotel, but he didn't want it. Together they burned their mother's body and paid their respects, and that was the last time Popo ever saw him."

My grandmother gathers up our empty bowls and dishes. I watch her make her way to the kitchen. When she thinks no one is looking, she reaches a quick finger up to dab at the corner of her eye.

47

The afternoon sun divides my room into lines and triangles, patches of light and geometric shadows. I'm sitting on my bed, trying to think through everything I've seen. Everything I know.

My mind is reeling. If I close my eyes, there's a strong sense of vertigo, like I'm free-falling through a huge, dark chasm. A deep gorge that marks where my family's world split, where the foundations tore apart. It's the breakage in the lines of my family's history. The breakage widened by my mother turning into a bird.

My eyes hurt. A pressure has wrapped itself around my skull, like hard chains coiling and tightening against my temples.

I try to ignore the headache, fight it away via sheer force of will. My fingers gather the T-shirt strands together and begin to weave my net. It starts sort of like a braid, the material moving over and under like waves on a sea. I'm worried I won't have enough fabric to make the net as big as I need it to be, but that just means I'll have to be strategic about how I use it.

My phone chimes. There are new emails waiting for me.

One from my father, because I never responded to his first message.

> FROM: bsanders@fairbridge.edu
> TO: leighinsandalwoodred@gmail.com
> SUBJECT: RE: Check in
>
> Leigh, I've already spoken on the phone with your grandmother and given her this information, but my Hong Kong number is below, so feel free to give me a call. Or email. Let me know how you're doing.

I roll my eyes and archive the note. There's a more pressing matter—and that's the new message from Axel.

> FROM: axeldereckmoreno@gmail.com
> TO: leighinsandalwoodred@gmail.com
> SUBJECT: (no subject)
>
> Dory didn't know I was recording her. I came over to hang out with you but you weren't home for some reason. The door was unlocked, so I let myself in and Dory was on the piano. It was different from what she normally played. I peeked around the corner and it seemed like she was riffing off one specific melody. I recorded a good

chunk of it and paired it with some synths and
strings. Sometimes when I listen

The email ends there.

I click on the link at the bottom. Another MP3 track. It takes forever to load, but when it finally plays, a chill snakes its way down my spine.

It's Teresa Teng—the very song Waipo put on as we ate breakfast.

Behind my eyelids, I can see my mother's careful hands roving over the keys, feeling out the tune and its roots and its peaks, her eyes closed, the expression on her face suffused with the sepia hues of nostalgia, with viridian music.

I can see her.

I can see everything.

48

WINTER, FRESHMAN YEAR

It was the last morning of winter break. I made myself coffee using Dad's French press and sat alone in the kitchen for a good hour, trying hard to forget the dream with the two girls from the photograph.

Their words echoed in my brain: *Dory doesn't have a daughter.*

Being wiped away by those blackboard erasers had both itched and burned. The sensation was still in my legs. I couldn't shake the feeling of wanting to be known and remembered.

I needed a distraction. My fingers absentmindedly peeled open the Emily Dickinson book.

> *Pain has an element of blank;*
> *It cannot recollect*
> *When it began, or if there were*
> *A day when it was not.*

"What's that?" said my mother as she walked in.

I jumped in my seat. Coffee spilled over the lip of my mug.

"A book I found," I started saying, half hoping she wouldn't realize which book it was, half hoping she'd give something away in her reaction.

But that wasn't what she was talking about. She pointed at the pieces of jade around my wrist.

"Oh. I found it in the basement. Is it yours?"

She gazed at it for a beat too long, eyes dark and narrowed. Then her face smoothed into neutral. "Yes. It is very old."

"From when you were still…living in Taiwan?" I asked tentatively.

She nodded. "Yes."

"Do you want it back?"

"No. You wearing it look good." She pulled out the waffle iron and turned to me, her eyebrows a question.

"Yes, please," I said. "Can I have extra cream? You know, last day of winter break and all that?"

"Me too!" said Axel, letting himself in through the back.

"Me three," said my mother.

We got extra berry preserves *and* extra cream, and Axel made my mother laugh by telling her the story of how, the day after Christmas, he and his sister tricked his little cousin into thinking one of Santa's elves had moved into the basement.

"I don't know where Angie got those weird shoes with the bells on them, but she put those out, and left strands of 'elf beard' on the couch. Angie was like, 'Look, Jorge, if you wait here long enough, I bet he'll come back!' And Jorge was like, 'How do you know the elf is a he?' And then he waited in the basement for two hours. He even brought the elf a plate of pasteles! He's way more patient than I ever was."

"That's *so* mean," I said.

Axel shrugged and grinned. "Kid's got no siblings. *Someone's* gotta mess with him."

Later, when Axel had left, Mom sat down at the piano. Her improv was some of my favorite stuff—every performance was one of a kind. She had a handful of melodies in her arsenal that she'd made up or something, and she would play them again and again in different ways, sometimes with a little smile tugging at the edges of her mouth, sometimes with her eyes closed, looking wistful.

Things were almost normal. Except Dad had been gone too many days. Except Mom's eyes had turned glassy like she was trying to go somewhere far away in her head.

Caro was back from snowboarding, so I dragged Axel with me to her house. It was the first time the three of us were hanging out together outside of art class.

"My grandparents were *killing me*," Caro was saying as we went down to her basement. "Half the time they sat in the lodge making out. And Mom kept trying to check out other girls for me, which was too weird. Plus, you know, unfair to Cheslin."

I smiled.

"I'm pretty sure one girl heard her say, 'What about *that* chick? Think she's hot?' It was mortifying. But other than that, it was really fun."

"That's awesome," I said.

She tilted her head. "All right, out with it. What's up?"

"What?" I said. "What are you talking about?"

"You've been listening to me, but you haven't been a hundred percent present. Something's up." She glanced at Axel, who was sitting on a stool with his back to us, gazing at the wall of Caro's photography. There was a question in the look she gave me.

"Well, we went through all those boxes in my basement."

She didn't question the *we*. She and I had still never discussed Axel, though I had a feeling she'd puzzled out a good amount.

"I knew it!" she said. "You found something."

"A few somethings," I told her. I showed her the bracelet and the Emily Dickinson book. I saved the photograph for last. "I was hoping you might be able to tell...something. Anything. Like how old it might be?"

She turned the picture in her hands, examining the edges and the back before taking a real look at the subject. "Who are they?"

"I have no idea. If I can figure a possible time period... maybe that'll be a clue. Though Axel's convinced that one of the girls is my grandmother." I glanced at Axel's back. He'd been weirdly quiet since we got to the Renards'. It occurred to me that he might, in fact, be feeling shy.

Caro shook her head. "I don't know enough about the history of photography papers. I'd be able to give you a better idea if it were a carte de visite or like a cabinet card. All I can guess is...the oldest this could be is maybe like, early nineteen hundreds? But chances are it was made way after that."

I tried not to look disappointed.

"What about the Emily Dickinson book?" said Caro. "What's the copyright date on that?"

"It's not dated," said Axel as I opened the cover. "I already looked."

I checked anyway. "What kind of book isn't dated?"

"A super old one?" Caro suggested.

"So here we are," said Axel. "An old bracelet. An old book of poetry. And an old photograph. Anyone else have any ideas?"

"We need brain food," said Caro. "Then maybe we'll have ideas. I vote Fudge Shack."

"I'm allergic to fudge," said Axel.

"Oh," said Caro, clearly thrown off.

"He's not allergic." I rolled my eyes. "I once watched him eat six huge blocks of maple walnut fudge in one sitting. Paired with a liter of Diet Coke. At three in the morning."

"Right, and then I puked in your bathtub. An allergic reaction."

"We can go," I said, ignoring him. "We just have to monitor his intake."

"I'm not a babysitter, so I'm not monitoring anybody," said Caro. "But know this: Puke in *my* bathtub, dude, and I will end you."

Axel pounded a fist on his chest until a rough burp came out. "Acknowledged."

I hid a smile. They were going to get along great.

While we waited in line at Fudge Shack I looked up Emily Dickinson on my phone. The depressing thing? She published hardly anything while she was still alive. Nobody had any clue who the hell she was. She was just there, writing poem after poem. It was only after her death that she became relevant.

But also, apparently Dickinson asked her sister to burn everything she wrote. I guess she never wanted to become relevant in the first place.

The burning, though...that's what I didn't understand. Even if you didn't want to share your work with the world—even if you were private about it—wouldn't you want to be remembered?

Dad was home in time for dinner, and he found me curled up on the couch, shading a drawing while I waited for Mom to call us into the dining room. He sat down on the piano bench, facing me. He wanted to have An Important Conversation; I braced myself for it.

"That's interesting," he said, eyeing my art pad. This was a large one—it took up my whole lap and stretched wide past my elbows. It was pretty obvious that this specific piece—a more fantastical work with a melting sun and fish swimming through a sky of asteroids—had taken me a long, long time.

Funny word choice, on his part. He did not actually sound *interested*. When he opened his mouth again, I knew that whatever came out was going to annoy me.

"Is that all you've been working on lately?"

"Oh, I actually spend most of my time at school, you see. And when I get home, I have this thing called *homework* that won't do itself, despite modern-day technologies. So as much as I would *prefer* to not go to school and instead spend all my time drawing and sleeping, the answer is no, unfortunately. I've been working on life in general, lately."

"I just think," Dad said slowly, "that you're so full of potential, Leigh. Don't you see how this might not be the best use of your time? There are other things you could apply this energy to. Other things you could really excel at, that might help you figure out your path down the road."

Meaning, a path that was not art.

"Years from now you'll look back on this and what'll you have? Just...a bunch of these pictures. You probably won't even want them anymore. It's like my old Coffee Grind recordings in the back of the office closet—who the hell wants to listen to a bunch of derivative crap played by mediocre twentysomethings? Nobody. I really should just throw them out."

I heard him loud and clear: He thought my art was shitty. He thought it was just as shitty as his craptastic jazz band who'd recorded their EP in someone's garage. And normally this was the moment when I would pull on the gauntlets and steel myself for a fight, but I needed him in a good mood if he was going to answer any of my questions.

So all I said was, "Right."

I waited until after dinner, which was when we used to always sit together and eat Häagen-Dazs ice cream. Mom didn't like ice cream, so that was alone time with my father that I could count on. She was already heading upstairs, and I brought out bowls and spoons and a brand-new carton just as Dad was rising from his seat.

"Haven't done this in forever," I said.

He gave me a smile, but it looked a little more like sadness in his face. I watched him settle back down into his seat.

I counted through five spoonfuls, meditating upon the gentle clink of the spoon against porcelain and the way the ice cream numbed my tongue.

He opened his mouth, and I knew he was going to say something about art again. I had to stop him. I had to get my questions in before the chance got sucked away by a fight.

"So I've been going through the boxes in the basement," I said quickly. "For a project at school."

"Huh." He blinked. "It's about time someone went through those. They're ancient. Some of them are maybe older than you."

"Yeah, I got that feeling. I actually wanted to ask—I found an Emily Dickinson book. Was that yours? Or was it Mom's?"

Dad frowned. "Neither, I would think. You know my tastes—I don't have much beyond the Chinese classics. As for your mother...well, it would be strange if it *was* hers. She hates Emily Dickinson. Or *hated*, at least. It was one of the first things I learned about her when we started dating."

"Wait, what? I would never have guessed that."

"Yeah." A funny little half smile of nostalgia tugged the corner of his mouth. "I'll never forget the way she said it. 'I *hate* Emily Dickens!' And I went, 'You mean Emily Dickinson?' She said, 'Yes, exactly. Why would anyone read that? It is so *boring*.' And I remember laughing so hard because I had been so nervous—it was only our second date—and it was just hilarious to me that she had this random, intense opinion about Emily Dickinson."

I put down my spoon. "Did you ask her why?"

"Of course," he said. "But she didn't seem to have a real answer. I guess at some point some Emily Dickinson poem or maybe an Emily Dickinson fan just really offended her, and she never got over it."

"Maybe," I said.

"I even remember what she was wearing," he mused. "She had this amazing sweater—I wonder if she still has it. It had pink, orange, and green zigzags. It was pretty hideous, really. But when she wore it—man. She could wear anything, your mother."

A seed of something dark had begun twisting inside me. Nausea or sadness or anger, or some combination of all of those. I could feel it snowballing, taking up more space.

"Our first Valentine's Day she actually called me at eight in the morning—that was when she was back in Taiwan and I was still in Chicago—and she said she'd written me a poem and would I like to hear it. I told her of course, and she proceeded to read me this little ditty. It was about lips and flowers and bees."

My stomach was wringing itself out now. I sat very still, hoping the twisting and the nausea would just fade if I ignored them long enough.

"And I could tell immediately that it was Emily Dickinson, but I said, 'Darling, that's amazing! I can't believe you wrote that for me!' And then she was cackling with laughter on the other end for a good two minutes. When she finally recovered, she said, 'You cannot believe it, because I did *not* write it.' And so I said, 'But aren't you Emily Dickinson?' and she went laughing her head off again. It was so silly, but her laughter—that was the best sound in the world."

The question thrummed through my center Winsor violet: Why did it feel like our family was crumbling if we were still full of so much love?

Dad shook his head, still smiling. "Back then, long-distance calls between the US and Taiwan cost three dollars a minute. I spent every dollar I earned on those phone calls."

This was what Caro's grandparents would have called *romantic*. It was. There was no word better applied here. But it weighed me down in my seat. I should have brought up the topic at dinner after all. I wished that my mother could've been down here listening, helping to tell this story, smiling and laughing with him.

"Let's ask Mom to play something for us on the piano." I stacked our empty bowls.

Dad gave me a sad smile. "She's already gone upstairs. Some other night, maybe. I've got to pack."

"You fly out in the morning?" I said.

He sighed and nodded. "Ten o'clock. The car's coming at seven."

"Right. Need any help?"

He looked surprised at the offer. I hadn't helped him pack for anything since I was a kid. It used to feel like a scavenger hunt, digging through the closet to locate his fancy shoes, running down to the kitchen for the travel-sized toothpaste. I remembered swelling with fluorescent importance as he asked me to help him pick out ties.

"Thanks, Leigh, but I've got it."

I listened to the sound of him going up the stairs. *Thud. Thud. Thud.* Like the feet of a heavy giant falling hard on a ground so far away his eyes could no longer see it.

49

I'm going mad here, between the roar of my memories and the counting, and weaving, counting again, just seven days left, seven days to find the bird.

I'm sick of remembering. Weary of the shadows and storms being tugged to the surface of my mind, mauve spilling into raw umber. Tired of reliving the past, the mistakes.

I've been weaving the net much too tightly, so I have to undo it all and start again. Looser, I remind myself, because every time I get caught up in the memories I go all absentminded and my fingers curl and tug and tighten. I need bigger waves, a looser weave, a larger net. I have to get this right so I can catch the bird. A sigh of frustration, and fingers relinquish their grip. It's back to a pile of thin fabric strands, now beginning to curl at the edges where the scissors severed the fine weave in the cotton.

Someone else's memory—that's what I need. Something to refresh myself and shake me loose.

And that's how I find myself standing before the drawer,

pulling that box of incense out again. There aren't very many sticks left.

I don't look closely enough to count them; I'm tired of counting. But I know with just a glance that I'll run out soon.

The match is already lit when I remember that I need some kind of trigger. Like the tea leaves.

I shake the match till it's dead and cast about the room for something that might be good. The leaves worked because Waipo touched them herself, because tea is important to her, an element anchored to her past.

My eyes settle on the box from the bird—I haven't touched it since Dad walked out. Maybe now's the time to go through it again.

Photographs. Letters. I unfold a manila envelope and tug out the contents. There's a page covered in handwritten Chinese characters and, behind it, a piece of art. A drawing from years ago, one I have no memory of ever making. I must have been a little kid, because at the top, it says *For Dad* in the most atrocious handwriting I've ever seen, thick green strokes of oil pastel all jagged and off center.

What is *this* doing in the box?

I wonder what it would give me, if I burned this?

Remembering how the feather and the tea crumbled to ash makes me pause, because someone saved this drawing for a reason. I can't just sacrifice it for a memory.

But in the next blink, my room has changed and I can see the cracks again; they've made it halfway down the walls. The ceiling is missing pieces here and there, little gaping holes of emptiness. Even as I watch, another piece begins to crumble away. It disintegrates, the dust falling, leaving behind only the black.

There's a shrill screech, just like the one we heard outside the temple. The flapping of wings.

A burst of red between the cracks of the ceiling. Wings bearing a million different hues. Vermilion, crimson, the red of blood. A long tail gliding past.

One feather drops through the largest gap. It floats down like a sigh, coming to land on top of the drawing, and then vanishing.

I don't need to be told twice. My fingers are shaking, so it takes a few tries to light the new match. Flame to incense. Ember to paper. The drawing begins to burn. Ribbons of black smoke pitch forward, turning, sweeping, coiling.

There's the darkness.

Then come the spark and the flash.

50

—SMOKE & MEMORIES—

The sun is a fat coin embedded in the wide blue sky. I'm standing in the driveway I know all too well, with its crooked slant and the ridge that earthworms stick against on rainy days. A big yellow school bus pulls to a stop.

Behind me, my front door wheezes open, and I turn around in time to see a younger version of my father stepping onto the porch. I know from the smell and the sunny colors that it's one of his memories. He grins and calls out, "Whatcha got there, kiddo?"

A tiny girl with a mess of pigtails comes running across the street and up the driveway, waving a piece of paper like a flag.

I don't remember this at all.

"Look what I made!" the eight-year-old version of myself shouts.

I follow her into the house, where Dad spreads the paper out on the counter.

"*Wow*," he says, sounding genuine. "I think it's your best one yet."

"It's Mommy playing the piano!" little Leigh exclaims.

"I can see that," my father replies. "You did a spectacular job."

"It's for you, Daddy!"

"*Wow*, thank you. I think this should go here for now—at least until we get the chance to frame it!"

My heart twists at the way my younger self beams cadmium bright, the way my father's hands lovingly push everything on the fridge out of the way to make space for the drawing. Could Dad see the instinct in how I was already capturing the proportions and dimensions of the piano? Did he note the way I'd tried to blend different colored oil pastels in my shading?

"What do you think of that?" he says.

"Higher!" says my miniature self. "So Mommy sees."

Dad nudges it up another few inches. "Don't worry. It'll be the first thing she looks at when she gets home."

"Where is she?" Tiny Leigh cranes her head around to one side and then the other.

"Not home yet. Want a snack?"

"But she's *always* home now."

"She's running a few errands, but she'll be back soon. How about an apple with peanut butter?"

My memory-self makes a face. "I'm sick of that."

Dad yanks open the freezer. "Okay . . . how about mozzarella sticks?"

Little Leigh's eyes shine wide. "Mommy *never* lets me have those for an after-school snack."

My father shrugs. "It's your birthday. I don't see why today can't be an exception."

"Yes!" Memory-me leaps into the air, pumping a fist. I can't remember ever having so much energy in my life.

Dad is heating up the marinara sauce and the afternoon

sun is streaming into the kitchen and the house is filling with that delicious deep-fried smell. The front door opens.

"Mommy!"

My mother smiles from the foyer—it's an expression that cuts right through my center. "Happy birthday to you!"

"Where have you been?" My younger self jumps down off her stool.

My mother takes the wrapped, suitcase-sized box out from behind her and maneuvers it down the hallway. "I was picking up your birthday gift. Do you like to open now?"

"Yeah!"

Those tiny fingers tear at the paper, stripping it off with noisy gusto to reveal a beautiful leather case. Thumbs flip open the two shiny latches without hesitation—the top lifts and little shelves slide out, bearing perfectly lined up sticks of color. Cray-Pas on the left, and markers beneath those. Gel pens on the right; crayons on the lower level. And pencils. So many pencils. Sketching pencils with their different hardnesses, watercolor pencils—enough to make little Leigh's head spin.

My memory-self gasps, and can't stop gasping.

"Do you like it?" asks my mother.

"It's the best thing ever!" memory-me exclaims. "There are so many colors!"

And behind us, on the periphery, my father wearing a grin I haven't seen in a long time. A grin that presses hard into my ribs, that makes me feel simultaneously warm and sad.

A flicker, and a changing of colors, a changing of smells.

My mother wanders alone down the hallway of my high school. The whole building is set up for a student art show. Paintings and drawings line the walls of classrooms and halls.

Murals cover the lockers. Glass cases have been set up to display three-dimensional things: abstract wire sculptures, papier-mâché, glazed ceramic pots and vases.

Mom walks past every piece of art—even the ones that are obviously not mine—hunting for the corresponding placard and checking for my name. And every time she finds one of my pieces, she steps back to snap a photo on her point-and-shoot camera.

She swells with pride and loudly points out my drawings to anyone nearby. The last one she finds is the portrait of her. I hadn't shown it to her yet; it was a surprise. A photo-realistic pencil sketch suspended in glass. My mother at the piano, one hand grazing the keys, the other raised up to the page of sheet music with a stubby pencil to mark down the fingering.

"It is beautiful," she says.

The light changes, everything inverts, the smells turning, and when the colors return, I can tell by their faded hue that it's an older time. A memory from further in the past.

There's my grandmother—a version of her who is perhaps in her late forties, walking along the side of a road. She pauses outside a set of rounded steps that lead up to a doorway, where there's a pointed arch with an image of Jesus at the top. She does not enter, but leans against the railing, listening.

The colors and sounds settle and then I hear it, too: the notes of a piano, first lively and fluttering, and then slow and somber. Adept fingers dancing over the keys, adept heart drawing feeling out of the notes.

The music comes to its reluctant end, and my grandmother sighs. She shakes her head a little and then walks on, hurrying as if she does not wish to be seen.

The colors invert, and the memories swirl away.

51

The remains of the drawing line my palms with soft gray ash, silky between the pads of my fingers. I rub my hands and the dust falls away, turning to nothing.

Once upon a time we were the standard colors of a rainbow, cheery and certain of ourselves. At some point, we all began to stumble into the in-betweens, the murky colors made dark and complicated by resentment and quiet anger.

At some point, my mother slid so off track she sank into hues of gray, a world drawn only in shadows.

On the nightstand my phone begins to buzz. There's the quiet tinkling of notes—

That's strange. Who would be calling me?

But it's not a call. It's the track Axel sent me, the one of my mother playing the Teresa Teng song. How does my phone keep doing that?

The afternoon heat wraps tightly around me, and yet the music sends shivers into my center, drags other memories to the surface.

52

WINTER, FRESHMAN YEAR

It all ground to a halt. My questions, my investigating. The normalcy. The illusion.

It was a blustery February day, over halfway through my freshman year. I got home from school to find my mother horizontal on the couch. She looked tiny, like a rag doll.

"Hey, Mom." I let my backpack slide to the floor.

No response.

"Axel and Caro are coming over later. Can we order pizza?"

Still nothing.

I wondered if she was in a deep sleep kind of nap.

"Mom?"

I nudged her shoulder and she turned her face up. Her features scrunched like she was hurting.

"Are you okay?"

She didn't say anything, but I thought I saw her head shake slightly.

I nudged her harder. My mother shifted and something slid off the couch, thudding to the floor. Her cell phone.

I picked it up, searching for a clue. Her password was my birthday; I unlocked it with quick taps and the first thing that popped up was her call history. The last dialed number was 911—the call made just a few minutes ago.

"*Mom*," I said more urgently. "What's wrong?" I'd seen her like this before, listless and unresponsive, but this time it felt dangerous. It was an instinct that seized my body with fear.

The light in the room changed: The afternoon glow turned spiky. In stabbed flashes of red, flashes of blue. I spun around, my eyes shooting for the window. The first thing I saw was the police car. Then there was an ambulance and, pulling in behind them, a fire truck. I looked around the room, trying to take stock of everything around me. Nothing was burning. No alarm was blaring. Why was there a *fire truck*?

The knock on the door was a pickax chipping through my skull. I made my way toward the noise, but I couldn't remember my feet actually touching the ground. When I pulled open the front door, the cop took up my full field of vision.

"Good afternoon," he said. "We're responding to a call from a woman by the name of Dory Sanders."

"That's my mother," I said numbly.

"Is she here?" he said.

"I don't know what's wrong with her," I told him.

"Can we come in?"

"I guess, I mean..." I didn't have a chance to say more.

She didn't speak to them, and like a contagious effect, the cops stopped speaking to me. My questions went unanswered. They gathered her up into the ambulance and took her to the hospital, and I ended up sitting in the waiting room, wondering what the hell was going on.

I called Dad eleven times. He didn't pick up.

The waiting room smelled toxic white but felt traffic-cone orange. I dug my heels into the floor, hoping to leave a mud stain, or grind away enough of the ugly carpet to make a mark.

Rain check on pizza, I texted to Axel and Caro.

"Leigh?" It was the first familiar voice I'd heard in hours, and it wasn't at all who I'd expected.

"Tina," I said. Axel's aunt. Mom's closest friend.

"Hey." She gave me a weak smile. "Are you doing okay?"

"What's going on?"

"I picked up some medicine for your mom, and I'm here to drive you guys home." It wasn't a real answer. "You ready to go?"

The nurse came out then, pushing my mother in a wheel-chair. Mom wouldn't look at me. She wouldn't look at Tina.

"I got in touch with Brian," Tina said. "He got on the first flight he could."

My mother's expression didn't change. Her eyes were sunken, haunted, like she hadn't slept or seen the sun in days. Like someone had wrung the color out of her complexion. When had I last given that face a real look? I felt hollow.

All the way home Mom stayed silent and ghostlike. The nurse had taken the wheelchair back, so Tina draped my mother's arm over her shoulders and half carried her through the front door. I followed from behind, watching the way my mother's feet dragged, how she couldn't even hold up her own weight. She was like a puppet whose strings had snapped.

Tina had brought leftovers for us. She heated up a stew,

uncovered a huge plate of rice and beans, chattering away with forced cheer.

"Jorge's new thing is these glow-in-the-dark lizards. He keeps hiding them around the house, trying to scare me. I'll go downstairs in the middle of the night for water, and at the bottom of the steps, there'll be a plastic lizard glowing at me."

I was relieved when she went home to make dinner for her own family. My mother and I sat in the dining room with the stew ladled out into bowls, the rice and beans served on the nice plates that we rarely used but had been pulled out by Tina's quick hand. Mom didn't touch the food. One of the bulbs up above flickered and buzzed. It was the only sound to be heard.

Mom closed her eyes and slumped forward onto the table, burying her face in her arms.

We sat there like that for hours. I didn't do my homework. I didn't pull the blinds on the windows. The outside world grew dark and the streetlamps bloomed yellow. The neighbors stepped outside with their dog, and that was how I knew it had to be at least ten o'clock.

We sat there until all the other houses on our street winked out their lights. The world was going to sleep.

A car pulled into our driveway, and there was Dad, hauling his suitcase up the porch steps, coming in the front door. I had the fleeting thought that everything would be right again. He was here; he would fix it. Mom would go back to normal.

Inside the house, he kicked off his shoes and walked into the dining room.

"What happened?"

He didn't look at me. Mom didn't look at him. Slowly,

though, she rose out of her slump and pushed her back against her chair. Her eyes stayed closed.

"I'm okay," she said. Her voice came out in a scratchy whisper.

Dad stared at her hard. "Are you really?"

"I'm okay," she said again.

His expression changed. "Give me something concrete here, Dory. *Talk* to me."

Mom shook her head. She opened her mouth and closed it again.

Dad was shaking. His face was red and pinched and horrible. His feelings emanated like heat and debris from an atomic bomb. I was only a bystander and I was getting scorched.

"It's gotten worse again, hasn't it?" he said. "Why didn't you tell me?"

I had the feeling he was talking about something I didn't totally grasp. I watched her face carefully. She didn't say anything.

"It's a school night," he said finally. "We should all get to bed."

But I didn't go to school the next day. In the morning Dad was out—he left a note saying he was taking care of errands and getting groceries. There was nobody downstairs to make sure I actually left to catch my bus. I checked the garage; Mom's car was still there.

She was upstairs in bed, facing away from me. I could tell she was awake.

"Hey, Mom." My mother turned, tightening the blankets around her. She looked up at me with eyes like a little bird's, uncertain and fearful.

"Are you okay?" I said. It was obvious she was not.

She shook her head. There seemed to be nothing to do but get in bed next to her and crawl under the blankets. She curled toward me until our foreheads touched. I fell asleep like that, and when I woke up, my mother was no longer in bed, but my hair was wet, and there were dark patches on her pillow. She'd been crying. I crawled out of bed to look for her.

Mom was downstairs, leaning on the counter with a mug between her hands, peering into the hot chocolate.

I knew she'd heard me come down, but she didn't turn around. It was like she wanted me to notice the little orange bottle wrapped in its pharmaceutical label, perched on the edge of the counter.

"What's that?" I said, glancing at the pills through the orange. I had a strange sense of déjà vu—as if I'd seen her just like this before, standing next to a prescription bottle, her body shaped with defeat and gloom.

Or was it a vague memory, forgotten until now?

Mom knew what I was referring to. She didn't look up. "That is my new life."

I went and wrapped an arm around her shoulders, set my temple against hers. "If they can help, then it's a good thing. It's a good life."

I waited to feel her nod, but she never did.

At one in the morning a text came buzzing through my phone, and I realized I'd failed to respond to any of Axel's messages over the last seventeen hours.

Hey, I texted back.

Are you okay? What's going on?

I sighed and texted, *Can I come over?*

Of course

I had to sneak out of the house, which was easy enough. When I cut diagonally through other people's yards, it only took five minutes to run to Axel's, even with the snow ankle-deep.

In his basement, he slumped down on the couch next to me. "So what happened?"

"Ugh."

I fell over sideways so that the top of my hair was grazing the side of his thigh. It occurred to me that if I had shifted my body differently, I could've put my head right in his lap. Would that have freaked him out?

He gently nudged my shoulder.

It was easier to talk with my eyes focused on the little dots of light on his keyboard, the giant headphones lying in a puddle of cords. I didn't have to look at Axel. I didn't have to see his reaction.

I told him about going to the hospital. I told him how I found Mom in bed in the morning, and how in that moment it felt like I would be guilty of something if I just left her and went to school.

I didn't use the word *depression*, which had been thudding around in my skull all day.

"But I still don't get it," he said quietly. "Why did she call nine-one-one?"

I shrugged, which made my head bump against his leg. I could feel the static gathering in my hair. "I don't know, either."

I mean, I could have speculated. I didn't really want to.

"God. I'm so sorry, Leigh."

I let my eyes fall shut.

When I woke in the morning, I was still on his couch. A quilt was draped over me. I sat up slowly. Axel was asleep, curled up on his twin bed in the back corner. I watched his body swell and fall with each breath.

A cyprus-green pang struck me between the ribs. He'd removed himself from the couch. We could've fallen asleep touching, but he didn't let that happen. I guess it would've been weird.

But maybe really nice.

I stood up and stretched. Axel's watercolor pad leaned against the music stand on his keyboard. My fingers itched for it. I loved seeing his paintings. Sometimes he'd let me flip through, and he'd explain how each bold stroke or swirl of color was going to translate to a solo bassoon, the trill of a piccolo, arpeggios on a Spanish guitar.

I picked up the pad and thumbed through to find paintings I hadn't seen yet. The edges flew by too fast, landing on a page in the far back that was heavier and thicker than all the rest—

Here was a photograph, old and a little bent, glued in place. It took me a second to puzzle out who the four people were—I was too used to thinking of Axel's family as just him, Angie, and their dad. This was the Moreno family back when it was still whole, before Axel's mother walked out.

Sometimes it was easy to forget that Axel's mother existed; so much of his face came from his father. I wondered if that bothered him. If he felt like the lack of his mother in his own features made her seem too easily erased.

Here, in two dimensions, they looked so happy. But then, didn't everyone, in pictures? That was almost the point, wasn't it? To be able to look back and see yourself smiling, even if the camera had shuttered and clicked while you were standing there thinking about all the things that were wrong?

Axel's mom grinned with teeth that were slightly crooked. Her black hair fell in messy waves around her shoulders, and she wore an emerald dress that flattered her curvy hips. She looped arms with her husband. He stood awkwardly to the side, a couple inches taller than his wife, but shrinking inside a striped button-down that was a little too big.

Beside them: toddler Angie squeezing a plush elephant, and Axel in a plaid shirt, gazing up at his mother like she was the only thing in the world he needed.

I heard the rustle of sheets too late. Axel rolled out of bed, and I didn't have time to hide what I was holding. I turned toward him, suddenly feeling like I shouldn't have touched anything in the first place.

His eyes landed on the sketch pad. He sighed.

I knew that sigh. It was the sound of him deciding to forgive me.

"I'm sorry," I said immediately. "I realize I shouldn't have now, but I didn't think you would mind—"

Axel waved away the rest of my sentence and squeezed his eyes shut through a yawn. "You shouldn't have. But it's fine."

I nodded, my cheeks burning a little.

"I just found that the other day," he said, coming around to sit on the couch.

I sat down next to him. He smelled like sleep.

"You mean the photograph?"

"I don't even remember when it was taken," he said. "But I remember that dress. She called it her power dress and only wore it for special occasions."

"How old do you think you are?"

Axel looked over my shoulder. He stared at the photo for a while. "Maybe six? It was probably a year before she left."

"Could you tell?"

"Tell what?"

"That she was going to leave."

Axel sat back and let out a long, slow breath. "I don't know."

"Did it seem like your parents were falling out of love?"

His fingers traced the edge of a cushion that had begun to fray. "I don't know."

I slid down on the couch so that I was lying on my back, my legs forming a bridge over the cold floor. "I know emotions are all internal and whatnot. But I just wonder if it's visible on the outside. You can tell when people are falling *in* love. So there must be a way to see if people are falling *out* of love, right?"

Axel slid down so our eyes were at the same level. "Maybe, I guess."

"Do you think people can be in love but also unhappy?"

"Yes," said Axel, the most solid answer he'd given in a long time. "Definitely."

53

Once, Dad and I went to a choir concert where my mother was the piano accompanist. Everyone was watching the conductor, the singers, the soloists—but we kept our faces angled toward the far left of the stage. There, my mother leaned over the huge piano, her hands heavy as anvils when the voices stormed, fluttering light as a dove when the voices sailed low and quiet.

Her chords kept time like a clock. She turned her own pages, her hand flying so quickly it was like a magic trick; if you blinked you would miss it. Nobody but us watched her, but she was playing for all the world. She was a sea creature and the music was her ocean. It had always belonged to her. It was in her every breath, her every movement. She was the color of home.

54

N*i kan*," says my grandmother. *Look*. She points to a church. The rest of her words are far away, indistinct.

Feng steps so close to me her sleeve grazes my elbow, and the touch makes me shiver. "Popo says this is where your mother learned to play piano. She learned from a Catholic nun who saw that she was very gifted and would let her come during the empty hours to practice."

"Can we go inside?" My voice comes out all ultramarine. And as I ask, it dawns on me that I recognize this place. I saw it in the incense memories, saw how Waipo stood outside on the steps, listening.

We push through heavy wooden doors into a little foyer. A second set of doors slides open and then we're standing behind rows and rows of maple pews, the wood gleaming in the soft light.

It's so strangely quiet, like a bell jar has fallen over us, sealing away the sounds of the city, the rush of the traffic. There's only the gentle rhythm of our breaths. The shy clicks of our feet echoing off the marble floors. The most surprising thing about the place is how similar it is to the few churches I've seen back in the States—I guess I was expecting something different.

Waipo tugs my arm and points at a piano off to the side. Someone has draped a swath of forest-green velvet over the top to keep it from getting dusty. I wonder if it's the very instrument my mother used, her fingers learning the feel of the keys and the spacing of an octave, her hands working up and down scales.

I tug the velvet off, slide my fingers along the smooth surface.

"That's a digital piano," says Feng. "The piano your mother would've played must be gone now."

Murky disappointment sinks through my center, dark as mud.

"Shall we head to the night market?" says Feng. "The sun's about to set."

I follow my grandmother back out the sliding glass, past the heavy wooden doors, down the steps.

But just as Feng turns for the main road, a few lazily drifting notes of music catch my attention. A piano. I listen for a few seconds—it's definitely coming from inside the church.

"Leigh," says Waipo as I whirl around and run back up.

The music fades away just as I pull open the inner door.

There are the rows and rows of empty pews. There's the piano, the velvet crumpled on the bench, where I left it, forgetting to put it back. There's no one to be seen.

Outside again, Waipo looks at me questioningly.

Feng catches the expression on my face. "Is everything all right?"

"I thought I heard someone playing."

Feng shrugs. "A trick of the wind, maybe."

There's a rustling to the left, and when I turn a young man is standing under a tree mere paces away, watching me with a toothy grin. His baggy jeans are filthy, his orange T-shirt stained at the hem. Shoulders hunched up around his ears. Teeth yellow, some of them brown with rot.

"*Qingwen yixia…*" he says slowly. *May I ask…* He repeats it. "*Qingwen yixia…shi Meiguo ren ma?*" Every word comes out so slow and clear that I actually understand the whole question. *Are you American?*

I cross my arms, trying to make myself smaller. He stares at me expectantly, and so finally I give him a tight nod.

"Come on," says Feng, beckoning us away.

"What does he want?" I ask.

Feng shakes her head.

When we reach the intersection, I glance over my shoulder. The young man is still standing there. He cups his hands around his mouth and calls something out to us.

Waipo stiffens visibly. She glances at me and picks up her pace.

I nudge Feng. "What did he say?"

She rolls her eyes. "Just spouting nonsense. He said birds belong in the sky."

My heart skips. When I look back, the man is gone. There's only the tree, swaying in the breeze, and a strange bit of mist disappearing into its branches.

55

By the time we get to the Shilin Night Market the last of the light has leaked away. Purple-gray seeps into the sky as people fill the intersection. At first glance all there is to be seen are the lights and the crowd. Vertical signs hang on both sides of the streets—lit-up stripes in yellows and blues and pinks and greens, bearing logos and Chinese characters.

The night market feels like a special sort of festival, except Feng tells me it comes alive every night. People walk by holding sweets like shaved ice and red bean ice cream. I see some things I've never tried but Dad's told me about, like stinky tofu, and yellow wheel cakes filled with custard. One stand sells skewers of tiny brown eggs, and other kebabs that look dark and marinated. On either side of the crowd, there are stalls lined up in no particular order, some of them peddling trinkets and clothing and accessories, others smoky with freshly cooking foods—

"The snacks here are called *xiaochi*," says Feng. "That

translates to *little eats*, literally. *Mmm*—all my favorite smells in one place! You know, I always thought the most romantic date would be to walk through a night market together eating everything in sight." She skips beside me, grinning.

Waipo takes my elbow and leans close to me. She mutters something into my ear, but all I catch is *ni mama. Your mother.*

I shake my head. *"Shenme?"*

She says it again, slower, and this time I hear it. *Your mother's favorite night market.*

There's a family with two little kids heading in our direction. The youngest looks up at me with big, round eyes. He tugs on his sister's hand, points at me.

"Waiguo ren," his sister says. *Foreigner.* She turns to her parents, pointing her finger, too. *"Ni kan!"* Look!

I angle my face away, pretending to be very interested in a stand selling deep-fried squid tentacles. Do people really eat these?

"Hallo, hallo," says the squid merchant, peering at me curiously.

Too many people pressing close. How am I supposed to find my mother in this place?

"I bet you've never had anything as delicious as the food here!" says Feng.

Up ahead, someone starts yelling and the crowd pauses, heads tilting to look. The man's gesturing wildly with his hands, pointing to the sky as he shouts. He seems to be in charge of a steaming vat: Little golden rounds float on the surface of a dark soup.

Feng makes a noise of understanding. "He's saying that someone came and stole a bunch of the fish balls."

And then I catch what he's saying. *Did you see it? A bird—a red bird. Very big!*

"He says it was a filthy bird that came down out of the sky." Feng shakes her head. "How strange."

"Strange," I echo, my voice coming out ash blue.

"It's too bad. Waipo wanted to get some of these—they were your mother's favorite night market snack. Though the best fish balls are in Danshui. Your mom used to commute out there just to buy them."

Your mother's favorite.

The words turn around and around.

Your mom.

As if Feng knew her. As if she somehow, once upon a time, walked these streets alongside my mother.

Something in me snaps.

My body turns. My feet root down into the ground. Even as I'm telling myself to hold back, the words are boiling their way up, pouring out of my mouth. "Stop pretending you know about my mother."

"Huh?" says Feng.

It tumbles out of me, wretched and wild and black with rage: "As if you know a single real thing about her. As if you've traveled *back in time* and met her—"

I'm seething so much my stomach is clenching and my insides hurt and I want to spit out every furious thought that comes to mind.

Feng's eyes open wide. Her shoulders droop forward and she shrinks into a slight hunch. "I'm sorry, I was just try-ing to—"

"Stop it. You're not part of this family. You don't know *any-thing*. Why are you always here? I wish you would leave us *alone*."

Feng takes a step back, stumbling over her own feet. "I just want to help you. That's all."

I spit the words out so meanly I surprise even myself: "Why are you so convinced I need your help?"

"Leigh," Waipo says.

"It's okay," says Feng. She turns to my grandmother and tries to smile. *"Meiguanxi."*

I blink, and she vanishes into the crowd.

56

After Feng left, Waipo and I made our way back home in a gauzy silence.

It's quiet in the apartment now, everything so still that I can hear my grandparents shifting in their bed. There's a far-away cricket making its rhythmic count somewhere out on the streets. The occasional car swishes past. My guilty inhales and exhales loud as stormy waves crashing over rocks.

If Axel were here right now, he'd ask, *What color?* and I'm not sure I would be able to answer. Maybe it's a color I haven't discovered yet.

I try to shove the thoughts about Feng out of my brain.

My hands grab at the T-shirt strands. I start again with a braid, my knuckles directing the fabric, fingers curling to hold the weave loose. I focus on the over and under, on tying quick knots, and let my mind wander.

There was one weekend when Caro and I spent our entire Saturday reading about tetrachromacy and trying to figure out if one or both of us might happen to have it. It's this extremely rare thing that means you can see colors that other people can't. So, like, a regular person might call a sky perfectly blue while a tetrachromat insists that it's also red and yellow and green.

I wonder if seeing the bird is like that. If those of us who've seen her have something special in our eyes, in our brains, in our hearts—something that allows us to see into that other dimension of existence with sharp clarity.

Because the bird is real. She has to be.

I am as certain of this as I am of the fact that I was born. That I'm alive. That my name is Leigh Chen Sanders.

And then I remember how one article said that most birds are tetrachromatic.

That must be true for my mother, as a bird. It must be. I wonder if she can see colors I can't. If for her the sky is full of purples and oranges as she sails across. If the moon looks like a brush loaded with a million different shades of paint, waiting to be cleaned.

It's as if my thoughts summon some kind of magic. The colors of my room begin to deepen their hues, like flowers blossoming. Crimson in the corners. Cerulean along the southern cracks. Indigo by the window. Bioluminescent green tracing the creases of the wall closest to the bed. The things that are already black somehow take on a truer shade, pitch dark and empty.

I blink hard, and it clears for a moment.

But then it pours back in like an ink spill spreading quick.

On the shiny surface of the stain, I see hints of the past. The memories unfurl.

57

SUMMER BEFORE SOPHOMORE YEAR

I should've known something was up when Dad came and sat down in the kitchen and said nothing about the sketch under my hand. He was so quiet I wondered: Was he watching me work?

I set down my pencil to take a sip of tea. That was when he pounced.

"Leigh, how do you feel about going to camp?"

I paused, mug halfway to my mouth, and raised my eyebrows. "Camp?"

It was the end of June, end of freshman year. My summer had just begun, and later that day Axel and Caro were going to come over. I was ready to enjoy two months off.

I had no idea that in less than a year my life was going to flip upside down.

"Sleepaway camp," said Dad.

There must've been a look of horror on my face because he said, "Come on, it'll be fun. You've never done it before. It'll be a good experience. There's one in Upstate New York that looks perfect for you."

"What, about this"—I gestured to my pajamas, sketchbook, and half a dozen pencils strewn out next to my breakfast—"indicates that I'd want to go somewhere totally not interesting, and make fake new friends who I'll never speak to again, and be away from my *actual* friends, just to do a bunch of trust falls and get eaten alive by diseased mosquitoes—"

"It's an art and nature camp," said Dad.

I had to work hard to not roll my eyes. My father clearly thought that anything with the word *art* in it automatically won with me. At least he was making an effort?

But the wrong kind of effort.

"Can we address the elephant in the room?" I said.

His face shifted into something wary. "What's the elephant?"

My stomach tightened with irritation. "Okay, Mom? Is in no condition to be left alone." I hated the word *condition*, but it was easier than calling it what it really was. *A war.* Her depression was this big thing we were all battling together.

"She's not going to be alone."

"Oh, she's not?" I did a pretty good job of keeping most of the sarcasm out of my voice. Most, but not all. Luckily, my father missed the tone.

"No. I canceled the summer intensive I was going to teach, and I've postponed my trip to Beijing. So I'll be here."

Great. *Dad* would be here. *Here,* quote unquote. I imagined him shut up in his office for eighteen hours, submerged under papers, everything else in the house forgotten. *Here* still didn't mean he was actually *present.*

I unclenched my jaw. "Mom needs me."

"Actually, that's exactly why this came up. Your mother and I were thinking—"

"There's no way Mom had an actual thought that was in agreement with this," I said loudly over him. My mother hadn't uttered a real sentence in over a week. She moved like a zombie. Over the last couple months her piano students had stopped coming—either she'd canceled the lessons or they'd all sensed something was very wrong. Now she spent her days in bed with the curtains drawn. If I coaxed her long enough, hard enough, she'd sometimes eat a tiny bit of food.

"*We* were *thinking* it would be good for you to get out of the house for a little bit. Get away from this, go somewhere positive. And it'll give your mother a break so she can relax and have some peace and quiet—"

"Are you *shitting me*?"

"Language, Leigh," said my father.

I made a noise of disgust.

"We've already enrolled and paid for you to go—"

I stood up, all but slamming my mug down. "You *what*?"

"We'll be driving you there on Sunday. So you should probably start packing." He stood and pushed his chair under the table.

"Dad, you can't be serious."

"I am absolutely serious, Leigh. This'll be good for you."

"That's the biggest goddamn lie—"

He shot me the look of death. "*Language*, young lady. If you can't speak to me with respect, you're going to get yourself grounded."

"Oh, grounded for *four whole days*." I rolled my eyes. "Before I'm chauffeured straight to hell."

"That's it," said my father, throwing his hands in the air. "You officially *are* grounded. Which is perfect. Plenty of time for packing. I'll send you the website so you can see what they recommend."

"This is like the opposite of a kidnapping."

"Leigh, this is not meant to be a punishment. I did actually try to pick something you would like. I think you're going to enjoy it."

He was so very wrong. On all counts. It *was* a punishment. And no, I definitely *wasn't* enjoying it.

Camp Mardenn. Six weeks of hell. We lived in wood cabins, ancient and smelly, complete with plastic buckets if it rained and leaked. Every day we went out to "be with nature and make art"—I focused on the art of screaming silently.

I missed Axel and Caro desperately.

I missed my mother even more.

Was she eating? Was she shut up in the bedroom? Was Dad talking to her, maybe trying to make her laugh? She'd been totally unresponsive when I begged her to talk him out of sending me to camp. Was she any better now?

When my parents dropped me off, my mother had given me a tight and wordless hug. The pendant she always wore smashed up against my sternum; I imagined a cicada-shaped imprint in my skin, aching as it faded. I was surprised she even came. She'd spent the ride sitting slanted in the shotgun seat with her face pressed against the window. As I waved good-bye, her expression was almost apologetic. She wouldn't meet my eyes.

I'd survived two weeks of camp. Barely.

The bathroom smelled like a dental office, like the chemically sweet toothpaste dentists used for scrubbing your teeth. The kind that often pretended to be bubble-gum-flavored. Pretended, and failed miserably.

The smell made my head hurt, but it was worth the bit of privacy. At least it didn't smell like ass.

"That's it," said Axel, his voice coming in through my phone all tinny. "I'm coming to get you."

I snorted.

"I'm serious. You sound completely miserable."

"I just don't understand why he thought it would be a good idea to sign me up without even asking how I felt about it."

"Camp Mar...denn...Two *n*'s, right?"

"Axel, what are you doing?"

"I told you..." The volume of his voice warped and I envisioned him switching his cell to the opposite ear. "I'm coming to get you."

I rolled my eyes but also pressed the phone closer. "It's not like I'm some damsel in distress."

"No, but you have no way out. How would you leave? You need an accomplice."

There was the noise of footsteps outside, and I worried for a moment that someone was going to walk in. The sound passed. Tension flowed out of my shoulders. It was dinnertime, which was usually when the bathroom stayed empty the longest.

"Leigh?" he said when I had been silent for a beat too long.

"Sorry," I said. "What were you saying?"

"I'm taking the bus. I'll be there tomorrow."

"What? You can't be serious."

"I'm serious if you're serious. Tell me you really, truly want to stay at that camp, and I won't come."

I made myself think about it. I tried to imagine eating one more of those Boca Burgers that tasted like they'd been stored in the freezer for too many years. Sitting through another bonfire while people sang along to bad guitar strumming. Watching the awkward campers and their painful attempts at flirting.

Another four weeks of this without Axel, without Caro. Another four weeks of not speaking to my mother.

I'd tried calling home. It was always my father who picked up. When I asked to speak with Mom, he said, "Now's not a good time, Leigh."

What the hell did that mean?

The next night, Axel came, and I snuck out.

The hotel Axel had found for us was *very* budget. Not that I was about to complain. It was probably why they didn't even blink when Axel fed them the lie about losing his driver's license just hours earlier.

"I can try to find some other form of ID—"

"It's fine," said the front-desk clerk in a tone of supreme boredom.

There was barely any walking space around the one full-size bed. The towels were crusty and smelled strongly of bleach. One of the lamps wouldn't turn on. The chair legs were wrapped in duct tape. And the bathroom—well, it must've been cleaned a century ago.

It was going to be an interesting experience.

The thought hit me. How much was this whole mission costing him? Bus tickets? A car service? Hotel for the night? It couldn't be cheap. His very part-time job paid him eight bucks an hour. This had to be eating up several weeks' worth of work.

"Axel, I'm totally going to pay you back."

He paused, halfway through unzipping his backpack. "What? No, don't worry about it."

"Seriously, I can't let you pay for all this."

"Leigh, I wanted to come. If I didn't, I wouldn't have offered. Okay?" Axel dumped out the contents of his bag. "Provisions!"

We sat cross-legged on the bed and feasted on handfuls of Frosted Flakes and salt-and-vinegar chips.

"Sorry I don't have real food," he said.

"Are you kidding me?" I said through a mouthful of chips. "This is the best meal I've had in two weeks."

There were fruit cups for dessert. We didn't have spoons, so we fished out the chunks with our fingers and slurped at the juice. It was the taste of freedom.

He told me about the rock candy Angie had been making, how he kept sneaking in a drop of green food coloring to mess with her. His cousin Jorge had slathered half a jar of Vicks VapoRub on his belly to try to relieve a stomachache from eating too much mac and cheese. Tina had joined this new women's group, where she'd picked up new expressions like *Oy* and *Aye-yai-yai*—and both of those were the first things she said when Axel told her I'd been shipped off to sleepaway camp.

We laughed and joked and it felt almost normal again. But I had that unpleasant tickle of concern. A voice inside me couldn't help asking: *Why would Tina join a women's group, unless she and Mom aren't spending all their free time together anymore?*

"You want to change first?" Axel said, tipping his head in the direction of the bathroom.

I thought of the filth and cringed. "I don't want to be in there for a second longer than I have to. I think I might even skip the shower." My last glance had revealed the bottom of the tub to be brown and silty. No way was I stepping in that.

"Same," he said with a matching grimace.

"We could just change out here? Backs turned or whatever."

"Sure," said Axel. "That works."

The moment he agreed to it I was overcome with the fear that he would try to sneak a peek at me. *Why would Axel do that? Axel, your best friend, and pretty much the world's most upstanding person.* But I couldn't shake the paranoia. I didn't want him to note the extra flab around my midsection, or glimpse the smallness of my breasts. I all but jumped into my pajama bottoms and yanked my tank top over my head. Done in the span of three seconds. I whirled back around.

On the other side of the bed, Axel was taking his time. He had just tugged on a fresh pair of boxers. Half a second earlier and I definitely would have seen his ass. The realization made hot embarrassment bloom in my cheeks. I should have turned away to offer him the same respect and privacy he'd given me, but I was rooted in place. I watched as he pulled a pair of loose athletic shorts up past his knees and over his small hips. The muscles in his back stretched and bent, cupping brown shadows and light.

His shoulder bones were sharp, sculpted, like they were designed to be attached to wings. Axel had a nice back.

Really, Axel had a nice *everything*.

Somehow in the last few years his wiry limbs had thickened and toned up. You could see the muscles starting to trace the edges of his upper arms. And his butt. I'd never spent so much time staring at a boy's butt.

He stopped moving, like he could feel my eyes on him. "All right, are you done? I'm turning back around."

"Okay, yes, me too, I'm done," I said too quickly, all in one breath. I bent down to pick up my socks and hide my face.

Sleeping was something else entirely. Axel and I had slept in the same space plenty of times. But usually it was one person on a couch, the other on an air mattress. Or both of us in sleeping bags. And we'd sat together on a bed for countless hours, playing games with a deck of cards so worn we knew the ace of spades and the eight of diamonds just by the creases on their backs.

But sitting together was different from *lying* next to each other on the same bed.

The mattress was lumpy and sunken in the middle. Every time I shifted in search of a more comfortable angle, my body slid a little closer to his side.

Finally our elbows were bumping, and Axel started laughing.

"What?" I said tensely.

"This is the problem with only children," he said. "You don't know how to share space."

"It's not my fault the bed's all sunken!"

"It's fine," he said, still laughing. "We can share the middle. Can you turn on your side?"

I turned my back to him, because even in the darkness I felt like he would be able to read my feelings in my eyes.

I could feel him scooting on the bed—it shook the whole mattress and sent me sliding down into the middle again. But then the shifting stopped.

"There," he said, and I felt his breath on my neck. He was facing the same direction I was. I willed myself to relax, to loosen my limbs. Mere inches away, the heat of his body scorched me.

We weren't touching, but we were so very close.

"Better?" he said.

I nodded first, then remembered he couldn't see. "Yeah."

We fell silent, and I listened to the sound of his breathing, so steady I was certain he was asleep. My body prickled, too awake and ultra aware. There behind me lay my best friend. Only a small strip of air separated us from full-on spooning. I pressed my hands together like in prayer, pinning them beneath my pillow so that maybe I would stop wanting to reach out and touch him.

A long while passed, and then Axel murmured something.

It sounded like he might've said, "What color?"

But I couldn't be sure. I pretended I was already asleep.

58

Colors flash like promises and black flickers like static, like memories, and everything is falling, falling, remembering,

falling,

remembering,

the two words synonymous.

59

SUMMER BEFORE SOPHOMORE YEAR

In the morning when I woke up, I realized my body had turned a hundred eighty degrees, and my temple was pressed against Axel's chest. He was facing me, his hand half on my ribs, half on my waist. Alarms sounded in my skull; I wasn't wearing a bra. Panic made me roll away. His fingers trailed over my stomach, and something surged under my skin. I slid off the bed entirely, waiting for the heat in my center to settle.

Here was my best friend, asleep. No glasses on, dark eyelashes shuttered down against his cheeks. His shirt riding up, exposing part of his thin midsection.

Those lashes fluttered open. "What's wrong?" he mumbled.

I shook my head. "Nothing. Um, what time is our bus?"

He sat up, rubbing his eyes. "Not till just after lunch."

"Well." I glanced at the hotel clock on the nightstand, with its demonic red dashes aglow in the shape of numbers. "It's almost noon."

Axel twisted around and snatched up his glasses. "Shit," he said. "We were supposed to check out by eleven. Shit, shit, shit."

On the bus I claimed the window seat in case I couldn't bear to look at Axel and needed somewhere to put my eyes. But things seemed to have returned to normal. We pulled out our sketch pads and drew each other's feet—mine in my worn sandals, the coral polish chipping off my big toes, his in a pair of gray socks and sneakers with green bottoms.

From the end of the bus line we caught a train to a town near Fairbridge. Axel called Tina to pick us up, because he knew her freak-out would be the mildest. He'd conveniently forgotten to tell anybody that he would be disappearing for a night.

Tina twisted around to look at us when we piled into the back of the car. "Axel, what were you thinking? Your papa was worried sick. You gotta learn to pick up your phone."

Axel waited until she'd turned back to roll his eyes dramatically. "I know, Aunt Tina, I know. Trust me, it was important. Leigh needed me."

Tina softened. "Leigh, sweetie, are you okay?"

"Yeah, I'm good, thanks."

"What about your mother? How is she?"

I stiffened. "You haven't seen her?"

"No, honey. She hasn't been returning my calls."

When she pulled into our driveway, Axel offered to help me get my stuff into the house, but I shook my head. I was certain now that my intuition had been right—something was up with Mom. Whatever it was, I wasn't sure I wanted Axel to see.

I rang the doorbell and immediately heard my father's heavy feet rushing down the hallway. He threw open the door.

"What were you *thinking*?" Dad's face flashed through the spectrum of expressions: shock, rage, relief, rage again.

"Well, I—"

"I got a call from Camp Mardenn informing me my daughter's missing, and suggesting that I talk to the police about putting out an Amber Alert—Leigh, what on earth made you think this would be a good idea?"

"Okay. I—"

"And then I started getting calls from the Morenos asking if we'd seen Axel—did he drag you into this disappearing act? You're grounded, by the way. For the rest of the summer."

The unfairness made my jaw clench. "What! Ugh—Dad—can you calm down for a second?"

"Calm *down*? We had to file *two* missing persons reports!" Dad shook his head, his eyes rolling up in an *I can't believe this* arc. He turned away, leaving me to untangle myself from all the straps of my bags. "Why the hell—?"

"Leigh?"

My head snapped up. My mother's voice, bodiless, drifting somewhere distant and overhead. She was coming down the stairs. It was the first time I'd heard her say my name in weeks.

"What is happened? Why are you so angry?" she said as she reached the bottom of the stairs.

"Nothing," said my father. He sounded exhausted. "Everything's fine. I was just speaking loudly."

"Leigh," she said with a soft smile. Her pale pink bathrobe gave her an angelic glow. She hugged me, and I was so shocked

I just stood there in her embrace, forgetting to hug back. "You have good time at your party?"

"Party?" I repeated, lost. I looked over at Dad, who wouldn't meet my eyes.

"I told her about the sleepover party," he said, scowling. It was a cue to play along.

After the two weeks of misery he put me through, I was *not* in the mood to help him.

But the sweetness in my mother's face made me think twice about picking a fight. I wanted her to stay happy. The darkness around her eyes seemed to have faded a bit, and she was standing straighter.

"Sure, Mom. It was great."

Dad's shoulders sagged with relief. He turned away and headed for his office.

Mom helped me with my bags. "Why you bring so much for party?" She laughed a little, and the sound was so musical and perfect my breath hitched.

"Oh, I don't know," I said airily. "I thought I needed it all."

My mother was about to go into the kitchen, but I stopped her and gave her another hug. She seemed surprised but wrapped her arms around me tightly. I squeezed my eyes shut and inhaled. She smelled clean again. Before I left, she'd had a stale and musty scent from days of not showering. Now her hair was buttery from her coconut shampoo. The shirt under my chin had that fresh laundry scent. All extremely good signs.

"I feel have not seen you for forever," she said.

"I feel exactly the same way," I told her, blinking hard to rid the stinging from my eyes.

My father had managed to avoid me all night. It was the next morning and I finally cornered him in the kitchen as he brewed his coffee.

"Okay. What's going on?" It took everything I had to keep my attitude restrained and my voice low. Mom was still asleep upstairs.

There were gray pouches under his eyes. He threw me a wary glance as he fiddled with the French press.

"What's up with Mom? Why is she so confused?"

"She's fine now," said Dad. "The confusion will pass."

She's fine now. Like something had changed.

Rage boiled up inside me. "What did you *do* to her? Is that why you sent me away?"

Dad shook his head and pinched the bridge of his nose between his thumb and finger. His voice dropped to a loud whisper. "Your mother is still recovering, okay? She's been going through treatment."

I almost exploded. *"What?"*

"Shhh." He held out both hands and spread the fingers wide.

"What kind of *treatment*?" I wanted to punch something. "Why didn't you tell me about it?"

"I didn't want to upset you, all right? There's a lot of stigma surrounding it, and there was the possibility of side effects—"

"What. Was. The treatment."

He rubbed his temples and sighed. "Electroconvulsive therapy."

I stared at him. *"What?* Is that—is it what I think it is?"

"Otherwise known as shock treatment," said Dad.

"I can't *believe* this."

"Now, Leigh—"

"You sent me to camp so Mom could go through *that* by *herself*?"

"Listen to me—"

"You can't just treat us like we don't know how to make decisions for ourselves. You dropped me off like you were leaving a dog at a freaking kennel! You didn't even ask what I'd want. Did you ask Mom if she wanted to go through electro—whatever?"

My father sat down. "Yes. I took her to the doctor, and we talked about it together. She explicitly consented to it. She could've changed her mind at any point, but she didn't. Your mom was in a bad place, Leigh. She wasn't eating. She wasn't talking. If she kept it up, she was going to die." His voice cracked on that last word.

I shook my head. My mother was not going to *die*. My mother with her sunny voice, her strong piano-slaying fingers, hugs that melted your heart. My mother who made the best waffles, the best pastries. Who had smiled so sweetly at me just last night.

He cleared his throat. "Electroconvulsive therapy changes the brain chemistry fast. It can bring a person out of really bad depression when other things aren't working."

I stared at the kitchen tiles. I imagined my mother in an operating chair, hooked up to a million wires, getting zapped over and over again. Body lighting up blue and white, eyes rolling in the back of her head, mouth open in a soundless scream.

"It's really not what it sounds like," my father said, as if he could hear my thoughts. "Shock treatment is very much misunderstood. I needed the doctor to explain it to me, too. They gave her a muscle relaxant, and they put her to sleep. Then they applied an electric current to induce a quick seizure, change the brain chemistry. She doesn't even remember it."

"Was that the only option?" I asked.

Dad drew in a shaky breath. "The doctor said it was a *good* option, because she's been treatment-resistant. She's tried psychotherapy. She's tried so many medications. They work well for a lot of people, but they haven't really worked on *her*."

"Right," I said, though this was news to me.

"Leigh...we didn't want you to worry. But—well. This whole thing was not...a recent development. Your mother's been fighting depression for many, many years. I'd guess longer than you've been alive."

I'd figured out that much, lying in my bed sleepless for countless nights, running through the backlog of my mother's behavior. The months when it seemed she'd forgotten how to form a real smile. The long naps she would take, often forgetting to do something she'd promised. The conversations when she was barely responsive.

I realized that I'd known for a long time without truly understanding. Her illness was something I'd been afraid to look at head-on.

But there was also the fiery, lit-up version of my mother. How could a person like her be depressed? She was full of energy and life and passion. The word *depressed* made me think of this group of kids at school who wore all black and thick eyeliner and listened to angry music and never showed their teeth. The ones who people sometimes called *emo*, making it sound like a bad word.

My mother wasn't like that. Not at all.

And then a small voice in the back of my head whisper-wondered: Was it my fault? I was the one who was around her the most. Was I somehow preventing her from getting better?

"When was it?" I asked. "The treatment?"

"The last appointment was the day before yesterday. She's gone six times over the last two weeks."

I sucked in a fast breath. *Six times.* "You should've told me. I could've handled it. I could've been here to *help*. You can't just send me away like I'm a task on a to-do list that someone else can check off."

He bowed his head. "I'm sorry, Leigh." It was probably the first time in my life my father had ever apologized to me.

I sat down. My stomach uncoiled and exhaustion took over, seeping into my limbs.

"The confusion and short-term memory loss are just side effects. But she's been coming out of it fast. It worked—and better than I'd hoped. As far as I can tell, she's really only confused about these last couple of weeks."

I nodded slowly. "Does she remember—what she was like before? How she used to feel?"

"I think so."

The floorboards creaked overhead and both of us fell silent. We listened to the noise of my mother's feet, easing from one side of the room to the other. We listened as she made her way down the stairs, one slow step at a time.

I got up and started boiling water for tea.

That was where we were when my mother rounded the corner into the kitchen. Me dipping a tea bag into a mug, watching the water change. Dad at the table, sipping his coffee with one hand on the edge of a newspaper.

"Good morning," she said. She was still in her bathrobe, but she'd brushed her hair until it was shiny and sleek. She beamed at us, and I felt so certain in that moment that everything was going to end up just fine.

60

When I finish weaving the net, it's nearly as wide as the smallest wall in my room—thank goodness I over-packed on baggy T-shirts and stretchy sweatpants. It's just large enough that it might be able to hold the bird and stop her from flying off again, if I can figure out the right way to use it. Tomorrow I'll figure out where to set it up, and how I'm going to launch it.

But still I can't sleep, and my room is too quiet, the night too heavy, the hours dragging by.

The harsh words I said to Feng keep echoing back to me. I thumb through the box, looking for a distraction from the brown and muddy guilt clouding my mind.

What I pull out is a beige piece of paper, stiff and pebbly, folded up. The memory of the assignment bursts to the surface. I'd partnered with Axel, and we'd folded the sheet in half so that I could sketch him on one side, and he could sketch me on the other. We weren't allowed to look at what the other person had done until we were both finished. When we unfolded the page, it looked like our black-and-white selves were smiling at each other.

We'd laughed about it, and then I never knew what happened to the actual paper. I didn't realize anyone had bothered to keep it.

What memories will I find in here? I tug out a fresh stick of incense, and bring the match to its bright and flaring life.

61

—SMOKE & MEMORIES—

I'm standing in the master bedroom. The very bedroom where it happened.

My eyes go to the spot in the carpet where I saw the mother-shaped stain. But it's not there. Of course it's not there.

"I don't think it's a good idea to encourage her," says my father. He's sitting up against the headboard, pinching the bridge of his nose between a thumb and index finger. Next to him, the lamp on the night table buzzes.

My mother lies beside him, curled up and facing the wall. She says nothing.

"I just worry about her, you know?" says Dad. "She has no siblings. No cousins. She has, like, one friend."

"A good friend," my mother says, her voice muffled and slow. "One very good friend can be all she need."

"Well, and friendships change," says Dad.

My mother is silent again.

"This art thing is getting so intense. It's all she does."

"She has passion," my mother says defensively.

"And that's great," he says. "But hobbies change, too. And there's the question of, will it provide for her? Will it make her happy?"

"She should do what she loves."

Dad turns his face toward my mother's back. He says, very quietly, "You do what you love. Are *you* happy?"

She doesn't answer.

"Dory," he says after a long moment.

There is only the sound of my father drawing in a deep breath. He sighs, clicks the light off.

A burst of new colors.

In the darkest corner, the hands of the living room clock glow slightly, little moon-green blades showing that it's past midnight. Light slants in from the hallway—enough that the rest of the room is dimly visible. My mother's on the couch, eyes closed, a cushion under her head, blanket sliding off her shoulder. At first it's hard to place the memory in time—over the years there were so many nights when she slept downstairs because the bedroom had become a cave of insomnia.

But then my father steps lightly into the living room, wearing his favorite vest from my middle school years. He leans down over the couch to slide the blanket up, tuck it under my mother's chin, nudge a lock of hair out of her face.

He turns to leave the room but stops, his eye catching on something: a piece of art resting against the sheet music on the piano. I remember that drawing—it was from the end of sixth grade. Mom had gotten me an extra special pack of artist's charcoals and I'd shared them with Axel, who couldn't afford anything that nice but hated what Mrs. Donovan had in the art room. The prompt was to sketch shoes, and Axel and I traded to make our subjects more interesting. He drew my new but already-stained purple Converse. I drew his off-brand sneakers that were so old they'd turned the color of dust, and there was a crack near the toes of the left one.

The flaws in Axel's shoes made my drawing especially interesting—I became obsessed with getting the shading just right, replicating the grime perfectly.

And then I'd set it on the music stand so Mom could see, as usual. I didn't expect Dad to even notice it. That year he'd already stopped paying as much attention to my art. Or so I thought, at least.

Now I watch as he carefully brings the picture into the hallway light, leans down to gaze at the details I captured, his eyes tracing the laces, the worn heel, the cracked rubber.

On the couch behind him, my mother's eyes open. She shifts inaudibly, tilts her head back, watching him.

"Hmm," he murmurs to himself. He goes to the kitchen, pulls an old camera out from a drawer, and snaps a photo of the drawing before setting it back and tiptoeing away. The golden light clicks off, but I know my mother's eyes are still open, still looking.

The colors change.

My mother, making waffles on a Sunday morning. I must not be awake yet, because Axel is sitting there at the table alone, turning a mug of coffee around and around and around.

His hair is a mess, sticking out in funny directions.

"You two are a good pair," my mother says, spooning fresh whipped cream onto his plate.

"Who?" says Axel. "Me and Leigh?"

My mother nods. "She cares about you very much, you know?"

Axel laughs uncomfortably. "She's my best friend."

Mom nods again. "It is rare you find such strong friendship."

Axel makes a big show of cutting his two waffles into minuscule pieces. "Is there syrup?" he says.

My mother pulls a small jug from the fridge. "I'm glad she has you," she says with a half smile.

The kitchen flickers and vanishes.

62

Forty-three days.

Six left.

I think of that last memory—Mom trying to talk to Axel about me. It clouds my head with sepia tones.

Why did I need to see it? To remember how much we've broken between us? I don't get how this gives me anything useful.

I try to shake the fog from my head. Everything's looking jagged and cracked, speckled with black ink. I know it's just my insomniac haze, and not the actual world. But I can't help feeling like everything is starting to break.

This morning there is no one beneath the gazebo in the park, so Waigong and I have claimed one of its benches.

All around us: the chorus of cicadas, the conversations of little birds.

On the wooden table, there's a square tablet made of stone, with white lines etched into it, drawing a system of grids.

There are Chinese characters carved across the center. It *is* a board game. I wonder what the pieces are—if they're round like coins, if they're engraved with the hooks and strokes of more Chinese characters.

My grandfather runs his fingers over the board.

And then I have an idea. I pull out my phone and swipe past the first two screens until I find the right app. "Look! Want to play?"

Waigong doesn't say anything, only frowns at the phone.

I hold up four fingers. "All you need to do is get four in a row. Then you win." I point to myself and then place the first piece. I take his finger and tap the screen to make Player Two's move. It's the quickest game, and I let him win since it's just a demo.

There's a spark behind his eyes. I think he understands.

"Okay, so now let's play for real," I tell him.

As soon as it loads, he's jabbing at the screen with his thumb, placing his piece right in the center.

We go back and forth. I'm so focused on strategizing that I'm careless, and suddenly he's got four in a row and he's won.

My grandfather glows, his cheeks rounding, mouth opening wide with quiet laughter. He rocks back and forth, looking pleased as linden green.

I win the next two games, but still he grins at me, totally thrilled, as if he's the winner no matter the outcome.

The trees along the path reach up into the clouds, leaves gently swaying. We walk slowly, searching again for the perfect flower. I look carefully in every direction, trying to come up with an idea about how to use my net. I wonder if the bird ever comes here.

It's on our way back that Waigong stops me with an arm and points to something on the thick branch of a tree at just about eye level.

A lone brown cicada, this one alive, swelling and pulling, swelling and pulling.

It's molting.

We watch, transfixed, as it pushes its way out of the back, where the shell has opened like a costume unzipped. Slowly, the fresh body wriggles out, a pale summery green. The new legs kick a few times, inky eyes shining like they know everything of the world. Wrinkled, cabbage-like bunches unfurl themselves from the sides, smoothing out into long wings, green at the edges and translucent in the centers, tissue paper soft.

Its husk, brown and stiff, clings to the branch. A ghost left behind.

63

Did my mother ever get to see a cicada molting?

Did she wish that she could do exactly that? Shed her skin and be someone new?

There were the days when she seemed to transform into something quieter, darker. Her colors deeper but also muted. Both her truer self, and not.

Or maybe it wasn't a transformation. Maybe it was a momentary reveal. A peeling back of the protective layers.

A sharpening of a pencil, bringing the tip to its most focused point.

64

Back at the apartment, everything seems quieter. Waipo smiled at this morning's flower—a single stem shooting off into a patch of tiny coral blossoms, so cheerfully star-shaped—but still. Today she looks especially tired. Her features drooping, her eyes a bit darker.

As she ladles fluffy white congee into bowls, she glances at the door.

She misses Feng.

Her somber mood is my fault. The guilt drops heavily into the pit of my stomach, and shame wraps around me like the prickly side of Velcro, sharpens the thought that I've done so much wrong.

Naphthol red—the color of an angry pen marking the errors I've made.

In the living room, I watch Waipo scrape at the head of a match. In her other hand, the long stick of incense trembles. For a millisecond, the tip takes on its own little flame before

260 • EMILY X.R. PAN

dimming to a vague touch of light and heat. A whisper of life, issuing ash and smoke, salting the air.

Waigong leans back on the couch, watching music videos with the volume dialed all the way down. There's a singer dressed like a pirate, holding a miniature version of himself in his palm. I blink, and in the next moment, he's dancing with a posse of guys in masks.

"Waipo," I say. "*Lai.*"

She looks up at me.

"*Lai kan.*" I have an idea for how to distract her, how to make her feel better.

"*Kan shenme?*" she asks. *See what?*

But I don't know how to answer with words. I pull her by the elbow toward the guest room. We slide past inky cracks that stretch along the walls wider and higher than I am tall. We walk past a huge, gaping hole in one corner of the apartment. An abyss so black and empty it makes me shiver. The ceiling above almost completely cracked. Thin black lines fissure outward.

Of course, my grandmother doesn't see any of this.

It's my insomniac sight—I think of it as a superpower. The thought almost makes me smile.

When we get to my room, Waipo slumps down to sit on the bed.

"*Deng yixia,*" I tell her. *Wait.*

When I open the box, the first thing I spot is that photograph again—the duplicate of the one on Waipo's altar, propped against the edge of her fruit bowl.

Two girls sitting, the ornate wooden chair backs rising high up behind them, their legs dangling. One of them a little taller, a little older.

My fingers trace the edges. This one's crisp, as if it's been carefully preserved all these years. Not like the worn copy Waipo must pick up every day, with its softened edges, its greasy fingerprints.

"Tamen shi shei?" I ask, holding the photograph out to my grandmother. *Who are they?*

She squints at it and answers with a fast roll of words I don't know. Well. At least there's another way I might be able to understand.

I shove my handmade net aside, because it's taking up the whole top of the set of drawers, and pull out the box of incense, feeling suddenly self-conscious, anxious. For a second, I wonder if the bird *didn't* bring these sticks, if the incense belonged to my grandmother all along. I show her the box, point to the characters printed on its lid. She shakes her head. She doesn't seem to recognize it.

Waipo watches me fiddle with a match. Stick to flame. I take the embering incense tip to the corner of the photo and watch it burn.

Black smoke spurts out. Not the gentle wisps from before. Not the wavy ribbons. This is a violent spewing, and I realize: The smoke doesn't like this. It doesn't like that I've brought another person.

The photograph is plucked from my fingers by an invisible wind, swept high into the air, where it explodes in a crackle of lightning and rains down ash.

When I turn to look at my grandmother, her eyes are wide.

There is no flicker.

There is no flash.

The colors do not invert.

Beneath our feet, everything shudders, and I wonder if there's an earthquake. It shakes so hard the already-cracked walls fall down; the ceiling crumbles. Waipo yelps as the bed drops out from under her.

The floor's gone. Gravity has disappeared. We are drifting through that black abyss, turning in somersaults. All I hear is the sound of our breathing.

"Leigh," says Waipo.

Her voice is like a light switch.

The black vanishes. We slam down into the ground, the impact tremoring up our legs.

65

—SMOKE & MEMORIES—

A green field. A sky of sherbet. That's where we are.

What the hell is this place?

Waipo points at the grass up ahead, and it's like her finger summons a wind. A huge gale sweeps past us, blowing hair all around my face and making my grandmother's tunic billow violently.

It's when a photograph skims past my ankles, flipping and bouncing on a breeze, that I realize there are things strewn all over the field. Pictures. Letters. Envelopes addressed in Chinese.

Then I spot the box, turned on its side, my name scrawled across the top in bold black marker.

The things the bird brought me. The box my grandparents said they burned. And all around it, broken sticks of the blackest incense. What have I done?

Waipo reaches for a crumpled piece of paper on the ground

near me. The moment her hand touches it, there's the telltale flash.

Colors out. Colors in.

The ground gone from under us, replaced by the old beige carpet of my father's office. The room is dimly lit and smells like fresh laundry, and we're standing right beside his desk, where he's scribbling on a loose piece of paper with a fountain pen. What flows from the tip isn't English. Strokes and swoops shape themselves into Chinese characters. He writes with beautiful, practiced ease.

The fountain pen makes a harsh, scattering noise—black ink soaks into the paper in the rough shape of a dog bone.

Beside me, my grandmother gasps. She gestures emphatically, pointing at the spilled ink. It takes me a moment to understand: She recognizes that piece of paper.

Could he be—? The thought drops like a weight into my stomach. Is he writing to *her*? To Waipo?

Dad shakes his head at the wide spot of ink but continues writing around it. He finishes the letter off, signs his name in English, fanning the page to dry the ink quicker.

He gathers together things from his drawers: various photographs of me (I must have been in the seventh or eighth grade), of my mother, and a few of our entire family together. And the final addition: a collection of my artwork—most of which I don't remember. A self-portrait. Baby squirrels done in oil pastel. My mother's hands roving over the piano. A charcoal sketch of Sunday waffles.

My father carefully folds these things into a protective folio, paper-clips his letter to the outside, and slides it all into a large yellow envelope. There's already an address on the front of it, written in Chinese, with *Taiwan (Republic of China)* printed neatly at the bottom.

"Brian?" The voice of my mother out in the hall.

Dad hurries to push the thin package into the shadowed area behind his computer monitor.

The knock comes then—soft knuckles rapping twice—and the door slips open.

"Dinnertime," says my mother, poking her head through.

Waipo sucks in a tight breath of air.

My father turns toward the door with a smile, his fingers hovering above his keyboard as if in midthought. "I'll be right down."

A stream of lights and colors, wavering, buzzing a few beats longer than usual.

Then the darkness. Then the flash, and the colors return muted. I think we've jumped back in time.

And suddenly I'm hyperaware of everything I'm seeing and hearing and feeling. Thinking, too—I can sense people's thoughts.

Inside an old kitchen made of plaster walls, a young woman sings, stirring a dented pot with a wooden spoon. With a happy sigh, she settles into a woven bamboo chair. Her free hand cradles her belly, swollen with child.

It's Yuanyang. No longer the little girl, but also not yet the Waipo I know. She's somewhere in between.

Her husband swings into the kitchen with a grin. He wears a dark uniform, hair trimmed close to the scalp. Waigong, so young I barely recognize him.

"I can't wait," he says. "Why can't the baby come already?" It's so strange to hear him speak, to remember he once had a voice, too.

"He won't be a toy to play with, you know," says Yuanyang. "He'll be a living thing."

"She," says Waigong.

"How are you so sure it's a girl?" says Yuanyang.

"How are *you* so sure it's a boy?" says her husband.

Yuanyang shrugs. "Just my guess." She has never borne a child; how is she to know?

"It's not a guess for me," Waigong tells her. "I *dreamed* it."

Heavy darkness. A flash of light. New colors:

A scene much like one the incense has shown me before: a woman on a bed with a blanket over the hump of her stomach. Yuanyang again, though she's a few years older than in the last memory. Her eyes tired but shining. The same husband at her bedside, cradling their newborn child. It's another girl, already full of music, cooing and grunting and blinking up at them.

He goes to rewrap the ragged blanket around the infant, and I glimpse a little brown patch in the soft rolls under the baby's chin. The same birthmark I grew up seeing in the hollow of a pale neck. That's my mother.

"Jingling, come and meet your new sister," Yuanyang calls.

Sister. Sister sister sister. The word bounces in my skull, wrapped in the cottony gauze of disbelief. My mother is a younger sister. The black-and-white photographs of the two little girls— that's who they were. My mother and my aunt. Dory and Jingling.

A four-year-old girl emerges from the dark corner where she's been standing quietly. She chews shyly on the end of one of her braids.

"Look, Jingling," says her father. "Your sister looks a lot like you did when you were born."

Jingling straightens up, trying to see better.

"Can you believe you were this tiny once?" Her father grins. Sweat coats his face, making the color of his cheer shine all the brighter.

The midwife rushes into the room, giving commands, wrapping the new baby in fresh rags.

"Jingling," says the midwife. "You're a big sister now. You have a very important role to play. Are you ready?"

Jingling's eyes are wide and unblinking.

"Today your life has changed. Now you have someone to take care of. The first thing you can do as a new big sister is go and prepare the kitchen so I can boil some water. Then we'll be able to sanitize and wash everything."

Jingling nods and disappears out the door.

Yuanyang takes the baby back and kisses the flat nose. What a magical little thing, beautiful and warm.

She is alight with happiness, but she is also thinking of her own mother holding her like this, fresh out of the womb—her mother making the decision to sell a newborn child. Yuanyang shifts the baby closer, inhaling deeply. Her new daughter smells wonderful, better than the best tea leaves on Alibung Mountain.

"They will be best friends," says her husband, beaming. "Our two little girls."

"Yes," says Yuanyang, warmed by the thought. "Best friends."

A flicker. The light changes.

In a living room I don't recognize, Yuanyang paces in a troubled circle around the two brocade armchairs. She's aged by a couple decades. Her hair is short and wavy; silvery strands wink in the light. The edges of her eyes starting to pouch and wrinkle.

"Please, Jingling," says Yuanyang. "Talk to her. She is unhappy."

This memory feels different. It takes me a second to realize: It's from Jingling's perspective. It's also fuzzy—blurrier than any of the incense memories have been. The faces are hard to see clearly. There's a sweet floral smell—the feeling of being inside Jingling's head.

She's grown into a young woman. Her hair arranged in a neat bun. A simple dress hanging from her shoulders, the sleeves fat and billowy.

Yuanyang sighs. "You were never this much trouble. You did everything so well. You were always so focused."

"You shouldn't always compare the two of us," Jingling says quietly.

Yuanyang shakes her head. "She will listen to you. Tell her to work harder. Tell her she must understand her priorities."

"I will," Jingling says to mollify her mother. But she knows her little sister has a different kind of spirit, bursting with a different kind of ambition. Her sister has so much more in mind, even now, as she comes up on the end of high school. Dreams that stretch beyond being a perfect child, a perfect wife. Her sister, with the right support and intention, could be a real artist.

Jingling believes this with absolute certainty: Her sister could be successful, could be famous, could be loved by the world if only they knew who she was. The way her sister mastered entire piano sonatas and concertos with nothing at home to practice on but a broken kitchen table—that was true magic. There is something heavenly in her sister's fingers. Something the rest of the family doesn't understand.

"Thank you, Jingling," says Yuanyang, her voice brimming

with relief. "You always know what to do. She'll listen to you. I'm certain of it."

Jingling is certain, too, because she knows what she is going to tell her sister: to work hard, yes. To understand her priorities. But also to know that if her priorities are different from those wished upon her by their parents, that's fine. If they need time—years, even—to understand those priorities, Jingling will at least be there to support her, to make Mama and Baba see that some things are worth dropping everything else for.

Everything gives out, buzzing like static. The darkness comes, then the flash, flipping to a new memory.

Outside the Zhongzheng International Airport, Jingling squeezes her little sister's wrist. Dory is all grown up, a university girl now, and about to leave the country for the first time. Jingling can hardly believe it. Yuanyang stands behind them, her face twisted with obvious disapproval.

"You've got everything you need?" says Jingling.

Dory nods. "I wish you would apply for a program abroad, too. So that we could be in America at the same time."

Jingling smiles apologetically. "But if I can get through the bulk of my thesis this summer, I'll be able to graduate early. Save that tuition money."

A sigh. "I know. You're right."

"Go study your music. Go be inspired. The summer will disappear, and soon you'll be home again." Jingling's face is shining with pride for her sister. "I have a present for you."

Dory's eyes light up. "What is it?"

"A surprise." Jingling draws a small box from her pocket. She watches her little sister tug at the cream-colored ribbon, slide off the top. There, shining in smooth stone, in cloudy hues of dark and pale greens: a jade cicada. So intricately carved it looks alive. Any second now it will begin to sing.

"Jingling!" Dory gasps.

"I went to six different merchants to get the perfect cicada," says Jingling. "I know they're your favorite."

"It's incredible! I've never seen one as beautiful as this." The glittering chain hangs the cicada right in the center of my mother's sternum, over her heart.

"Mama found the chain," says Jingling, gesturing toward their mother. "See how it twists? It's a very special one."

Dory and their mother lock eyes for the briefest of moments. Yuanyang is the first to look away.

"Thank you," says Dory. "I'll wear it every single day."

The sisters beam at each other.

"I have something for you, too," says Dory. "We think alike." She produces her own little box, a rich and lucky red, the top folded like origami.

Jingling grins as she undoes the lid. Pinned down against a little bed of dark velvet: a bracelet of jade ovals like little flower buds, each piece framed in gold.

She clasps the bracelet around her wrist. It looks perfect on her.

Everything is shuddering, earthquaking. The colors inverting. A staticky buzz grows into a roar so loud my ears hurt.

The lights and colors flicker on and off, on and off.

On.

Off.

66

Fall down. Slam into the floor. Cough through the cloud of ashes.

Ashes everywhere, dusting the walls, coating every surface of my room. The floor covered in mounds and swirls, all of them a dead, muted gray.

Sister. My mother has a sister. Where is she?

My grandmother pushes herself up off the bed, looking shaken.

"Waipo," I start to say.

My mind is fuzzy and aching. What are the words that I need in order to ask my question?

Staggering to her feet, my grandmother crosses the room and lets herself out.

Strewn throughout the ashes: flame-eaten letters, leftover corners that used to be whole photographs. A singed length of string that must have tied together a bundle of envelopes. The original box from the bird, destroyed.

Almost all the incense has been smashed or burned up—I can see the snakes of gray where they fell and embered down to the very end. The few precious sticks that do remain are broken, their lengths uneven.

That net I wove from my shirts has been half consumed, and what's left of it is charred and disintegrating. Even as I try to see what I can salvage, the fabric breaks apart in my fingers.

I wasn't supposed to do this, to bring Waipo in; the incense memories were meant only for me. How was I supposed to know?

Each breath is tight, like there's thick rope wound over my ribs, binding my bones together. A storm starts behind my eyes, shooting a monstrous headache across my temples.

I gather up what I can: just three pieces of incense. Three more chances to call up the memories, see the colors of the past, and try to understand.

67

My phone chimes to alert me to a new email and I couldn't be more relieved. This is what I need right now. Exactly this kind of distraction, something to take me away from the feeling of ruin and failure.

There are six messages in a row from my father, lined up in my in-box like a checklist. Most of them I haven't bothered to open. There's one saying we've been in Asia for a week, and how much longer do I want to be here? I'm feeling the slightest bit guilty for my radio silence, so I tell him I'm fine, I want to stay another week. Want, I say, not *need*, though that's the word pounding in my chest.

What I *need* is more time to follow these memories and understand them. What I *need* is time to gather materials and weave a new net, set my trap for the bird. But obviously I don't say any of that.

Then I click into the newest email, the one that brought me the alert. A message from Axel.

FROM: axeldereckmoreno@gmail.com
TO: leighinsandalwoodred@gmail.com
SUBJECT: (no subject)

There was this one day last summer when we
sat in Caro's car outside those woods. We talked
about the idea of being in love, and there was
something weird there. I always wanted to ask
you about it. I never figured out how to ask.

I squeeze my eyes shut. Is he asking now?

68

SUMMER BEFORE SOPHOMORE YEAR

How about I teach you, Leigh?" said my mother. She sat on the piano bench, twisting to look at me. "Just some basic."

I pushed up off the couch and shook my head out of habit, softening it with a smile. "Not today, Mom."

She watched as I gathered up my pencils. The guilt was settling over me; should I have said yes? I'd been turning down the offer for years. It wasn't like I didn't want my mother to teach me. I was just never in the right mood. And I worried that I wouldn't be good enough.

"Maybe you go out with Axel and Caro," she suggested. "You sit in here with me too much."

The guilt tripled. Could she tell that I was just itching to leave the house? I'd been grounded for the whole summer, *for that ridiculous disappearing act*, said Dad, even though it was his fault I ended up at that camp to begin with. I hadn't seen Axel in ages—the part of my punishment that felt the most unreasonable—and the thought of him was a cobalt bruise I kept bumping.

After my mother's treatment at the beginning of the summer, I'd ditched my plans to find a job and started spending all my time with her. I would've done that even if I hadn't been grounded. The smile she'd been wearing for the last few weeks—so genuine, so radiant—had me convinced that she was really recovering. But I also worried that once I was gone every day, when school started again, she'd sink back into her darkness.

I couldn't shake the feeling that I had to give her as much of myself as I had, that I was the pillar holding her upright.

"Go," she said, like she could see the internal war I was waging. "Your summer almost over. Enjoy your time."

I made myself nod. Things were, after all, a bit better. Mom was seeing a therapist. She was a month into a new medicine. Dad and I were breathing easier.

So I sent off some texts, feeling guilty as the responses that came so immediately sank a cool relief into my bones. Caro had the idea to go out near this creek we always passed on the way to school. She wanted to take pictures under the moonlight.

The August evening was hot and muggy, though not as bad as earlier in the day. The sky was already brown like a river, with streaks of fire chasing the clouds. Fireflies were out and winking, making their slow weave through the air.

Caro popped the trunk to pull out lights and tripods and swaths of gossamer. Axel and I carried sketch pads and clip-on lights just for the hell of it, and Cheslin lagged behind us with a pile of thrift-store dresses in her arms, all velvet and satin and taffeta, pearl buttons and shiny ribbons.

We trudged through an overgrown field, the stiff grass

reaching up to our thighs. Caro led us into a dark copse of trees where the hawks were always flying in and out, and we could hear the gurgling of water.

"This is nice," Axel said, so quiet I was pretty sure he meant it just for me.

"It is," I said.

"We haven't done anything like this in a while."

Could he see it in my eyes, the color of my missing him?

"Here," Caro called out, stopping where there was a gap between the thick trunks. "This is perfect."

We all helped drape the fabric. We wedged flashlights between branches, set collapsible reflectors on the ground to redirect the beams. By the time we were done, the sun was gone. The moon had emerged, though it stayed half swallowed by the clouds. It made for an eerie sight, pale beams crisscrossing through branches, lighting up the gossamer.

Cheslin powdered her face and started pulling dresses on over her tank top and shorts. Caro moved her half into the shadows, and in front of the camera, Cheslin became a ghost.

"It's a new series I'm working on," said Caro. "Called Dead Girl Cheslin."

Axel and I found a fallen log to sit on, but it was too dark and both of us were too distracted to actually draw. We looked on as Cheslin became a goddess, a sylph, a creature of resurrection. We watched as Caro's world narrowed down to Cheslin and Cheslin alone. The camera wound and shuttered.

At one point, Cheslin began to shed her clothes. Off came the shorts, the tank. She unhooked her bra—

"Whoa," said Axel, his one syllable puncturing the air.

"Oh," said Cheslin, turning her face. She blinked as if see-ing us for the first time. "Does it bother you?"

He coughed and waved his hands out in front of him as if to say, *Continue.*

Cheslin shrugged. "It is, after all, just a body."

Caro grinned.

My face burned. Did Axel think Cheslin was hot? She was nymphlike, with those elegant limbs and that long, honeyed hair. She had a natural grace to her that I would never have. While she shimmered, I was stained in charcoal.

Cheslin threw her hands wide and rolled her eyes upward. She looked like something out of a horror movie. A breeze poured her hair to the side.

"Yes," Caro was saying. "Yes, that's perfect."

My body was tightly wound, tuned up like a piano string. I was pretty certain that I wasn't interested in girls, but sitting there watching this felt voyeuristic. Heat funneled through my center, pooling in my stomach. I wanted to feel what Caro and Cheslin were feeling. I envied their thrill.

"Let's go," Axel said to me, standing up abruptly.

Simultaneously reluctant and relieved, I followed him out of the trees. Caro and Cheslin didn't even notice us leaving.

It was stuffy in the car; we settled into the back and left the doors wide open.

"Sorry, it was just getting a little weird for me," he said.

My eyes took in the amount of space between us. There was plenty of room for us to spread out, and yet somehow we'd ended up close enough to feel the heat of each other's bodies, drawn together like magnets.

I swallowed. "It was kind of weird."

Mere inches away from him. I thought of what Cheslin had said: It was just a body.

Ignore the fact that it's Axel's body. Ignore the fact that you saw that body almost naked just a month and a half ago. Ignore the fact that you want to see that body again.

Just. A. Body.

"It was almost like we were watching them have sex or something. Only they weren't even touching."

The word *sex* bloomed in the air like a match.

I shifted in my seat a little so I was in less danger of accidentally leaning into him. "You know, I used to see Cheslin occasionally—way before Caro had told me who she was. I'd see her in the street, or getting into a car, or just walking around in her uniform. Back then I would've guessed she was just a basic prep school girl. Goes to show how surprising people can be when you get to know them. Those two—they seem so different on the outside. It's lucky they found each other."

"Could just all be lust," said Axel.

That surprised me. The crudeness of it seemed unlike him. "They've been together for a pretty long time. It's got to be more than lust. At least on Caro's side—I think she's, like ... actually in love."

"Wow," said Axel.

"What?" I turned to look at him. "You sound skeptical."

"I guess I just—don't know what that's supposed to feel like. Like how does Caro know?"

"How does anybody know?" I felt defensive for some reason. "You just know."

I turned my eyes out to that spot in the woods where we could see the crisscrossing lights through the trees. "You know it when you miss someone you just saw an hour ago. When you can't stop fantasizing about kissing them. When you feel irrationally happy simply standing in the same room. When you're addicted to just ... being around them."

Axel was watching me; I could feel it. I was afraid to look at him.

"But like, how can you be certain all of that isn't just a passing thing?"

"You can't, I guess." I shrugged, and the motion made my elbow brush against his arm.

"You sound so sure about it. Like you've experienced it or something."

"Maybe I have. Maybe I haven't." The words felt silly, and that pitched me into silence. Then, "Maybe it's hard for you to buy into because of your mom." *Because you don't want to be left again.*

He tensed and I immediately regretted what I said. I watched from the corner of my eye as he willed his shoulders back down, drew in a slow breath. "Maybe," he said.

I thought about my father spending all his money dialing long distance to Taiwan to talk with my mother. I thought of Mom's stories about the goofy things he did on their first few dates. Badly executed magic tricks and jokes that made no sense. We used to laugh so hard about it we couldn't breathe, our stomachs close to bursting.

Was it just a passing thing? Were my parents still in love? Did they even know, themselves?

"I don't think so, though," said Axel, reeling me back to our conversation. "I buy into it."

"You do?" I said, surprised.

"Yeah. Because all the things you described...I think I get those feelings, too."

The full weight of what he was saying slammed into my chest and crushed me under the sharp heel of an invisible boot. Who did he fantasize about? Who made him irrationally happy? I imagined another Leanne Ryan coming into his life. Was this going to be his pattern—start every school year with a new girlfriend?

"Oh." My voice sounded so very far away.

"I just never know what to do about it," he said. "When I feel that way, I mean."

My mouth formed words that I didn't even know I was saying. "Well, you'll figure it out."

"Yeah," he said. "I guess."

69

Sometime close to dawn, I fall asleep.

The strange thing is that I know that's what it is. There's the cool darkness wrapping around me. The pounding in my temples finally subsiding. The blissful nothingness.

And then my eyes are wide open and I'm wrapped in a gray fog, in a twisting storm, and the wind is picking up, and I can hear the chaotic flapping of wings.

It's a dream it's a dream it's a dream.

I know it's just like the dream from before, and yet I can't stop it. I can't wake up.

"Mom?" I call out.

"Leigh!" Her voice frantic. Her flapping erratic.

She shrieks.

"Mom!" I can't see her, but I reach out all the same.

There's a flash of red, a puff of feathers bursting into my face. The storm sucks them away.

Flash of lightning. Deafening boom. The thunder strikes

just in front of me. Everything lights up in a blinding stab of white, and I see her silhouetted against the clouds.

She screeches. It's a cold, terrible, animal sound. It slices through me. I can smell her flesh burning. With my next inhale, I swallow a bit of storm cloud.

Dusty ash coats my mouth.

70

The next day my grandmother doesn't say a thing. Every time her eyes meet mine they're distant and distracted. Is she thinking about that world where the smoke took us? The memories we saw? I wish I could ask what color her thoughts are.

I go out walking around the city on my own, my every step heavy and ultramarine, hoping to find some sign of the bird. But today there's nothing. I waste away the day obsessing over what I need to do.

In the back of my head, circling like a vulture, the chant I can't stop: *Forty-four days. Forty-four days.*

Images from the dream flicker behind my eyelids with every blink. I can still smell the bird burning; I can taste the ash on my tongue.

Dinner comes earlier than usual, and we eat in silence. Waigong's gaze swings back and forth between me and my grandmother like a pendulum. He can tell something is off.

"Feng," I say—masochistically, experimentally, or maybe for no damn reason at all.

Waipo looks up.

I swallow the sigh. It scrapes on the way down.

"*Wo...men...qu...*" My broken Chinese feels like an insurmountable wall. I finish with *"zhao ta,"* praying I got the tones right, hoping that the idea gets across.

Let's go find her.

Because I'm tired of messing everything up. If I hadn't felt so guilty, I wouldn't have brought Waipo into the smoke, and if I hadn't done that, I wouldn't have destroyed everything.

But maybe this is something I can fix. It's weird without Feng here—and I'm ashamed to think it, but I desperately need her help. She knows Taipei, and she knows my family—she can help me make a new and better net, and figure out the best way to lure the bird down.

I try saying it again: *"Qu zhao ta."*

My grandmother blinks at me; I'm not sure she understands. It takes a lot of coaxing to get her to pull on shoes and follow me out the door.

The sun has already swung around to the crease of the horizon. The air slightly cooler, shadows soft but still out to play. It's a good thing I held on to that piece of Hello Kitty stationery with Feng's address spelled out in Pinyin—Google Maps shows it isn't too bad of a commute.

On the train, Waipo pulls the wooden beads off her wrist and rolls them between soft, cabbage-wrinkled hands. Her gnarled fingers find the head of the bracelet, where the guru bead is tied off by an elaborate looping knot. She closes her eyes and thumbs past each piece, one by one, turning the whole circle until she reaches the head. I wonder if she's praying for us to find the bird.

A soothing voice announces the name of each stop in four languages. Mandarin and Taiwanese. English. The fourth must be Hakka; I think that's what Dad said. The voice cycles through the languages like a song. Like a spell. I wait for the right name to charm us off the train. When it finally does, the sky has gone dark. The clouds dragging that nighttime veil over themselves like a blanket. The pinks and oranges diminished to the umber of dusk.

Waipo follows me as I study the map on my phone and walk us toward the pin that marks where Feng lives. We cross wide intersections where mopeds scrape past bearing tired passengers, bags of groceries, some of them with pet dogs perched in the foot wells between the riders' knees.

Feng's apartment is in a residential alley, tucked deep inside a tangle of narrow roads. I march us right up to the wide concrete step and double doors of shiny steel, and buzz number 1314.

There's no answer. Push it again, holding that dusty square button a few beats longer. Still nothing.

I check the address to make sure I've got the right apartment. Maybe if we just wait awhile, she'll come home.

We watch the sky turn to purple turn to black, watch the winds ushering the clouds overhead. I wonder: If you peel away all that darkness, would you find that deep YInMn blue? Maybe that's where all the other colors are hiding—in a dimension of the world we just can't see, between our sky and the rest of the universe.

Then I start to think about the possibility of other

dimensions. Maybe they're layered together, stacked like the thin pages of a book so that you can't see them unless you're looking from a specific angle. Dimensions between realities. Dimensions between life and death.

Maybe those are the places where ghosts live.

Waipo sighs and slowly, carefully, makes her way down off the step, heading back toward the road.

"Wait," I say, the word automatically coming out in English.

My grandmother turns and gives a sad shake of her head. She's tired of waiting.

Everything in my body is heavy and disappointed and the color of dust as we walk down the alley and round the corner. I draw in a deep breath, tasting the air.

"Leigh?"

The sound of my name like the cold blade of a key turning in a lock.

"What are you doing here?" Feng stands behind us, half of her carved in shadow, half of her pale beneath the streetlamp. Even in the dark I can see the pattern of bluets on her blouse.

Waipo's gaze yo-yos between us.

"We came to find you," I answer.

For once, Feng seems at a loss for words. "Why don't we go get something to eat?" she says finally. "There's a night market nearby."

We wind through the alleys, walking in silence, listening to the cars and mopeds rolling past. The occasional conversation leaking through screen windows. The hiss and pop of a wok sizzling with oil.

In the next alley, a large family has set up a line of tables, laden with tall red candles and freshly cooked food. Cellophane stretches over the tops of dishes. Fried rice, eggplant, a mix of bamboo and mushrooms. Three whole fish in a puddle of sauce, draped with scallions. Bean curd and pot stickers and fluffy white buns and more.

Every plate stabbed through the center with incense. A stick through the breast of a chicken, through the rounded meat of a peach. Sticks piercing the cellophane windows, standing upright in mounds of sticky rice, in clumps of noodles.

And off to the side, a metal barrel, swollen with flames. Children race around the table, gathering pieces of paper that are bright with red ink and gold foil, and tossing them to the fire.

"Ghost Month offerings," Feng explains. "The joss paper is ghost money."

"Offerings? Like, that food is cooked for the ghosts?"

"Of course. Ghosts want to eat, too, you know. They're the hungriest of anyone."

We know we've reached the night market by the crowd. The colorful signs and lights. The smoke of foods being grilled and fried.

Waipo grabs my elbow and points to a stand where a man is brushing sauce onto a rectangular treat on a wooden stick and then rolling it in peanut flour.

"Pig's blood cake," Feng explains, and at first I think I've heard her wrong. "Have you tried it?"

My grandmother nudges me again and moves to get in line.

I shake my head quickly. "Uh, that's okay."

"*Hao chi!*" says Waipo. *Delicious!*

I shake my head again.

Feng smiles a little. "Come on. Let's go over here."

Through smoke, through the throngs of people, past stalls selling fried foods, past the next intersection, where blockades cut off the cars—we finally stop again before a large barrel of soup crowded with fat, snowy pearls.

"It's a sweet fermented rice soup," says Feng. "With rice balls."

"It's fermented?" I raise an eyebrow.

"It's really good. Trust me." She puts in the order, and we sit down at a table on the side.

Two bowls immediately appear before me and my grandmother. Grains of rice and cloudy wisps of egg float around balls of white and pastel pink. Waipo hands me a spoon.

"What about you?" I ask Feng.

She shakes her head. "I'm actually not hungry. I just thought it would be a nice snack for you to try."

I set my spoon down and swallow. "I'm sorry."

Feng looks down.

"I shouldn't have said those things to you. I was way out of line. You've done nothing but help."

"It's okay," she says.

Beside me, Waipo slurps at her soup, either oblivious to the tension or purposely ignoring it.

"People who are grieving often can't help themselves." Feng's words come out in a tone that says she knows from personal experience.

I wait to see if she's going to say more.

"I know what that's like," she says slowly. "I've . . . well, I lost my family, too."

The smoke from a nearby stall gusts toward us. In the street, a dog without a collar wags her tail, hoping someone will drop some food. The mother at the next table over chides her toddler, who's knocked over a bowl.

"I'm so sorry," I say. "I didn't know." There's that awful curiosity, and I try to imagine what she means. *My family.* Her entire family? Is she the only one left? It feels rude to ask.

"It's okay," she says. "It's fine." Her expression is hard to read.

Then I remember how she said she's been away from home for a long time. I wonder if that has something to do with it.

"It just makes me think about the few threads left that keep me tethered to them. I take a lot of comfort in seeing the Ghost Month offerings—it always helps me feel like there's still that connection to my family. You know, because ghosts are still here."

I know what she means. "It's easier knowing that they're still part of this world, somehow."

"Exactly." Feng gives me a sad smile. "Go on. Eat."

The rice balls are sticky and filled with sesame paste that melts out like a runny yolk. Delicious. The soup itself is sweet, slightly tart, with the hint of an alcoholic tang.

"So good, right?" says Feng, cheering up a bit. "My favorite thing about it is the texture. My sister used to argue that the best way to eat it was to bite a hole in one of the balls, and eat the filling first."

I pause with the spoon halfway to my mouth. "You have a sister?"

Feng blinks. "Yes. I had a sister." She looks away. "I didn't mean to bring her up."

My throat is scratchy when I tell her, "My mother has a sister, too. But I didn't know. I only just found out recently."

A woman in a stained apron reaches between us to remove a stack of dirty bowls and spoons, and we fall silent for a long moment.

"Actually. I wanted to ask Waipo about this. Could I, um? Could you translate? I just... I don't know anything about my aunt."

Feng turns to my grandmother, speaking in a low voice. Waipo's eyes light up. She pushes her soup aside and begins to speak.

"Your aunt loved to eat. She loved discovering new treats. Popo says she's never seen another girl who could eat so much—it was... Jingling's favorite thing. If she went hungry for too long, she'd become angry and stubborn."

My face stretches into a smile.

"She tried so hard to be a good older sister. Smart, reliable. A good teacher. Anything she was passionate about, she wanted to share with the world. Like American poetry. She was obsessed with a poet named Emily Dickinson."

The name rings in my ears like a gong. "Emily Dickinson?"

"Yes," Feng continues. "She was always reciting this poem, that poem. Whenever she tried to teach your mom about American poetry, she lit up like a fire—it was her greatest love."

My mother had that same passion. The way she'd shout, *Yes! Exactly!* after a piano student nailed a run. Her face full of lilac eagerness whenever she suggested I sit down for a first lesson.

"Sisters are very lucky," Feng says quietly. "They get to be family and they also get to be best friends. Even in the afterlife, I think they recognize the presence of the other better than anyone else."

The afterlife. I wonder if Feng's felt the presence of her own sister?

"Can I ask you something?" My voice is nervous and hesitant.

"Of course," says Feng.

"Have you ever seen a ghost?"

"I think people see ghosts all the time," says Feng. "And I think ghosts *want* to be seen. They want to be reassured that they truly exist. They drift back into this world after passing through the gates of death into another dimension, and suddenly they hear every thought, speak every language, understand things they didn't get when they were alive."

I nod.

"What about you?" Feng asks. "Have you seen a ghost?"

"I'm not sure about ghosts, specifically. But I guess that's the closest thing to it. If I told you . . ." I pause, tasting the words before they come.

Her eyebrows pop up. "If you told me what?"

"Would you believe me if I said I've seen my mother?"

Feng is silent as she considers the question. She picks up a napkin and begins folding it like origami, into quarters, then triangles, making creases with her nails. "Yes," she says finally. "I would believe you."

I lean back in my chair, feeling somehow a bit lighter.

Feng gives me a sidelong glance. "So where did you see her?"

"Here. And back at home, a couple times. She's—" I pause

because I know it sounds ludicrous. "Um. I see her as this . . . well. She's this huge red bird."

"A bird," Feng repeats.

My grandmother makes a sound that gets our attention. I watch as she slowly bends to pick up something in the dark, shadowy corner beneath her side of the table.

She holds up a long, silky feather, the color of a rose.

71

I thought I would be able to sleep after tonight, but instead all I can think about is that feather, and ghosts, and other dimensions. And what's real.

And colors.

I see colors in the dark now. Sometimes they form shapes, or even faces. Sometimes they get angry with me, turn a dirty, boiling crimson. Sometimes they try to soothe me, drawing themselves like crystals in a pale dusty blue.

I don't even have to close my eyes. The colors are just there, floating above me, like little truth tellers. Wherever my thoughts go, they follow.

I desperately want to sleep. I would even take a nightmare.

The colors shape themselves into a face. Like a sketch made with oil pastels. I know those eyes. That nose. That chin.

"Mom?" I say softly.

She vanishes in a cloud of red, and the colors crumble away to nothing.

72

FALL, SOPHOMORE YEAR

The late September chill was just beginning to set in. My sophomore year Art II was ninth period—the last period of the day—and as I packed up, Dr. Nagori pulled me aside to say he'd called my house.

At first I thought I was in trouble with my favorite teacher.

"I wanted to speak with your parents myself so they would take this seriously," he said.

"Both of my parents?" I needed to know how much damage control was ahead of me.

"Your mother answered the phone. I told her I think you should submit a portfolio to Kreis in Berlin."

I blinked. Understanding was slow to set in. There was only one thing I registered with certainty: I was not actually in trouble. "Berlin?"

"Kreis—*Raum für Kunst,*" he said. "Remember those slides from that young artists series last week? Those were shown at Kreis, an art gallery for young emerging artists."

I did remember, but I still didn't get what he meant. I wasn't German. I wasn't a real artist. I was just a high school student.

"They're doing a new thing next summer: an international show for artists under the age of eighteen. It'll be a juried exhibit. You have to submit a portfolio by the beginning of June. The theme is surrealism—your work would be a good match."

June. That felt so far away.

I didn't know that by June everything would flip upside down. That somehow, in a blink, everything could change.

Or not a blink. In a few swallows. In four slashes.

"The months will go by quicker than you think," Dr. Nagori told me. "I would encourage you to begin working seriously now. The stuff you've been doing is excellent. It's like the summer gave you a new pair of eyes, a new perspective. I want to see you expand on this last set. . . ."

I wondered if he realized what I was up against. If he could even begin to guess that my father hated the amount of time I spent with my sketchbook.

If Dad found out about this, there was no way in hell he would let me do it. I could hear it already: *You are absolutely not going to waste your time on this. Leigh, if only you took this energy and applied it to studying for the SATs! Or tried to bring up your chemistry grade. It's not that you don't work hard—it's that you focus on the wrong things.*

But only if he found out. Which maybe he wouldn't.

"If the submission fee is a problem, I think I can maybe persuade the school to cover it," Nagori said kindly, quietly. He was trying to guess at my thoughts, and it occurred to me that the expression on my face was probably not the most positive.

"Thank you." I forced out a smile. "I'll...talk to my parents about it."

Staying to talk to Nagori caused me to miss the bus, but it didn't matter. Axel had just gotten his license and Tina's old car. The ancient Toyota Camry was dark blue with boxy corners, and waiting for me in the back of the junior parking lot. The engine ran with an eternal growl, but it was the smoothest thing to drive. He'd already let me try it out.

I told him what Nagori said.

"That's amazing, Leigh!" he shouted, swinging right at the circle to take the fast way home.

The windows were down because he liked the roar of the wind blowing past his ears, no matter how cold it was. I climbed halfway out of my seat to reach for his hoodie in the back. It smelled like Thai food, but I slipped it on anyway.

"I guess," I replied. "He sounded so serious. It didn't seem like a good thing."

"That's just your brain in shock trying to balance it out," Axel shouted against the wind. "You deserve this."

I curled up low in the seat. "But why did he only talk to me? What about you?"

"C'mon, Leigh, you can't expect everyone to be good at everything. Face it. This is something you're really great at. Nagori sees the talent. Anyone would, from a mile away."

"But *you're* good. You should submit, too. Your watercolors—"

Axel shook his head. "Art is *your* thing. It's not my thing. Sure, I like it. It's fun. But for me it's all about the music—you know that. The visual just helps me get there from a fresh perspective. If God told me, *You've maxed out, you can't have any more art*, I'd get over it. But if someone tried to take art away from you—I think you'd shrivel up and die. You'd turn into, like...a raisin. We'd have to bury you in a matchbox."

When I was silent, he turned to look at me. "Come on. What color?"

I shrugged. I didn't know.

It wasn't until later that I realized what was bothering me: Art had always felt like *our* thing. Not *my* thing. Something we shared. We spent summer afternoons meandering through the woods, finding new stuff to get down on paper. If school was canceled for snow, Axel came over to trade portraits.

As he dropped me off that afternoon, he wished me luck for the conversation I'd have with my parents. Slamming that car door shut, I felt a strange sense of separation. When Dr. Nagori singled me out, he severed something between me and my best friend. I wanted my art; I wanted to be good. But I wanted Axel, too, exactly the way I'd always had him. As a partner in crime. Not a cheerleader.

My mother was sitting on the piano bench with her back to the instrument, like she'd been waiting for me to walk in. There were bags under her eyes; I wondered if she was having trouble sleeping again. She stood up when she saw me.

"Dr. Nagori called," she said.

I slid my backpack off, let it thud to the floor.

"How do you feel about art show?"

"Excited, I guess." I sounded anything but excited.

My mother raised her eyebrows. "Dr. Nagori said you make good work. He said this is opportunity you can get noticed. Do you want to get noticed, Leigh? Do you want to go? To Berlin?"

"There's no way Dad'll say yes. So it doesn't even matter." I sank into the sofa.

"No," my mother said firmly. "It does matter. You want to go, you will go."

"I haven't even submitted a portfolio, Mom. That's the first part. I have to *be accepted* first. They're only picking, like, twelve people."

"Ahhh," said my mother, her voice rounding a hill. "I see. You are afraid."

"I'm not *afraid*," I shot back with so much contempt even I had to concede it was a lie. My cheeks went warm.

Mom came and sat beside me, perching on the edge of the seat. "It's okay to be afraid. But not okay if be afraid means you do nothing. You must not do nothing. That's not life worth living."

I tried to swallow, but my throat wouldn't work; there was something stuck in it, dry and methyl violet.

Later I wondered: Was that how my mother felt? That she was *doing nothing*? That her life was not worth living?

"Have you ever been afraid to do something?" I asked.

"Of course," said my mother. "I was afraid marrying Dad. I was afraid coming to US. But look now: how happy I am here. How happy I am, I have this wonderful daughter, so dedicated and talented."

I rolled my eyes like I was acting out a part. Why did I do it? Some terrible requirement of being a teenager is being absolutely awful when your parents are being lovely.

I saw the way my mother tried to shake the eye roll off like it was only water, like it wouldn't sink through her skin. She smiled, but her eyes looked far away and wistful, as if she were filling up murky brown.

"You will make portfolio. You will go to Berlin."

Other things were changing, too. Axel was doing more music than ever, since he'd enrolled in band. The music room was right around the corner from my locker, so we started up a habit of walking to art together after he got out of eighth-period jazz. Which was great. Until Leanne started walking with us.

I should've realized we hadn't seen the last of her. Apparently she played the alto sax—who knew? I guess he didn't find her so annoying anymore. There were, like, seventeen kids in the jazz band, and between them they all had varying degrees of chumminess, depending on what instruments they played. I tried to figure out how Axel fit into this equation. He mostly stayed on electric bass, but I knew he occasionally switched over to piano. It seemed, though, that his closest friend in that class was Leanne.

One day the two of them rounded the corner to my locker, laughing obnoxiously hard. I could barely follow the story they were telling.

"—And Mr. Chiu set his mug down right next to the trombones," said Leanne, the cadence of her voice dramatizing the whole thing. I wondered if her eyes were going to pop out.

Axel snickered. "So we do this epic run through the coda—it's the first time this piece has gone at all smoothly—"

"We're going to be late for art," I interrupted loudly.

"Okay, okay, walk and talk," said Leanne.

Axel's grin was so wide it was about to break a window. "The trombones are all into it, and Chiu is shouting, 'Yes! Yes!' Like he's just had the best sex of his life or something."

Leanne was cackling.

"And Darrell Hudson leans right over the desk and empties his spit valve into Chiu's mug." Axel exploded into laughter, tears squeezing out of his eyes.

The bell rang, and we ran the rest of the way, Leanne to study hall, me and Axel bursting into the art room. Nagori rolled his eyes at us. We started the day's assignment, and Axel was still laughing, and I was curling into my piece of paper, hoping he couldn't see the bit of hurt that was seeping through me Prussian blue.

73

It's Feng's idea to go. "We should visit your mother's university," she said after I told her about the bird, after I explained why I was trying to go to the places that had been important to her. Feng promised to help me come up with a new plan, said she doesn't think we need to make a net. She thinks that visiting my mother's spots is exactly the right thing, but that we need to look harder.

"If the bird told you to come to Taiwan, then there must be something she wants you to do or see," Feng said. "Something more than just finding her."

I think back to the note my mother left crumpled up in the garbage can.

~~I want you to remember~~

We take a car up Yangmingshan, which Feng says was

once called Grass Mountain, for the silvergrass that grows tall and flowers on its highest slopes. We snake through winding roads, through pockets of sulfurous air. Outside the window, in every direction: a million shades of green. And behind all the flora: the mountains like watercolors. Layers and layers of blues and grays and greens rolling into one another.

And when we finally get to the Chinese Culture University, to the music building with its slate eaves and pagoda-style rooftops, we climb up to the fifth floor, to all the practice rooms where my mother must've sat and trained for hours. We find one with *HELLO* scratched above the knob. It happens to be the one door that's unlocked.

There isn't much space, but the three of us pile inside anyway. The black piano gleams with our reflection; I lift the cover to let it smile with its shiny teeth, like my mother would prefer.

Feng pushes open the only window; the smell of sulfur sweeps in, and something compels me to get a photo of the view. I guess I want to capture what my mother must've seen when she looked out there after hours of practicing. When she was only a student, without the burden of a family. When she was—I hope—happy.

As my finger taps the button to get the picture, a screech pierces the sky, stabs right through me.

Waipo grabs my wrist and points with her other hand just in time for me to see a red tail gliding away.

I press into the window, lean myself out as far as I can, but she's gone.

"Did you get a picture?" says Feng in a hushed voice.

"I don't think so." But I check my phone anyway. On the

screen I see the eaves of the roof. The watercolor mountains in the distance. The faraway trees like broccoli.

And on a balcony floor a couple stories down, in one sunlit patch of stone: the shadow of a bird.

I've been shivering nonstop since our visit to the school. And as the day progresses, the hallucinations are flaring up again. Colors brightening and mixing. The edges of things sharpening then blurring. Inky cobweb lines returning.

Everything around me looks shattered.

The seconds tick their way toward midnight, which will mark the end of the forty-fifth day.

But we must be getting closer. A tiny voice in my brain screams, *Closer to WHAT?* The rest of me swells defensively.

Closer to seeing her again. Speaking with her. Hugging her.

I want you to remember

She has to tell me what it is. Before she runs out of time.

We're so close. I'm so certain of it that it feels like I can justify using one of the precious remaining incense sticks. I pull open the drawer and reach for the two photographs I was able to salvage from the ashes. Both of them are a bit damaged, but whole enough.

I choose my parents' wedding photo, slightly bent, one edge discolored by heat, one corner entirely missing. There's my mother in her modest white dress, a delicate veil flowing down her back. My father young and handsome in his rented suit. It's a posed portrait, but the happiness in their faces is real.

With shaky fingers, I light the shortest stick.

Touch the ember to the photograph, watch it begin to burn.

Flicker and flash.

Flicker. And flash.

74

—SMOKE & MEMORIES—

The smoke has brought me to a large room sort of like the college student community center where Dad used to take me to play foosball and get lemonade from the vending machine. The room's packed. Most of the people are college-age, clustered in little groups, some appearing friendlier than others.

In the center of my vision: young Dory and young Brian, being introduced by friends. She's looking shy in a lavender dress. Giant plastic glasses perch on the edge of her nose. My father in his baggy button-down shirt leans in to say something funny. The rest of the room is too loud for me to hear them, but it's enough to see my mother laugh, her face erupting like a firecracker, eyes squinting, thin fingers coming up to hide the wideness of her grin.

Flash.

Dory and Brian in an empty auditorium, sharing the piano bench. He watches her fingers move. Her eyes are closed, and Schumann pours out from her hands, one sneakered foot pressing and releasing a golden pedal.

Flash.

Dory outside Brian's apartment, clutching at the jade cicada that hangs from her neck. Her face tight and shuttered. He opens the door.

"Dory, it's—God, it's three in the morning. What is it?"

"I'm sorry," she says. "When they call me it was one o'clock afternoon time for them, and after I have to find somebody to drive me here—and they're all asleep—"

"Slow down," says Brian, taking her wrist and tugging gently to bring her inside. "Who called?"

"My parents," says Dory. "They call because—they call about—"

Brian waits. His eyes are full of fear. Dory shakes harder and he guides her to a chair.

"My sister," she whispers finally. "Dead."

My heart seizes, turns to ice.

"What? Oh my god, Dory." He wraps his arms around her. That's when her face crumples. "I'm so sorry."

Dead. The word is cold and flat, aquamarine like the thick buildup of frost, and it fills my body with that color, with that echoing syllable, *dead dead dead.*

Jingling died. My mother had a sister, and my mother lost her sister, and no one ever told me.

"They don't know what happen. Her roommate found her on the floor. She only look like she just faint." Dory waits for the shaking to stop, waits for a pause in her heaving breaths. "I fly back to Taiwan tomorrow."

"Tomorrow," says Brian. "When will you be back?"

"I'm not coming back," she tells him.

He pulls away as understanding settles over his face. "But...there are still three weeks."

"I have talk to the program director already. I—I'm finished."

"Okay," says Brian slowly. "Do you want me to go with you? To Taiwan?"

She looks confused. "Why?"

"Well. Um. I know the timing is terrible. But this...is important to me."

"This?"

"Us." He gestures toward her, then toward himself. "You and me."

"It has only been few months," says Dory.

"So?"

She's silent.

"Tell me what you want," he says, and his voice cracks the tiniest bit. "Please. Just be honest. Because I know what I want."

"What do you want?" Dory's voice is barely audible.

He looks at her like he can't believe she's even asking. "I want us to be together. For starters."

Flash.

There's my mother again, still college-student young, wearing a loose cotton dress and perched on her suitcase on the curb outside the airport. A yellow cab winds through other cars to pull up in front of her. The man who steps out on the street side is barely recognizable at first, but then I notice the turned-down corners of the eyes, the strong jaw. This is a much younger Waigong. The other door opens, too, swinging slowly out above the curb. Waipo steps out, her eyes bleary, her face ashen.

"Did they figure out the cause?" asks my mother. The quality of her voice is different; she must be speaking in Mandarin, though the smoke once again allows me to understand her perfectly.

"An aneurysm," says Waigong. His voice is low and hoarse.

"She had symptoms," Waipo adds. "Nausea. Headaches. But she thought it was only a virus."

My mother's head droops, her shoulders slumping like she's given up.

"I told her to rest, but you know your sister," says Waipo shakily. "Always working. We even saw her for lunch that day."

A strange wave of relief shudders through me. An aneurysm. Not intentional. Not like my mother.

Flash.

My mother standing in a corner, cradling a chunky plastic phone between her ear and shoulder. Her face is toward the wall, where nobody can read her expressions. She pushes the spirals of the phone cord onto her index finger, loop by loop, stacking them until her knuckles are completely swallowed. The sound of a young man's voice comes through the receiver, the voice slightly thinned, so that it takes me a moment to realize it's my father.

"But how are you doing?" Brian asks.

"Am fine," says Dory, her voice a little quiet, a little shy. I realize then that Waipo is standing mere paces away, in the kitchen, listening closely to the exchange with a strange look on her face.

"I miss you," says Brian.

"I miss you, too," Dory replies softly.

"Can your parents hear you talking on the phone?" he asks.

"Yes. But they don't understand. It's okay."

There's the sound of him drawing in a breath. "I'm coming to see you."

Dory pauses. The set of her shoulders changes. She reaches a hand up to grip the phone tightly. "Really? You come to Taiwan?"

"Yes. And if your parents would be willing to meet me—I'd like to meet them."

She nods slowly, speechless.

"Dory? Did you hear me?"

"Yes," she answers finally, her voice thick with emotion.

Brian's voice drops lower. "Are you all right?"

She nods again, though he can't see. "Yes. Am fine. I need to go now."

"Okay. Goodbye, Dory."

"Goodbye," she practically whispers.

When she hangs up, Waipo has stepped out of the kitchen to stand directly in front of her. "Who was that? Who were you talking to?"

"A classmate," Dory answers.

"What classmate? An American classmate? From the summer?"

"Yes."

"Why did you sound so strange?" Waipo demands.

"I didn't," says Dory, but she doesn't make eye contact. She makes a show of glancing up at the clock. "I'm going to the market now, before the best vegetables are gone."

Waipo says nothing but turns away scowling.

As Dory pulls on her shoes, she pretends not to hear the conversation between her parents in the other room:

"Who was that?" says Waigong.

"She said it was a classmate." Waipo doesn't sound happy. "I think it was *him*."

"The American?"

"Yes," says Waipo. "She was speaking to him in English."

"She can't have this American boyfriend. She must marry someone Chinese. She *must*."

"*You* tell her," says Waipo. "She's being strange."

Dory closes the door behind her as quietly as possible and runs down the stairs.

The light changes. The memories retreat.

75

Jingling. She died so young. How did I never know?

And my grandparents—I never realized they had such strong feelings about who my mother loved. It's hard to imagine them so stern, so overbearing. Why did it matter if Mom married someone who wasn't Chinese, or Taiwanese, or Asian at all? And what do they think of me, then, the product of their daughter and a white man?

I wonder if Waipo and Waigong still feel that way. I wonder if that's why Dad walked out of the apartment—if it was unbearable to be with them.

How did my parents think they could build a family around so many secrets? It's like setting a house on top of a network of ditches and loose ground, and praying the foundation holds. No wonder we fell apart.

My phone chimes.

FROM: axeldereckmoreno@gmail.com
TO: leighinsandalwoodred@gmail.com
SUBJECT: (no subject)

I click it open, and it takes a while to load.

No words in the body of this email. Just an image I've never seen. A watercolor Axel painted of the cat on the kitchen counter turning her whiskers up toward my mother's chin.

The two of them gazing at each other like there's nobody else in the world.

76

FALL, SOPHOMORE YEAR

The trees had changed, many already letting loose their browns. Crunchy pieces of autumn sprinkled across our lawn. The air nipped at me, a good ten degrees or so lower than I was ready for.

Halloween decorations had taken over the world. Scarecrows in the fields we passed to get to school. Decals of ghosts and witches and Frankensteins in every other window. Pumpkins carved up, some of them aglow with candles in their bellies.

So when I got home that chilly afternoon, I didn't even blink at the cat on the piano bench. My mind shuffled it back into the deck without a thought. It was another decoration, a creature as black as they come, perfect for witching hour.

I took off my jacket and the cat pounced on it. *That* got my attention.

"Um, hello?" I called into the house.

"Shit!" Something heavy thudded to the floor. "Ow, *crap*. Ow ow ow."

"Dad?" I was surprised to find him here. His flight wasn't supposed to bring him back until the next morning. Part of me was disappointed; it meant I wouldn't be able to spend the night sketching in peace. But I tried to summon some good cheer. It was rare to have him home on a Friday.

"Leigh!" My father rounded the corner of the hallway, and his face lit up with relief. "You're just in time. I persuaded your mother to go run errands, but she'll be back any minute. Come help with this."

He beckoned me into the living room, where this weird geometric structure had fallen over on its side. I helped him push it back up, and he clicked something on the bottom into place.

"There. What do you think?"

"Uh. It's great?" The structure was taller than me. There were carpeted platforms and columns wrapped in what looked like rope.

"It's a playground. For Meimei."

I raised my eyebrows. "Who?"

The cat meowed then, like she knew we were talking about her.

"It's a surprise," said Dad, picking up the creature.

"You got us...a cat?" I tried to tamp down my shock. He traveled so much we couldn't even keep track of his time zones. He should've been the last person in the world to be making decisions about getting a pet.

"I just figured...well. I worry that Mom's been lonely. Seems like she could use some company."

"What about me? What about her piano students? We're just chopped liver?"

"Her piano students," my father repeated, his face strange. "Right." He was suddenly very busy fiddling with the cat playground, which already looked fully assembled.

"Dad. Is there something you're not telling me?"

"Hmm?" he said innocently.

I thought of my mother, tired and drained when I got home. I'd been taking the late bus every day—Nagori was letting me use the art room to work on my portfolio for Kreis. It used to be that I had to listen through at least four piano lessons after school. But these days I got home so late I missed it all. .

Unless there wasn't anything to miss.

"She *is* still teaching, right?"

My father said nothing.

The anger boiled up so fast it surprised even me. "She stopped? Again? When was anyone going to tell me?"

And how did *Dad* find out first?

"Listen, she's just having a difficult time—"

"How are you supposed to know what kind of time she's having? You're barely even *here*, Dad," I said, more harshly than I meant to.

He winced visibly.

I crossed my arms. "She's been getting worse again. She needs help."

He was silent for a long stretch. Finally, he said, "You're right. I'm not here enough. I need to change that. One more year of this and I'm done. No more conferences, no more traveling. I'm booked through next summer, but after that, I'll be home and sticking to a normal—and local—teaching schedule. All right?"

It was my turn to be silent. I didn't know what to say. Did I believe him? I couldn't be sure. It sounded too good to be true. And worse, a dark and horrible part of me wasn't sure I wanted it to be true. Because if my father stayed home, I wouldn't have the freedom to work on my art. He'd be nagging me constantly. He'd tell me to focus on the practical things. He probably wouldn't let Axel come over so much.

"And she is getting help," he said, his voice dropping lower. "Her doctor just switched her to a new medication. Sometimes that can make things a little worse for a while. But we're keeping a close eye on it."

I pressed my mouth into a thin line so I wouldn't blurt out anything about the irony of the pronoun *we* and the phrase *a close eye*.

I threw myself down on the sofa. It didn't make sense for me to be the last to find out about things like this. Wasn't I, compared to my father, the way more reliable support system? I had to work to keep the disgust off my face.

We heard the garage opening then, the motor humming as it pulled the door up. Dad straightened with excitement. He placed Meimei at the top of her playground.

Mom walked in and the cat meowed.

"Surprise!" Dad half shouted, throwing his arms out.

"Oh," she said, "my god. Is that cat?"

I'd been under the impression that my mother hated cats. She mentioned a long time ago that she thought cats were evil and tried to suffocate humans in their sleep. But the moment Mom reached out a tentative hand, Meimei pushed her head right into my mother's palm and began to purr. The two of them took to each other like they were meant to be.

Dad flew out again, and I wondered if he felt any guilt for having upped the head count of those he was leaving behind. As the days grew cold, Mom started sleeping more and more. I was an expert at taking care of myself by then. In the mornings, I rolled out of bed exactly seven minutes before Axel nudged his Camry into our driveway. Just enough time to throw on clothes, brush my teeth, grab an English muffin, and walk out the front door.

It was impossible for me to know how late my mother slept in after I had left for school, but it reassured me that she at least got up to feed Meimei, put out clean water, sift through the litter box.

That dark and horrible part of me envied the cat. I'd learned to be self-sufficient; it was a habit forced upon me by my mother's condition. But here was a creature who was helpless, an animal who didn't deserve the name of her species because she couldn't even be called upon to kill a cockroach. *She* was the one to get my mother out of bed. She was the reason my mother changed into real clothes, the reason my mother rose to brew a pot of tea.

Sometimes I watched from the other room as Meimei found Mom in the kitchen and went about winding figure eights through her ankles. When Mom bent down to pet her, she flopped over, lifting her fluffy belly to the ceiling and closing her eyes for a good rub.

The cat was the one who reminded her that life was a real thing. All the rest of us might as well have been mannequins on display in the window of a museum.

"It's funny, I never thought of you as a cat person," said Axel, pressing chords into his keyboard. It was on the electric guitar setting, and the notes came scraping through the tinny speakers of the headphones hanging around his neck.

I was on the couch, sketchbook propped up by my knees, and shading with a nub of charcoal. "I'm really not. I don't understand Meimei at all. Like, she'll rub up against me to make me pet her. And then halfway through the petting, she whips her head around and swats at me to stop. See, look." I held out my hand to show the scratches on the back. "I just don't understand what she wants. But whatever. She's my mother's cat."

"I didn't peg your mom for a cat lady, either."

"She's not, really."

"When I think 'cat lady,' I think of, like, Leanne's mom, who used to be a breeder and now judges cat shows."

"Sounds like a thrilling life," I said sarcastically.

Axel raised his eyebrows. "So why'd your dad get Meimei in the first place?"

I shrugged, flipping to a fresh page in my sketch pad. "Who knows? Maybe he thought a dog would be too much work."

"But why a pet at all?"

"To give Mom a reason to get out of bed and do shit."

Axel was quiet. The chords stopped. He turned on his squeaky seat so that he faced me. "Is she okay?"

I shrugged again.

"Will you please talk to me about it?"

Something in his tone made me pause and look up. I set down the charcoal.

"There's something you haven't been telling me, isn't there?" he said.

"What do you mean?" I said, and a neon-red sign flashed dangerously in my head: *Bullshit bullshit bullshit.*

"Come on, Leigh. I'm worried."

Axel crossed his arms, and I waited, silently counting to thirty, hoping that maybe he'd give up. He didn't.

"She's been . . . struggling," I told him.

"With what?"

"Everything? I'm not sure."

He gave me a look and I threw up my hands. "I'm being serious! Really. I don't know. She won't talk to me about it. But it feels like every little thing is this insurmountable wall for her. And when she's down . . . it's pretty bad."

He nodded me on.

"It's the reason they sent me to that awful camp over the summer. So I would be out of the way while she had treatment."

"What kind of treatment?" said Axel.

"Electro-whatever it's called. ECT. Like, shock therapy."

"Whoa."

I let a breath out through my nose. "Yeah."

"You could've told me, Leigh."

My eyes drop to the floor.

"So she's . . . she has . . ."

I could practically hear the gears turning in his head as he searched for a label, a name, a descriptor.

The word *depression* bounced around in my head. *Depression depression depression.* Was that even what she had? I knew that there were other mood disorders out there, other conditions and chemical imbalances.

Depression, I opened my mouth to say, but the word refused to take shape. Why was it so hard to talk about this? Why did my mother's condition feel like this big secret?

Axel looked at me expectantly, still waiting for me to fill in the blank.

"She's forgotten how to be happy," I told him.

But that felt wrong, too.

77

Day forty-six. We're headed north, to Jiufen.

When Feng told me where Waipo wanted to take me, I didn't understand. "So you're saying that my mom never spent any time there...but we need to go anyway?"

"There's someone in Jiufen that Popo wants you to meet," she explained. "I think it's really important."

All I could think was *We can't afford to waste a single day.*

"But I don't have time. I need to come up with a new plan to catch the bird."

"Trust me, I really think this will help," said Feng. "Your train leaves in two hours, so you should probably work on packing your overnight things right now."

"Wait, you mean *our* train, right?"

She fiddled with her sleeve. "I'm not going. I can't."

"What? Why not?"

"It's not a good time for me to go," she said.

"But I need you to help me," I told her. "I need you to translate."

"I just can't, Leigh. I'm sorry." And then she left.

When Waipo and I get off the train, there's a man about my dad's age waiting with a minivan to pick us up. He doesn't look happy, but he opens the door for us anyway, slinging our overnight bags into the trunk. They land with a thud that I feel against the back of my seat.

There's a rapid exchange in Taiwanese as he pulls out of the train station. I can tell he and Waipo are talking about me by the way she glances toward me a few times.

"Hi," he says abruptly. He turns his face, and I notice for the first time a pink birthmark spread across his cheek like a painted cloud.

"Um, hi," I answer back.

"I'm Fred," he says, his syllables curbed by a bit of an accent.

"Leigh." I give him a small wave in the mirror.

"Nice to meet you," he says without looking at me. It sounds like a lie.

He falls silent, and I turn my attention out the window. The road swells like a wave, winding dramatically so that the view is by turns mountain and sea, and by turns a bustling town. Tourist shops line the edge of the streets. Here and there we see a collarless dog ambling along the side of the road, a stray cat perched on a low wall, another one curled up on an awning.

"I don't know why you come here," Fred says suddenly. "They threw the ashes north. Not here."

My skin prickles. "What ashes?"

My mother my mother my mother.

"Chen Jingling ashes," he says, and Waipo looks up sharply.

Not my mother. My mother's sister. My aunt.

"They scattered her ashes here?"

"*No,*" says Fred emphatically. "North. Farther." He sees the look on my face. "Don't tell my wife. She thinks you just normal customers."

My brain is spinning, and I glance at my grandmother, but her face is turned out the window.

"You know who I am?" Fred says then, his voice a little softer, less gruff.

I shake my head.

He says nothing after that.

Around us, the mountains rise higher and higher in dusty blues and purples. The farther up we go, the more water I can see, a calm, still blue-gray that stretches on and on.

We turn off the main road, our car crawling up a steep hill to pull into the alley between two buildings.

"Come," he says. "I'll show you your room."

He demonstrates how to unlock a heavy front door and leads us past a wide space with tables and chairs, and down a hallway to a room labeled A3.

"Here's the key." Fred raises a hand, gives the wood three sharp raps with his knuckle.

"This is our room?" I ask.

"Yes."

"So why are you knocking?" I immediately feel embarrassed for asking.

He looks at me for a beat. "*Gui yue hui peng dao gui.* You know the expression?"

My grandmother makes a face at him.

I shake my head.

"It means, during Ghost Month, you will run into ghosts. You should always knock before going into the room at hotel or bed-and-breakfast, to be respectful to ghosts. And now especially—because right now it is Ghost Month."

He pushes the door open, hands us the key, and then we're on our own.

The room is small and well lit. Waipo kicks off her shoes and changes into the slippers provided for us. I follow suit.

On the other side of a decorative folding screen are two low beds and a nightstand. Above them, on the wall: two huge, beautifully painted accordion fans. One featuring a pair of red-crowned cranes, the other a lone phoenix beginning to dive down, its tail feathers teardrop-shaped like peacock quills, long and draping.

Birds. My hairs stand up on end.

A knock at the door makes me jump.

When we open it, Fred says, "Here is a map. See this? This is back of old street. Walk down steps and turn right, there is old street. Lots you can eat—*xiaochi*. Do you understand?"

Little eats, I remember Feng telling me. "Yes."

"If you go to front of old street, there is a Seven. Convenience store."

Seven. As in 7-Eleven. Right.

"Breakfast from eight to ten, right here." He points down the hall. "Have any questions, call me." He points to a number scrawled at the bottom of the printout. And with that, he shoves the paper at me and starts to pull the door closed.

Waipo calls out something loud and angry.

Fred's face twists, a mix of rage and indecision. "Fine. You see first star on the map? Wait for me at the teahouse. I meet you after I finish my work."

He pauses, and for a moment there's something nervous in his expression. "Don't talk to someone about Chen Jingling. Okay? And tell your grandmother: no funny business."

He turns away and slams the door.

78

L ight rain pricks its way down into the narrow alley
between the little shops and stands. It's impossible to take
two steps without running into someone, but the crowd thins
as the rain picks up. Red lanterns swing overhead in long lines.
The sound of rhythmic drumming winds its way down to the
street. Outside a shop selling carved stamps, a little dog with
floppy ears and caramel fur sleeps snugly curled, oblivious to
the bustling around him.

In the teahouse, we sit all the way up on the third floor
against the windows, peering out over the town and the water.
The waitress brings us a glass pot filled with a reddish tea.
Dried fruits crowd the belly of the teapot. Cheerful little goji
berries swim just below the surface.

Waipo peers out the window, distracted.

I sip at the tea, slightly sweetened by the fruits. That heavy
feeling is returning, that thick fog creeping into my brain.

With each blink, it takes a bit longer for the world to resettle and sharpen.

Careful not to get anything wet, I turn to a fresh page in my sketchbook and start a portrait of my grandmother. Her faraway, wistful eyes. Thin, pensive lips. Flowy tunic draping down the rounded slopes of her shoulders. Soft fingers wrapped around a cup of tea. Fat wooden beads and a glassy jade bangle knocking together on her wrist.

It's hard to imagine her arguing with my mother. It's hard to think that their relationship could fray to the point of breaking, to the point of someone snipping the thread between them clean in half, deciding to never look back.

With just the one pencil, I try to capture all the colors of her aliveness in gray scale.

By the time I finish the portrait, the sun has gone to bed. It was tricky, the way the shadows against her face kept shifting. But she was good at sitting still. That must've been some bottomless thought she got stuck in.

"*Hua wo a?*" says Waipo. *You drew me?*

"*Shi ni,*" I confirm.

"*Gan ma hua wo?*" She laughs a little and shakes her head.

Outside the window the sky has gone black. There are the lights of the town, flickering in oranges and yellows and blues and greens. The fat red lanterns are lit up, festive and bright. And more lights are out over the water, their reflections twinkling faintly. Proof this little world is still wide awake.

My grandmother summons a waitress, who brings us a menu. Waipo points to the photographs of the dishes, asking questions about each one, gesturing with her hands as she speaks. I listen to the rolling cadences of their conversation, busy myself with a doodle of our second pot of tea.

It's not long before platters arrive: dumplings, stuffed lotus root, sautéed yam leaves, noodle soup, a bamboo basket full of steamed buns.

"*Baozi,*" says Waipo, pushing the basket toward the center, where we can both reach. A little white napkin unsticks itself from underneath the bamboo structure.

Actually, not a napkin. A square of paper, half soaked with the condensation from the steam, so I can see that there's text on its underside. It takes a few seconds and a few careful fingers to peel it off. Handwritten in blue pen:

> If I could see you in a year,
> I'd wind the months in balls,
> And put them each in separate drawers,
> Until their time befalls.

That's all. Nothing else.

What the actual heck?

I know only through pure, unshakable instinct: It's by Emily Dickinson.

"*Shenme?*" says Waipo, seeing my face.

I have no idea how to answer her. The tremors start in my toes, making their way up the rest of my body. I am an earthquake. Any second now, I'm going to split apart.

Gripping the poem hard, I slide out of my seat, searching for the waitress who served us. "Hello? Excuse me?"

A different woman comes over and says something to me in Mandarin.

"I need to know who gave this to us," I tell her, holding out the wet square of paper.

She gives me an uncertain look.

"Do you speak English? Is there someone who speaks English?"

"*Deng yixia*," she says, and she turns back, click-click-clicking away from me fast in her heels.

I try to still the panic.

My grandmother has stood up, too, now. She takes the poem from me, her eyebrows scrunching together at the sight of the English words. "*Shenme?*" she says again.

Minutes later, it's Fred who appears. He scowls at us. "I told you to behave like normal customer!"

Before I can say anything, Waipo starts spewing words. She points to the piece of paper in my hand.

"I'm trying to figure out who brought this to us," I say. "It was under the *baozi*."

Fred snatches up the paper and reads it, his eyes scanning impatiently from side to side. "What is this?"

"I think it's an Emily Dickinson poem."

"Emily Dickinson," he repeats slowly. Again, even slower. "Emily. Dickinson."

"Right. Do you... know who that is?"

He shakes his head. But then, a moment later, his eyes widen. He pulls up a nearby stool and sits down at the end of our booth. "I know this name, Emily Dickinson. We burned the poem by *Emily Dickinson* for the wedding."

"What wedding?" I ask sharply.

His voice drops. "When I married the ghost of Chen Jingling."

I stare at him, speechless.

"You don't know?" he says, reading the expression on my face.

I shake my head.

"Okay." Fred sighs. "I don't want to talk here. First you have to see."

"See what?" I ask.

He points out the window. "Look at those trees."

I squint through the lights reflected in the pane, through greasy smudges of fingerprints on the glass, try to find something in the dark outside to focus my eyes on. After a moment I see the silhouette of trees, a cluster of them not too far from the teahouse.

"*Kan dao le ma?*" asks Waipo. *Do you see?*

What am I supposed to be seeing?

"Energy flow through trees," Fred says quietly. "Watch the leaves."

And there it is. The sharp, silhouetted edges shifting and melting, forming the shapes of animals and humans. The shadows extract themselves from the tops of the branches, pull free, and drift upward into the sky, turning to a pale mist before vanishing into the darkness. Every time I blink, my eyes have to resettle, refocus, find the edges all over again.

"Where there is a shape, there is a spirit," says Fred. "People have those statue of Guan Yin and they know there is something there, filling the shape. But then those people forget about the original shapes made by the earth. The trees hold spirits, too."

"*Gui?*" I ask, looking at Waipo. *Ghosts?*

She nods.

"You should never shine a torch at trees," Fred tells me. "The light disturb the spirits. Right now because it is Ghost Month we can see them clearly here, so close to Jilong. Most people try not to see the ghosts. They just burn offerings and ignore signs. But if you look and try to see, you will see."

There's something beautiful about the way the shadows move. Like contortionists. Like dancers. Like brushstrokes across a canvas.

I watch carefully to see if there's a large bird. If there's a silhouette that might be my mother.

Fred reaches across the table for the last bun. He crams the whole thing into his mouth. "Now we drive back so your grandmother can rest. Then I'll tell you everything."

79

On the third floor of Fred's bed-and-breakfast, there's a balcony with chairs and a table situated right up against its stone wall. Overhead, the vague shapes of gentle giants shift across the sky, clouds veiled by night. We sit here in the quiet dark, Fred on one side of the table with an unlit cigarette between his fingers, me on the other, leaning on my elbows and gazing out over the town. Breezes whisper past our faces. For the first time since arriving in Taiwan, I find myself feeling cold.

He slides the cigarette behind his ear and pulls out a box of matches. "You have the poem?"

I hand it to him and watch as he cracks open a flame and touches it to the scrap of paper, drops it into the porcelain ashtray.

"This came from a ghost. Now we send it back." He holds the cigarette in the small fire until it catches.

If I squint my eyes, I can just barely make out the lines of the mountains. I can see the sparkle of lights like gemstones on the surface of the water.

"Many years ago, when I still live in Taipei, I go to Shilin to visit my sister. I was walking to her apartment, and I saw a red pocket on the ground. Someone dropped it." Fred pauses and looks up at me. "You know red pocket?"

"They have money in them, right? They're given for, like, Chinese New Year?"

"Yes," Fred says. "I pick up the red pocket, and think how lucky I am. I really need money! But inside, instead of money, there is—how do you say it? Hair. A pinch of hair?" He gestures with his fingers as if they're stroking along silky strands. "A bunch of hair?"

"A lock of hair?"

"Yes! A lock of hair. It was tied using ribbon. Then your grandfather stepped out from behind a corner. He was hiding. He told me the hair belong to his daughter, Chen Jingling, and I have to marry her."

"But she was dead?"

"Yes. So I have to partake in a ghost wedding."

"But couldn't you say no? They couldn't force you to do it, right?"

"I did it because they were grieving. So they could have peaceful hearts if they know their daughter has a husband. But, you know, see this?" He points to the birthmark on his cheek. "If someone is marked by the universe, there must be a good reason. I think to myself, this is part of my destiny. Also, if you have a ghost wife, sometimes she will bring good fortune."

"Do you think she did?"

Fred's eyes grow wide and he nods. "Yes. Definitely.

Everything I have now, I have because of Chen Jingling. That's why I still keep my apartment in Taipei. I only go back a couple times a year. But I keep the apartment for her, because of everything she help me." He sighs. "I should go back to Taipei again soon probably. Always have things to take care of there."

I try to imagine a life touched by a ghost. Changed by a ghost.

A fresh breeze gusts past, and as if summoned by my thoughts, I think I hear the faraway beating of wings. I look to the sky, search for a sign, a silhouette, anything.

The wind recedes. Everything stills once more.

"What was the wedding like?" I ask.

"It's like normal wedding, but they made, like, a doll for her. Using bamboo and paper. She wear real clothing and jewelry. And afterward, everything was burned. We send it all to the spirit world."

"At your wedding, did you—" I pause. Wait for the words to settle on my tongue. "Did you meet my mother?"

Fred shakes his head. "No. Your grandfather mentioned that Chen Jingling has a sister. But I didn't meet her. Why didn't she come with you to Jiufen?"

The question comes so unexpectedly that the breath hitches in my chest. "She, uh. She couldn't."

"Too bad," he says. "Next time."

"Next time," I echo.

He takes a pull on his cigarette, tilts his head back to blow the smoke upward.

A new thought occurs to me. "Have you ever seen Jingling?"

"I tell you, she died, that's why—"

"No, I mean"—I lean in a little closer—"you know. Her ghost? Her spirit?"

He wrinkles his eyebrows. "I see and hear and feel enough to know she is there."

"Have you ever seen any other ghosts?"

Fred looks angry again. He flicks at his cigarette with the tip of his thumb. A chunk of ash falls onto the table. "Why you asking this?"

"You seem to know a lot about ghosts."

"Of course," he says almost defensively. "I was married to a ghost." He looks out over the water, and something in his face softens. His voice grows quiet. "It's Ghost Month. Not a good time for ask these questions. Especially here."

"Why especially here?"

"We're near Jilong. The Ghost Festival there is so big it brings the attention of many ghosts. And because of higher concentration of ghosts, they are more noticeable to the living. Like when you can see in the trees. When ghosts come up here, they become more visible. I tell you before. *Gui yue hui peng dao gui.*" Fred mashes the end of his cigarette into the edge of the balcony wall and stands up. "I'm going to sleep. You want to stay here?"

"Yeah, I think I'll sit for a bit longer."

"Okay. Just close the door when you leave. Don't stay out too late. Remember—it's Ghost Month."

I listen to the sounds of his feet on the stairs diminishing, until all that's left is the noise of the wind rustling the trees, the occasional car or moped wheeling past on the road below.

I stay until the shivers set in, and my skin is cold to the touch, goose-bumping. I'm about to leave when I hear something.

The sound of wings. Wind, coming in pulsing waves.

I blink, and there's the bird, just as huge and beautiful as the first time I saw her. The reddest feathers turned almost purple by the darkness, slick with oily moonlight, long and sharp and curling. She swoops low. She turns in circles overhead, in figure eights, carving her way across the sky.

Every time she goes so far that I'm sure she's gone for good, she circles back.

There's urgency and joy in the way she soars. With each powerful beat of her wings, she gains height. She arcs in the air and dives back down. The longest feathers trail behind her like a kite tail, like a dancer's ribbon.

I stand up, jump with all the force I can, swinging my arms overhead.

Why won't she come down and talk to me?

I want you to remember

It's impossible to tell if she's seen me. But I can't help believing that she *knows* she's being watched. She dives, turns, flips.

"Mom," I say, the word finally crawling its way up my throat.

The one syllable breaks the spell.

High up in the air, the bird falters, just for a millisecond. She dips down one more time, and then she flies away.

80

All the colors around me are oversaturated and melty. Neon blues dripping out of the sky. Deep greens spilling into the sea, onto the roads. My head pounds. My ribs ache. I guess this is why they tell you sleep is important.

The forty-seventh day has flashed by in a blink. Breakfast. A temple. The bus. Train. Metro. Transfer to another line. Walk home.

Time, gone.

"Did you find anything in Jiufen?" Feng asks.

Two days left. Two days to find her.

I need sleep so badly; I couldn't sleep at all last night after the bird flew away. I sat there watching the sky until morning. The sun crawled up over the water, pricking the world awake, and there were long curls of mist rising up the mountain like a trail of spirits. The bird didn't come back.

"I met Fred. The one who married Jingling's ghost," I tell Feng.

Her fingers tug at the hem of her daisy-print blouse, where a thread has begun to unravel. "Poor Jingling," says Feng. "She—well. I bet she would have wished for the chance to fall in love before she died."

The sky is a velvety indigo with the hint of dark silvery clouds.

My mother once told me: *The clouds you see at night hold promises.*

"I saw the bird, too," I tell Feng. "And I think she saw me. But she didn't come down. She didn't—"

My voice cracks and suddenly I need to gulp down air.

"Maybe she didn't need to," Feng says very quietly. "Maybe it was enough."

"What do you mean? She told me to come to Taiwan—she has something to tell me."

"Maybe what she really needs," Feng says, "is just to remember. And to be remembered."

Smoke dances through the air at the night market, drifting past in sheets. I slurp at a bowl of soup full of wide squares of flat rice noodles—a savory treat Feng ordered for me. It's just the two of us here, sitting on a bench, watching children playing with a dog. They're crouched on the ground, giggling at the floppy, silken ears.

Then one of the kids jumps to her feet and starts to shout.

"Agong! Agong!"

Their mother rushes over to shush them. She unspools a long string of words, all of them too far out of reach for me. She looks distraught.

"What's happening?" I ask Feng.

"The girl says she sees their grandfather. Her mother's saying that's impossible."

"Why?"

Feng shrugs. "The mother says their grandfather is in the sky. 'No he's not,' says the little girl. 'How do you know?' says her mother."

The girl is shaking her head.

In just a few more hours, the forty-seventh day will be over.

"The little girl says, 'Because only angels can go up into the sky.' And now . . . the mother's saying that her grandfather *is* an angel. But the girl doesn't believe it."

We watch in silence as the mom leads her daughters away. The older one—the one who made the outburst—won't stop looking over her shoulder, her gaze fixed on something in the distance.

"Children know the truth," says Feng, her voice going very quiet.

I turn to look at her. "What? What do you mean?"

"They haven't learned to walk around with a veil over their

eyes. That's a habit that comes with adulthood. Kids always know what they see. That's why ghosts can't hide from them."

Ghosts can't hide from them.

I think of the bird and her feathers and my awful dreams of her suffering and disappearing.

I look out into the city, at the cars and mopeds, at the glass and lights. The distant buildings twinkle and shine, a collection of artificial stars.

We watch a young couple walk through the night market, bumping shoulders, fingers threaded together. They share a dessert and trade smiles and laughter.

"Have you ever been in love?" Feng asks.

"I don't know," I answer, but it feels like a lie.

Love. And what do any of us really know about that?

81

FALL, SOPHOMORE YEAR

It'd been almost two months since Nagori told me about the Berlin young artists show, and Dad hadn't said a word. My guess was Mom wasn't planning to tell him. What would happen would happen.

June felt like a long way off, but Nagori was nagging me about my progress.

"What the hell am I supposed to *draw*, Axel?" I flopped onto his couch facedown, pressing my nose into the tweed. My sketchbook was on the floor, where I'd flung it so I didn't have to look at the drawing I'd begun. "I don't know how to make a goddamn portfolio."

"What's wrong with the things you've been making?" he said, pressing chords into his digital keyboard. He'd turned the volume way down low; I could hear the tap of the plastic more clearly than the actual notes. "Haven't you been working on stuff in the art room after school?"

"None of it's good enough. I can't just keep doing these

weird, surreal, sketchy ... things. If I want to get into the show, I need to send in pieces that are more ..."

"Profound?" he offered.

"Yes! Exactly. Profound and, like, more polished."

"Polished just takes time. But I'm not sure you can really *try* to be profound. I think that's how you end up doing ... pretentious hipster crap."

"Hipster? Really? That's coming from Mr. Opera Electronica."

He put his hands up. "Hey, I'm not going out of my way to try to be 'profound.' I'm just trying to do something genuinely interesting to me. Which was what *you* were already doing before you got your suspenders all in a twist over this Kreis thing."

I raised my eyebrows. "Suspenders?"

He shrugged. "Just trying out some alternatives. *Panties* is annoyingly sexist. But anyone can rock suspenders."

"True," I said.

Axel pushed a button, and the little red lights on the keyboard died. He shoved my feet aside and sank into the couch next to me. "I thought Nagori just wanted you to expand on the stuff you've already shown him."

I tried to forget about the warmth of his hands over my socked feet. I loved how familiar the gesture was, loved that he was comfortable enough to just reach out and touch.

I reminded myself that the touch probably meant very little to him. In fact, it definitely meant absolutely nothing.

"Yeah, but what does *expand on* even mean?" I threw out air quotes with my fingers. "It's not like a pet cow that I just need to fatten up for the state fair."

"What if you tried working in more than just charcoal?"

I lifted my head and glared at him. "You know how I feel about that. I'm not practiced enough. I'll botch it."

"Pretend you're a kid again and you don't even know what's good. Just try for the sake of trying. For the sake of having fun."

I shook my head. "I'm sticking to charcoal."

It took me another week to finally get (A) an initial sketch that sucked slightly less, (B) brave enough to show it to Nagori.

Unintelligible sounds crawled out from his mouth. "Mmm." He tilted his head. "Hummm."

Maybe he was trying to commune with the zombie spirits who haunted the art room.

Or maybe he just had no idea what to make of the picture I was showing him.

My fingers twisted together under the table. "It's supposed to be more abstract." I could see Axel hovering by the door outside the classroom. I'd made him promise to wait in the hall until I was done.

"It's like matryoshka," said Nagori.

"Like what?"

"Russian nesting dolls. You've seen them, I'm sure. They're painted with faces on the outside, and hollow on the inside to hold increasingly smaller—".

"Ah, right. Got it."

"It's a beautiful concept," he said. "The image replicating itself and changing subtly each time."

"But?" I could hear the word dangling in the air between us and it was pissing me off. My knee jiggled hard, like it was winding up a generator and prepping for takeoff. I pressed a firm palm down on the leg to stop it.

"But...I think the piece lacks emotion."

I swallowed hard. "Emotion," I repeated.

Axel was peeking through the window again. I shot him a glare and turned my attention back to the drawing.

"That's what's so strong about these other works you've been doing, Leigh," said Nagori. "The nostalgia, the sadness. I want to feel...something. Right now when I look at this, all I feel is, huh, cool philosophy. But nothing stirs *here*—" He placed a hand over his sternum. "You see what I mean?"

I tried to swallow again, but my throat was dry enough to be splintered apart and used for kindling. "Yes. I see. I think."

"It really is a great concept. Don't scrap the idea—just try again. See if you can capture...more."

"More," I said, because I was turning into a goddamn echo machine.

"Right," said Nagori. "These links—that is a bracelet, yes? What made you want to draw it? Find the emotion."

I spent the weekend in Axel's basement with all my supplies, trying to *find the emotion*. The lighting wasn't great, but Mom was having one of her episodes. The slightest noise—even the mere turning of a sketchbook page or the light *scritch-scratch* of my pencil—would set off her temper.

"I can't *think* with your noisy," she would say in a mean voice.

Or, "Drawing *supposed to be* quiet activity, Leigh."

Or, "You turn the page so loud!"

It was better to escape, and Axel's made for the perfect haven.

I was redoing the picture I'd shown Nagori. It felt easier to start over from scratch, so all I had was a fresh sheet with light pencil outlining what I wanted.

Emotion, I scoffed. This was surrealism. What did he mean, *emotion*? This was just supposed to be about the fantastical merging with reality.

Axel sat in front of his keyboard with most of his back to me. Giant headphones hugged his ears, but I could see enough of his profile to tell that his eyes were closed. He curved in toward the keys, shoulders rounding as if to form a hollow in which he could collect the music.

I turned to a fresh page. My hand was moving fast, drawing Axel, doing bold and geometric lines for the keyboard, getting the sound and movement out in graphite.

I hadn't done anything realistic in a long while. I sank into the meditation as my pencil explored his body. The broad shoulders. The graceful elbows turning as his hands mapped the terrain of his piece. He was self-taught, but he looked beautiful and confident when he played. My mother repeatedly offered to teach him, but he refused to take a free lesson. I guess it felt too much like charity.

The sound of keys stopped and Axel swung around. I looked up at him, my hand hovering above the page.

"What?" he said.

"What?" I felt some strange and heated mix of guilt and embarrassment, like he'd caught me doing something bad.

"Why are you giving me that look?" he said.

"What look?" I prayed that he wouldn't come over and see. It was a quick study, but it was obvious what I'd been sketching. I'd done a decent job capturing the expression in his body.

His face cracked into a wry grin. "You were *drawing* me."

"Was not."

Axel stood up and I flipped my sketch pad shut.

"Let me see," he said, holding out his hands.

"No."

"Leigh, come on, why are you being all weird?"

"I'm not." I felt parrot green and five years old again. "I'm not being weird."

Even though I was. I *was* being weird. How many times had we sketched each other? How many times had we sat side by side, drawing each other's feet?

I guess the difference was, when he didn't know I was drawing him, it felt voyeuristic.

He laughed a little. "You are *totally* being weird."

I stood up and began packing away my pencils. I didn't really want to leave, but I also didn't want to continue this conversation.

"What color?" he said, and I paused.

I looked up at him, standing there beneath that sad basement lightbulb with his sleeves rolled up to his elbows. His expression was unreadable. I opened my mouth and hesitated against the truth.

Axel skipped toward me in a tackle that threw us both onto the couch. Most of my back landed against the seat, and Axel's body was on top of mine for a moment that lasted both forever and no time at all. I was so aware of his smell, of the fleshy inside of his arm grazing the exposed part of my midsection where my shirt had ridden up.

My sketch pad slipped between us—and before I could react, he was already holding it far away where I couldn't reach. My torso was pinned under the back of his right knee—not that I was fighting all that hard to be free of him. Axel was already turning the pages.

"Aha!" he said, triumphant, landing on the sketch.

I could see his expression from where I lay smushed into the corner of the couch, my neck uncomfortably bent. I saw the wide grin on his face, and I also saw the way it faded as self-consciousness seeped in.

He fell silent as he gazed at the picture. I wondered if he could see what I had allowed to crawl out of my heart and down my arm and out my fingers. The lines of his body sketched with such care and longing. The shadows in his skin filled in by a hand that wanted nothing more than to trace those dips and edges, those muscles and those angles.

"This is really good, Leigh," he said very quietly. "You've gotten a lot faster."

I felt his knee loosening above my midsection, and I pushed myself up into a properly seated position. His leg slid off me, taking with it the warmth and the thrill.

"Thanks." I felt a million miles away.

"Do you have any others?" he said.

"What do you mean?"

"Like"—he dropped his gaze—"have you drawn me before? When I didn't realize? I'd really like to see them."

It took a beat too long for me to process the question and then summon the best answer. "No." I wondered if he could see the lie burning in my face.

"Oh," he said.

For a moment I almost convinced myself that he sounded genuinely disappointed.

When I went home that night, I could still smell him from

when his body had covered mine like a blanket. I lay in bed, my fingers retracing the places on my body where he'd made inadvertent contact. I imagined an Axel who might touch me on purpose, who might touch *more* of me.

What would that feel like?

A memory bloomed like a flame, ablaze and sharper than everything: Axel's almost naked back on that summer night in that crappy hotel room. The tantalizing heat of his body as we almost spooned, that inch-thick layer of nothingness crackling between us.

My right hand ended up down between my legs and I wondered about sex. I thought of all the skin you saw in R-rated movies and the way bare limbs just slid together like they were made to be entwined. I thought of Axel, imagined us sitting on his couch and taking off our clothes.

I fell asleep full of wanting.

82

Why the hell did anyone ever invent a ticking clock?
I can't shut out the incessant sound. Everything lines up to match its demanding rhythm. My inhales and exhales. The pulse between my ears. That vague drumming that I'm almost certain is only in my head.

Tick. Tick. Tick. Tick.

Who'd have thought a clock would turn out to be my worst enemy?

Sometimes when Mom was cooking she sank into this deep pool of quiet, and it seemed like the clock in the kitchen grew louder and all her movements fell in sync with the ticking.

Whatever she was chopping, her hands took on a steady rhythm. Her lips pressing in concentration, eyebrows knitting toward each other. She would silently drift from one side of the counter to the other like a dazed cat, her limbs soft, her gaze slightly unfocused.

Tick. Tick. Tick. Tick.

How I wish I could rewind to one of those days and step up beside her as she julienned peppers, as she drained the water from a glassy pile of mung bean noodles, as she stirred a pot of soup. I would touch her elbow and ask what she was thinking about.

Was she happy? Was she sad?

Was she thinking about a red bird?

Tick. Tick. Tick. Tick.

My sketchbook is open to a fresh page on the bed, but I'm too restless to draw. Too anxious. It feels like the valves of my heart are jammed with muck, working extra hard to pump the blood. My lungs losing elasticity, fighting the air I'm trying to take in. My head fogged up all Antwerp blue.

I have two days, and two sticks of incense.

As I lean toward the nightstand to grab the matches and my last photograph from the box, my mother's cicada pendant swings to the side and thwacks me in the shoulder.

The cicada. The pendant she wore every single day of her life.

My fingers reach up to find the jade, feeling the carved ridges and the smoothness of the underside. There's the comforting weight of it hanging from my neck, the stone warm from sitting close to my heart.

My reluctance is smothering, the necklace heavy as an anvil.

I can't.

I should.

My fingers are trembling the slightest bit as I put the photograph back, because the pendant is so much more important—there's got to be something crucial in this piece of jade.

I unclasp the chain from my neck, feeling strangely certain now. My fingers trace the curves and edges of the carving one last time. After this, it'll be gone; the cicada will burn up, turn to gray silt, disintegrate.

I wish I had a longer piece of incense, but this'll have to do.

83

—SMOKE & MEMORIES—

There's my father, so young, stepping out of a cab. He's wearing a button-down shirt and a blazer. His hands cupping a bold bouquet of roses. He walks slowly, carefully, up the steps of an apartment building to the third floor. He checks the address in his pocket and presses the button in the frame of the entrance, which spews out the melodic trilling of robins.

"Doorbirds instead of doorbells," he mutters to himself, smiling a little.

My mother cracks open the door, bright-eyed and breathless. "You're here!" she exclaims. She looks nervous, one hand clutching the pendant against her sternum.

"I told you I'd come."

She inhales deeply. "Wait for a moment—"

From inside, behind her, I can hear the voices of my grandparents.

"Who is that?" they demand.

My mother turns away to answer. "There's someone I want you to meet."

Waigong appears behind her, and his face shifts from neutral to dismayed to disgusted. "Who is this?"

"He speaks Mandarin very well!" my mother says quickly, anxiously. "He wanted to come here to meet you and—"

"He is not coming in," says my grandfather in a terrible voice. "He is not welcome here."

My mother's face contorts and flashes with rage. "But you haven't—"

Waigong takes her by the elbow and nudges her out of the way. He doesn't even look at my father as he shuts the door.

I can't help the gasp that slides between my teeth, the cerise punch landing in my gut. How could my grandparents not even give Dad a chance? What was so wrong with him?

He lowers the flowers. He knocks, presses the bell again. There's no answer, only the sound of arguing from the other side. He sits down on the steps, settling in for a wait.

A burst of light, and the colors tilt.

Brian and Dory pushing through the doors of the courthouse and running out to greet their friends. Brian smiling so wide, carrying a huge black umbrella overhead. Dory's veil catching on a breeze, her jade cicada bouncing against her sternum. Her gaze slides downward for half a second, and in that moment there's the slightest hint of grief. A tug between the eyebrows. When she looks up again, her features have fixed themselves, and she's glowing with happiness once more.

One friend blows fat bubbles through a pink plastic wand. Another tosses rose petals. Brian and Dory laugh and grin, holding hands everywhere they go, like their new marriage is a lifeline to be tightly gripped. It's drizzling, but sun squints through the droplets. Someone shouts to look for the rainbow that's sure to come.

Darkness, and a spark.

My mother hums in the kitchen, wrapping dumplings. Chopsticks snatch up raw filling. Nimble fingers pinch the skins.

"Oof." She pauses to rub her large belly, smiling at the roundness that separates her from the table.

"Too bad you'll never meet your aunt Jingling," she says to the mound beneath her hand. "These dumplings were her favorite."

A burst of light.

My mother and my father, pausing in the middle of a hike. Trees around them tall and spotty. It's early morning—dew catches on their sneakers, stray blades of grass cling to their ankles. My mother cradles her belly, imagines her child floating in the hollow of a conch shell, bathing in gradients of sunrise.

"But think of our kid," says my father. "Think of her growing up missing a whole set of grandparents. Two people who are still alive. Imagine her in ten years, twenty years, resenting you for keeping her cut off. She'll be curious—anyone would be."

"Brian," my mother says sharply, "it is not for discussion. It is my decision. You do not understand."

He runs a hand through his hair and turns in a circle of frustration. "You're right. I don't."

"She will have everything else," says my mother, almost begging. "But I cannot do what you're asking."

The pain in her voice stabs at me, shards of something turquoise and broken lodging under my skin, jamming in my throat.

"Ever?" says my father.

My mother considers this. "One day, perhaps. I go to see them again. One day you and Leigh go to meet them. But I need time."

My father presses out a long, sighing breath. "Okay. Fine. One day."

New colors.

A baby bouncing over a knee above a familiar leather sofa. Across the room, deft hands mapping out black and white keys. A living room bursting with magenta warmth and dandelion cheer and all the hues of love, invisible but undeniably there.

I know that baby's face only because of the photographs hanging in my father's office. That's me. Little Leigh, daughter of Dory and Brian, back when all three of us were still in love with one another, before things had gone horribly wrong.

Or had things been wrong to begin with?

Flicker.

My mother stands in the kitchen with an apron wrapped around her. Her hair shoulder-length, the few white strands tinted red with her favorite henna dye. She pauses halfway through chopping a block of bean curd. The knife falls from her hand, tumbling heavily into the sink. Nobody's there to ask what's wrong. There is only my mother in the kitchen, hands shaking, brine edging out of her eyes. Eyes that see nothing but the knife.

Flash.

My mother, waving me out the door as I run to catch the yellow bus, and turning back to collapse on the sofa. The expression on her face like that of someone haunted.

Flash.

My mother in the basement, holding a bottle of OxyContin and a jug of bleach. She heard once that it takes ten seconds for something swallowed to reach the stomach. But how long to digest? How long if it's liquid?

Flash.

My mother, rising from her bed in the middle of the night. She walks quietly, slowly, avoiding the creaks in the floor. Down in the garage, she slides into the sedan and sits in the driver's seat, car keys biting into her palm. She's thinking. Debating. If she turns on the car. If she doesn't open the garage door. If no one in the house wakes, and she falls asleep at the wheel. The vehicle doesn't even have to move. She could sleep forever.

Flash.

My mother, on the floor of the bathroom, curled like a child, face pressed into the tiles, fingers stroking the carved wings of her jade pendant.

Flash.

My father, dragging his suitcase out the front door to leave for his first conference. His first week away from us. He kisses my mother and she smiles, but it's not real. Not a full smile. It doesn't shine in her face.

Dad doesn't notice. He's too excited. How does he not see?

He rolls his suitcase out to the waiting car and beams his grin at us while the driver loads the trunk. One last wave and he's pulling away.

Flash.

My mother, opening the back door and standing barefoot in the freshly fallen snow.

Her thoughts fluttering by like the pages of a book caught in a rough wind. Thoughts of the snow. Of how the cold is not so bad. The shivers will distract her from other things.

And after a while, she'll just fall asleep. Peaceful. Numb to the world. Dreaming one last dream in the hollow of a snow angel.

Flash.

The colors disappear. The light vanishes.

I hear a sob, and realize it's me. But when I touch my face, my cheeks are dry. I'm not actually crying. I've never felt more dried up in my life.

Long before I lost my mother, my mother lost her sister. My mother lost her parents—or at least, that's what she believed.

Believing is a type of magic. It can make something true.

Long before doctors put a label on her condition and offered slips of paper bearing the multisyllabic names of pharmaceuticals. Long before my father started leaving on his work trips.

Long before everything: She was already hurting.

84

I blink the memories away, and the world returns in colors made harsh by sleep deprivation.

Why is the smoke showing me all this? Why summon such grief, when I've already lost so much? So many of these things seem better off forgotten.

The ache of it all is stuck in my lungs.

I look down for the gray silt, but there is none. No dust, no ash.

Instead, there's the jade, sitting in my palm, looking the same as always. It wasn't burned up. The relief slams into my chest, and I suck in a deep breath.

It's still here. I get to keep it.

The only evidence of the incense and the memory is that the silver chain looks scorched. Sections of it dark and oxidized. But the links still hold strong. I clasp it around my neck once again, glad for the pendant's comforting weight, glad that after everything, I still at least have this.

85

WINTER, SOPHOMORE YEAR

Winter break started with the chain of Mom's cicada necklace somehow falling apart. She was bent in half, reaching for something in the cabinet under the kitchen sink, and the jade went clattering to the floor, no rhyme or reason. She immediately went out and bought a new chain until she could get the original fixed, but it wasn't the same. The silver tone was a bit too shiny, the length of it a little too short, and the links themselves boxy in a way that just didn't look right.

It felt like an omen.

I would think back on that later and realize it should've flagged my attention that I was already looking for something to blame.

Omen or not, it was a weird break. Axel went to visit family in San Juan for the first time in years, and Caro was snowboarding again. Dad was actually supposed to be home for a decently long stretch, and Christmas Day started off promising.

Dad pulled up a chair as Mom was wrapping dumplings.

"I'll help." He took a stack of the doughy skins and began scooping filling into the centers, folding in their edges.

Mom's face looked brighter than it had in weeks. She even hummed a little—a few lilting lines of melody that I recognized from one of her favorite sonatas.

I couldn't remember the last time I saw Dad help with the cooking. I loved watching them together, my mother's adept hands pinching off three dumplings for every one he clumsily finished.

On the kitchen counter, I opened my sketch pad to a fresh page. The charcoal was between my fingers and sweeping across the blankness, capturing knuckles dusty with flour, a tray of raw dumplings.

I listened to the rhythm of them plopping onto the tray, the light *scritch-scratch* of my stick, the way we all inhaled and exhaled in tandem.

And then, of course, the moment ended. Dad turned to see what I was doing. "Leigh, why don't you put that away. Come spend quality time with your parents."

I tried to push down the fight that was already rising up. "Uh, I *am* spending time with you. I'm right here, as you can see."

"It's not good to always be so internally focused," said Dad. "Come help with the dumplings."

I shook my head at him. "I'm drawing *you and Mom*. Generally I draw things that are *outside* of myself. How is that *internally focused*?"

"Art is an independent pursuit," Dad said, the tone of his voice changing, too. "And this is a family occasion. We need you to stop drawing and participate."

"*Participate?* Seriously? Like this is a goddamn classroom?"

"Watch your language when you're—"

"Stop," Mom said quietly, and the syllable shut us down like a finger on a remote. "No fighting. It's Christmas." Her flour-dusted hand flew to her chest for a moment, landing too low before she remembered the necklace was shorter now, that her jade pendant sat higher up.

I flipped my sketch pad shut and went upstairs, where I hunched in the corner and tried to draw new things to show Nagori.

When I came back down later to eat and open presents, Dad pretended like the exchange had never happened.

Christmas carols were playing. The tree was blinking its multicolored lights. I went first, handing each of my parents a flat, rectangular package. It'd actually been a long time since I'd made drawings for Christmas.

"Oh, Leigh," said my mother. "This is beautiful."

I'd put hers in a simple black frame so she could hang it up. Dad's was just flat, sprayed with fixative and stored between pieces of archival tissue.

"Wow," he said. "Great."

It was hard to get a read on what he actually thought.

"I didn't frame yours, since you travel so much—I thought, well. Maybe you'd want to bring it with you or something." It sounded silly now that I was saying it out loud. I could tell he didn't love it. It probably was just making him worry even more about my future.

"You make us look so real," Mom said. "There's no photograph like this."

I shook my head. "It just came from a memory."

"I actually remember that day," Dad said, surprising me.

"I do, too," said Mom.

I'd drawn—and then duplicated—the three of us on a playground in Village Park, where we used to go every night in the summers to take walks and throw a Frisbee around. There'd been this one evening when we found the playground totally empty and we took over the seesaw. Mom and Dad sat opposite each other on the seats, and I stood on top of the plank in the center, trying to stay balanced while they went up and down.

No colors. And not even charcoal. I'd done this one in the clean lines of a pencil. Mom throwing her head back, laughing. Dad with his goofy grin. Me, wobbling in the middle, on the edge of a smile.

"Thank you," said Mom. "I will hang over the piano."

She went next. Dad got a merino wool sweater custom-made by a knitter who was internet famous. I got an amazing set of high-end gouache paints that I'd been eyeing for forever.

"You use colors now, okay?" she said. "No color in your pictures for so long. But now you have good paint."

I hugged her and promised I would try them out.

And then it was Dad's turn. He surprised Mom with a little black velvet box. My mother didn't wear much jewelry, except for that jade cicada, which still looked totally off. For a moment, I worried that Dad had gotten her something to replace it, but then she popped open the box, and fat blue pieces of topaz winked at us—a whole string of them in a silver bracelet.

"Wow," said Mom. She seemed speechless; when had he last given her something so shiny?

"Your turn, Leigh," Dad said quickly, maybe because he was feeling weird about the splurge of a present, too.

Mine came in a box. It had a nice heft to it. I tore at the reindeer wrapping and picked the top off, and in the middle of a bunch of tissue paper was a book. It had a white cover and neon block-letter words.

FIGURE OUT
WHAT YOU'RE
DESTINED FOR

I felt the corners of my mouth already lifting into a laugh in the same second that I realized Dad wasn't joking. This was *actually* his gift to me.

"Um, thanks," I said, fighting really hard not to make the word a question.

"Look inside," said Dad. He seemed almost giddy.

I turned through the first few pages until I found what he wanted me to see. On the title page, the words DESTINED FOR had been circled a million times and were sandwiched between handwritten text. On the left it said, *For Leigh, who is,* and to the right of the title was scrawled, *GREAT THINGS!!!!*

The author's name—Wilson Edmund Sharpe IV—was crossed out by a thick black marker. The flourish of a signature had been added below that, barely readable but for the sharp edges of the Roman numeral, *IV.*

"I met him at a conference," said Dad. "He was promoting this book, and when I heard him speak, I knew I had to get you a signed copy. The guy lit up the whole room. You know, I showed him a picture of us, and he said you look like you have your mother's genes and must be very driven. He's right, of course—"

"Excuse me? I look like I have my mother's genes? So he was stereotyping," I said flatly.

Dad cocked his head. "What do you mean?"

I pulled out my fingers for air quotes. "I 'must be driven' because I'm half Asian? Do you know how often I get that? Or how often people ask if I have a 'tiger mom'?"

My father paused for a long moment. "Well. At the time I didn't think he meant it that way. Really, though, I bet this will be life-changing for you. Give it a read, see if it helps you figure out what you want to do."

"What I want to do," I repeated slowly.

"You know," said Dad, "help you find a direction."

"Okay," I said. "Thanks."

He looked all around the room, as if there were answers to be gleaned from the air. He clasped his hands together. "You don't like it."

I shrugged slowly. "I don't think I *need* it? But I . . . appreciate the gift?"

Was I being horrible? I couldn't tell. But the fact that he refused to believe in me was wearing me down. I was so very tired of these conversations.

"What exactly do you see yourself doing? In, say, five years. Twenty years. The rest of your life."

"Making art." It felt good to say it out loud. "I've been thinking that . . . maybe I'd want to go to art school."

"Leigh, you need to be serious."

I wanted to scream, but I didn't. "I *am* serious."

"And how are you supposed to make a living with that?"

I looked at Mom, who was watching our back-and-forth with a lost expression on her face. "I don't know. I could always teach?"

"You need a stable career. Something that will provide you baseline happiness."

"*Art* makes me happy," I said sharply.

Dad opened his mouth again, but thank god Mom interrupted him.

"Don't talk about this now," she said. "We should be enjoy Christmas."

We moved on to playing Uno, with Dad and me speaking to each other as little as possible. I found myself wishing he were flying out to another conference soon. I longed for the way the house expanded each time he stepped out the front door, filling with new space and air for me to breathe.

Early the next morning while my parents still slept, I sat in the kitchen drinking mug after mug of peppermint hot chocolate, watching the cat stare out the window. The quiet was getting to me. It felt like it was taking Axel nine hours to respond to every text. I tried not to be offended; he had a big family, and apparently they had a ton of holiday traditions.

I thought about how different things had been last Christmas. How Dad had been gone, but somehow that had been better. How Axel spent winter break helping me sort through those boxes.

And with that thought, my feet carried me downstairs. I wasn't sure what I wanted to do, but I was restless and I was remembering the bracelet, the Emily Dickinson book. I'd taken those up to my bedroom, along with that black-and-white photograph of the two little girls. The other stuff was still where I'd found it.

In the basement, the boxes were exactly how we'd left them, open and askew. There were even letters on the floor from when Axel and I had separated them into piles. A part of me wondered at my carelessness in leaving these out. Anyone who'd come down would've seen immediately that I'd been digging, snooping.

Maybe that's what I'd been hoping for. Maybe I'd thought that if my mom or dad saw what I'd been looking at, they'd confront me, open up a dialogue. Finally talk to me about my grandparents.

But nobody had been down here. Not in an entire year.

That night I let myself out onto the porch and stood on the steps, face angled up toward the cloudless sky. The moon was a fat, glowing coin. It had a face. Kind, and almost smiling. I wondered if my grandparents in Taiwan were gazing up at the same plate of light, trying to make eye contact with that pale and beaming man.

86

How am I supposed to find the bird? How are these frag-ments of the past supposed to help?

Forty-seven goddamn days since the stain. In the morning it'll be forty-eight. I'm almost out of time.

Earlier I made Feng translate for me and ask Waipo if there's anywhere else we might visit. If there's a place my mother loved that we haven't gone. Waipo shook her head, said that we've gone everywhere she knows.

Part of me wonders if she's lying to me, and then I feel the need to shake myself, because why would I think that? There's a knot of resentment somewhere in the back of my skull. Would my mother have turned into a bird if my grandparents hadn't been so against her marriage to my father? In their faces I try to search out a hint of that old disapproval...but all I see is exhaustion. Skin gone spotted and soft. Wrinkles that trace the paths of something that might be regret.

Even when they smile, there's something sad lingering in the corners of their mouths.

I think of my mother saying to my father, *One day you and Leigh go to meet them. But I need time.*

One day. As in now.

My father's sigh hisses in my ears.

My father. Dad.

Maybe he's the missing piece. Maybe if the bird sees that he's here, with me, then she'll come down. She'll tell us.

I want you to remember

I give myself a minute to think about it, until the certainty settles over me disazo scarlet, a color as bold as her feathers. Then I draft the email.

FROM: leighinsandalwoodred@gmail.com
TO: bsanders@fairbridge.edu
SUBJECT: Urgent!!!!!!

Dad, I need you to come back here ASAP. Please. It's an emergency.

87

Right as I'm about to close out of my email, my phone chimes. At first I think with grim satisfaction that Dad's replied already, because he has the tendency to freak out and respond within milliseconds.

But it turns out to be a new message from Axel.

FROM: axeldereckmoreno@gmail.com
TO: leighinsandalwoodred@gmail.com
SUBJECT: (no subject)

So much happened in the winter. So much I wish
we would talk about. I feel like I somehow failed.
   Something I've been wanting to ask you for
forever: What the hell happened at Winter Formal?

The email spins a web of muddy colors inside me, smearing everything stil de grain brown.

Sometimes Axel could be so dense it made me want to shake him. As if I were the one who'd gone off and started dating someone else. Someone awful. Twice.

Screw Axel. And screw Leanne. I hope the two of them are happy.

The rage trickles down into my hands.

I flip through my sketchbook and tear up the drawings I've made for him on this trip, listening to that coarse, satisfying noise as the paper rips. Shredding each of them, smudging the pieces with the oil of my fingers.

What the hell happened? *You* tell *me*, Axel.

And then my brain is going there, dredging up those recent months again, churning them to the surface, remembering.

88

WINTER, SOPHOMORE YEAR

We turned the corner into the new year. The break ended, and it was announced that for the first time ever, our school was holding a Winter Formal at the end of February.

"I'm totally taking Cheslin," Caro declared at lunch a week later.

"Really?" I said. "You actually want to go to that?"

"Why not?" she said.

"It's...I mean. It's just another school dance."

"It's more than any old dance," Caro said. "It's a formal. It's like *prom*, except open to everyone."

I shrugged. "I'm not even sure I'll go to prom."

Axel slid into his seat and shoved three fries into his mouth.

"What about you, Axel?" said Caro. "Are you going to Winter Formal?"

I was expecting him to make a face and roll his eyes, but he didn't. His chewing slowed. He swallowed and made a show of popping open his Snapple and taking a few gulps. He bit into three more fries.

"Take your time," Caro said drily.

He shrugged. But what he finally said was, "Maybe. There might be plans for that in the works."

I had to physically hold my jaw back from falling open. Axel? At a dance?

Caro raised her eyebrows. "You move *fast*, dude."

It was her reaction that made me rewind and play back his words in my head.

What did he mean, *plans*? Did he have a date?

But it didn't come up again, and after that, I forgot Winter Formal was even happening. There were other things to worry about, like my portfolio. Like how each day I dreaded going home, where I knew I would find all the shades drawn, everything dark, the air stale and thick with the stench of cat litter that desperately needed sifting. Mom's current default was insomnia and migraines, which made her either explosively angry or quiet as a slug.

Dad was still traveling, though not as frequently as he used to. During the periods that he was home, his new mission was to convince me that art school was a bad idea.

"Don't you see how you'd be limiting yourself?" he said as I swept a charcoal stick across the page.

"I could go to a regular school that has a good art program *and* other things, too," I said.

But it seemed that if I compromised the slightest bit, he pushed harder.

"What if you went into the sciences? You're always

spouting off random science facts, like remember when you were telling me all about pigments?"

The frustration was heating up my face. "Because I'm interested in scientific things that have to do with *art*. Do you even remember what my science grades look like?"

"Well, you could even study, like, accounting or economics—and just take an art class for fun. You don't want to box yourself into an impractical profession—"

"Tina majored in philosophy and now she has her marketing job, which she says has nothing to do with her college degree."

"There are always exceptions. But imagine how difficult it must've been for Tina to get that position."

"And what about *you*, Dad? Are you going to tell me that your East Asian Studies major was the most practical thing?"

He opened and closed his mouth a few times. "At the very least, it offered solid options for working in academia."

It wasn't like art school was my number one goal in life, but the more Dad pushed against it, the more I wanted to prove him wrong. Wrong about something. Wrong about me.

Mom was never around for these conversations. I started to wonder if Dad purposely waited until she wasn't in the room. Maybe he thought he'd hurt her feelings, because she *had* pursued her art. She embodied the exact opposite of what he wanted me to do.

"The only people who succeed in artistic fields are the ones who are incredibly lucky *and* phenomenally talented," Dad said another day. "And even then, they struggle. It's not going to be good for you."

"Got it, Dad. You don't think I'm talented enough. Or lucky enough, or whatever."

"It's also hard work, Leigh. Have you ever worked so hard at something there was nothing else you could do? *Truly* worked hard?"

I thought of the art show in Berlin. I thought of Nagori singling me out, warning me the months would disappear quickly. He'd been right about time. And Dad was right about the work. I hadn't been working hard enough. Was I capable of it?

That last conversation with him lit the match: I was going to prove my father wrong. I could work hard. If Nagori believed I was good enough, I was good enough. But I would do everything in my power to be better than good. I wanted to be one of the best.

Dad flitted off to the other side of the world again and I bought a new art pad, larger than what I normally worked on. When I sat down to begin, though, I found I couldn't think. The darkness in my house pressed up against me. When Mom was quiet, our home felt like a pit deep in the ground. When she was loud and irrationally angry, our home was a storm cloud holding tightly on to all its thunder.

While Dad was unbearable with his arguments about art school, his being home seemed to buffer the storm, quieting my mother. I was enormously glad but also hated to have him be gone again.

It was on a Wednesday that Axel came and met me at my house right as I was getting off the late bus.

"Make good progress today?" he said, gesturing toward the art case tucked under my arm.

I shrugged. "Nagori seems to be liking the direction better."

"Cool," he said.

It wasn't like it was weird to see him, but there was just something strange in the way that he stood there, watching me unlock the front door. He followed me inside, kicking off his shoes.

"Is your mom upstairs?" he asked.

Most of the lights were off and it was quiet. "Um, I assume so."

He came to sit on the sofa so that he was as far away from me as possible. I heard the inhalation before he spoke, as if he were steeling himself for something. "You planning to go to the thing on Friday?"

I had no idea what he was talking about. "What thing?"

"You know. Winter Formal."

I felt my body freeze up, and my face must've looked funny because then he said, "Are you okay?"

"Uh, yeah. I mean. No, I wasn't planning to go."

"Why not?" he said. He was staring so hard at my feet I wondered if there was something wrong with them. I rubbed my toes together self-consciously. "We could go together."

"To Winter Formal?" I said, not certain I'd heard correctly. He nodded.

I heard the floorboards upstairs creaking slightly, which meant my mother had gotten herself out of bed. The last thing I wanted was for her to hear this conversation. I pushed up off the couch.

"Sure," I said.

He stood up, too. "Great."

My expression managed to stay neutral as he left, but the moment the door closed I seemed to lose control over my body. I burned like a star and smiled until my cheeks were sore.

Later, the terror settled in: I was going to a dance. How did dances work? And what if I did something wrong?

❧

I had no idea what people were supposed to wear to this kind of thing, and it didn't help that I basically had only one day to figure it out. In the end, Caro got Cheslin to lend me some of her dresses, and I chose one that was delicate and airy, the aquamarine chiffon draping down to my ankles.

I stood in front of the full-length mirror as I blow-dried my hair, trying to get it to fall straighter.

What had Axel meant by asking me to go with him? Were we just going as friends, or was this something more?

He was weirdly quiet when he picked me up, and he stayed that way even as we got to school. He didn't say anything about my dress, or the lip gloss I'd taken from my mother's drawer. I wondered if he hated it all.

I studied him out of the corner of my eye. Over his black button-down, he had on a dark vest with subtle gray stripes, and a silvery bow tie. He'd used some kind of product in his hair.

The lights of the gym were dimmed, and someone had strung white lights up in the creases of the ceiling. We found Caro immediately—she stood out in her tuxedo dress.

"You look amazing, Leigh," she said.

"You really do," Cheslin agreed. She was still a bit shy around us, but she smiled sweetly at me, her fingers tugging at the skirt of her vintage lace dress. "You should keep that. It's an amazing color on you."

"Really?" I said.

"Definitely. It even goes with that color in your hair."

"Wait a sec—did you two come *together?*" Caro's gaze bounced back and forth between me and Axel.

My face went hot.

"I'm gonna go get a soda," said Axel. "You want anything?" I barely had time to shake my head before he vanished into the crowd.

"Did you?" Caro pressed.

"I'm not sure it's what you think it is," I said, my stomach starting to twist. I didn't really want to talk about this. At least not here, with a couple hundred other people around us.

But then the DJ put on a crowd favorite, some song that I barely recognized, and Cheslin grabbed at Caro's arm to go dance.

Axel came and found me again. There was no soda in his hand, but I didn't say anything about it. We leaned against a wall and talked for a long while about silly things in an awkward, stilted way. My fingers were itching for my sketchbook. Why hadn't we thought to bring a couple pads and pencils?

When Axel excused himself to go to the bathroom, I went and found myself a chair so I could sit.

Why were we here at all?

I thought of my mother alone in the house, eating cold leftovers by herself in the kitchen. Or worse, not eating at all, but back in bed and wrapped up in a million blankets.

I thought of the new pieces of art I'd started that I hoped might come out good enough for Nagori to finally say I was finished with my portfolio.

It occurred to me after a while that Axel had to be done in the bathroom and was maybe having trouble finding me again. I checked my phone, but there were no texts, and I couldn't be sure if it was the reception crapping out. Just as I left the gym and started toward the main foyer, where I could get a better signal, I heard a voice I recognized. It sounded almost hysterical.

"I can't believe you came with *her*. I thought you said there wasn't anything between you two."

I couldn't help myself. I tipped my head just enough to look around the corner. It was Leanne Ryan.

And she was talking to Axel.

"There really isn't," he said. He sounded absolutely certain.

As quickly as possible, I made my way back to the gym. Everyone was dancing in a long train at that point, and I couldn't stand to be there any longer. I pushed out through the back door into the biting February cold and rounded the edge of the wall in search of privacy.

"Oh, hey, Leigh."

My eyes were stinging and everything felt greenish brown, muddy and cold, and the last thing I wanted was to interact with another human. I squinted to see who was standing beneath the outdoor lamp. It was a guy from Nagori's art class last year. A senior. It took me a second to remember his name: Weston.

"Hey," I said.

"It's pretty ridiculous in there, huh?" he said.

I was trying really hard not to shiver. "Yup."

"Hey," he said, "are you cold?" Before I could answer, he took off his jacket and slung it over my shoulders.

"Uh, thanks."

He leaned close to me to reach into a jacket pocket and pull out a steel flask. "You can't have this, though," he said, chuckling. He unscrewed the top and took a swig.

The flask made me nervous, but I tried to smile the feeling away.

"Just kidding," he said. "You can have some if you want."

"No thanks, I'm good," I said.

"You're good?" he said.

"Yeah."

"Nah," said Weston very quietly. "You're beautiful."

It was the two words I'd been hoping Axel might say when I ducked into his car. Or when we walked through the parking lot toward the gym. Or just at some point tonight. It was strange, now, to hear it from someone else.

"Thanks." I looked down.

The cold was cutting through the jacket and I was starting to shiver again. Weston pressed close and started rubbing his palms up and down my arms.

"You ever been kissed?" he said.

The question caught me totally off guard. I should've left then, but he held a strange fascination for me. He was so forward, in a way that Axel never was.

And I was terribly curious what kissing was actually like.

"No," I told him. "I haven't."

I guess I knew what was coming. His face loomed close, his lips first finding the edges of mine before sliding in toward the center. He was eager with his tongue, and he didn't taste great. There was a filminess in his mouth and an unpleasant tang that must've been the alcohol.

He was a little breathless as he pulled away. "You're so beautiful, you know? You're, like, exotic."

Every muscle in my body went taut. "I'm not," I said flatly. "I'm American. That's not exotic."

He raised his hands. "Didn't mean to offend. I'm just saying, you're gorgeous."

Weston leaned in again, but I moved aside before he could make contact. I handed his jacket back to him and turned away.

Axel was standing right next to the door when I stepped back into the gym, like he'd known that that was where I would be. Had he seen me with Weston? Every inch of me filled with rhodamine red.

"I'm ready to go whenever you are," he said, not meeting my eyes.

"Oh, sure," I said. "We can go now."

If I'd thought the ride to the formal was weird, the ride back was worse. Axel said nothing at all to me until he pulled into my driveway, at which point the only words he spoke were "See ya."

Upstairs, I shed Cheslin's dress and fell back on my bed spread eagle. I ran my fingers over my lips and felt my stomach curling tighter and tighter. There was some strange misery twisting inside me, and it took me a long time to figure out what it was.

For the last five years, I'd been convinced that Axel would be my first kiss.

89

Sleep.

Heavy, empty, clear, dark sleep. Buttery and soft and gentle and delicious sleep.

Melting into the blackest black. Thank goodness.

First comes the laughter. It's a bright and melodic sound. Happy as a fresh bouquet.

It echoes.

Echoes.

Echoes.

And somewhere in the echoing it begins to change. The melody warps. The laughter stumbles and chokes and slips into a sob. The quietest sob. But it gets louder, turns hoarse and gasping.

"*Leigh*," the voice cries.

And the blackest black begins to fade. It starts to glisten. The color shifting and turning until it's the deepest red. The slick, wet, pulsing red of an artery letting go.

90

The sun rises. Forty-eight days.

Dad hasn't responded to the email. I wonder if his phone is dead. I wonder if he got so caught up talking with a colleague or working on some project that he's lost track of time.

When I slide out of bed, everything blackens and blurs; the floor shakes just the tiniest bit. Soft morning light casts my shadow onto the wall, and I see my silhouette morph into a winged beast. The wings stretch wide, and just as suddenly they fold in again. My shadow shrivels back down to the shape of myself.

I can still smell the blood. I can still hear the sobbing.

Only a dream only a dream only a dream.

"Leigh."

My eyes sting and my head hurts. I need more sleep—

No, I'll sleep after I've found my mother.

Open the door and a weird smell hits me in the face, dark and earthy and aged. I step slowly into the hall. That scent gathers in the corners, trying to stick my attention. It's got me—I have to find the source. The smell reels me in, down the hallway and toward the bathroom, where it's the strongest. Someone left the door open, and I can hear a waterfall roar before I even step inside.

The water is crashing and steam rises above the shower curtain, which has been pulled all the way across the bathtub.

"Hello?"

Nobody answers me. What am I going to find back there?

Mucky dread pools in my stomach. I count to three, and yank the curtain aside.

Water...and blood.

No, not blood. What my eyes are seeing is not liquid. It's not puddling or congealing. There in the bottom of the tub is a thick layer of feathers, dark and drenched, sticky and shining red. The water drums them flat with hard *splats* that make me cringe. I wonder if there are enough feathers down there to coat an entire bird.

"Waipo," I call over my shoulder. *"Waipo!"* I hear her shuffling down the hall as fast as she can.

My grandmother's still in her pajamas. *"Shenme?"* She blinks the sleep out of her eyes, looks down at the tub and back at me. Her forehead knits tightly together.

I remind myself: *It's not blood. Just feathers.* But the image of blood is still there in my mind, stuck like gunky residue. The tub still looks grisly.

My grandmother places her hands on my shoulders; she can see the panic in my face.

I don't understand the meaning of a bathtub full of feathers. I don't want this to be some kind of goodbye message. An ending to the note my mother never finished.

Where the hell is the bird?

"*Lai chi zaocan,*" says my grandmother. *Come eat breakfast.*

Doesn't she see all the feathers? She smiles at me uncertainly, gesturing in the direction of the dining table.

"*Wo bu e,*" I tell her. *I'm not hungry.*

I pull on my sneakers and let myself out of the apartment. Is this what it's like to go crazy? Why can't Waipo see the feathers?

Am I just completely losing it?

The air is so wet and sticky I immediately begin dripping with sweat. The morning light pale and watery . . . and shattered. Broken into a million pieces. Everything outside the apartment cracked, like someone took a sledgehammer to the world. The breakages are marked by inky black. Jagged lines stretch across the sky. The clouds, cracked. The trees, cracked. My grandparents' alley, cracked, ready to crumble at any moment. With each step I take, the cracks in the ground double, triple, black lines fissuring outward, the sound like ice breaking.

I make my way to the park slowly. Even the people I pass look broken. Their mopeds about to fall apart. Their bodies shattered like mirrors, heads like crushed eggshells. The inky lines run down their noses and mouths, but they don't even seem to notice.

There's a noise high above me. I look up to see something slowly falling my way, drifting a little. It's a deep dark red. A perylene maroon.

A feather.

It lands in my outstretched palm. Something is unlocked by my catching it. The sky turns purple. It begins to rain feathers. Every shade of red. Scarlet and merlot and opera rose and

Venetian and ruby and mahogany and sangria and blood and currant reds. Long, sharp contour feathers, fluffy down feathers, even the small, hairlike filoplumes.

I run along the sidewalk collecting them, gathering them off the ground, plucking some out of the air, taking all the ones I can before they're stolen away by a breeze.

Why are these falling? Where is the bird?

The thought hits me: *I've broken something.*

What if I wasn't meant to unlock all those memories? What if those things were supposed to stay tucked away, hidden and eventually forgotten?

Is this what my mother—before she turned into a red and winged beast, back when she still wove magical worlds over the piano keys, and delighted in the look of a perfectly done waffle, and called my name in her warm bismuth-yellow way—is this what she would've wanted? For me to chase after ghosts? For me to uncover whatever answers I could, and try to stitch together the broken pieces of my family history?

I think of Emily Dickinson, asking her sister to burn all her words.

I think of my mother's note.

~~I want you to remember~~

Maybe Mom crossed that out because she changed her mind.

Maybe I wasn't supposed to do all this, and the cracks are her way of striking out all that's left.

It begins to rain. All the colors swirl together like a dirty paintbrush plunging into a cup of water.

91

I sit in a shattered park, beside shattered trees, under a shattered sky. I even feel the bench crunching when I shift. Rainwater snakes its way through the crevices of the broken ground. The only thing that hasn't cracked is my own body. My limbs are whole, unscathed. I'm the last person out here who isn't about to crumble.

In my left hand, a bouquet of the feathers that fell from the sky. I bury my face in them. They're soft and buttery, just like my mother's hair used to be. Warm, springy, with a hint of coconut. They don't have the wet and rotting musk of the red-filled tub. They smell like Mom. The way she smelled in life.

"Those are some beautiful feathers."

Feng's standing next to my bench. I didn't expect to see her here. She's not broken, either—a huge relief. I'm not alone.

"Mind if I sit?" she says.

"Go ahead," I tell her.

"I've only got a few minutes, actually. Then I have to go run an errand."

"Okay."

Feng takes a deep breath and lets it back out in a slow sigh. "I like to come here, too. It's so peaceful. The mosquitoes don't even bother me anymore."

"It's been forty-eight days," I tell her.

Even though I've never told her I was counting, I can tell by the expression on her face that she knows exactly what I'm talking about.

"I came all the way to Taiwan to find the bird. But what if I don't? I'm almost out of time."

"Are you sure she wants to be found?" Feng says gently.

"Not anymore."

"What are you planning to do if you find her?"

The question annoys me. "How am I supposed to know? It's not exactly like I intended for all this to happen. She's the one who sent me a box of clues. She basically *told* me to come."

"Maybe that's all she wanted," says Feng. "Maybe it's enough that you're here."

I shake my head. "I have to find her."

"I have faith that you will," says Feng. She stands. "I'm really sorry to cut this short."

"No, it's fine."

"You'll find her. I know you will. But when you do, promise me you'll let her go."

"What?" I look up.

"Let her go. Let her be. That's the greatest gift you can offer a ghost."

The words echo in my head, titanium white, turning and turning. *Let her go. Let her be.*

Feng hesitates for a long moment. This time, when her voice comes out, it sounds just as cracked as everything around us. "I saw the bird, Leigh."

"What?"

"She spoke to me. She told me to go home."

"Go home?" I repeat. "Why did she talk to you? And what—are you going to listen to her? Are you going to leave? Where is 'home'?"

"I don't know. I kind of like it here." She smiles at me. "But anyway. Don't worry about it for now."

I have no idea what to say to this. I'd kind of thought that her home was here. That she'd...settled.

"I have to go run my errand. Goodbye, Leigh."

I look up at her. Her head and limbs and body solid and bright against a shattered, cracked world.

She smiles. "See you later."

As she walks away, I note how quietly she moves, so small and so light that the broken ground doesn't make a single noise beneath her footsteps.

I turn on my phone. No new email from my father. My thumb pulls down on the screen to refresh.

Nothing.

Refresh again.

The chime of a new message. I straighten up; the wood creaks treacherously. But when the new email loads, it's not from Dad.

FROM: axeldereckmoreno@gmail.com
TO: leighinsandalwoodred@gmail.com
SUBJECT: (no subject)

I almost don't click into it, because I'm still not sure how to feel about his last email. But curiosity gets the best of me. It turns out to be another one of those messages that has no words. Only a picture. A watercolor he made—I immediately recognize his style. But I can't figure out when he would have painted me like this.

Because in the picture, I'm sitting curled up on his dusty tweed couch, wearing his favorite hoodie, hugging a giant bowl of popcorn, my face open and luminous and full of laughter. The stripe in my hair is blue, but I've done blue so many times that that tells me nothing.

Something about the way he painted me is so incredibly intimate. The colors soft and sensual. The careful strokes highlighting the curves of my thighs and the angles of my face.

Heat rises to my cheeks, thinking of him staring at me so closely. As if his brushes were hands that had traced every part of me.

I miss him. I miss the way things used to be. I miss sitting close enough to feel the heat of his body, smell his shampoo. Being able to tease him. Knowing his every thought just by the slightest twitch of his lips or the gleam in the corner of his eye. I miss the ease and the warmth. And the history. Everything between us that made us, *us*.

92

SPRING, SOPHOMORE YEAR

A part of me had hoped that with the seasons changing and the days growing longer, other things would melt away with the snow. Like my mother's increased moodiness, which seemed to be dictated as much by the taste of the air as it was by her migraines. And the weirdness between me and Axel, still lingering from Winter Formal.

But it only got worse. I started to feel like I could no longer just walk into the Moreno house. I still saw Axel during art, but that was basically it. And Leanne had started eating at our table, which pretty much ruined lunch for me.

I let my portfolio take over—no art project had ever so consumed my life. I worked late into the nights and often fell asleep atop loose pieces of charcoal, waking up with my skin and clothes totally smudged and stained. I swam deep into the drawings until it seemed that all I breathed was the dust trailing my careful fingers, and everything in my vision became smears of black and gray.

I found my knuckles tracing things I never thought could be captured on paper. The delicate lines of my mother's depression. Shadowy resentment toward my father. The negative space of our family's gaps and divides. The bold, heavy wanting I had for Axel.

I made multiple drafts of everything, finessing my strokes, changing the light and dark, altering the focus. All I needed for the application were three strong pieces, just a sampling from a hypothetical series. Three pieces. It felt like a new mantra. *Just three good pieces.*

I emerged out of my sea of charcoal and paper just as the spring air was starting to boil. I traded my smock for a tank top and shorts and found myself down in Caro's basement for the first time in ages.

"Have you talked to Axel lately?" I asked.

"Sort of," Caro said. She sat on a stool in her basement, fiddling with the dials on an old camera. "You guys have been weird with each other."

"I know."

"Maybe you should talk to him about it," she said.

"I'm not sure he wants that. He's not the most confrontational." I'd been doing a quick pencil study of Caro and her long torso curving over the stool, but she moved and now the light was different. I turned to a fresh page.

"You should still try."

I shrugged, even though Caro was usually right about things.

"How are you and Cheslin doing?" I asked. Then I realized it sounded like I was comparing me and Axel to her and Cheslin. Except Axel and I had only ever been friends with a pathetic side of unrequited feelings. I chewed on the inside of my cheeks, hoping she didn't think anything of it.

"We're great," said Caro. She grinned a little. "We decided we're ready to . . . y'know. Go all the way."

"Wow," I said.

"I had this worry that we would outgrow each other. Sometimes that's just what happens, you know?"

I couldn't tell if she was also talking about me and Axel now, but I hated that thought. I didn't like the idea that he and I might one day not need each other.

I needed him. I needed him so much more than he knew.

"But things are good," Caro went on. "It's kind of scary how good."

"What do you mean, scary?"

Caro shrugged. "I mean. Our whole relationship is the payoff of being brave enough to go for something we both wanted. But we have to stay brave."

I felt simultaneously happy for her and sad for myself. *Brave* was a word I'd never really thought about in the context of relationships. But it was exactly what I wasn't. I wasn't brave enough to tell Axel how I felt.

"Hey, what happened with that portfolio Nagori was helping you with?" said Caro.

"I literally *just* sent it in," I said.

"Oh, awesome. I didn't realize you'd finished."

"I almost didn't think I would," I told her. It was true. The deadline had been just a few days ago, and I'd wasted so much time in the months leading up to it. I'd finally found my momentum, except that I'd had to pause whenever Dad was home. I slid my work under my bed and tried to avoid getting into an argument. He sat in the kitchen talking at me while I baked cookies or cleaned the fridge, keeping my hands busy to ward off the anxiety of not working on my art, my heart tattooing *just three pieces* against my ribs.

At some point in there, I'd cleaned up my crap, too. Beneath the piles of clothes and sketches and pencils, I'd once again unearthed the things we found in the basement. The bracelet. The Emily Dickinson book. The letters. The photograph.

Really, those had driven the rest of my portfolio.

"Hey, you're staying for dinner, right? My grandparents are over."

"Sure," I told her. "That'd be great."

As usual, Charles and Gaelle did their hopeless-romantic thing.

"I like Cheslin very much," Charles was telling Caro. He said Cheslin's name like it started with *Sh* instead of *Ch*. "She is smart. Beautiful, too."

Caro rolled her eyes a little. "Thanks, Papi."

Charles grinned. "One day maybe you will decide she would be a good life partner."

"Oh god," said Mel, "not the marriage talk."

Gaelle spooned bread pudding onto my plate. "And how are you, dear? How are those *wonderfully romantic* parents of yours?" She winked.

My stomach churned and I smiled weakly. "Um, good."

"What about that boy of yours?" said Mel.

For a second I thought she was talking about me kissing Weston, and I was both confused and terrified that anybody knew about it.

"Axel?" Mel added.

"*Mom*," said Caro, looking mortified.

That moment confirmed that Caro knew exactly how I felt about Axel, and worse, she and her mom and probably even her grandparents had talked about me and him. Him and me. They'd talked about Leigh and Axel, and maybe even how sad it was that Axel would never return Leigh's feelings. It was probably a dinner table topic, complete with Gaelle mewing sympathetically and Charles offering advice to an ear that was not present.

I felt sick.

As soon as dinner ended, I excused myself and headed for the door.

"I'm sorry," said Caro, following me down the hall. "I'm sorry, I'm sorry, I'm sorry."

"It's fine," I said, though I could barely look at her.

"I didn't actually directly say anything, but a couple months ago Mom just straight up asked me what was up with you and—"

"It's *fine*." *You and Axel.* That's what she'd been about to say. The phrase made me want to throw up. "I'm not mad," I told her, which was not a hundred percent true.

"Listen," she said. "While we're on this subject."

I groaned and rolled my eyes.

"No, really. There's something I need to tell you. Axel and Leanne got back together."

I blinked at her, stunned.

"*She'd* actually asked *him* to go to Winter Formal, and there was a whole kerfuffle over that. So it's not like ... a particularly sudden development. I just thought you should know."

The words punched me in the gut. The expression on Caro's face was so terrible, and I understood then that this was something she'd been hiding from me. She looked like she was in agony.

It was nowhere near how I felt.

"Wow," I said. "Okay."

"Leigh?" said Caro.

"That's. That's great. How long has it been?"

"Kind of a long while now," she said. "They've been... playing it down at school. But Axel told me."

I scoffed. "Why would they do that? Why bother?"

"Are you okay?" said Caro.

"I'm just peachy," I told her.

"Really? Truly? You're being honest?"

Why was everyone in my life so demanding? "Really," I said, just to get her off my case.

"Okay, then promise me something."

I sighed. "What?"

"Let's go to Fudge Shack tomorrow? Please?"

I shook my head at how random that was. But it seemed she thought that going to get fudge together could reset things. "Okay. Fine."

"Three o'clock," she said. "Okay? Just meet me there. We'll get maple walnut. Your favorite. And they'll have their Saturday Sundae samples."

I didn't remind her that maple walnut was actually Axel's favorite. Not mine. "See you then."

I should've known what was going to happen.

I walked to Fudge Shack because I didn't want to ask anyone for a ride. It was only twenty minutes from my house, and they went by fast enough. I had earbuds plugged into my phone, and

twenty minutes was almost exactly how long it took me to listen through all four of Axel's Lockhart Orchard tracks twice.

Inside, it was packed. I remembered why I hated going
there on weekends. The Saturday Sundae samples were over-
hyped, but everyone went for them. It was the only place in
town that offered samples in actual miniature cones. Plus they
had good seating options. On a normal day, at least. Today
every table was full.

I did a circuit to see if Caro was already sitting somewhere
and ended up finding Axel. He leaned over one of the window
tables with an empty chair across from him. He had a weird
look on his face and was staring intensely at his slice of maple
walnut. I was pretty sure he'd seen me.

"Hey," I said, walking over.

"Hi."

"What are you doing here?" I said. If there was one person
who hated weekends at Fudge Shack more than I did, it was
Axel. I caught myself looking around for Leanne.

"Um, waiting for Caro," he said.

"Oh." At first I thought I heard him say "Leanne" because
that seemed the most logical to me. And then my brain
replayed the words and I heard it clearly. "Oh."

"Let me guess," he said, and it must've dawned on him, too.

I checked the time. "Yup. It's three oh six."

Caro was never late. She'd set us up.

I wanted to kill her. I wanted to hug her. I was going to
maybe do both.

I sighed. "Uh, do you want to go outside? It's a little loud in
here."

"Sure." Axel pushed back his chair. Five years of best-friendship, I thought to myself. How had things gotten so ruined?

Or maybe they weren't ruined. I prayed he was going to actually talk to me.

We pressed our way through the throng—"What's up, Moreno?" and "Hey, man," some of the guys from school called out, Axel waving back at them—until we had made our way through the heavy door and out onto the sidewalk. I sipped in the spring air.

The sun was tucked behind some clouds and a crisp breeze was kicking up. Tall bushes rustled behind us, shaking out rain-like noises. I crossed my arms against the chill and tried to find a place for my eyes—the parking lot, the grass, my shoes—anywhere that wasn't Axel's face. Caro's words echoed around me. *Axel and Leanne got back together.*

"Want some?" He held out the fudge, a pale rectangle on a slip of white wax paper.

I shook my head. "No thanks. I just want to talk."

"Okay," he said. He wrapped the paper around the fudge, and when he stopped fidgeting, he turned his gaze up expectantly.

I opened my mouth and closed it again. I sucked in a deep breath.

"It's just," I started at the same time that Axel went, "Listen—"

"Go ahead," I said quickly. I wondered if he was going to bring her up.

He kicked at a pebble on the sidewalk. "I feel like things have just been really weird. Like, we haven't been the same."

"Yeah," I agreed. A new breeze swelled up, and I tried to ignore the way it played across his dark hair.

"Can we, like, try to reset?" he said.

I nodded. "Absolutely."

"I'm not sure it's possible to totally go back to normal. Or at least, *normal* as defined by how we used to be. I don't know."

I nodded less fervently, pretending there was something I understood in that sentence. Was it because of Leanne? Was she the reason why we couldn't go back to normal?

"But I've really missed you. You—you're my best friend."

The words stung a little. I breathed them in and swallowed them down.

"I've missed you, too," I said softly.

"Well," he said. "I was starting to worry."

I rolled my eyes but couldn't help smiling a little.

"And I've really missed your mom's chive dumplings."

"I knew it," I said. "You've been using me this whole time just to get dumplings."

"And waffles," he added. "I was a good guy once. The waffles were my downfall."

My smile faded a little. It was just a few hours ago that I'd been in our kitchen making waffles by myself, even though it was the wrong day for them. When I went upstairs into the master bedroom to try to nudge my mother awake, she only knotted herself tighter in the sheets. I ended up sitting there at the kitchen counter, eating cold waffles with sour berries and missing Axel while Meimei slinked between my legs, winding back and forth, back and forth.

"Well." Axel cleared his throat. "Sorry, but I actually have to go. I told Caro I couldn't stay long—"

"Oh." I tried not to look disappointed. I barely managed to stop myself from asking if it was because he had to go meet Leanne.

"I'm sorry, it's just, I promised Angie we would practice for this Father's Day surprise we're doing—it's kind of silly."

I let out a slow breath of relief.

"But. Never mind that. You know what I remembered this morning?" he said.

I shook my head.

"Tomorrow is Two Point Fives Day."

"Oh my god." Warmth bubbled in my stomach. It was, wasn't it?

It was the day that was exactly two and a half months after Axel's birthday, and two and a half months before my birthday. It was our annual thing to get together, make some weird form of sweet-and-salty popcorn, and draw each other's feet. A celebration of us, and a celebration of school ending, because it was always more or less the week before summer vacation started.

"I can't believe I forgot," I said, feeling dazed.

"So, come over? We'll hang out in the basement, make some popcorn?"

"Yes," I said with a real smile. "Definitely."

93

By the time I get back, the cracks have made their way into my grandparents' building. Up the stairs and onto the landing and in through the front door. I slip off my shoes and watch the way the floor breaks under Waipo's steps. People are speaking to me, but the sound is like rushing water. Or static on a radio. Loud. Empty.

I stare at the cracks. Black, spreading, fissuring.

"Leigh," I finally hear.

It's my father. He's standing in front of me, holding my shoulders. He didn't respond to my email, but he's here. His entire body is cracked, too, the pieces of his face barely hanging on.

"Dad," I hear myself say.

He looks down at the bouquet of red feathers in my hand, and his mouth draws a grim line. "Are you okay?"

There's a wrong kind of noise. The tiniest little snap.

I realize: There should be light coming through the windows, but there isn't. The living room is dark as midnight.

There's just one little sliver of brightness pouring through from the corner. Enough to show how the windowpanes are glistening, distorting. I blink fast to clear my vision, but it takes a long moment for my brain to process what I'm seeing.

The windows. They're melting.

As they slide down off the walls, the liquid glass turns to black ink. It pools on the floor and spreads toward me, runny and fast. I step backward quickly, hitting a wall with my shoulder. On impact, there's a shattering sound. The wall cracks into a million more pieces. New ink oozes from those fissures, running down to join the puddle on the floor.

A small feather slides out from my handful and turns a slow somersault in the air before drifting directly into the inky darkness. The feather sizzles and crumbles, turning to ash and then vanishing. Instinct tells me: We can't touch the liquid black.

My mother's dying soaked down through the carpet, through the wood. When it was done with the bedroom, it took over our house, and then it moved on to me. It soaked through my hair and skin and bone, through my skull and deep into my brain. Now it's staining everything, leaking that blackest black into the rest of the world.

"Leigh?" says my father.

"Come on," I tell him. I look over at my grandparents sitting at the dining table. "Waipo. Waigong. Tell them to come, too."

"Come where?" says Dad.

When I pass the kitchen, that same darkness is pouring out onto the tiles, dripping down the cabinets, overflowing from the drawers. The ink seems to sense my presence; it comes snaking toward me.

"*Run*," I call out.

Nobody moves.

"Come *on*," I say, nudging my grandfather's elbow and wrapping my hand around Waipo's wrist.

My grandparents move so slowly I'm about to have a heart attack. We make our way down the hall and into my room. The ink follows us all the way. I don't know how much time we have, but the black is creeping close when I slam the door shut.

"Leigh, what on earth are you doing?"

The only thing I can think to do. My best guess at stopping the cracks:

I strike a match, light the last stick of incense. Touch its firefly end to the handful of feathers, and watch them begin to burn.

94

—SMOKE & MEMORIES—

The black smoke explodes. Everything around us tilts and turns, beginning to spin. We're trapped in a storm, a cyclone of heat and ash. It's far worse than when I lit the incense with Waipo. Everything has disappeared. There's no room, no door. Just the four of us and the darkness, the wisps of black smoke winding around us, burning our eyes, filling our lungs.

We fly through darkness. We wing through light. The air around us turns to ice, then to fire.

It begins as whispers: the same whispers that first called me to the incense. The smallest, most hushed of voices. They increase in volume, like someone's turning up a dial. I recognize them: My mother, sparkling and bell-like, talking to a piano student. My father, chanting silly rhymes I haven't heard in a decade. Waipo's quiet laughter. Then others that I know only from memories. Waigong's deep tones. Jingling's round and optimistic cadence.

The voices wrap around us like the softest blankets.

And then we hit the other side of the storm. It tosses us high, and I get separated from everyone.

"Dad?" I call out, but it's a vacuum, my voice simply sucked away.

I land, by myself, in a seat at a table draped with a white tablecloth and laden with food. Younger versions of Waipo and Waigong sit with Jingling around the same table. It's a fancy restaurant, and totally packed. None of them are eating. The memory smells strongly of flowers.

"How long have you known?" says Waipo, her voice severe.

"Only a few weeks." Jingling sighs.

"Why didn't you tell us about this immediately?" Waigong demands. His fingers are wrapped so tightly around his teacup I can see the tendons bulging in the back of his hand.

Jingling shakes her head. "I didn't think there was anything to worry about."

"But now you're worried?" says Waipo.

"I don't think he's good for her," Jingling says slowly. "We were supposed to talk on the phone, and she never answered my call. She didn't pick up for four days in a row." The hurt is plain in her words, straining the timbre of her voice. "It's not like her to do that. We used to talk every day. And when we finally spoke . . . she brushed it off. I think he's a bad influence."

"She told you she's been spending all her time with this secret American boyfriend?" Waipo presses.

"Yes."

"This relationship has to end," says Waigong. He finally sets down the porcelain cup. "Tell her she must break up with him."

"She's too stubborn. She won't listen to me if—" Jingling winces. Her eyes squeeze shut, and she cups a palm to her face.

"What's wrong?" Waipo pulls her chair closer.

"Nothing. My eye has been hurting a little," says Jingling. She drops her hand away and blinks several times as if to clear her vision. "I'm fine."

"She'll listen to you before she'll listen to us," says Waigong, sighing. "How did we come to have such a disobedient child? Why couldn't she be more like you?" He picks up his chopsticks, prods at a sliver of bamboo shoot, sets the chopsticks back down. "You have to tell her."

Jingling sighs. "She's in love."

"No," says Waigong, the fury reddening his face. "She doesn't know what love is. She will love a good Chinese man with a good family, who can give her a good life. Next time you call her, tell her to end this."

The colors flicker and change; the vague and chemical scent of dryer sheets wafts through the air.

A room I don't recognize. There's my father in a wooden chair, his posture stiff and tense. Before him, little clay teacups send wisps of steam up into the air.

On the other side of the table, Waipo and Waigong sink into their brown couch, their eyes downcast. They're older than the last memory, and they seem very tired, in a permanent way. Worn down.

My mother is nowhere to be seen.

Dad visiting my grandparents on his own? The idea leaves me stunned. Cold numbness settles under my skin.

So many secrets. So many omissions.

"I've continued to write to her," says my grandfather.

"I know," says Dad.

"Has she read the letters?" Waipo asks. She turns her face up with a hopeful expression.

"I don't know," my father answers, though it's clear he does.

The smile on my grandmother's face is full of pain. "And Leigh. What is she like?"

"A lot like her mother. Strong. Stubborn." He smiles a little. "She's very talented."

"A pianist?" says Waigong.

My father shakes his head. "She draws. I brought a few of her pictures—"

He opens his briefcase wide and pulls out a folder, passing it over the tea.

Waipo's shaky fingers carefully extract the loose pages. She stares at each one for a long time. She pauses on a charcoal drawing. "Who is this?"

"Leigh. It's a self-portrait."

My grandmother hovers her finger over the paper, tracing the dark lines in the air.

In the picture, I'm wearing Axel's old headphones, curled up on the arm of a sofa with a sketch pad in my lap. I remember making it based off a photo he'd taken on a crappy camera. We hadn't known each other for very long, but already we were best friends.

"You can keep those," says my father. "She won't notice. She draws so much. Nonstop. I'll send you more."

"How long are you in town?" asks my grandmother.

My father wraps his hands around a cup of tea. He sips. "Nine days."

"You travel often?" she asks.

"Not too much, currently. This is only my second trip abroad since the last time I saw you." Dad sets the tea down. "I hope I'll get to travel more in the future."

"Is she happy?" asks Waigong.

"Leigh? Yes. She's . . . in love with her art."

"And her mother? She's happy, too?" My grandfather's eyes are unblinking.

"I think so," says my father. He draws in a breath and sighs. "I hope so."

"That's all that matters," says Waipo.

Waigong closes his eyes. "Did she tell you what we said to her? When she decided to marry you?"

My father looks embarrassed. "Yes. She told me."

"We never should have said that." His voice is gruff, his eyes slightly red. "It was our fault. We only thought it would stop her from leaving."

Colors dim. Light flashes.

My mother and father sitting with a younger version of me at the kitchen table, holding spreads of cards in their hands. My hair has a streak of purple. Was I in seventh grade?

"It's your turn, Leigh."

My memory-self lays down a card and Mom gasps. Her lips stretch into a wide grin.

"Dory, you're giving yourself away!" says Dad.

My mother shrugs. "So what?"

"You're supposed to bluff."

Mom squints at him. "Bluff?"

"You know," memory-me says. "Try to trick us."

"Oh, well, I am tired. Let's eat cake. You want cake?" My mother stands up.

"Um," Dad begins to say.

"Sure," memory-Leigh replies, and they all set their cards aside.

Mom brings out the freshly baked pan of chocolaty goodness.

Dad crams a piece into his mouth before my mother has had a chance to properly serve them. "These are actually brownies, you know."

"What's difference?" my mother says. "Brownies just like chocolate cake."

"There's a big difference—" And with that, Dad launches into his explanation, waxing poetic about the denseness, the ratio of chocolate, the various optional ingredients.

Dad's always been a dessert person, and I can't help but smile as this memory unravels around me. This was back before he started flying all the time, before work took him away from us.

"Okay!" my memory-self says. "Can we play? The game's almost over."

"Yes, okay," says my mother. She gathers up her cards.

"Go ahead, Mom," says memory-me.

Dad finishes the last of his fourth brownie, brushes the crumbs off his fingers, and reaches for his cards.

"Oh, me?" My mother looks delighted. "So here! Look!"

She lays out her final hand.

"I win!"

"What!" Memory-me throws her hands up in the air. "I was *so* close."

Dad furrows his eyebrows at the spread he's holding. He looks down at the table. "Hey, wait. Those were mine! You stole my cards!"

"Nope," says Dory. "You said I need to bluff. So I bluff. So I win."

"What a cheater!" Dad cries. He reaches over to tickle her in punishment.

My mother curls away from him toward the side of her chair and collapses into giggles.

"Cheater, cheater, cheater," Dad chants, his face glowing.

My memory-self rolls her eyes. "You guys are ridiculous."

Darkness. New light.

There are my parents, standing in the kitchen. They're even younger than the last memory. I'm nowhere to be seen. My mother's shaking her head at something in my father's hands.

Dad's holding plane tickets. Three of them. Destination: Taipei.

"Why do you do this?" Mom's voice is low and raw in a way I've never heard.

"Don't you think it's been long enough?" says my father very gently. "They deserve to see you. You deserve to see them. *Leigh* deserves to *meet* them."

"No. They don't deserve to meet her. You don't know them. *I* know them. They're *my* parents. They have only disappointment in who I am. My entire life. Disappointment."

"It's been so many years," my father says. "Enough time for everyone to think about what's happened. To regret what's been said."

"Yes," says my mother, her voice shaking even harder. "I have lots of time to think. All I do is remember what they say. They say, 'You are supposed to marry Chinese man. If you marry that white man, this is no longer your home. You are no longer our daughter.' How can someone say that to their child?"

Dad wraps his arms around her; she holds her hands in tight fists between her chest and his. "They didn't mean it."

"They did," says Mom, weeping now. "They mean it. I know they did."

"Dory—"

"They blame me. They think if I never come to America, if I never meet you, Jingling would be alive. Why everything always my fault? Maybe I blame them. They ate lunch with her the day she died. They should see how sick she was. Why everything my fault? Why not their fault? They will never meet Leigh. They will never hurt her like they hurt me."

Dad doesn't say anything after that. He holds her, and she buries her face in his neck, her shoulders shaking.

The memory flickers and dies like a lightbulb going out, the floor dropping from my feet.

95

Iland on the moon.

Not the whole moon, but just a patch of it. A moon broken into pieces; this is all that's left. The ground is bleached and sickly, and when I walk a few paces forward, I stop short, because the edge drops away like a cliff. I'm peering down at an entire world. Spread out before me is a blackish indigo, and it glitters with stars, specks winking here and there.

I have the thought that if this chunk of moon just tips forward the slightest bit, I might find myself tumbling down into that emptiness to be scattered among the constellations.

The sound of flapping turns my attention upward.

There's the bird, soaring, bright as a flame. Just like that night in Jiufen, she circles and she dances. She winds through the sky, tracing the stars, connecting the dots. She dives and skims so close to my patch of moon that I'm certain she's seen me. She knows I'm here, knows I'm watching.

In that moment, I think of a poem I found in that Emily

Dickinson book, and it's like I can hear someone reading the words to me:

> *My cocoon tightens, colors tease,*
> *I'm feeling for the air;*
> *A dim capacity for wings*
> *Degrades the dress I wear.*
>
> *A power of butterfly must be*
> *The aptitude to fly,*
> *Meadows of majesty concedes*
> *And easy sweeps of sky.*
>
> *So I must baffle at the hint*
> *And cipher at the sign,*
> *And make much blunder, if at last*
> *I take the clew divine.*

I try to feel what she feels, my mother, the bird, sailing across that sky with her eyes closed, so certain of every turn and every angle that she doesn't need to see. I inhale deeply, try to catch the scent of her.

Here is my mother, with wings instead of hands, and feathers instead of hair. Here is my mother, the reddest of brilliant reds, the color of my love and my fear, all of my fiercest feelings trailing after her in the sky like the tail of a comet.

I hear that musical, sunny voice, so far away and quiet.

"*Leigh*," she calls out to me.

My name echoes across the sky. *Leigh, Leigh, Leigh.*

My mother says, "*Goodbye.*"

Goodbye, goodbye, goodbye.

The bird rises higher and higher. She turns and arcs.

I watch as she bursts into flames.

My heart seizes. My breath stops.

She burns like a star.

The wind comes, just a breeze at first, growing into an insistent gust. Then the storm returns, just as wild and furious as before. I try to find something to grab on to with my hands, but there's nothing. The ground is too slick. The wind slides me right off, tossing me over the edge.

A scream tears out of my throat, but there's no one to hear.

I'm falling. I'll be falling forever. There's no end to this.

I crane my head around to watch that star. That bird. My mother.

Her light flickers out, and then there's only ash and night.

Cold, inky black swallows me up, and there's nothing left to see. Nothing at all. No galaxies. No constellations. Just me and the abyss.

96

TWO POINT FIVES DAY

Two Point Fives Day. How did we end up on that couch? Maybe it was inevitable. Maybe we were two magnets the universe had been drawing together all this time.

Axel's house was empty that day. There was only him and me, and we filled the space with our laughter, let our relief spill everywhere. Relief at being friends again. Relief that we were together and alone for the first time in forever.

Why weren't we at my house?

We made popcorn and poured melted chocolate on top, drizzling it in the shape of a star again and again until fudgy brown blanketed everything. When Axel tasted the first piece, it made such a mess he had to lick the chocolate off his lips. I watched the way his knuckle brushed at the corner of his mouth, the way his darting tongue caught the candy.

He held the bowl out to me, and our fingers touched. The electricity crackled between us pyrazolone orange; he must've felt it, too.

Where was my mother?

Down in his basement, we sat shoulder to shoulder, and I could feel the slight shifting of his body with each breath he took. We drew each other's feet. It was all so achingly familiar. That scar on his ankle where he'd gotten stitches as a little kid. The way he liked to flex his toes, tap them in time to his music.

I turned to a fresh page and changed my perspective to get his legs, too. I wasn't sure I had ever sketched those strangely perfect knees.

We were inches apart, both too close and too far.

My mother, making her way up the stairs.

I fumbled with my stick of charcoal and ended up dropping it. That was how it started. It fell into the crack between the couch cushions, between us. We reached for it at the same time, bumping knuckles and bumping heads.

"*Ow,*" he said.

"*Are you okay?*" I automatically reached a hand toward his temple, toward where I imagined to be the source of his pain.

My clumsy fingers knocked his glasses askew, left his forehead smeared and ashy.

"*Hey,*" he said, but he was laughing.

"Hey yourself," I said, grinning.

He wiped the charcoal off and reached for my face with soiled fingers, seeking revenge. We were laughing together then, a sound so musical and warm my ribs stretched with happiness.

My mother, trying to write a note.

I grabbed his wrists to stop him from getting the soot on my face, and we ended up in some kind of arm-wrestling situation. He was the stronger one, so I leaned toward him to gain the advantage of weight—

And ended up bumping into his face. My nose against his nose. My lips brushing his lips.

I yanked back like a spring released.

I could pinpoint the exact spot where my mouth had touched his. It was a speck of the hottest fire.

His wide eyes were twin suns burning into me. We stared at each other, our hands still on the other's arms, knees touching, breaths short and fast but in sync.

Axel was the first one to let go. There was coldness left on the parts of my arms where his hands had held me. Ultramarine waves pouring through my body.

Then his fingers were sliding off his glasses.

He pressed in close.

I could feel that gentle breath against my lips.

I made myself gaze straight on and watched as his face loomed so large I couldn't see the edges anymore.

We kissed, and I was every color in the world, alight.

97

My fall through the darkness slows until I'm just drifting, afloat. It's freezing. This is the blackest black. My eyes take in nothing. I can't even see my own hands, but there are times when I hear and feel things. Voices somewhere above me. Something cold on my forehead. A drop of water trickling down my temple.

A burst of light, and suddenly I see my room in my grandparents' apartment. Everything too sharp and oversaturated.

There's my father, helping me up to sit. Somewhere behind him, I can hear Waipo muttering in Taiwanese.

Two pills on my dry tongue. I sip at a glass of water.

My body is so, so heavy. I just need to close my eyes. Just for a second.

I'm falling again, fast and hard, spinning through the black.

The wind picks up, pressing against my skin as I drop. At some point, the darkness begins to pale. The black turns to a murky indigo. Indigo fading to dioxazine purple, shifting to cobalt blue, then cerulean, and taking on a shine like a water-color wash. The palest bit of rose seeps in like a touch of sunrise. Swirls of white blossoming, unfurling, expanding like an inhale.

I'm drifting through a sky.

"Hey, Leigh." It's Dad. I turn to try to find the source of his voice, but I can't see him anywhere. "How you feeling, kiddo?"

He hasn't called me kiddo in years.

"I'm okay," I answer.

As the air warms, I hear the tinkling of a piano. It grows louder, until I can pin down what the music is: *Pavane pour une infante défunte* by Maurice Ravel.

"Remember this piece?" Dad whispers.

"Ravel. One of Mom's favorites." She used to play this one when she was in a quiet but good mood. *Pavane for a dead princess* is how the title translates. I always wondered: Who is the dead princess?

The music ends, and the sky goes quiet. Something settles into the space between my ribs. Something that feels full and achy and sad all at the same time.

I can tell Dad's feeling it, too, when he says in a quiet voice, "Remember how if you did something weird, she would say, 'Oh! My god!' like it was two separate phrases?"

I laugh a little. It feels strange but good. "Yeah. And remember how if you tried to make a joke? She would shake her head and say, 'You are a funny man, but you are not funny.'"

Dad snorts. "Yeah."

"Remember when you gave her that first waffle iron for Christmas and she looked so confused when she opened it—"

"*You* remember that, Leigh? That was ages ago. You must've been four."

"She said, 'It's for making the cake that looks like a fence?' And then she called it 'fence-cake' for the longest time."

"I don't think she even liked waffles at first," he says, and I can hear him smiling around the words.

"I remember she kept trying to improve them by adding ingredients from the Asian grocery store."

"Oh yeah," says Dad, chuckling a little. "Like the waffles with the red bean paste, and sesame seeds on top."

"And then the ones she made with the matcha powder. They were pretty good."

"Those *were* good! And she only made them that one time."

I feel my face stretching into a smile of my own. It warms my body. "We could try making some ourselves."

"And then she started doing those waffle sandwiches?" says Dad.

"Wow, I'd totally forgotten about that."

"She tried to make that BLT with cheese, but in between two waffles?"

"I think it would've been good if she hadn't used the Kraft singles," I tell him.

He starts to laugh in his belly, and it's such a good sound. Warm and reassuring, something I haven't heard in a long time.

The sky turns cadmium orange.

98

I blink, and there's no sky at all. There's a ceiling. My father, sitting backward in a chair, his arms resting on top. I'm in bed under a thin blanket, and suddenly I'm too hot. Sweating. I kick the blanket off.

"You're looking better," says Dad. He puts his hand on my forehead. "Your temperature's gone down."

"I had a fever?"

"For like three days."

Three days.

I missed the forty-ninth day. My eyes sting.

"You crashed hard," he says, and I can hear the concern lining the edges of his voice. "You had us all pretty worried. Your grandmother said you weren't really sleeping—insomnia can do some pretty severe things to the mind and body, you know."

I think of the cracks spreading across the ceiling until the world around me shattered.

"Though it sounds like you still managed to do a fair

amount of exploring." Dad smiles. "You went to a couple of my favorite temples." He sees the question in my eyes and explains. "She's been calling me with updates here and there."

"You shouldn't have left." It's not the thing I was planning to say, and so the words surprise me, too. "It was shitty that you just walked out of here when you couldn't deal."

His head droops. "You're right. I'm sorry."

"What were you guys even arguing about?"

"It was ridiculous. Your grandmother made a joke about, I don't know. Something about how if we'd come years ago, things could be different now. I didn't even fully process what she was saying—I think the joke might have ultimately been about food? Really, I just took it as an accusation, and I exploded, and she exploded right back. It was a mess. I'm sorry, Leigh. I really am. And I've apologized to your grandparents, too. Emotions were just...running high. For everybody."

I don't know what to say to all that, so I drop my gaze and let my eyes wander. I look over at the nightstand, suddenly remembering the photograph—the last one from the box. The one I never burned. Dad picks it up for me. It's a little bent, the edges charred.

It's a color photograph, but everything is so faded that at first glance it almost looks like it was taken in black-and-white. There's my mother with long, looping braids that hang down against her shoulders. Jingling has a short bob that barely reaches her chin. The two sisters sharing secret smiles. They look like they're not even teenagers yet. And behind them, Waipo and Waigong, gazing into the camera, mouths straight but not unhappy.

"Why didn't you tell me I had an aunt?" I ask.

Dad's face tightens, looking angry and guilty and sad, the color of burnt carmine. "It wasn't for me to say. But I should've made your mother tell you. You deserved to know."

"What about me? Like—" I struggle to find the words. "When did you tell Waipo and Waigong that...I...even existed?"

"I went to see them—you were just about two years old at that point. I was on a trip to Taiwan for work, so I brought them photographs of you."

"You just showed up? Why did you wait so long?"

"I only went after I opened a letter they'd sent to your mother. Your waigong said they wanted to make amends. I thought maybe I could help fix things." His face was full of anguish. "Everything that happened after Jingling—" Dad lets out a heavy breath. "Your mother blamed herself for it. She kept saying she should've realized that something was wrong. That Jingling was sick."

I blink. "How could she have?"

"That's what I said. But she was convinced. And after, your grandparents pressured her to stay in Taiwan. They wanted her to quit music, do something practical. Something Jingling would've done. They wanted her to marry someone Chinese or Taiwanese. I flew to Taipei to meet them, and they shut the door in my face. Your mother was terribly wounded by that. When I got back to the States, I called her, and she was so upset. Impulsively—and maybe foolishly—I proposed. When she said yes, it was her way of running away from home."

I imagine my mother making the decision over the phone, no hesitation, already throwing the few things she would need into an empty suitcase.

Dad goes on. "For a while, I wondered if she only said yes to rebel—whether she would've said no under better circumstances. And then I felt so guilty. Maybe if I'd just given her time to forgive herself a little. Maybe if I'd had more faith in us. I was just so in love, and so afraid I was going to lose her."

He shakes his head. "I never wanted her to divide up her family. But she felt that without Jingling, there was nothing to close the rift between her and her parents. And I—well. I couldn't bear to make her do anything that might make her miserable."

I swallow hard. "So you—you still—loved her? *Love* her?"

"Of *course*. I never stopped, Leigh. Never."

I turn my face away because it's too hard to look at him. "It's just. You were gone so much. You...changed. You turned into this career guy, and then Mom and I were just that family tucked away in the back of the closet."

Dad inhales sharply.

"Sometimes it seemed like you were just pretending everything was fine, like the problem might fix itself. But things like that don't go away on their own."

He makes a sound like he's quietly choking.

My voice cracks. "We *needed* you, Dad." There's both a pain and release in saying it out loud. I spent so much time trying to convince myself that it was better when he wasn't around. That we didn't need him. That Mom and I were a complete unit on our own.

Now that I've said the words, I don't even feel angry anymore. Only sad.

I listen to his thick inhalations.

When he speaks again, his words are shaky. "I never meant to let my work take over. But you're right. And when I finally realized something was broken...I didn't know how to make it better. Every time I came home, there was this unbearable weight. It was easier to be gone, you know? To be a family via the phone. Like we were in our twenties again, keeping it up long-distance, separated by the Pacific."

His voice gains speed, as if he's rushing to pour out the thoughts before he can take them back.

"Sometimes it really felt to me like you two were better off when I was gone. I didn't know how to change that. I just—" He squeezes his eyes shut. "These aren't excuses. I know it's my fault. And I can't take any of it back. If I had been a stronger, better person, your mother would still be here."

"No," I tell him. "You can't blame yourself. It's not your fault. Just like it wasn't Mom's fault that Jingling died." As the words come out, I realize they're true. I actually believe them.

He's still shaking his head. There's a helpless misery in his face.

"Anything could have happened, even if you'd been there for all of it. Mom was sick."

"I just wish—" He stops and presses his lips together, swallowing the words.

I get it. There's no point in wishing. We can't change anything about the past. We can only remember. We can only move forward.

It hurts so much I feel barely stitched together. I have to work hard to push down the knot in my throat. "Tell me about when you guys met."

Dad goes quiet, but his face changes.

"Tell me," I urge again. "It was at a students' mingle event, right?"

When he finally speaks, his voice is soft and slow. "She was the only one in the room I wanted to talk to. She lit up the place. She was like this torch. I could've talked to her forever."

Dad smiles then, but it's a painful one. "When she mixed up her idioms, she made me laugh so hard. She never cared about being wrong—she would just laugh along with me. And when she played piano—god, this is going to sound so corny—it was like her body just melted into the sound. It was like music was where she was born, and when she played the piano, she was home again."

I think of my mother swaying on the black bench, her body rolling with the wave of the melody, fingers precise and certain on the counterpoint. There's that twinge, that soreness. The regret that I never let her give me a lesson.

Dad reaches behind him, pulls a folded square of paper from his back pocket.

"What's that?"

He unfolds it wordlessly and holds it up so I can see.

It's the pencil drawing of our family on the seesaw in Village Park, looking as old and worn as a treasure map. It must've been folded and refolded a million times.

"Wow. I kind of thought you were going to stick that in a folder and forget about it."

He takes his time replying, like the words are difficult to come by. "I've kept it with me since you gave it to me for Christmas. First I packed it in my suitcase so I could look at it while I was away. And then it just became habit to carry it in my pocket. It made me feel better."

"Wow," I say again.

"I'd be on a plane, and I'd unfold this and just marvel at

what an amazing job you did—the emotion that you captured in our faces. Every time I looked at it I felt like I remembered that day even better. It's remarkable."

My eyes sting. "Thanks, Dad. That means a lot."

"You have a gift. I'm sorry if it ever seemed like . . . I thought otherwise. Your mother was so incredibly proud of you, and she had good reason to be."

We fall silent, and I wonder if he's realizing the same thing I am: that we just had our longest conversation—without fighting—in a long time.

The ache for my mother is still there. It's never going to leave. But it's tucked deep inside layers and layers of remembering. Some of it good, some of it bad. All of it important.

The door creaks and my grandmother steps into the room, bringing me a glass of juice. Her eyes light up when she sees that I'm awake.

"Leigh," she says, followed by a string of something fast and melodic.

I turn toward my father expectantly. "What did she say?"

He smiles a little. "She said your name is powerful. It's just like the Mandarin word for *strength. Li.*"

My grandmother smiles, too. "*Li.*"

99

Hold your finger to the sky with so much force it length-
ens like a spine. Look up to the point of it and beyond.
There. That tiny patch of the world, no bigger than the tip of
your finger. At first glance, it might just look like one flat color.
Blue, or gray, or maybe even orange.

But it's much more complex than that. Squint. See the
daubs of lilac. The streak of sage no wider than a hyphen. That
butterscotch smear and the faint wash of carnelian. All of them
coming together to swirl at the point just above your finger.

Breathe them in. Let them settle in your lungs. Those are
the colors of right now.

100

Dinner is a little too quiet, and that's when it suddenly occurs to me:

"Where's Feng?" I turn to Waipo. *"Feng zai nali?"*

She gives me a confused look. She says something I don't understand.

Dad looks just as puzzled. "What's Feng?"

"Feng," I say. "Our friend Feng!"

My grandmother shakes her head. *"Shei?"*

"That's an interesting name," says Dad. "What tone is it? The word for *phoenix?*"

"That's just . . . I don't know."

"What does she look like?" he says.

The question catches me off guard. What *does* she look like? As I open my mouth to describe her, I realize I don't know anymore. All I remember is her paleness, and her bright floral prints.

Dad shrugs. "Waipo says she doesn't know anybody named Feng."

I bolt into my room and tear through everything, searching for a sign of her. She existed. I'm sure of it. My phone still works—it's still on that Taiwanese network. The SIM card she gave me was real. I look for the selfie we tried to take at the top of Taipei 101, but all I find on my phone is a blurry picture with half of Waipo's shoulder. But the pastry bag—the one with the red bird logo—it's still there in my drawer.

Is that all? No other traces? She was so deeply embedded in our lives for two weeks. I return to the dining table, scanning the apartment for any other signs of her.

"Dad, can you ask Waipo about the box of stuff that was sent to us—it had, like, tea and pastries in it. It had my SIM card in it. *Feng brought us that box.* Ask Waipo if she remembers."

I watch the two of them conversing, the way my grandmother points to him, the way he shakes his head as he responds.

"Leigh," he begins slowly, "she says that the box was delivered by mail, and that it had no sender listed. She'd thought that *I* was the one who sent it."

"But you didn't. You weren't. Right?"

"Right," he says, looking concerned. "I never mailed you anything."

Back in my room, I carefully fold up the gift bag that held the pastries and tuck it into the back of my sketchbook.

Feng was real. I'm certain of it.

But somehow, nobody remembers her. Nobody but me.

"Dad, can you look at something for me?" My fingers tighten on the lid of the small marigold-orange box. The edges of it are burned up from the day I brought Waipo into the smoke. But the characters are still readable.

This, I know, is also real. Which meant the incense had to have been real. Which meant the memories were real.

He finishes unzipping the worn corner of his suitcase and throws the top open. "Sure, what is it?"

I show him the incense box and point to the characters in red:

最
難
風
雨
故
人
來

"*Zui nan fengyu guren lai*," he reads. "Oh. It's a phrase from the Qing Dynasty. A line from something a scholar wrote, basically a poem."

"What does it mean?"

"*Zui nan fengyu guren lai*," he says again, more slowly. "*Zui nan* means *the hardest*. *Feng*—you know *feng*, right?"

I blink for a second. Feng? Does he suddenly know who she is after all?

He continues. "It means *wind*. I thought I'd taught you that, but maybe I didn't. And *yu* means *rain*. So *fengyu* means *wind and rain*—in other words, bad weather, and metaphorically, bad times. *Guren* means *loved ones*, friends and family, and *lai* means for them to come. String it all together, and it means it's an incredible blessing to be able to see your loved ones during the most difficult times."

101

Iremember it all. The bird. The incense memories. The way the world began to fill with black cracks. The falling. Feng.

And since the forty-nine days have passed, something has changed. Dad is different. During those absent years, his presence had turned a hard and icy blue, but now he brings with him a warm, reassuring yellow ochre. He's been trying really hard. We're learning to actually talk again, the way we used to. Inside jokes are resurfacing. We're remembering how to smile together.

It was the final gift the bird could give us: the remembering.

The pieces of my family history glued back together, so that I finally know and understand. And a reminder of the love that we've always had, even in the times when it was stormy, when it was hard to see.

I want you to remember

I will. I'll remember.

102

One day I make the commute back out to Feng's address. I step up in front of those steel doors and push the same button: 1314.

After what feels like forever, I hear the sounds of feet coming down the stairs. One of the doors creaks open and a man pokes his head out.

I recognize the birthmark before anything else. The watercolor cloud on his cheek.

"You again?"

I take a step back. "I'm sorry. I didn't mean to bother you—"

He scowls at me. "So why do you press my doorbell?"

It wasn't Feng's address that she'd left in that box, on the pink Hello Kitty stationery. It was Fred's.

"I'm really sorry." I'm already down the steps and turning away.

"Wait for a minute," he calls to me. "I have something for you."

The door clangs shut and I hear the sound of him climbing back up the stairs. A few minutes later he comes back holding a red envelope.

"I can't accept that," I tell him. The thought of taking cash from—

He shakes his head. "It's not money. It's Chen Jingling hair. I never burned it. You can have it, for you to remember her."

Then the red pocket is in my hand, and he gives me one last look before shutting the door.

I guess that's that. There's no Feng here. But still, I can't quite bring myself to leave. Standing at the corner where she found us before, I thumb open the red pocket and look. There's the dark and shiny loop of hair, tied off with an elastic and a ribbon. There's also a photograph. An old one, but in color. Two young women, standing in a park, smiling straight into the camera. On the left, my mother, in a simple yellow dress. I recognize those plastic glasses from the memories I've seen. This must've been taken when she was already a university student. And beside my mother is her sister, Jingling, wearing a dress covered in flowers of varying reds and pinks and purples.

Jingling. Or the woman I knew as Feng.

Now I remember what she looked like. Now I can see it, clear as day. Jingling's face was fuzzy in every memory—but still. How did I not realize it before?

I scroll through my phone again for that blurry photo from the day we went to the top of Taipei 101. It was Feng's idea to take the picture. Was that her attempt to tell me that she was a ghost?

The sky is beginning to darken, so I know I have to go home. I turn in a circle, looking one last time. Hoping for a glimpse of a floral blouse. Hoping she'll materialize and offer to take me to try some new delicious food at the night market, and explain to me everything that's happened.

She doesn't.

"Bye, Feng," I whisper.

A breeze gathers up before me, and it rustles the leaves of the trees.

The next morning, we hire a car that drives the four of us to Danshui, to the sea. My father carrying a small wooden box he's hidden from me all this time. My grandmother carrying the ceramic urn with the blue dragons.

There, in the water, we scatter the ashes. My mother's. Jingling's.

The wind rises up to claim the gray.

And then it's gone. We're left with the colors of after. The colors of now.

103

Dad decided to let us stay for another week. We've gone with my grandmother to the hot springs, despite the ridiculous summer humidity. We've sat beside my grandfather and watched wrestling and game shows and music videos. And he's gotten pretty good at Connect Four.

We've gone back to a couple night markets to eat all the foods. In memory of Feng, I've been more adventurous—I've tried pig's blood cake, chicken feet, oyster omelets, barbecue eel soup, even fourteen-day-old stinky tofu. They're surprisingly good.

On the days that we've accompanied Waipo to the market, I've learned that the sweetest papayas are those blushing a bit of red. The best pomelos are found by smelling them, feeling for the heaviest ones. Some dragon fruits are white on the inside; some are red. The bunches that look like grapes but with tough brown skins are longan fruits—"dragon eyes"—and their peeled centers are candy-sweet. The most delicious part of a guava is the very middle, dotted with crunchy seeds.

Though I can't understand much of what Waipo says, I love our quiet moments together. I like to sit at the dining table and watch her cooking in the kitchen, watch the careful way she has with each ingredient, like it's something precious. And I can tell she loves listening to my conversations with my father, even if she doesn't follow. She sits beside me in the sunny afternoons, looks on at my fingers sweeping charcoal across the sketch pad, pours me cup after cup of tea.

Sometimes Waipo says something, and I can feel Dad tense up beside me. In those moments, even though I don't understand exactly what's being said, I know it's something about Mom, something he doesn't like. I nudge my hand close, so he remembers that I'm there with him. And then I watch his shoulders unwind just a bit.

There are still things to be worked through. There's no way to speed through the grief.

There's still a mother-shaped hole inside me. It'll always be there. But maybe it doesn't have to be a deep, dark pit, waiting for me to trip and fall.

Maybe it can be a vessel. Something to hold memories and colors, and to hold space for Dad and Waipo and Waigong. And Feng, even though she's gone.

I can't tell if Waipo remembers the bird. If she remembers that day that I pulled her into my room and lit the stick of incense.

During our last few days, I sketch out what I can recall of the bird. Of the memories I saw. Feng, from different angles. As much detail as I can manage. When I show my grandmother the sketchbook, her hands turn the pages slowly. I watch as she stops for a long time on the picture of her and Feng kneeling in the temple. There might be a glimmer of recognition in those eyes. It's impossible to know for certain.

But something between us is different. There's a special connection.

I'm starting to pick up more Mandarin. I'm remembering things that I knew a long time ago. Sometimes I hear something and the translation pops into my mind; I instantly know what it means. Dad's promised that when we get back he's going to sign me up for a Mandarin class. The deal he offered: He'll pay for it if I'll give therapy another try. I countered with: deal, *if* I can see someone new, and *if* he also finds *himself* a therapist. We came to an agreement.

I'm hoping that by November I'll be able to actually hold a real conversation in Chinese. That's the goal—I want to surprise Waipo and Waigong, who are going to try to come visit us for Thanksgiving. It'll be a tough holiday, but having them as guests will make it better.

Mom won't be there to make the turkey and her special stuffing recipe with the sticky rice and the mushrooms chopped into ear-shaped pieces. Instead, I'll be the one cooking. There are a few of my mother's recipes I'm pretty sure I could make, especially if Axel helps.

Axel. I still haven't called him. Haven't emailed, haven't texted.

If I'm honest, that's part of the reason I don't want to go home. There's still an arrow between my ribs. I'm pretty sure it'll always be there.

I think of that first message he sent.

Goodbye.

But we can't just stop being best friends. Axel knows me the way nobody else does. Axel is the only one who gets all my colors.

104

Our plane lands ahead of schedule, but it's still late at night when we finally pull up to our house. The stars and the crickets are all out and calling us home. Our curtains are drawn, but a soft glow pours around the edges.

A familiar pang hits me. This is how the house used to look when I came home after dark and Mom was in the living room, trilling away at the piano.

If I don't walk inside, maybe I can just stand out here with my suitcase and feel like she's still there, waiting for me to go in so she can shout a greeting over the music without stopping her fingers. I can pretend that when she finishes the Rachmaninoff, she'll swing her legs around the piano bench and leap up to give me a hug.

And in a few days, when it's Sunday, I'll roll out of bed and find her in the kitchen making waffles with berries and whipped cream. I'll hear that sunny voice chirp "Good morning!" to me while I'm still shaking off the fog of sleep, and I'll grunt back in response, remember to smile at her, offer to help mix the batter.

I'll do all the things I constantly forgot to, all the things I wish I could go back and add in like another layer on a watercolor painting.

"You coming, Leigh?" says Dad.

Our driver pulls away from the house, and then there's just me standing in the driveway with my suitcase, staring as Dad fiddles with his keys on the front porch.

I let loose a long, slow exhale. "Guess we forgot to turn off the lights, huh?"

"We didn't," he says, and the two simple words send my heart racing. Because what could that mean, except that Mom *is* actually alive and home and waiting for us right inside?

My heart speeds as I drag my suitcase up to the porch and haul it in, trailing after Dad through the soft yellow light and into our house.

"You're home! Welcome back!"

Arms wrap around me, and it takes a moment too long for me to process the shoulder pressing into my cheek, the soft shirt against my skin, the smell of deodorant and shampoo all wrong.

"Axel." I blink quickly so he can't see how close I am to crying.

"Anything drinkable in the fridge?" says Dad, who's already kicked off his shoes and is heading for the kitchen.

"I just made some lemonade, actually," Axel replies.

"Good man," says Dad. "Come on. Let's all have some."

"Of course I knew you were in Taiwan," says Axel. "Who did you think was going to take care of Meimei?" The cat winds a figure eight between his legs.

Guilt cuts through me chromium-oxide green. How

could I have forgotten about my mother's cat? Of course Dad would've called Axel or Tina.

"We're best friends now, aren't we, Miss Cat?" Axel says in an adorable voice I'm pretty sure he would never use in front of anyone else. He leans down to scratch behind her ears. The volume of the purring kicks up a few notches.

The phrase *best friends* echoes around and around, bouncing off the walls inside my skull. That's what *we* are, right? That's what we'll be, forever?

Dad yawns long and hard. "Thanks again, Axel. It means a lot." He gets to his feet. "I'm gonna go try to beat the jet lag, but you two kids hang out as long as you want."

Really? Dad, letting Axel stay at the house past midnight?

We listen to my father's socked feet padding up the stairs, creaking on the top step, turning down the hall. The door of his office closing behind him.

Too much silence. It crawls between us, digging a deep pit that feels increasingly harder to jump over.

"So," says Axel. I hate the way that word is a tiny island of thought, packed with questions and expectations.

My brain jumps to a subject to break the weirdness. "Dad should've paid you. For cat-sitting, I mean."

"He tried to," Axel tells me. "I wouldn't take the money."

"Axel—" I start to say, but he cuts me off with a shake of his head.

"Let it go, Leigh. I did it for myself as much as I did it for you. It was nice to be here, alone with just the cat and the memories."

Memories. I think of the incense smoke, and the flashes of the past.

"How are you doing?"

I know what he means. It's been about two months now since my mother died.

Died. That word.

I guess she really is gone.

"A little better," I tell him, and it's the truth. "You?"

He nods. "Same."

I draw in a deep breath. "Can I ask you something?"

Axel shifts in his seat. "Of course."

"Those emails." I pause, because I'm not really sure how to frame my question.

"Emails?"

"Yeah. Um. What was up with those?"

He gives me a funny look. "What?"

"I mean." My face is growing hot and I'm already regretting bringing them up. "They were pretty weird. Some of them…there was just no context. Not that everything *needs* context, but just, like. They were kind of random?"

"Leigh," he says. "I have literally no idea what you're talking about right now."

I can't decide if he's being cowardly or actually dense. "The emails."

"Right, I got that part. What emails?"

"All of them?" I'm starting to get impatient. "Everything you sent me while I was in Taiwan."

His forehead scrunches down. "Ah. I see. I don't know what you're talking about…because I sent you zero emails while you were in Taiwan."

I squint at him. "What?"

He looks back at me. Is he joking?

I pull out my phone and open my in-box, jabbing my finger at the screen, growing more furious by the second. My hand pauses as the app works to load—

What if those emails weren't at all real? What if I actually imagined them?

But no. The messages are there, thank god. The anger rushes back, hotter and louder than before. How much more cowardly can he possibly get? "These emails." I shove the phone in his face. "Do you remember *now*?"

Axel takes the phone from me. He clicks through them one by one. I watch as his eyes read the words, trace the watercolor brushstrokes. When he gives the phone back, his face is strangely pale.

"Leigh, I need you to believe what I'm going to say, all right?"

Suddenly, I feel oddly calm. If this is the game he's going to play, there's nothing to do about it. "You're about to tell me you didn't send me those emails."

"I didn't send those emails."

"Even though I have proof of them right here."

"Let me finish," he says. He scratches at his bottom lip with one thumb. "I wrote those emails. But I never sent them."

"How does that make *any* kind of sense?"

"They were in my drafts. I—I do this thing." He swallows. "I write drafts. Emails that I sort of—fantasize about sending. But I never actually send them. I just draft them and let them sit there."

I watch his face closely, waiting to catch the slightest bit of bullshit.

"I swear to god, Leigh. I'm—I just. Right now I'm absolutely mortified you saw these." He huffs out a shaky laugh.

"You said goodbye—" I pause because I'm not sure how to ask my question.

"What?"

"Your first email. It said 'goodbye' and it linked to the last track you wrote for the Lockhart Orchard set. What did you mean? Why were you saying goodbye?"

"That...I meant." His voice grows very quiet. "I was saying goodbye to your mom. But I realized later that it didn't really fit in with that set, even though I used the same structure and instruments. What did you think it meant?"

I don't know what to say to that.

"So," Axel says finally, "you believe me? About how I didn't send the emails?"

"Show me your drafts," I tell him.

"What?"

"Take out your phone. Pull up your drafts folder. I don't have to read them. I just want to see that they exist."

"God." He makes a hissing noise of disbelief. But even so, he pulls the phone out of his pocket.

I watch as he navigates to his email. Try to memorize the features in his face. Is this the last time we'll talk to each other like this? Is this the end of everything? He can't try to take back what he's sent. Things changed irreversibly that day on his couch.

"Um." His eyes bulge. "What the hell."

"What is it?" I ask.

"All my drafts are gone! Everything I wrote. And instead— there's just. There's this." He hands the phone to me.

It's a photograph of a bird's shadow over my lawn. The very lawn outside the house we are standing in.

"I've never seen that before," says Axel. "I have no idea how that got on my phone! This is the weirdest thing."

The bird. The incense. Feng. Nothing feels so weird to me anymore. Not after all that.

"Okay," I say.

He looks dazed. "Okay what?"

"I'm allowing it. I accept your answer." But now I need to go and sit alone in a corner and reread all his emails with this new knowledge. My chest aches at the thought of it. "I should really go to bed."

Axel stands up. "Wait. I want to show you something."

"Right now?"

"Just upstairs," he says.

And for a moment I have the terrifying thought that he's going to make me go into the master bedroom and walk over the stain. I know it's not technically there anymore; the carpet has been stripped, though no one uses that room now. Still.

"Leigh?" I can hear the uncertainty in his voice.

"Yeah?" I tip my head up to meet his gaze. "Where exactly are we going?"

"Your bedroom? Is that okay?"

Relief pours through me.

Then a whole other species of panic creeps in. We've been in my bedroom loads of times before. But it's one thing to end up there casually, and another thing for him to lead me there intentionally.

I hear myself say, "Oh. Okay. Sure."

105

Upstairs it's quiet. Dark. The lights are all off, and Dad's already snoring. Axel treads lightly, knowing which creaky steps to avoid.

At the top, we turn left and he stops me outside my door.

"Close your eyes," he whispers.

I give him a look. "Do I have to?"

"Shhh."

I can feel the air from his whispery breath on my face. That's how close we're standing.

That wall of electricity—it's back, charging up as strong as ever. I feel my weight shifting from foot to foot, and all I can think is: *Don't lean forward. Don't fall into Axel. Don't touch him.*

"Just close your eyes," he whispers.

I roll my eyes dramatically, to try to prevent him from seeing the nervousness in my face. It's bad enough the way my pulse is fluttering. I'm sure he can hear it.

Behind my eyelids, there's still light, little flickers trapped like butterflies. I hear Axel's hand at the knob, pushing the door open. I hear the click of the light switch. He takes my hand, and I barely manage to stop myself from jumping at the touch.

Axel guides me into my bedroom. I've spent a huge fraction of my life in this room—so why does it feel like foreign territory? I hear the sound of the door shutting behind us, and all I can think is: *We're alone we're alone we're alone.*

The last time we were alone together—

"Okay," he says. "You can look now."

It's not my room at all. I mean, it is, but it looks completely different. While I've been away chasing after ghosts and memories, Axel has been busy painting my walls. The Creamsicle streaks from my poor attempt at whitewashing have been replaced by vibrant colors, bold strokes curving and sweeping around the room. Even the back of the door has been painted to blend seamlessly into the walls. Mango yellow and cobalt blue and jungle greens and luscious reds. It's a study in movement. There are waves and crests . . . like in music, I realize.

It feels like the inverse of what he usually does—making music out of images. This time he's captured a world of sound in two dimensions. It feels like one of Mom's piano sonatas described in paint.

Some of the colors sweep into vague shapes that could be the silhouettes of things. The more I notice them, the clearer they are. I pick them out like a kid searching the clouds. There's a tree, a cat. A plane. A pair of feet.

There is, at the top of the southwest corner, a red beast with wide wings, a dark beak, a long trailing tail. I freeze in place, because there's no way he knew about the bird.

"So?" he says. There's that dreaded word again.

"Oh my god, Axel," my voice coming out brilliant violet.

"I'll help you paint over it if you hate it," he says quickly. "I just thought you could do with a change, get some colors around you—"

"*No*," I say, maybe a little too forcefully.

He stops and looks at me.

"That's not what I meant at all." I struggle to find the words. "It's . . . this is amazing. I can't believe you did this for me."

"There's so much that I would do for you," he says.

I turn to face him.

"More than you realize, I think," he adds softly.

My blood is going into overdrive, pounding and rushing through my veins. I have the ironic thought that I might die of a heart attack before getting the chance to play out the rest of this conversation.

"Same here." My words are so inadequate I can't help but cringe. "What I mean is—you're so important to me. And I'm so sorry I didn't talk to you after she—"

I can't even say it, but Axel nods me on.

"I shouldn't have shut you out. I should have told you about—well, everything. Because you're more than just a friend—" Cringe again, because that's too much of an admission. Did I basically just confess all my feelings? Panic courses through my body in traffic-cone-orange waves. "I mean, you're my *best* friend." That's not much better. My eyes squeeze shut. "I'm being super inarticulate right now."

Axel laughs, and the sound washes over me like a warm bath. He beckons me over to the bed, and we sit side by side on the edge. I quickly estimate: seven inches of space between us. Seven inches that might as well be the Atlantic Ocean, for how far away he feels. Fine. It's better this way. Inhale, exhale.

"Let me try saying what I have to say first," he says. His voice is all soft, and it occurs to me that *he* might be nervous.

That thought changes everything. I watch how he struggles to figure out where to put his hands. How he keeps removing his glasses and fiddling with them. How he repeatedly runs fingers through his hair. His eyes meet mine, then flick away again, like it's hard, for the first time after years of best-friendship, for him to maintain eye contact.

"Part of why I painted all this was because I missed you so much it hurt. Before you left, I was trying to give you space. I hoped that when you came back from Taiwan, we could talk again. But I couldn't stop thinking about you. I couldn't stop thinking about—"

The pause here is the longest pause in the world. I catch myself holding my breath, waiting for the words that are coming next.

"I couldn't stop thinking about kissing you," he finishes, sending his eyes down toward his hands instead of at me. "It just—it felt so right."

Yes! my mind is screaming. *It did!*

"But—well. I shouldn't—"

I interrupt him because I can see the fight on his face, the struggle to spit it out.

"It's okay," I tell him, even as I cut myself on the words. "I know about Leanne. And—I won't say anything to her. I won't ruin your relationship."

"Our—*what?*"

"Caro told me," I begin to explain.

He shakes his head adamantly. "No, no—I broke up with her. *Weeks* before Two Point Fives Day. That whole thing was a mistake. The biggest mistake."

When I open my mouth, what comes out is:

Absolutely nothing.

"Look, I never explained what happened in the spring," he says. "I wanted to, but I just. Things got so weird. They spiraled out of control."

I nod like I'm understanding. I really don't.

"While I was in Puerto Rico over winter break, I talked a lot with my cousin Salvador. I told him about you."

He told his cousin about me. I don't know why the idea is so surprising.

"Sal's an old romantic. Kind of like Caro's grandparents, you know? While I was talking to him . . . I realized I was falling for you. And he convinced me I should tell you how I felt. But then when I got home . . . I couldn't do it. And then at Winter Formal, I saw you kissing that guy Weston. And I just didn't know what to do after that. It felt hopeless. And at that point, Leanne was around so much, and she was clearly still into me, and we were getting along better than we had in the past. She was—well, for lack of a better word, she was a distraction."

Leanne. I suck in a deep inhale. He'd said before that things couldn't go back to normal. Was this what he meant?

"Then when I kissed you. God, I mean. I could tell it freaked you out." Axel's voice speeds up again. "And if you never want it to happen again, I totally get it. I will respect that. I know I crossed a certain line—"

"No," I blurt. Good. Not mute anymore. The panic has

pushed the gears back into place. "It wasn't just you. *We* crossed that line together." Still not exactly what I want to say, but it's a start.

I try to keep going, but Axel is shaking his head, looking at his feet now. "I'm sorry, Leigh, if you feel like I made you do something you didn't want. I would never, *ever* try to push you...."

My face goes hot as I remember all the conversations that have come up in sex ed about consent and how it applies to everything, not just going all the way.

When I look up, he's pressing a thumb against his lips like it'll prevent anything else from coming out.

"You've got it all wrong," I finally manage to tell him.

That's when he turns and meets my eyes again. They're so sad, so defeated.

"Axel. I wanted you to kiss me. More than anything in the world. I've wanted it for years." Deep inhale. Slow exhale. I make myself say it: "I still want it."

There. I said it. The words didn't kill me.

"You do?" His voice is hoarse.

"So much. But. I can't stop thinking about that day—"

I don't have to say more; the ashen look on his face tells me he knows exactly what I mean.

"If I hadn't been in your basement. If we hadn't been." *Kissing.* The word lodges in my throat.

"It wasn't your fault, Leigh," he says softly.

I squeeze my eyes shut against the tears that are clawing their way up through my body.

"You can't blame yourself. You can't just let that day put a freeze on everything else."

My eyes are still shut, my lungs compressing. "And I've

been afraid." The words come so fast and so quietly that for a moment I don't believe I've actually said them.

"Leigh. Look at me. Leigh?"

I force my eyes open.

He stares at me for a long time, his eyes searching my face. I notice every single time they drop to my lips. His gaze makes me feel warm and buzzy.

"Your mom told me something once. It was a waffle Sunday. You hadn't gotten out of bed yet, and I was helping her mix the batter. She said that coming to the States to marry your dad was the scariest thing."

I squeeze my eyes shut.

"She said it was terrifying to leave her family, and she hadn't known your dad that long, but some instinct made her feel like it was worth it. She said it was like jumping over a canyon and hoping where she landed would be amazing."

Like the grass always being greener on the other side? My hands twist together in my lap. Mom's analogies were like her idioms—hard to sift through. And often not at all reassuring.

"Leigh."

I open my eyes again.

"She said that it was one of the best decisions she ever made. The bravest thing she'd ever done. She said she hoped that I would have that kind of opportunity in my life. I remember her words: 'Once you figure out what matters, you'll figure out how to be brave.' I think a part of me knew, even back then, that she was talking about you and me."

Brave. The same word Caro used.

Mom always had been rooting for us. She never said anything to me, but it was obvious.

I force myself to meet Axel's gaze. In the last five years, I thought I'd learned to read every expression that could possibly fill those features. I thought I knew them better than anyone. I was wrong. The look he's giving me now—that hope in his eyes, that bright wishing—I've seen it before. But I never realized it was meant for me.

"I understand if you need to think about it. And I understand if, after you're done thinking, you decide it's not a good idea. I just want you to know—"

"Axel," I tell him. "Shut up."

And then I do possibly the bravest thing I've ever done:

I close the space between us and kiss him, hard.

He's surprised for only a fraction of a second. Then my hands are at his face, peeling his glasses up over his head and tossing them onto my nightstand. My body, drawing him down onto the bed. His lips, between my teeth. Our legs, sliding against each other.

My heart bursting with manganese blue and new gamboge yellow and quinacridone rose.

I pause and draw back.

He smiles up at me. It's the perfect antidote to my panic. I look at his soft eyes, at the upward tug of his lips, and I feel the tension melting out of me.

"What color?" I ask him.

Axel strokes my arm for a long moment, still gazing up into my face.

He huffs a quiet laugh. "All of them."

106

The day after we get back, the post office delivers all the mail they've been holding for us. That's when I see the letter: The date stamp shows that it was delivered right after we left for Taiwan. Sent to our house all the way from Berlin.

KREIS—RAUM FÜR KUNST is printed up in the corner.

"Well?" says Dad. "Are you going to open it or are you just going to stand there?"

"You open it." I shove it toward him.

"No way. That thing is *yours*. Take pride in it, no matter what the outcome is."

I pause. "Do you actually know what this is? Did Mom tell you?"

"Yes," he says. "She did."

My hands shake so hard I practically destroy the envelope in the process.

Dear Leigh Chen Sanders:
   It is our great pleasure to invite you to join
our international show for young artists here at
Kreis—Raum für Kunst.

I start screaming after that first sentence. When I finally calm down enough to read the rest of it, a weight drops into my stomach. I look up at Dad, waiting for him to tell me this is impractical, that it's not something worth pursuing—

"What's wrong?"

"I really want to go," I tell him.

"Of course you're gonna go," he says, grinning. "And I'm coming with you."

"Are you being serious?"

"I'm a hundred percent serious."

My heart explodes into a million tropical colors, and I jump to hug him.

And then, obviously, I call Axel.

"I *knew* it," he says.

"I'm screwed." I let the panic spool out. "I was in Taiwan the whole time I should've been putting the finishing touches on the rest of the series."

"How many pieces are you bringing total?" he asks, ever the voice of logic and reason.

"I had to submit three samples, and I can bring up to seven pieces in addition to those three. So up to ten total."

"But you don't have to send those in ahead of time, right? You just bring them with you?"

"Right, but—"

"And when is the show?"

"It runs for a week at the end of the month.... I'd literally get back the day before school—"

On his end of the line, there's the noise of fumbling and shuffling. "Okay, so August..."

"Axel, what are you doing?"

"Looking up plane tickets, of course."

"You're... coming? To Berlin?"

"Are you kidding? I'm not missing this. Do you realize we'll be there for your birthday?"

"But all your savings—"

"Are mine to do with however I please. Anyway, you've got this, Leigh. 'Up to ten' doesn't mean you *have* to bring ten."

I sigh. "There's no way I'm going to be one of the winners."

"So what? That's not even the point. I mean, okay, maybe it was the point originally. But you're *in* the show. That's a huge deal."

"Ugghhhh."

"It doesn't have to be about winning anymore. Now it's something different. Now you're just doing this for yourself. You can't chicken out."

"I know," I say. "I know. I'm going to do it. I *have* to do it. I'm just..."

"Scared?" Axel offers.

"All I have are works in progress! Everything with Mom... it kind of brought me to a halt."

"So why are you still talking on the phone? Get to work."

I sigh again. "Okay, okay."

"I'll talk to you when you've done enough to deserve a break."

"*Uggghh.*" I flop down on the couch, going totally horizontal. "But at least I know what I have to do."

"What?" he says, though he sounds like he knows what I'm going to say.

"I have to break out the colors."

There's a grin in his voice. "Yes. Yes, you do."

107

Dad insisted on paying for Axel's ticket to thank him for taking care of Meimei. Caro and her family are in France for the month, but all four of them are coming to meet us in Berlin for the show.

And somehow, I've put together a portfolio. A series that I think Mom would be proud to see.

The three of us take up a whole row on the airplane: Dad in the aisle seat, Axel in the middle, and me on the inside, next to the window.

I think of the pictures I made, stored safely away in my artist's folio in the overhead compartment. Twenty-two hours until the gallery opens. The plane slants up into the sky, skating through the air, the pressure tipping us back against our seats. I take Axel's hand and turn to look out the window. Below us, the ground shrinks away. The cars are toy-sized, then ant-sized, then nothing.

Cottony wisps stream past. We cut through their layers.

We level off above the clouds into an unbelievably bright expanse of blue.

The plane angles and tilts, and I fight the gravitational force, leaning to press my face into the glass. I catch a glimpse of the clouds below, and the edge of our shadow upon them, shaped like a bird.

108

THE REMEMBERER SERIES

Eight Surrealist Drawings by Leigh Chen Sanders

Each 61 x 91 cm

Charcoal and gouache

#1. FAMILY TREE

#2. PIANO

#3. EMILY DICKINSON

#4. INCENSE

#5. RED BIRD

#6. CRACKS IN THE SKY

#7. SISTERS & GHOSTS

#8. CICADAS

Artist's Statement:

What is memory? It's not something you can physically hold, or see, or smell, or taste. It's just nerve impulses jumping between neurons. Sometimes it's a matter of choice. Other times it's self-preservation, or protection.

This series is a memoir of sorts, born out of the excavation of my family history. Each piece represents a different memory found. The gradual introduction of color from one piece to the next is meant to illustrate a developing epiphany. All of them culminate in the final piece, *Cicadas*, which is a surrealistic mosaic piece done in full color:

A mother, father, and daughter seesawing together on a park playground. Giant bird flying through a wide sky. Man on a plane. Girl in an apple tree.

Memories that tell a story, if you look hard enough. Because the purpose of memory, I would argue, is to remind us how to live.

Author's Note

This novel first began taking shape in 2010 and has made its way through several different iterations, most of them vastly different from one another. The only thing in common across all the drafts was how it was always a story about family and identity and the different facets of love.

Then, in 2014, my family lost one of our own to suicide. Half a year later I began rewriting this book for the umpteenth time, and the complicatedness of that grief stuck in my brain and glued itself to my words. I didn't mean for all this to work its way into my writing, but novels like to develop minds of their own.

Here are a few statistics:

Someone dies by suicide every 11.9 minutes.

It's the tenth-ranking cause of death in the United States.

For every death by suicide there are twenty-five attempts.

Those were taken from the American Association of Suicidology's official data in 2015—the most recent I could find.

It was important to me that while Leigh's mother had experienced some terrible things in her life, there wasn't a *reason* to explain her having depression. She, like so many people all over the world, simply fell victim to a terrible disease. It's a disease we are still learning to fight.

Depression manifests differently in every person; the symptoms can vary. Not every depressed person will act the way Leigh's mother does. Treatment can help so much—it can lower or even eliminate the risk of suicide. Strong social support has also been proven to play a big role in preventing suicide. If you suspect someone in your life of being suicidal, please reach out to them. Please, talk about depression. Talk about other forms of mental illness.

Talk about suicide—research has shown that talking about it does not increase ideation or risk, and actually *can* make a significant difference.

I grew up witnessing firsthand the effects of depression, and watching how my family let the stigma surrounding it become one of the darkest, stickiest traps. That stigma can and does kill. That stigma is perpetuated by not talking.

RESOURCES

SUICIDE PREVENTION

National Suicide Prevention Lifeline:
  suicidepreventionlifeline.org
In a crisis, call their free and 24/7 U.S. hotline:
  1-800-273-TALK (8255)
Contact their Crisis Text Line:
  text TALK to 741-741
National Hopeline Network:
  hopeline.com / 1-800-442-HOPE (4673)
American Association of Suicidology:
  suicidology.org
American Foundation for Suicide Prevention:
  afsp.org
Suicide Prevention Resource Center:
  sprc.org

FOR SUICIDE LOSS SURVIVORS

Alliance of Hope for Suicide Survivors:
　allianceofhope.org
American Association of Suicidology survivors page:
　suicidology.org/suicide-survivors/suicide-loss-survivors
Friends for Survival:
　friendsforsurvival.org
National Suicide Prevention Lifeline survivors page:
　suicidepreventionlifeline.org/help-yourself/loss-survivors/
Suicide Awareness Voices of Education:
　save.org

UNDERSTANDING MENTAL ILLNESS

Mental Health America:
　mentalhealthamerica.net
National Alliance on Mental Illness:
　nami.org
National Institute of Mental Health:
　nimh.nih.gov

Acknowledgments

I remember knowing when I was just seven years old that I wanted to tell the world my stories, and see my own books sit on shelves in libraries and stores. It took a little over two decades for that dream to begin to come true. Two decades, and the help of a lot of incredible people. I'll try to cover most of them below.

First, my brilliant and tireless agent, Michael Bourret, to whom I could easily write an entire tome of thanks. I don't know how you have the energy for all that you do—clearly some part of you is made of magic. Thank you for being so kind and passionate and human, and for championing this story so hard. I truly won the agent lottery.

Thank you as well to Lauren Abramo, Erin Young, the rest of the DG&B team, and Mary Pender-Coplan at UTA—I'm thrilled to be represented by the absolute best people.

Alvina Ling, my wonderful editor, helped me shape this book into what it always wanted to be. Thank you for believing in me and my words, and for loving these characters so much.

Thanks to Kheryn Callender for being an important friend and assistant extraordinaire throughout this wild ride.

Thank you, Nikki Garcia, for so precisely and gracefully handling all those logistics and details.

And to the rest of the Little, Brown family—especially Russell Busse, Michelle Campbell, Jackie Engel, Elisabeth Ferrari, Shawn

Foster, Sasha Illingworth, Jess Shoffel Maglio, Annie McDonnell, Emilie Polster, Elizabeth Rosenbaum, Carol Scatorchio, Andrea Spooner, Victoria Stapleton, Angela Taldone, Megan Tingley, Ruiko Tokunaga, Valerie Wong, Danielle Yadao, Elena Yip, and any other LBYR team members I didn't learn of in time to include here—I'm endlessly grateful for all that you awesome people do.

Christine Ma and Rosanne Lauer were my excellent freelance copyeditor and proofreader.

The artist Gray318 and the above-mentioned Sasha Illingworth and Angela Taldone made my cover so beautiful I can't stop staring at it.

Thanks must also be sent across the ocean to my UK editor, Samantha Swinnerton, and the rest of the fabulous team at Orion Children's Books, including Thy Bui, Nicola Goode, Helen Hughes, Dominic Kingston, Lucy Upton, plus anyone else making magic happen for this book.

I've had some amazing teachers who left a permanent mark on me, and I would not be the writer I am without them. In particular I want to name: Susan (Hartmann) Nabors (fifth grade), Cindy Stone Murphy (sixth grade), Tery Solomon (eleventh grade), and Rachel DeWoskin (college). You taught me that I have what it takes. I thought of all of you so often as I was drafting and revising.

I began this novel while I was in Chuck Wachtel's workshop during my first year of NYU's MFA program. It was Chuck's steadfast belief in me and in the seed of this story that made me try again and again until I got it right. Thanks, Chuck Laoshi.

The Writers Room on Broadway provided the most quiet of places to focus, and all the peanut-butter-filled pretzel nuggets I could possibly desire. I spent many hours there revising.

Here's a group hug for the Kidlit Authors of Color, and for the Electric Eighteens, who offered much-needed cheer and commiserating.

Kim Blanck, Mia Garcia, Britt Lockhart, and Kayla Rae Whitaker were among my early readers and feedback-givers—you guys are the best.

Wang Shengfei and He Jiawei and Joyce Ge, who live on the other side of the world, kindly answered a thousand questions via WeChat as I was deciding what conventions to follow for the Pinyin.

I'm indebted to the terrifically generous Sisi Guo for the guidance and the psychologist's perspective.

The very final draft of this book was completed during my residency at the Djerassi Resident Artists Program, the most beautiful and soul-nourishing place I've ever been. The fantastic Djerassi staff kept me well-fed and inspired, and even plucked a faulty smoke detector off my ceiling at two in the morning. My fellow April 2017 residents braved the trails and ticks and spiders with me—and their pep talks and fancy-dessert-making skills carried me through my last revision.

Delilah Kwong fed me wine and chocolate and other treats, and kept me buoyed with constant love and excitement.

These badass women offered camaraderie and encouragement throughout the publishing process: Renée Ahdieh, Sona Charaipotra, Preeti Chhibber, Dhonielle Clayton, Zoraida Córdova, Sarah Nicole Lemon, Kaye (aka Karuna Riazi), and Marie Rutkoski.

Tiff Liao and Anica Mrose Rissi are magical beings of light who gave me crucial sanity checks, and always told me exactly what I needed to hear at exactly the right times.

Aisha Saeed, Joanna Truman, and Anna Jarzab are razor-sharp storytelling rock stars who were kind enough to read and give extensive comments on multiple drafts. Their texts and emails boosted me up when I needed it most.

Nova Ren Suma is one hell of a mentor and the greatest cheerleader, whose friendship and generosity have been so huge to me. I'm grateful for your amazing belief in me, and for your feedback early on that dug right down into the heart of my story. Thank you for your emails full of exclamation marks, and for making me feel like all this could ever be real.

Bri Lockhart is the eponym of Leigh and Axel's apple orchard, as well as the gin to my tonic, the Nutella to my everything, my girl gang co-captain, and one of my very first champions. Thank you for reading that super-early draft on your vacation and messaging me about it from across the Atlantic Ocean.

Special thanks to my many aunts and uncles in Taiwan who helped with pinning down the details and logistics that went into my research and, in turn, this book. And to the rest of my extended family—thank you all so much for your love and support.

I'm grateful to my own waipo, the real Yuanyang, who I made into Leigh's grandmother, and whose incredible life journey gave me the spark to begin this novel.

To my parents, Alex Pan and Beatrice Yu-Pan, I owe more thanks than there are words in all the languages combined. Thanks, Mama, for helping me find the line by Qing Dynasty scholar Sun Xingyan that's printed on Leigh's box of incense. Thanks, Baba, for staying up late to talk about superstitions and Ghost Month. Thank you both, for the battery-draining phone calls, and the millions of questions you answered as I was revising. Thank you most of all for supporting my wildest dreams.

Loren Rogers—my husband, best friend, partner in life— thank you for absolutely everything. For cooking all the meals and doing all the laundry and listening to every inane thought that bubbles out. For pushing me to chase this dream life. Thank you for believing in me, and letting me hear that belief so loud and clear. Thank you for every hug, every squeeze of the hands, every laugh, every reminder of how damn lucky I am that I picked the right night to go to Milk and Cookies. You inspire me every single day.